ELDAR PROPHECY

THE ONCE MIGHTY eldar craftworld of Kaelor floats through the darkest reaches of space. Home to a once glorious people, the eldar race is now in the twilight of its existence. When the warrior Naois comes of age, he is unaware of a prophecy that has been placed on his shoulders. Armed with his deadly training from the ancient Aspect Warrior Temple of the Warp Spiders, Naois seeks to rebuild the lost prosperity of his once great family and when his actions begin to fulfil the dark prophecy, he sees an opportunity to exact revenge on his enemies and bring them to their knees.

CS Goto's mythic tale of the Craftworld Kaelor eldar includes an extensive Appendix.

A WARHAMMER 40,000 NOVEL

ELDAR PROPHECY

C S Goto

For the monster that follows the path of Ihnyoh
around the garden.

A BLACK LIBRARY PUBLICATION

First published in Great Britain in 2007 by
BL Publishing,
Games Workshop Ltd.,
Willow Road, Nottingham, NG7 2WS, UK.

10 9 8 7 6 5 4 3 2 1

Cover illustration by Paul Dainton.

A CIP record for this book is available from the British Library.

ISBN 13: 978-1-84416-451-6
ISBN 10: 1-84416-451-9

Distributed in the US by Simon & Schuster
1230 Avenue of the Americas, New York, NY 10020, US.

See the Black Library on the Internet at
www.blacklibrary.com

Find out more about Games Workshop
and the world of Warhammer 40,000 at
www.games-workshop.com

Ancient and mysterious beyond the comprehension of men, the eldar are enigmatic aliens who stalked the stars when mankind's ancestors were crawling from the primordial seas of Terra. Their magnificent empire spanned the galaxy: their whims decided the fate of worlds and their wrath quenched the fiercest suns. But many millennia ago, these Sons of Asuryan fell prey to pride, decadence and depravity – this was the Fall of the eldar. From the miraculous potency of their degenerate dreams, a sickening and obscene god was born – the Great Enemy. The psychic implosion of its birth-cries tore out the heart of the eldar empire, leaving a pulsing, bleeding afterbirth of pure Chaos in its place – the Eye of Terror.

And now, in the time of the Imperium of Man, the eldar are all but extinct – the last fragments of a shattered civilization plunged into constant warfare as they flee the ever-lustful reaches of the Great Enemy, struggling to suppress the deathly light of their fiery emotions lest the Enemy find them again. Those who managed to escape before the cataclysmic Fall did so on mighty living vessels called craftworlds; it is on these world-ships that the last remnants of the eldar civilization drift amongst the stars as a scattered and nomadic race.

Only a few of the wisest eldar farseers know how many craftworlds escaped from the Fall. One such craftworld, which fled out into the darkest reaches of the galaxy, hiding in glorious isolation from the Great Enemy in the blindness of nowhere, was Kaelor – the Radiant Eye. It drifted far from the touch of civilization, turning in on itself and incubating its own psychoses until the gravity of its intense psychic resonance gradually drew the attention of precisely those eyes from whom it sought to remain hidden. This is the story of Kaelor.

PROLOGUE: ABOMINATION

She blinked and the congregation flinched involuntarily.

The flash of sapphire from her radiant eyes shimmered through the darkness, touching the soul of each of the Yuthran sisterhood as they stood in ceremonial attention around the perimeter of the Ring of Alastrinah. The long, red robes of the seers floated like veils of lost innocence, caught in the eddies of a swirl of faerulh – the ethereal soul-wind that breathed out of the very spirit of Kaelor.

The little abomination sat in the centre of the fluttering, diaphanous circle. Her head had been freshly shaved, making her peaceful, smooth and uncreased features appear to gleam like a white pearl. Her face was elegantly elliptical, and her youthful cheeks already betrayed the signs of a resolute jawline. She

looked to all present like a statue of exquisite artistry
– worthy of Vhaalum the Silver – only her startling
blue eyes seemed to radiate life from deep within
her, like the light of Isha herself.

Little Ela blinked again.

Watching from her position in the circle, in the
shadowy Alastrinah Sanctum of the ancient Seer
House of Yuthran, Cinnia caught her breath and
leaned forwards, as though afraid that even the
slight motion of breathing might be enough to
extinguish the painfully pristine sapphire light in
the sleehr-child's eyes. For that moment, the seer
saw the infant's gaze as a solitary candle in an infinite darkness.

Cinnia's red robes rippled faintly with her aborted
motion, betraying her concern to anyone who might
be watching. But all eyes were trained on the vaugnh
– the abomination, as Cinnia called the eerie child
seer under her charge.

The infant's eyelids closed for a moment and then
fluttered open once again, defining starbursts of
blue in the shifting nebula of red robes that surrounded her. Despite their disdain for the childling,
the seers of the Yuthran sisterhood sighed almost
inaudibly, each of them transfixed by the vision of
the little female, who sat in such captivating tranquillity before them. Each of them was caught in the
discomforting space between awe, revulsion and
fear.

Little Ela appalled them.

Very slowly, the perfect and beautiful face turned,
as though independent of its neatly seated body. Its

sapphire eyes twinkled like diminishing stars as their gaze swept around the crimson circle, scanning past the faces that had become so familiar over the last several years. Ela looked through them as though the Yuthran were ghosts of nothingness.

Cinnia watched Ela's brilliant gaze patrol the ring, touching each of the sisterhood with a dab of her radiance. Not for the first time, the young Yuthran seer felt that she was merely a spectator, standing around the margins of this little abomination's life, meaningful only when beheld in those glittering sapphire eyes.

For a moment, Cinnia remembered the first time that she had seen the tiny sleehr-child, wrapped in the luxurious robes of Lady Ione, as the matriarch of Yuthran had brought her into the sanctity of the great seer house. In some ways, Cinnia's own life had begun on that day. At the very least, it had changed forever. Ione had presented the wide-eyed childling to her, as though entrusting her with the greatest treasure of Kaelor. From that moment on, despite her own youth, Cinnia had devoted herself to the training of the girl, placing herself into the shadows of the tiny abomination. Ione had never even said where she had found the childling, but Ela's origins seemed clear to everyone.

The memories sparked a feeling of profound marginalisation in Cinnia's dhamashir-soul, sending a shiver arcing through her spine. Not for the first time, she forced herself to disregard the deep unease that Ela provoked in her thoughts. The childling was under her tutelage.

Just before Ela's gaze reached hers, she lowered her eyes involuntarily, as though suddenly self-conscious, letting her gaze drop to the immaculate, polished, wraithbone floor that had defined this sacred space for generations. Subconsciously, she sought a haven in the ancient, unchanging material structure of her house, hoping that her gesture would appear as deference to the others.

There was no hiding from that gaze. It did not bridge merely the material space between Ela's eyes and Cinnia's bowed head, but rather it breached the materium itself, cutting through the unseen dimensions in a parallel course directly into the seer's mind.

In that moment of psychic contact, during which Cinnia steeled herself against the gaze that seemed to pierce to the very depths of her being, rapidly closing off her thoughts lest the little abomination would see too much, an image of Ela appeared in her mind. She was older, but recognisably the same. Her hair was suddenly long and white, like a mane of Mhyrune psychotropic silk, but her sapphire eyes were gone. In place of her gleaming stare there were two caves of darkness set into her perfect skin, and a cascade of blood poured out of the sockets like a river of tragic tears. Yet, even in the image, Cinnia could feel the touch of the sleehr-child's gaze in her mind, as though the loss of her eyes had made no difference to her sight: it was wraithsight. Was Ela the ehveline? Was that why Ione had saved her?

In that instant, just as Cinnia became conscious of her own wandering thoughts, the infant abomination in the centre of the ring of seers let out a cry of anguish, as though she had shared Cinnia's appalling vision of her future.

Lifting her eyes from the twinkling depths of the wraithbone floor, Cinnia saw Ela's radiant but unfocused eyes flash and flare, as though the child had seen something startling in an indefinite space before her. She was sitting bolt upright with her eyes wild, staring directly towards Cinnia, but her gaze neither focused on the seer nor passed through her. The line of sight was simply impossible to discern, as though little Ela was looking at an entirely different world from the one around her.

None of the Yuthran sisters moved to offer assistance or strength to the suddenly tortured childling in their midst. They stood with a tensely maintained calm as the breeze of faerulh continued to dance through their gently billowing robes. They watched, intrigued, repulsed and transfixed by the unusual event that transpired. The Rite of Alastrinah had never been performed by one so young, and had never been permitted until the Farseer's Court had pronounced an initiate ready by passing her through the Ritual of Tuireann.

An unspoken understanding swept around the ring of seers, like a sickly emulsion of sympathy and revulsion. They were not insensitive to the childling's suffering, but there was something about her very existence that they found offensive. She was dangerous. She was unbalanced and unnatural, and more than one of the Yuthran sisterhood agreed that it would have been far better for everyone if the Lady Ione had let her be executed with her father at the end of the House Wars.

However, the Lady had never done anything without good reason, and none would dare to question her farsight, even now.

Another anguished cry twisted into a scream, and the wraithbone floor pulsed and crackled with energy. Ela's eyes widened suddenly as threads of sha'iel radiated out from her, rippling through the floor and sparking into tiny stars of light as they tore through the psychically bonded tropes, leaving ghostly veins shimmering just under the polished surface.

The wraith-tendrils quested through the deck, lashing and flickering as though reaching for the feet of the seers that stood ringed in awestruck curiosity. None of the sisters of Yuthran moved, rooted by their own trepidation.

Not in thousands of years had anything like this been recorded in the seer house.

Images began to ripple and flow through the floor, dropping away from the reflections of the seers, intertwining and intermingling with the veins of sha'iel. They were vague at first, but compelling in an incomprehensible way, dragging the reluctant gazes of the seers down into them as though soaking their minds in a heavy liquid.

The abomination, the warp energy, and the hall itself were an intoxicating and lethal mix. Still standing around the perimeter of the ring, Cinnia stared at the scene in uncomprehending disbelief, feeling the atmosphere in the chamber swirling and condensing around Ela. It was as though the circular chamber was a cauldron, boiling the emotions and psychic energies of the seers inside.

The circular hall of the Ring of Alastrinah had been constructed in the Radiant Age of Gwrih the Founder, and its architecture was unique in all of Kaelor. The wraithsmiths and bonesingers of the day had worked closely with the farseer to fashion a perfectly psycho-conductive space, modelled on the fabulous ring that the farseer had once presented to Alastrinah. Although the chamber served to amplify the power of those within its centre, it also focused that power *into* the centre, containing it like light within a reflective sphere. Because of this intriguing and elegant design, the farseer had been able to give the Seer House of Yuthran an exquisite gift without also giving them any power of practical use beyond their own walls.

Cinnia saw the fire before the others did. It started as the merest hint of an ember, smothered under the hidden darkness of the floor. Then the ember flared into a spark of gold, and a breath of faerulh seemed to ease into it, fanning the spark into flames. After a matter of moments – no longer than the wing-beat of a tiny aereb-beetle – the flames billowed into an inferno, unrolling within the floor with such vivid ferocity that Cinnia had to control her instinctive urge to lift her feet away from the non-existent heat. She forced herself to remember that this was an illusion, merely the projection of Ela's vision into the perfectly conductive floor.

The suggestions of figures squirmed and writhed between the flames in what might have been agony or ecstasy, or both. They were dark, like silhouettes or the negatives of ghosts, flitting through the flames like lost dhamashirs, or like daemons.

The realisation struck the sisters of Yuthran all at once. As one, they gasped at the images that were pouring out of Ela's young mind. The little abomination was unleashing a torrent of visions into the Ring of Alastrinah, flooding it with scenes of death and carnage, of daemonettes of the Great Enemy dancing in the burning boulevards of Kaelor. The images seared into their minds even as the raging flames licked ineffectually and coolly at their feet.

Cinnia shrank back, staggering slightly under the force of the sensual barrage. She had never before seen images of such violence unleashed in that sacred chamber, and certainly never before during the Rite of Alastrinah.

She could feel her own thoughts heating insistently until she no longer felt that she could keep hold of them. It was as though the flames in the floor were simultaneously in her head. Her thoughts burned at the inside of her skull, boiling her mind like a soup. They started to melt, curdling together until she could no longer tell one from the next, rendering her mind into a swirling psychic emulsion.

For a moment, and for the first time since she had passed through the Trials of Menmon a number of years before, Cinnia felt genuine horror grip her soul. It was as though this childling were actually burning away her identity and filling her mind with flames and daemons.

In a sudden flash, Cinnia saw the image of the sleehr-child once again, sitting in calm stillness in the heart of the fury. Her eyes were vast caverns of darkness from which all the flames were erupting. Rivers of blood gushed out of them, cascading down her blistering and singed skin. She was not alone. Behind her with his arms outstretched to his sides, as though wearing the daemonic fire as a cloak around him, stood Ela's brother, Naois. His hands were thick with blood and his eyes glistened with an impossible, maniacal darkness.

The picture of the appalling siblings flashed for the briefest of instants, like a subliminal pulse, but there was no way to tell whether it had been real, whether it had been seen by the others, or whether it had been entirely within Cinnia's own mind. Her grip on the boundaries between these dimensions had failed almost completely.

Another wail of anguish washed out from the seated figure of Ela, but this time its pitch rose instantly into a whistling scream, just on the edge of hearing. The noise seemed to shatter the images that filled the hall, like a streak of lasfire slicing through glass.

As the roil of pictures and visions vanished from sight, leaving the hall suddenly cool, calm and silent once again, the abominable child in the centre of the ring collapsed forwards onto the ground, spent and exhausted.

Her eyes were closed at last.

One by one, the sisters of House Yuthran turned away from the childling and walked quietly out of the chamber. The initiate was supposed to be left to recover using her own resources. That had been the tradition since the time of Alastrinah herself. As they left, the seers attempted to effect an air of normalcy, as though this was how they had expected the rite to transpire, as though nothing exceptional had happened at all, but none could hide the unsteadiness in their strides.

After only a few moments, the Ring of Alastrinah was empty except for two silent figures. Little Ela lay motionless on the wraithbone. A tiny trickle of blood eased out of the corner of her mouth and began to pool on the floor next to her pearl-white cheek. Cinnia remained standing in her ceremonial place, somehow unable to turn away and leave the abomination on her own, yet unwilling to stoop forwards and go to her aid. The same question tumbled over and over in her mind until it made her nauseous.

Is this the ehveline?

PART ONE:
THE MISREMEMBERED

CHAPTER ONE: IONE

THE GOLD AND green banners of House Teirtu fluttered proudly above the heads of the warriors as they dashed out of the Sentrium and fell into formation before the Rivalin Gates, the last great barrier between the primitive styhx-tann and the cultivated Knavir eldar of the court. Dozens of Teirtu House Guardians filed into perfect, disciplined lines as though performing a drill. In the gathering darkness of this sector's down-phase, their polished armour burst with reflected light from the Farseer's Court behind them, silhouetting them to their foes amidst a flood of radiance, as though they rode the grace of the farseer himself, while the icon of the Serpent of Iden glistened in the heavy shadow that fell across their chests.

Yseult did not need to push her way through the lines. They parted automatically as she strode

19

through the gates towards the front of her troops. As a passageway opened up before her, a shaft of light rushed past her through the gap, carrying her long shadow out into the battlefield beyond. The head of the giant, elongated shadow reached almost to the feet of the crimson enemy's front line.

'You are not welcome here, spiders of the warp,' she muttered, taking a step forward of her own lines until she stood alone. The ranks of house Guardians closed up behind her, erasing her shadow with their sheet of blackness. 'You will turn back.'

Her voice carried no volume, which made her tone seem casual and disinterested, but her eyes shone with focus. Her armour was immaculate to the point of appearing ceremonial. She wore no helmet, and her long black hair fell over her deep green cloak of rank, which cascaded down from her shoulders like a silken mane. The long, two-handed hilt of an ancient diresword, protruded from under folds of fabric, fastened to her belt with a golden, serpent-headed clasp.

The assembled Aspect Warriors opposite her made no move. There was no answering call from their commander, and not a single eldar stood forward of their lines. They stood immobile and implacable in the face of the Teirtu House Guardians and the flood of light that gushed out of the Sentrium through the great Gates of Rivalin. In the intense brightness, their crimson armour shone like a warning beacon.

Yseult narrowed her eyes slightly, staring across at them. Could it be that they had simply not heard her? She had carefully calculated an appropriately indifferent volume, intending to cause offence not deafness.

She sighed inwardly, aware that the protocols for initiating combat differed between the various Aspect Shrines. The rules for battle between the Great Houses had been codified and consolidated during the House Wars over the course of the last hundred years, but it was not clear that these rules should also apply to the Aspect Temples, who had deliberately played no part in that terrible conflagration, or at least no open part in it.

During her own cycle of training in the Temple of the Dire Avengers, Yseult had embraced a dignified and honourable etiquette. It was entirely plausible that the deceitful Warp Spiders did not share her code of conduct. However, she realised that she was behaving without the necessary respect.

You are not welcome here, spiders of the warp. You will turn back, or we will turn you back. Realising that vocalising her words may have been unnecessarily insulting, she repeated herself, this time without giving voice to any of the words. Instead, she pushed them across the intervening space and directly into the minds of the Warp Spiders.

Who are you to refuse us welcome, servant of Teirtu? The reply was firm and powerful, and it resonated violently in Yseult's head. She could not tell whether it was audible to her Guardians. Part of her hoped not.

'I am Yseult Teirtu-an,' announced Yseult, taking another step forward of her own lines so that she could be clearly seen by both sides. She spoke the

words out loud, accepting and cultivating the defiance that such a move implied. Whether or not they
had intended it, her opponent's words had stung her,
even though it was true that she was merely pledged
to the House of Teirtu and not part of it by birth.

'I am duly empowered to welcome our friends, and
I am more than capable of repelling our enemies,'
she added, letting the tone of antagonism float across
to the Warp Spiders. It was all part of the ritual of
commencement.

We have no desire to fight you, Avenger Yseult. The
crimson front line of the Warp Spiders parted and a
magnificent figure strode forwards out of the formation. She was a full head taller than her Aspect
Warriors and her shoulders were set with power, as
the wash of light from within the Sentrium crashed
against her armour like water against a rock. Like
Yseult, the exarch had no helmet, indicating that the
formalities had not yet been exhausted. *You are not
unknown to us.*

Yseult smiled, raising one eyebrow in faint amusement. She was surprised to see that the exarch was
there amongst her warriors for this encounter, but it
certainly explained the psychic power of the voice
that had thundered across the no man's land
moments before. She was still more surprised by
what appeared to be a conciliatory tone. Was Exarch
Aingeal really trying to avert a battle, or was this
merely part of Warp Spider etiquette?

'You honour me, exarch,' she replied, still speaking
out loud so that her incredulous tone could be heard
by her own warriors. If Aingeal's attempts at

conciliation were insincere, Yseult did not want to be caught out. Besides, when given a choice between diplomacy and combat, a Dire Avenger should choose battle every time. She did not come to guard the Gates of Rivalin just to bandy words with this Warp Spider, exarch or no exarch. 'I wouldn't want to fight me either!'

There is no need for more Kaelorian blood to be spilt this day, Yseult Teirtu-ann. The hands of the houses are soaked enough already. We merely seek safe passage to the Shrine of Fluir-haern. That is all.

Yseult's eyes narrowed again as a burst of ruby light flashed off the exarch's ancient armour. This was not how the rituals of commencement were supposed to evolve. During the House Wars, Yseult had become accustomed to striding to the fore, announcing her name, and then launching into battle with a worthy opponent. The champions of each force would fight the first encounter and then, depending on the manner of the victory, the rest of the warriors would charge into the fray. Or they would retreat, conceding the superiority of the opposition. After so many deaths, the eldar of Kaelor had been forced to conceive of a way of battle that would not leave the craftworld bereft of eldar altogether. In the deepest recesses of their dhamashirs, they all knew that the children of Isha were a dwindling light in the galaxy, and none wanted to be responsible for extinguishing it completely.

And yet Aingeal's conciliations irritated Yseult. She saw deceit lurking in their depths, like a deadly snake poised in a flowering umbhala tree. The delay

appeared like procrastination or even cowardice. If
the Warp Spiders wanted to pass the gates, they
should simply make their move. All of this posturing
seemed vaguely insulting, and Yseult wondered
whether she was being mocked.

'You do not consider me worthy of your blood,
Exarch of Khaine?' Yseult found the reason for her
rising anger. 'You will not fight me?'

Behind her, from the ranks of the house Guardians,
Yseult could feel the bubbling of rising outrage.

I do not wish to fight anyone on this day of all days.

THOUSANDS OF ELDAR crowded the streets and boulevards that converged on the Plaza of Vaul in the heart
of the stately Sentrium sector, facing which stood the
Farseer's Palace and the Shrine of Fluir-haern. The
Sentrium was the grandest and most ancient sector in
all of Kaelor, seat of the Ohlipsean and home of the
Knavir eldar. The thoroughfares were crowded
beyond the point of congestion, as individuals
pressed up against each other in efforts to catch a last
glimpse of the body that had been laid in stasis on
the silver, ornamental anvil that marked the geometric centre of the craftworld of Kaelor. The anvil was a
monument to Vaul, the smith god, who was thought
to have been the favoured god of Gwrih the Radiant
himself. It served as a ceremonial altar on grand
occasions, but never before had it been graced by the
body of one from outside the Rivalin lineage.

Despite the pressing throng of eldar, there was a
heavy silence hanging over the Sentrium. Like all of
their kind, the Kaelorians were hostages to their

profound emotions. It was at times of such serious, communal grief that they lost themselves in the solidarity of their craftworld. None muttered even a single word of loss, but each felt the cumulative pain of the others, until the whole sector seemed bathed in grief and remembrance.

There had been no public announcement about the Ceremony of Passing, but the gathering of anguish and pain was a beacon that drew eldar from all over Kaelor to participate in the last moments of their beloved Lady. The Kaelorians felt drawn to the outpouring of emotion like moths to a flame, as though they gained strength and solidarity from the shared sorrow.

High up on one of the balconies of the Rivalin Palace, which faced into the plaza, Cinnia lifted her head and stole a glance around her. On both sides of her were the other courtiers of the Ohlipsean – the Circular Court – each of them with reverentially bowed heads. One or two had closed their eyes, as though they were consciously trying to attune their minds to the swell of grief that rose out of the plaza below them. The seriousness was oppressive.

To her surprise, Cinnia watched one of the other courtiers lift his gaze from the throng below. He glanced furtively around the balcony before noticing that Cinnia was watching him, and then he smiled a faint, embarrassed crease into his handsome, dark-skinned face. In that moment, Cinnia saw that his eyes were gleaming with gold, and she noticed the incredible luxuriance of his silk robes. Despite herself, Cinnia returned the smile, like an infant sharing a moment of recognition and daring, and then snapped her eyes away self-consciously.

Down below them, in the centre of the plaza, she could see the empty shell that was once Lady Ione's body. It had been carefully laid across the silver anvil in a theatrical manner that had clearly been designed to provoke heightened emotions from the assembly. The aesthetic was perfect, albeit shamelessly sentimental and manipulative, since the body was little more than a husk. It was a piece of theatre that would have been worthy of the riellietann, and Cinnia was instantly sceptical about whether the aesthetically stunted styhx-tann of House Teirtu could have conceived of this by themselves. For a moment, she wondered whether the farseer had been consulted on the best way to perform the ceremony. Despite his various faults, old Ahearn Rivalin certainly could not be faulted for his artistic good sense, and it was widely known that Ione had been one of his favourites.

A feeling of discomfort lapped gently at her face, and Cinnia glanced to the side again to see Celyddon Ossian still watching her with his golden eyes. His persistence was bordering on shamelessness, and it was certainly a breach of decorum at an event such as this. She looked away, not wholly displeased by the attention, but not wanting to encourage anything in this context. This was neither the time nor the place.

Murmurs and movement in the crowd below drew her attention back down into the plaza. A passage was opening through the assembly and a small group of eldar was emerging from the gates of the

palace directly beneath her. Bedecked in the green
and gold ceremonial finery of his great house, with
banners fluttering proudly above them, Iden Teirtu
led the contingent out through the crowd towards
the podium that had been erected for them next to
the anvil. Iden carried before him a folded cloth of
emerald green, as though he were cradling a child in
his arms.

For the first time since the end of the House Wars,
Cinnia felt the eldar of the Sentrium respond to the
sight of Iden with affection and sympathy. As he
climbed the podium, with his son Morfran at his side
and with the beautiful young Oriana behind them,
Cinnia felt a wave of emotion flood out of the assembly and wash over them. For the first time in many
years, Iden was the focus of positive emotion. No
matter how painfully the rest of Kaelor felt the loss of
Lady Ione, they knew that he must feel it more
intensely than anyone. She had been with him even
before his bloody rise to power in the Sentrium. She
had come with him from the outlying domains of
Teirtu when he had marched into the Ohlipsean and
wrested effective power from the farseer, and she had
given House Teirtu an air of sophistication in the
Court. Without her, the gruff Iden might never have
been accepted by the cultivated Knavir of the Circular Court.

They haven't even noticed that the farseer is not
there, thought Cinnia, shaking her head,
disappointed and thrilled at the ease with which her
fellow Kaelorians could be controlled. She reflected
that it was one of the many consequences of the

emotional nature of the Sons of Asuryan – as the eldar were sometimes known – and it was not something that could be wholly mitigated by the Eldar Path of Ihnyoh, despite widely accepted assertions to the contrary. Heightened rationality and discipline could not change the essential nature of the eldar dhamashir, they merely obscured it. Looking down at the thousands of eldar assembled in anguish and solidarity, Cinnia was momentarily appalled by their collective weakness for superstition.

The quality of the silence that filled the plaza suddenly changed, bringing Cinnia's thoughts back to the ceremony unfolding below her. She watched Iden stride forwards to the end of the podium, flanked on both sides by Teirtu standard-bearers. He approached the husk of Ione and the silver anvil, directly below and before him, with a pale and solemn face. Very slowly, he unravelled the emerald cloth that he had been carrying with such ritualistic care, letting it drop to its full length over the edge of the podium so that its glistening, silken sheen could be seen by the entire assembly. The glorious cloth rippled and fluttered like a standard, and the golden serpent of Teirtu shone from its centre. All across the plaza and in the streets that fed into it, thousands of heads bowed in reverence, as though Iden had unfurled an icon of the farseer himself.

Without a single word, Iden flourished the cloth into the air and let it settle down over the body of Lady Ione and the silver anvil, covering them both in the colours of House Teirtu. As she watched, Cinnia hoped that at least some of the assembled eldar would realise and resent the political aspirations of Iden's symbolic gesture, as the ostentatious fabric claimed Ione and the anvil for the great house.

As though in organic communion with Iden's movements, a path opened up through the crowd, leading from the anvil to the gates of the Shrine of Fluir-haern on the edge of the plaza, facing the palace. At the same time, a stream of uniformed Guardians flooded out of the gates and formed into perfect lines along the opening in the crowd, transforming it into a passage of emerald and gold for Lady Ione's final procession.

Opposite, on the balcony of the Rivalin Palace, Cinnia shook her head in disdain. Turning away from the scene below her, she eased her way between the other courtiers on the balcony, who remained bowed in reverence, and made her way back inside the palace, only to find Celyddon already in the reception chamber with two smoking glasses of blue Edreacian in his hands. With a grateful and relieved smile, Cinnia reached out and took one of the glasses.

YSEULT WATCHED THE exarch turn and melt back into the line of crimson Aspect Warriors that stood facing her detachment of Guardians. A flicker of anxiety flashed through her mind as she considered the possibility that the Warp Spiders were simply going to turn around and leave without a fight of any kind. Where would be the honour in that? The rituals of commencement had not resulted in a capitulation, nor even in the demonstration of obvious superiority

on one side or the other. To break off would simply
be insulting, as though the Warp Spiders did not
consider her or her Teirtu Guardians worthy of battle.
She could not return to Iden without a victory, and
she would not let an insult to her dignity stand
unchallenged.

She cursed the arrogance of the Aspect Warriors.

As Yseult's temper started to rise and her will
started to arm itself against the hint of an insult
being thrown at her, her hand dropped instinctively
to the hilt of her diresword. The cold metallic surface
sent a chill of vengeance through her arm, forcing her
to fight against an overwhelming urge to draw the
blade and charge forwards at the enemy. That sword
had been a gift to her from Lairgnen, the exarch of
the Dire Avengers. He had presented her with the
ancient blade when she had left the temple following
the completion of her cycle in the dhanir of the warrior. It represented a material continuity, a
permanent and physical connection with the Aspect
that she had served so loyally, and which had served
her so well. Even now, standing proudly beneath the
fluttering banners of Teirtu, Yseult knew that part of
her would always be a Dire Avenger. Looking at the
arrogant Warp Spiders before her, her mind raced
with alternative histories. She might have been an
exarch too, had she chosen differently.

The shining crimson line of Aspect Warriors had
not moved for the last several moments, but Yseult
could sense that a decision was being reached behind
the front line. The exarch was planning her next
move.

'I will not be denied!' yelled Yseult suddenly, fire spitting in her voice. 'Do you slight my name?'

Behind her, the Guardians pounded their weapons against the ground, thundering a note of intent, support, violence and warning.

I will fight you, Yseult of Teirtu, if you deem me worthy of your blade.

It was a new voice in her mind.

'Speak your name, Warp Spider, so that it may be recorded when there is nothing else left of you.'

'I am Fiannah, arachnir of the Warp Spiders and equal of Yseult.'

An unusually slender warrior eased through the crimson line and stood out before her brethren. She held her helmet in one hand and the characteristic deathspinner of her Aspect in the other. Her shoulders appeared unnaturally broad because of the warp-pack that she wore on her back, which made her exposed face seem small and delicate. Her hair had been cropped short, and it was tussled in the unkempt manner of a provincial warrior who knew no better.

Yseult smiled. An arachnir of the Warp Spiders was a worthy prize.

'Arachnir Fiannah, you honour me,' said Yseult, bowing slightly before taking another step forwards and unclasping her cloak. She flourished the rich, green fabric into a whirl around her, letting it fly back into the phalanx of Guardians behind her. In the same moment, she dropped low into a fighting stance and touched her fingertips to the hilt of her blade. 'Let us begin.'

The Warp Spider nodded matter-of-factly, dropping her deathspinner to the ground and casting her helmet aside. She tilted her head from one shoulder to the other, as though loosening the muscles in her neck, and then she reached up and ruffled her silver hair, as though trying to free what had been matted by the helmet before she had removed it.

The last movement drew Yseult's attention, since the gesture sparked a series of light-reflections that shouldn't have been there.

Powerblades, Yseult realised, eyeing the arachnir's forearms with a newfound respect. Now that she knew they were there, she could see them clearly: three little barbs running along the back of each forearm, and then long curving talons protruding out past the Aspect Warrior's fists.

The arachnir shook out her limbs casually, as though ensuring that there was no stiffness in her muscles. Then she stopped suddenly and an air of serious dignity descended on her. With a slow and deliberate movement, Fiannah folded her arms across her chest and bowed her head down between the powerblades.

Then she vanished.

Yseult blinked and then cursed – the wretched warp-pack! The Warp Spider was gone, leaving the line of crimson warriors standing unphased and implacable.

STANDING AT THE tall, elliptical window-bay in his tower, Ahearn Rivalin looked down into the plaza below. The great assembly for the passing of Lady

Ione was impressive, as it should be. The plaza was packed, and each of the tributary streets was congested with bodies for as far as he could see. Kaelorians had come from all over the immense, spacefaring craftworld; there were no longer enough resident in Sentrium to account for such large numbers.

With some discomfort, the farseer saw the banners of Teirtu hoisted around the empty body of Ione, which lay across the silver anvil of his forebears. The double incongruity of a non-Rivalin on the anvil, and then of the vulgar Teirtu laying claim to the graceful Ione made him shiver.

As he gazed down, stooped over the railing but with his weight supported on his gnarled staff, he heard the main door to his personal chambers crack open behind him, but he had been anticipating his guest for some time and he made no effort to turn and greet him. Somewhere in the back of his mind he had been conscious of when the guards outside his room had halted the visitor and challenged his purpose.

The guards; Ahearn smiled to himself. Iden had told him that they were there for his own protection, but the farseer was under no illusions about his situation. He was not exactly a prisoner in his own palace, but his activities were being very carefully managed for him by the head of House Teirtu. Looking down at the Ceremony of Passing in the plaza below, Ahearn could not deny that he would have liked to be there, since the Lady Ione had been like a daughter to him. She had certainly been like a sheet of silk amongst the rough, sackcloth of the Teirtu.

For a moment his thoughts turned to his actual daughter. He could see her down on the podium standing next to that Teirtu imbecile, Morfran, cradling his offspring in her priceless and perfect arms. His Oriana shone like a jewel amongst the crude and uncultivated eldar of that great house, and Ahearn furrowed his brow in displeasure at the way the Knavir of Kaelor had fallen so low that they must rely on these war mongering styhx-tann from beyond the Styhxlin Perimeter for their survival.

Times had changed on Kaelor. The House Wars had left scars through the very fabric of the vast edifice of the ancient spacecraft that the eldar called a craftworld. Looking out of his window, Ahearn could hardly recognise the place. He noticed that none of the Knavir courtiers had been permitted to join the ceremony, and he wondered whether they were also watching the proceedings from a balcony in his palace, somewhere below him.

'Radiant farseer,' muttered a voice from behind him. It was quiet and deferential, but it betrayed no hint of nervousness. There was assertion underlying the show of humility. It was the voice of an accomplished warrior, something that Ahearn was only just beginning to recognise.

'Lhir of Teirtu,' said Ahearn, smiling as he put a name to the voice without turning around. 'How good of you to join me at this difficult time.'

'I bring a message from the Zhogahn, my radiance.' Lhir's manner was clipped, professional and formal. He used the honorific title for Iden, which Ahearn had bestowed on the head of House Teirtu after its victory in the House Wars. Zhogahn: the vanquisher of sin.

Ahearn turned slowly, clicking his staff against the polished floor as he shuffled his weight around. He inspected the Guardian before him. Lhir was bowing deeply, with one knee and the opposite fist touching the ground. His long, silk cloak had been gathered and flung over one shoulder, an ancient ceremonial touch designed to expose his gun-belt and to show that his intentions were peaceful.

The golden glint of a shuriken pistol was visible in the deep shadow at Lhir's waist. The young officer had quickly learnt the value and the limits of ceremonial gestures.

The farseer nodded, impressed by the perfection of the young warrior. Some of these styhx-tann have promise, he thought as his eyes glinted with new possibilities.

'Would you care for a drink, my immaculate young Lhir?' asked Ahearn, wondering how the Guardian would respond. 'I have some excellent Edreacian. Have you ever tasted it?'

As he spoke, Ahearn shuffled over towards a plain-looking cabinet against the wall, with his staff clicking and scraping over the floor as he went. The cabinet opened with a dismissive gesture from the farseer, revealing a luxurious array of beverages and delicacies. A large carafe of simmering, blue liquid had pride of place. It was already half empty.

The Guardian did not move from his position, kneeling just inside the door. His head remained bowed towards the floor, but Ahearn could feel his hidden eyes tracking his movement across the room.

'I must inform his radiance that a detachment of Warp Spiders from the Temple of the domain of Ansgar are moving against the Court. Zhogahn Teirtu has dispatched a force of Teirtu House Guardians to repel the threat. They are making their stand outside the Gates of Rivalin, under the command of Yseult Teirtu-ann. They fight in your name, my radiance.'

'I see,' said Ahearn, pouring a small measure of the steaming blue liquid into a crystal glass. 'Are you sure that I cannot tempt you with a little drink, Lhir?'

'I take my leave, radiant farseer,' replied Lhir crisply, bowing his forehead until it touched the ground. As he rose to his feet, his cloak fell into cascades around him. He nodded once more to Ahearn, and then turned in an abrupt whirl of deep green fabric and strode out of the door.

The farseer watched him go, admiring the disciplined theatricality of the young officer. He could see why Iden had posted this particular Guardian to duty in the palace. There was very little to which even the Knavir courtiers could take offence in the cultivated manner of Lhir.

Rotating the shot of Edreacian thoughtfully, Ahearn wondered whether Lhir could be truly integrated into courtly life. In the myriad paths of the future, one always contains hope, thought Ahearn as he drained his glass.

Returning to the window, Ahearn looked down in time to see the funeral procession pushing through the crowd towards the Shrine of Fluir-haern on the far side of the plaza. Lady Ione's body had been draped with the green and gold serpent of House Teirtu, and lines of house Guardians flanked the route to the sacred gates.

While he stared, the scene faded into the background of his mind as his thoughts turned towards Lhir's message. The Warp Spiders again, he mused. It had not been so long ago that his own son, Kerwyn, had fallen into league with those Aspect Warriors during the period of escalation of the House Wars. Kerwyn had insisted that the warriors of that deceitful and secretive temple had been loyal to the farseer, but they had turned his mind against Iden and the Great House of Teirtu, and the consequences had nearly torn Kaelor apart. The Rivalin dynasty had become divided for the first time in its long, distinguished history. As a result, after he had routed the Ansgar and their treacherous allies, Iden had banished Kerwyn from the sanctity and sophistication of the Sentrium, sparing his life only out of respect for the farseer. Ahearn had never seen his treacherous and misguided son again.

What could the Warp Spiders want on this day of all days?

Down in the plaza, Ahearn saw the procession reach the gates of the shrine. There was a pause while the shrine-keepers performed the necessary purifications before they could permit the mourners into the sacred space within. In that moment, Ahearn saw the distance-diminished figure of Oriana turn her face away from the group and look directly up towards his window. Even though he knew that she was too far away to see him clearly, Ahearn saw something beseeching in her delicate manner that made him ache. In different ways, Iden had taken both of his children from him. It had been a high price to pay in exchange for the reimposition of stability and central power on Kaelor. Politics was a dirty and unpleasant business.

THERE WAS A faint hiss, like air escaping through a pressure-crack in glass. Then there was a scream, accelerating towards Yseult at an impossible speed. She dropped instinctively and rolled, coming back to her feet just in time to see the Warp Spider burst back into material reality and lash into a spin with her powerblades, slicing through the space that had been occupied by her own neck just moments before.

Without hesitation, Yseult unsheathed her sword and flourished it into a striking pose, held vertically above her head even as she sunk low into a combat stance.

Fiannah snapped to a halt, levelling her eyes and then her blades at the Guardian before her. She crossed her arms in front of her face and then lashed them down to her sides, as though shaking the blood of her kill from the blades that ran along her gauntlets.

For an instant, the two warriors stood motionless in the impromptu arena between their two forces. They were lit dramatically by the flow of light that washed out of the legendary Rivalin Gates – the site of so many of the greatest battles of Kaelorian history – and it eased over the lines of house Guardians that stood ready to defend them. Darkness hung over the ground all around them. It was as though the light-phase of Kaelor was striving to frame them a heroic stage.

Yseult shattered the tension. She lunged forwards suddenly, bringing her diresword down in a direct and simple strike towards the head of her opponent. The attack looked clumsy and obvious, but that was its purpose. As Fiannah easily sidestepped the blow, pushing out one gauntlet to parry the blade to a safe distance, Yseult let her strength fall out of the strike and used the force of the Warp Spider's parry to push her into a turn. Dropping almost to the ground, she swept out her leg and spun through a low sweep, catching the arachnir just before her weight had settled.

The Warp Spider's legs lifted under the force of the sweep, sending her crashing backwards onto the ground. Before she could regain her feet, Yseult was upon her. Her foot crunched down against the chest of the Aspect Warrior, pinning her, and she raised her blade into both hands for a vertical thrust down into her opponent's neck.

For a split second, the two warriors held each other's gaze, and then Yseult plunged down with her sword, forcing it down with all her strength and twisting her power into a scream of focus.

At the last moment, Fiannah vanished again, blinking out of the material realm just before the tip of the diresword touched her neck, leaving a fizzling crack of energy that vanished almost instantly. Yseult's scream was arrested as her blade was driven down into the rough metallic ground, burying nearly a quarter of its length. Her balance was thrown for a moment, as she teetered forwards on the hilt of her sword.

From her position just behind the front line of the Warp Spiders, Exarch Aingeal watched her arachnir reappear behind the unbalanced Guardian. She sliced rapidly across Yseult's back with one set of powerblades and then kicked out into her spine with a powerful thrust of her hips. The impacts made Yseult shriek in sudden pain and then flip over the hilt of her grounded sword and skid across the floor under the force of the kick, leaving her blade still vibrating in the ground.

The Teirtu Guardian sprang back to her feet, turning to face Fiannah with fury written across her features. With one hand, she reached round behind her to feel the deep slice that had been cut diagonally across her back, and with the other she tugged a short, black biting blade from her belt. A rapid flicker of her eyes betrayed her longing for the lost diresword.

Satisfied with the performance of her arachnir, Aingeal made a quick check of the other Aspect Warriors in the line, and then she turned and strode back away from the battle. She had more important duties on that day than battling the honourable Yseult. The Lady Ione had done the Warp Spiders a great service on the day that she had pleaded for the life of the young Ansgar heir, Naois. She had given a voice to the great prophecy. She had placed hope in the byways of the future, and Aingeal would not be deprived of the opportunity to pay her last respects to the beloved Lady of Hidden Joy.

Checking back over her shoulder towards the battle once again, the exarch activated her warp-pack and vanished from the scene. There had been no way that an entire detachment of Warp Spiders could have infiltrated the courtly sector of the Sentrium without detection – the sha'iel signatures around the Shrine of Fluir-haern were so closely monitored by the servants of the Rivalin Court – but a single warrior might yet pass unnoticed.

Meanwhile, Yseult stalked into an arc, patrolling around Fiannah with her black blade almost hidden in the near-darkness. She tossed it easily from one hand to the other, as though testing its weight and balance.

The Warp Spider turned on the spot, keeping her foe constantly in full view. She held her powerblades diagonally across her chest, and peered out from between them at the predations of the Guardian. Then, with a faint nod, an aura of energy pulsed around her and she vanished, leaving behind a purpling haze for a fraction of a moment.

This time Yseult was ready. The Warp Spider had appeared in the same orientation after both of her last jumps, and only an ork would have fallen into the same trap three times.

She waited for the crackle of white noise and the faint hiss of sha'iel escaping into material space through an abrupt breach. Then she darted through a tight circle, moving around behind herself. There was a sudden red haze and then Fiannah clicked into existence immediately in front of her, facing towards the point that Yseult had occupied only an instant before. Without a moment of hesitation, Yseult dashed forwards and thrust her dark blade into the Warp Spider's abdomen, forcing it under the warp-pack and into the arachnir's lower back.

Fiannah threw her head back and shrieked in shock and pain, but Yseult cut off the cry by ripping the blade out of her foe's flesh, springing onto her back and then dragging the biting blade across her throat.

While the Warp Spider fell like a dead weight, crashing onto her face on the ground, Yseult kicked free of the collapsing corpse, springing away towards her diresword and tugging it out of the ground. By the time the front line of Warp Spiders realised that their arachnir had been killed, Yseult was already brandishing her ancient blade and calling her Guardians into battle.

There was a brief moment of calm, and then the Guardians charged forwards towards the Aspect Warriors, with the light of the farseer bursting radiantly behind them. Before they had crossed even five metres of ground, the Warp Spiders blinked into their midst, deathspinners and powerblades flashing.

The Rites of Commencement were over.

THE INTERIOR OF the shrine was lit by a matrix of light-beams that criss-crossed the majestic space like an elaborate web. Despite the urgency and peril of her position, Aingeal smiled as she looked up out of the shadows that draped against a sweeping side-wall. She had only been inside the Shrine of Fluir-haern once before, but even then she had felt the power of the place. It was the oldest space on Kaelor, and the very first chamber of the vast craftworld to be built in the ancient and forgotten past before the Fall.

She knew the legends that suggested that the lattice of light was actually fashioned out of threads of sha'iel, constructed by the tiny, crystalline creatures that lived within Kaelor's Fluir-haern, its Spirit Pool, the infinity circuit itself. The threads appeared as luminous strands of a variant of wraithbone. It was said that if a place were saturated with the psychic presence of a sufficient number of souls for long enough, then the tiny creatures would begin to spill through into the material realm, hopping in and out of material existence and leaving microscopic crystalline fragments in their wake.

After uncountable eons, these fragments could build into breathtaking webs, just as single drips of calcium carbonate could build into stalactites and stalagmites. In her own temple, out in the domains of Ansgar, those tiny creatures were called warp spiders, and it was perhaps because of this that she felt so much at ease in the most sacred of all places on Kaelor.

Outside the heavy doors, Aingeal could feel the presence of the crowds in the plaza. They were almost silent, but such a tremendous concentration of eldar dhamashir-souls sent out powerful ripples through the immaterial dimensions. The exarch had skirted the concentrations, moving around the almost deserted edges of the Sentrium on her way to the shrine after invisibly breaching the Rivalin Gates.

Finally, she had approached the building itself from
the off-side, not using any of the tributary avenues
that arced around into the Plaza of Vaul. She had
made seven or eight warp-jumps to get there, and
she was certain that her presence would have been
detected were it not for the immense warp-
disruption caused by the grieving masses in the
Sentrium and by the battle raging in front of the
fabled gates. Not for the first time in her long life,
Aingeal praised Isha for the psychic resonance of the
eldar soul. The very same communal forces that had
once given birth to the Great Enemy could also
conjure a roiling maelstrom of interference. The
Warp Spiders had learnt to hide in the shadows cast
by the flaws of their brethren, the Sons of Asuryan.

There was movement outside. Aingeal could feel
the approach of the cortege, and she realised that
she had no time to linger in the glorious tranquillity
of the shrine. She realised immediately that she had
leapt into the wrong part of the shrine, her route to
the altar blocked by hundreds of strands of glistening thread. Surveying the interior of the shrine
carefully, she took mental note of the exact location
of each of the columns, the statues, and the sub-
altars that were arrayed in deliberately symbolic
patterns. As she stared, she noticed two cloaked and
hooded figures for the first time. At first she thought
they were statues, standing guard symbolically on
either side of the main aisle facing the doors, silent
in their perfect stillness. Then she observed the way
the light fell against the fabric of their cloaks, and
she noticed a faint glow reflected from their hidden

eyes: shrine-keepers. They had not yet noticed her intrusion.

Activating her warp-pack, Aingeal leapt from the shadows in the ambulatories directly into the central aisle that led up to the farseer's Tetrahedral Altar, where the original and only legitimate access point to Fluir-haern was housed. She appeared directly behind the shrine-keepers and, without hesitation, she reached forwards and snapped the neck of the nearest before he had even turned. The other spun in surprise and Aingeal saw the fear widen in his tranquil eyes just before she struck him in the throat. His eyes rolled back under the blow and he lost consciousness immediately, slumping into a cloak-covered pile on the ground.

Aingeal knelt to check that he was still alive and then glanced up towards the towering doors before her, as though to reassure herself that they had not yet begun to open. Then she turned and dashed along the aisle, stopping three steps before the podium on which the altar rested, and dropping to her knees.

Muttering a poem of ceremonial purification, Aingeal lifted her head and admired the flawless craftsmanship of the altar. It was said that the perfectly smooth block of wraithbone had been fashioned by the peerless eldar smiths of Jauin-zur in a time when the Children of Isha had lived on the surface of planets, before the Fall. Although it looked like a regular tetrahedron from every side, it had in fact been constructed so that the centre point, from which all the vertices were always equidistant, was

not located in material space at all, but rather was
locked into the immaterial realm, anchored in the
infinity circuit. The symbolism was clear: Fluir-haern
was the virtual vertex, always equidistant from every
point on Kaelor, no matter how the craftworld might
grow or change. The optical result was that it was
almost impossible to behold the altar completely. It
seemed to defy close inspection, as though the pressure of a gaze were enough to make its form slip and
alter.

The unique and matchless design also served a
practical function: because the altar existed partially
outside the material space of the shrine, it also provided a bridge between the substantial world of
Kaelor and its spirit pool. A small, tear-shaped socket
in the front face provided a point of access to the
bridge, and it was into this that the spirit stones of
fallen eldar would be placed for the Transference of
Dhamashirs. This was the destination of Lady Ione's
spirit stone. The destiny of her undying soul lay
within the Fluir-haern, where it would join tens of
thousands of her forebears in pristine sanctity.

In a moment of reverence, Aingeal considered her
memories of the Lady of Hidden Joy. She could still
remember watching her standing at the side of Iden
Teirtu on the balcony of the Farseer's Palace, overlooking the Plaza of Vaul at the end of the House
Wars. In the square, next to the silver anvil, Bedwyr
Ansgar stood with Kerwyn Rivalin and the Ansgar
marshals, held at lance-point by the victorious Teirtu
Guardians. Standing before their father, hardly old
enough to stand unsupported, were the childlings,

Naois and the tiny Ela. Just as Iden had raised his
hand to signal the executions, the fair Lady Ione had
interceded, dropping to her knees on the balcony
before all of Kaelor and pleading for the lives of the
infants. She talked of mercy and dignity. She talked
of grand purposes and fateful destinies. She talked of
the greatness of House Teirtu being measured not by
the death and destruction that it brought to Kaelor,
but by the life and rebirth that it held within its
power. She gave voice to the prophecy.

At that moment the eldar of Kaelor had taken the
Lady of Hidden Joy into their souls as an icon of
hope for the future. Iden himself had paused, uncertain and confused by the sudden actions of his
consort. He had been unable to deny her, and the
childlings were dragged away from the plaza by their
hair, leaving their father to face the executioners with
his loyal warriors. Just as Bedwyr had died without
uttering a word of remorse or fear, the childlings had
passed out of the plaza in eerie silence.

Not long after that, the lady had made the long
journey to the ruined domains of Ansgar and laid the
sleeping Naois on the steps of the Temple of the
Warp Spiders, leaving the orphaned heir to Aingeal's
care.

A crack of sound jolted the exarch back into the
present. Behind her, the doors to the shrine were
opening slowly. Without hurrying, Aingeal bowed
forwards and touched her helmet to the face of the
Tetrahedral Altar, and then rose to her feet and
bowed sharply once again. As the doors finally
opened behind her, she reached forwards and placed

a small runic icon on the altar as an offering to the Fluir-haern, whispering an incantation of the Warp Spiders' esteem and gratitude for Lady Ione.

The exarch could hear the rushing of feet and the bracing of weapons as the Teirtu Guardians spotted her and dashed through the open doors, hastening into the interior of the shrine. Unhurried, Exarch Aingeal of the Warp Spiders turned to face the intruders. A spread of Guardians had secured the only exit, and she could see the banner-draped husk of Ione being held in the doorway by the honour guard. Ahead of them, flanked by his personal bodyguard, Iden Teirtu stepped forwards along the aisle towards the altar. Then he stopped and looked up into the eyes of Aingeal, with furious hatred written in his gaze.

Then Aingeal vanished.

CHAPTER TWO: SCILTI

A PSYCHIC SCREAM echoed through the interior of the Shrine of Fluir-haern, ricocheting between the wraithbone statues and interweaving with the intricate webs of sha'iel that glistened impossibly in the darkness. The sound spoke of agonising frustration. It also contained pain, but overriding all the other emotions was a crescendo of violent rage. It sent ripples and shockwaves pulsing around the temple, making the glittering matrices shiver and quake.

The tall, powerful figure of Iden Teirtu stood before the Tetrahedral Altar and howled curses into the sacred space around him. Holding his arms out to his sides in a cruciform, he roared with fury, leaning his head back to give his voice full reign over his body.

He railed until his was the only voice audible near the shrine. All of the eldar in the Plaza of Vaul outside the gates were silent, listening intently to the anger of the great patriarch. His fury seeped into them like a faceless contagion, and unrest began to flicker through the crowd like an indignity. The emotions curdled into their grief, and before long the assembly felt wronged and affronted, without any idea of why. The Kaelorians of the Sentrium knew only that something had disturbed the ritual purity of the Ceremony of Passing. They knew only that Lady Ione's last moments in the material realm had been blighted, and they shared instinctively in the rage of their Zhogahn.

Iden's rant finally subsided. He dropped his arms to his sides and lowered his gaze back down to the cortege that stood around Ione's shrouded body, just inside the doorway to the shrine. His rotund son, Morfran, gazed back up at him with a wet smile gleaming over his face. His eyes shone with a touch of hysteria, as though his father's anger had thrilled him to the point of excitement. His rich, green robes were ill-adjusted, and his exposed skin shone with ornamental graftings and piercings. Despite his fury, Iden felt a faint wave of revulsion towards his kin. He couldn't help it; Morfran's physical presence, which was such an affront to the austere warrior ideals of House Teirtu, made him physically sick.

The delicate Oriana stood next to him, looking up at Iden with shock and fear written into her exquisite features. At her feet, the crumpled shrine-keeper suddenly groaned and twitched, alive but in pain, but

Oriana hardly noticed the suffering next to her. Her wide eyes shone with disbelief and she had turned her slender body slightly away from the Zhogahn so that the infant in her arms was partially shielded from him. Fury was more appalling than pain.

As for the others in the party, Iden didn't even spare them a glance. He could sense their shock at his reaction to the sight of the Warp Spider in the shrine, but there was nobody there worth his attention. There was nobody to whom he had to explain himself. Only Oriana's gaze demanded anything from his conscience.

Iden composed himself for her benefit. He smoothed down his heavy robes and straightened his dark jade cloak. Then he gathered his long, silver hair and arranged it over one shoulder, in the manner of the Circular Court.

He smiled sadly and nodded, as though acknowledging Oriana's right to judge him. Despite everything that had happened over the last several years, despite even his victory in the House Wars that had brought his great house to such prominence in the Sentrium itself, Iden still felt the innate superiority of the Rivalin line. No matter what he did, he would always see the eyes of Oriana or her father watching him critically.

She simply stared back, her horror undiminished.

Am I really so abhorrent to her, wondered Iden? Are the ways of my house really so brutal? His eyes drifted back to Morfran's excitable features, and not for the first time he saw the incongruity of the couple. It was simply impossible to imagine two more

different eldar on all of Kaelor. In the contrast
between them, as they looked up at him from the
central aisle of the Shrine of Fluir-haern, framed
between the corpse of one shrine-keeper and the
twitching remains of another, he saw himself as the
Knavir eldar of the palace must see him. He wondered whether their cultivated sensitivities would
even appreciate the difference between him and his
son. He even makes *me* sick, he thought.

A heavy sadness sunk into Iden's soul, a type of
profound loneliness. Standing on the steps before
the Tetrahedral Altar, in the most ancient and sacred
heart of Kaelor, he looked down on the daughter of
the farseer, standing side-by-side with his own son.
Such had been the stuff of his dreams during the
long and bloody down-phases of the House Wars,
but now the scene left him cold, as though something in the universe conspired to reject the
situation. It felt offensive.

He realised that he offended himself.

Many of the Knavir had refused to join the Ceremony of Passing, despite their obvious affection for
Ione. She had been the one member of his house
who had been truly accepted as an equal amongst
the courtiers. She had been trained in the ancient
Seer House of Yuthran, and had come to him in his
home domains in the years before the House Wars,
speaking of a prophecy that would see his house rise
to new heights of power. She had arrived in the
pledge-lands of Teirtu at the turning of the tide, when
the eldar of the neighbouring sectors had been close
to starvation. They had turned to Iden for aid, calling

on him to oppose what they called the tyranny of the
Rivalin Court, which they claimed had siphoned off
the wealth and sustenance of the outer domains for
long years, merely to feed its own taste for luxury.
Iden had heard the calls of his kinsmen and neigh-
bours in open sessions, but it had been the private
counsel of the Lady Ione that had finally inspired
him to take his courage in his hands. When House
Teirtu had first arisen as the sword of the Farseer's
Court in the outer reaches of Kaelor, Iden had led the
fight against the rebels with Ione at his side.

That was when it had all begun. That was when
military power had stealthily crept onto the political
stage of Kaelor for the first time since the Craftwars.
After eons of peace following the coming of Gwrih
the Radiant and the establishment of the Ohlipsean,
power seemed to be shifting away from the ceremonial grandeur of the Circular Court and towards the
less cultivated great houses of the outer reaches. For
the first time in its long and glorious history, the
Rivalin Dynasty needed more than symbolic authority over Kaelor. It needed military force to keep the
increasingly discomforted craftworld in line. In hindsight, the process was obvious. At the time, it had
been unthinkable. It was still unthinkable to many of
the Knavir courtiers.

Iden tried to hold Oriana's gaze for a moment, but
the young Rivalin averted her eyes almost immediately. She despises me, he thought, and she has good
reason. She was part of the price that old Ahearn had
paid to retain the power and the service of House
Teirtu. She was the promise of their future in the

court; the child of Morfran and Oriana would be both Teirtu and Rivalin.

Yet the match had not brought acceptance. It had merely served to emphasise the Morfran's vulgarity. Only Ione had been accepted. None had been able to deny her a place on even the highest of tables. The farseer himself had taken counsel from her on many occasions. She had been loved. Morfran was despised. Iden himself despised him.

Now, Ione was gone, and the Knavir of Kaelor held the Teirtu in such contempt that they had not even bothered to participate in her Ceremony of Passing. At the last, despite her popularity and integrity during life, she had been damned by association. He had seen them during the congregation in the plaza, up on their balcony in the palace, watching the proceedings with disapproval. He could only imagine the way that they would talk about the thousands of styhx-tann eldar that had crowded in the Plaza of Vaul for a last view of Ione's husk. They were above such things.

By Khaine, fumed Iden, his ire raised yet again by his unspoken chain of thought, the arrogance of the eldar! It caused such incredible suffering and inequality. Even the cyclical and ostensibly egalitarian Eldar Path could not mitigate it. Because the Knavir could control aesthetic standards, it was also up to them to determine the best path for the best dhanir to follow, and it was not the dhanir of the warrior, that was for sure! Although the Knavir may no longer be in touch with the realities of military power on Kaelor, they still managed to hold on to moral and aesthetic authority, and, given the character of the eldar, this was ultimately more important.

Iden exhaled deeply, bringing his thoughts under control. None of these things should be permitted to ruin the Passing of Ione. He would not be responsible for ruining the ceremony and he would not be responsible for providing the Knavir with further evidence of the vulgarity of House Teirtu. Things had gone so smoothly until that cursed Warp Spider had shown up in the shrine and disturbed the elegance with flecks of death and reminders of the House Wars.

He nodded towards the cortege, as though to signal that everything was under control, and then turned around to face the altar. He changed his hair from one shoulder to the other, just as he should, and then dropped to his knees, quieting his mind into a reverential meditation. He began the prayer of purity in a barely audible whisper, preparing the way for the passage of Ione's dhamashir into Fluir-haern. With the shrine-keepers incapacitated, he would perform the rite himself, as he had done for fallen warriors many times before.

Just as his mind was at rest, he saw a small tablet resting against the foot of the altar, as though it had been placed there as an offering in advance of the ceremony. It was a small, metallic disc, and it glinted faintly in the half-light of the shrine.

Furrowing his brow as the object broke his concentration, Iden tilted his head to one side so that he could see the little icon more clearly. An instant later, he sprang to his feet and ripped the long, heavy

sword from its holster on his back. He was crying
with renewed fury as he swung the broad, coruscating blade around his head in a giant arc, smashing it
through dozens of delicate, glittering wraith-webs
and shattering them into dust. The blade seemed to
thrill at the discharge of destructive energy, as though
it were feeding on his bloody intent.

Down in the main aisle, Morfran's eyes widened
with excitement as he watched Iden's rage explode
ruinously around the interior of the shrine. He eyed
the great sword with almost sensual pleasure, recognising it as Dhamashir-dhra, the Soul-Slayer, the
ancient blade that had been presented to Iden by one
of the eldar rangers that had fought the rearguard
action against a tyranid splinter that had pursued
Kaelor for several years before the House Wars.

Those battles against the tyranids had yielded
much of benefit to House Teirtu, including the trust
of the farseer, and the great sword was both a symbol
of Iden's mastery of war and a potent weapon in its
own right.

The legend said that it had been fashioned out of
organic material reaped from the chitinous bodies of
slain tyranids and then infused with wraithbone by
the peripatetic Bonesinger Yureelj, forging a blade
that seemed to come alive at the touch of its master.
In reality, the exquisite blade had been wrought
entirely from wraithbone, but its appearance was so
close to that of a tyranid bonesword that the
rumours of its alien origin had taken on a life of their
own. This in itself was testament to the skill of
Yureelj. Once or twice, Morfran had even caught Iden

talking to the blade, as though it were a living creature.

With a swift step, Iden moved down from the altar and into the aisle, letting the weight of his blade turn him as he descended. Dhamashir-dhra fizzed as it swept through the shadowy air, bleeding a trail of psychic energy in its wake. Then, as Iden's cry grew into an abrupt scream, the blade struck squarely into the base of the Tetrahedral Altar, provoking an explosion of dark-light that pulsed out from the altar in concentric shockwaves.

Despite herself, Oriana screamed in shock and fear, seeing the manic hysteria of the old warrior's soul laid bare for the first time. Then she turned, clutching her child, and ran back along the aisle, bursting out into the light of the Plaza of Vaul like a drowning youth struggling to the surface for air.

Breathing hard, with his long hair hanging in ripped curtains over his face, Iden watched Oriana flee. His billowing cloak was speckled with the shards of shattered wraith-webs, and a strong gust of faerulh whipped through the shrine, as though fleeing in solidarity with Oriana. Even as he looked down the aisle and out of the doors at the pressing congregation in the plaza outside, Iden's sword was still held out behind him, pressed against the side of the altar where it had struck, glowing and chittering with psychic force. Just beneath the tip of the blade, at the base of the still unblemished altar, the runic-icon of the Warp Spiders lay shattered and disintegrated.

Biting down on his anger, Iden looked straight past his son at the shrouded husk of Ione and spoke to as though to the dead. 'Mark this, the Warp Spiders will pay for the ruination of this sacred day, and if I find that the old athesdan farseer has made the same mistake as his son, there will be none to plead mercy at my feet. Not even you can save him from my blade, my lost lady.'

THE UMBHALA STAFF flashed through a tight crescent, arcing directly towards Naois's head. He had learnt the folly of parrying a staff many times before – the staff has two ends, and you cannot block them both – so he dropped his weight under the tip and smacked his own staff up behind it, accelerating the strike beyond its intended focus.

Overreaching slightly, Scilti felt his balance shift. This was a new tactic from Naois, but Scilti was not about to be bested by a cheap trick. He let his balance fail, and then, just on the point of falling, he sprang, cycling through a roll and flipping over Naois's dropping form.

Both tyro-combatants regained their feet simultaneously, turning immediately to face each other with their staffs held before them like swords, defining their striking distances. Their eyes met and their gazes locked as they patrolled around each other like predators, waiting for a glitch or an opening for the next attack. They feinted and faked, twisting through the various set pieces they had learnt in years of hard training, but neither seemed able to gain the advantage. Each gesture from one provoked the perfect counter from the other, so neither was willing to follow through.

Abruptly, Naois stopped moving and lowered the tip of his staff, letting it click down into the thin layer of sand on the hard floor. He let his shoulders relax, rolling them a couple of times to loosen the tension, but his silver eyes retained their glint of menace as he tracked Scilti's still prowling figure.

There was a measure of physical resemblance between the two warriors. They had similar builds, and they both had the shaven heads of temple acolytes, but Scilti was a full head taller than his younger cousin, and his shoulders were broader. He carried his staff like a weapon rather than a toy, and his fiercely set eyes spoke of a profound hunger that was yet unknown to Naois. It was as though a longing for death had touched his soul with a bloody hand.

He circled slowly, half turning his face away from Naois so as to keep his quarry on the edge of his sight, caught by the more sensitive receptors of peripheral vision. Naois remained motionless. His head was angled towards the ground, but the glint of his eyes betrayed an alert awareness. The tip of his staff defined tiny, imperceptible circles in the sand, as though he was doodling. Despite Scilti's physical advantage, Naois gave no sign of being intimidated. He was simply waiting, knowing that his older cousin would have to make his move.

Scilti completed his circle and then paused, studying Naois's casual posture as though inspecting an unimpressive but troubling underling. His face

snarled delicately, and a flicker of frustration crossed
through his gaze, making him blink. For an instant,
his eyes strayed to the edge of the small arena. He
could see the tall, slim figure of Adsulata, the arachnir that had been charged with overseeing his
training. She was standing in silent stillness in the
shadows by the crescent shaped doors. Sitting next to
her on a lush red cushion was the distinctly eerie figure of Ela'Ashbel, with her eyes glowing softly blue in
the half-light.

His thoughts lingered on the child seer for a fraction longer than his eyes did. She shouldn't be here,
he thought. She changes things. Her presence makes
this different. She already knows who has won, it has
already happened. They should have kept her in the
Seer House of Yuthran. She is not welcome here. A
new word arose spontaneously in his head: vaugnh –
abomination.

A dull shock punched into Scilti's stomach, taking
him by surprise. He let the blow push him backwards, tumbling back out of range of the follow-up
before planting his feet for the counter, but Naois
appeared not to have moved. He remained standing
in the centre of the arena with the tip of his staff still
caressing the sand. However, Scilti could see the rush
of footprints and the skidding of sudden motion in
the dirt, and he bit down on his tongue in self-
reproach. He knew better than to lose his
concentration, especially in front of the uncanny
young Ansgar.

Spinning his staff over his head and then turning it
into a braced position, caught under one arm and

held firm against his back, Scilti stalked forwards once again. He closed the gap on Naois with slow deliberation, passing the circumference of the circle that he had been patrolling before and stepping within the death-zone, within the ring defined by the striking range of Naois's staff.

He was sick of waiting outside the zone for an opportunity to dart in, and he was sick of Naois forcing him to make his move from the conventional distance. At this intimate range, doing nothing would be even more risky than ploughing in at the wrong time. After years of training, Scilti had finally learnt when to force the situation.

For a few moments, nothing happened. Naois and Scilti stood frozen, face-to-face, their uneven breaths mingling between them, each gazing off at the ground next to the other. The atmosphere in the arena shifted instantly as waves of tension, discomfort and anticipation flowed out from the poised warriors.

From her cushion near the crescent doors, Ela felt her brother's irritation. She could see his mind suddenly seethe at the intrusion into his space. This was not how he had been taught to fight. Adsulata had told them to keep the correct distance. His thoughts were racing with aggression, and Ela's eyes widened slightly as she saw Naois's body bulge perceptibly, as though the sense of injustice itself had taken on a physical presence.

Scilti also seemed to recognise a shift in Naois, and he reacted instantly. He pushed away from his cousin with both hands, even as they clutched around his horizontal staff. As the gap between them increased to the appropriate distance, Scilti twisted his hips and brought one end of his staff sweeping round towards the head of the stumbling Naois. Unbalanced, Naois could do little more than raise his own staff to block the strike as he tried to plant his feet in the fine, shifting sand, but Scilti's staff had two ends, and he could not block them both. As the staffs collided with a solid thwack, Scilti was already reversing his hips and swinging back the other way. In a flash, the other end of his staff smacked into the back of Naois's shoulders and sent him stumbling forwards.

'Stop!' commanded Adsulata, stepping out of the shadows and into the ring. 'That is a death blow. It's over.'

Scilti snapped around to face the arachnir, dropping his staff to his side and bowing smartly. Having regained his balance on the far edge of the arena, Naois did not turn. He stood with his head down and his back to the others.

From her position near the doors, Ela looked past the beaming Scilti and watched her brother's back anxiously. She could sense his rage building. It glowered in his mind as though needing only the briefest of breezes to fan it into an inferno. She could see his shoulders quivering, as though he were fighting his own instincts to turn around and reap destruction on Scilti and on the arachnir that had told him to keep proper distance. A forceful perception of injustice shimmered around him like a poisonous aura.

Ela shivered, realising that she was the only one who could feel the chill descending over the arena.

The scene glimmered and then hazed before her, fracturing like a faulty hologram. The images and figures swam for a moment, curdling in her mind as though she were mixing them into new formations. When they settled again, the new scene was shocking. She saw Scilti in the armour of a Warp Spider. She saw the temple around him in flames. She saw the domains of Ansgar smouldering in ashes. Then she saw Scilti lying dead at the feet of her barely recognisable brother, as blood poured from his hands into pools of burning ichor on the ground. She saw a violent maelstrom of warp-fire engulfing Kaelor.

'No.' She whispered it to herself, firmly but almost inaudibly. She had to learn to control these visions, now that the Yuthran had abandoned her, and the slight effort of vocalising sound was enough to bring her back to the present.

Without knowing why, Adsulata peered back over her shoulder at Ela, checking to make sure that the childling was all right. The little seer made everyone uncomfortable, and the Warp Spiders were not uniformly pleased that she had returned to the domains of her father and placed herself in the trust of the temple. She had turned up unannounced and unescorted, a solitary, wandering infant in the volatile lands of the styhx-tann. However, after many interviews with the exarch herself, little Ela had still refused to reveal why she could not return to the Seer House of Yuthran, and Aingeal had finally given her leave to stay.

'But,' continued the arachnir, turning back to Scilti, 'do you understand why it was a victory?'

The youth looked down into the ground, unsure whether this was a question that required a response. He had won, and that was the important thing.

'The victory is not the point, young Scilti. The point is that you fought today like a Warp Spider. You kept your distance to survey your prey, as though weaving a web around him, and then, once he was caught in the centre, you closed the distance suddenly and made the kill. This, young Scilti, is precisely the purpose of the warp-pack, it enables you to take control of the proximity of combat. That control must always be yours. Never surrender it to another.

'The moment when you realised that the regular engagement distance for the staff gave neither of you an advantage was exactly the moment for the warp-pack. Tomorrow, your staff may be a deathspinner. Leap in close and finish your prey with your powerblades: the fangs of the Warp Spider.'

'Yes arachnir. I understand,' replied Scilti, lifting his gaze to look at Adsulata. Was she implying that he was to be given his armour and weapons? She had mentioned the warp-pack, the deathspinner and the powerblades. Could this be the day? His eyes flashed with renewed hunger.

'Come,' she said, turning her back and leading the way to the crescent doors, 'we have much to do to prepare you for the Rites of Vhaenom.'

Ela saw the gleam pass over Scilti's face as he realised that he had finally done it. He had finally proven himself ready to join the ranks of the Aspect Warriors of the Warp Spiders. She watched her cousin dash along behind the arachnir as the web-encrusted crescent doors slid silently open to permit them exit, and she noticed with sinking dread that neither of them paused to consider Naois.

After the doors had clicked closed once again, the silence in the arena felt dense and heavy like ice. Still seated cross-legged on her cushion, little Ela looked over at her brother. His back was still towards her, and his head remained inclined down towards the ground. She could see it moving slightly, as though he were talking to himself, but there was no sound. His shoulders seemed to quake, as though momentous movements were passing through his body just below the surface.

It's not fair. The thoughts were childish and almost petulant.

Suddenly, Naois turned. His silver eyes were wild with fury, and tiny flames of blue seemed to flicker in their pearly opacity. His ferocity lashed out across the arena like a force whip, crackling over the thin layer of sand and disrupting the grains. Holding Ela's gaze for a moment, he spun his unbreakable umbhala staff up into the air. Then, with one magnificent movement, he caught it horizontally in both hands just as he brought his knee up to meet it. He yelled out in pain and defiance as his knee cracked through the shaft, splintering the hard wood into two. As the pieces broke into each of his hands, he dropped his weight to his knees and plunged the two shafts down into the ground, driving them half their length into the hardened floor of the arena as he yelled.

Ela flinched under the onslaught and thought that she experienced in those moments something of the fear that the Yuthran sisters had experienced in her own presence.

IDEN'S MIND WAS racing with the implications of the recent events. The Ceremony of Passing had not gone as smoothly as he had hoped, and certainly not as smoothly as he had needed. There were precious few opportunities for him to demonstrate his sensitivity to the refined customs and practices of the Circular Court, and this had been by far the most high profile. The Knavir had loved Ione, just as the Teirtu had done. She had been a figure of unity, and her passing should have been an occasion to consolidate that. The eldar of Kaelor should have been united in their grief for the fallen Lady.

But somehow events had conspired against him. It was as though the gods themselves were opposed to his victories, as though they were working silently and subtly against him to engineer his fall. He looked up at the glorious statue of Khaine, the Bloody-Handed God, which he had brought with him from his root-lands. Long years before, Iden had taken Khaine as his patron, even before he had gone through a cycle of training in the Temple of Dire Avengers. He had known even then that the god of war was a fickle master, but the glory of victory and the thirst for combat had been enough to swamp those subtle confusions. It was only when he had marched triumphantly into the Sentrium that Iden had really understood the consequences of his vows and his allegiances.

Thinking back to the Mythic Cycles, Iden knew that Kaela Mensha Khaine was a misfit god. He had torn the heavens apart and visited ruin and tragedy on his siblings. He had stripped Isha of her children and chained Vaul to his anvil. He had stood against the Sons of Asuryan until the last, when he had been rent asunder standing valiantly and defiantly in their defence against the Great Enemy.

It was small wonder that the effete Knavir looked at Khaine's blessing as a curse, and at those who received it as flawed and debased, but Iden had not properly realised the depths of their disapproval until so many of the courtiers had refused even to stand with him at the Passing of Ione, despite their love for the Lady herself.

Then there had been that damned Warp Spider. Iden couldn't believe her audacity. For her to show up in the Sentrium at all after her involvement in the House Wars was bad enough, but to appear within the Shrine of Fluir-haern on the day of the Passing of Ione was simply unconscionable.

The Knavir would not even deign to descend out of the Farseer's Palace, but the Exarch of Khaine, Aingeal, risked her life to be present in the shrine. It was the precise opposite of what he had wanted. It was the inverse of what he needed. The Passing of Ione had not brought him acceptance at the court, but it had brought the Warp Spiders back into the Sentrium for the first time since the execution of Bedwyr and his treacherous Ansgar warriors. Rather than distancing him from the affairs of Khaine, the events had thrown him back into those bloody hands.

And what had been the meaning of that icon? The little silver-black disc that Aingeal had left against the Tetrahedral Altar; it had been carefully decorated with an intricate web, containing a fanged spider in its centre. What was the meaning of it? Was it supposed to be an offering for Ione? Or was it a sign, left in the shrine for an accomplice to see and then act upon?

Iden's first instincts told him to suspect the worst of all things. He had not become the military master of Kaelor by ignoring the signs.

'Redouble the guards in the farseer's tower, Lhir,' he said, without turning to face the Guardian who had been kneeling patiently behind him while his mind had run through the possibilities.

'As you wish,' replied Lhir crisply, rising to his feet immediately and nodding a curt bow. He paused for a moment. 'You suspect that the farseer is in league with the Warp Spiders, my Zhogahn?'

Iden turned away from the asymmetrical, curving window that dominated the outer wall of his reception chamber. He had rapidly become accustomed to standing in that window to contemplate the strategies and vagaries of courtly life since he had taken up residence in the Sentrium. The view of the sector was unparalleled, and it gave him a sense of dominion.

'Suspicion is never without sense,' he said, smiling in an avuncular manner at Lhir. 'Whether or not it is justified, it is better to be prepared.' Besides, he thought, Ahearn's cursed son, Kerwyn, had once thought it expedient to ally with the Warp Spiders against him, and he would be dull-witted fool not to consider the possibility that the old farseer might harbour sentimental designs in that direction.

'One further matter, Teirtu-ann, send word to our forces in the Reach of Guereal that an extra tithe will be expected from the domains of Ansgar this year. Tell them to collect it early. Tell them to collect it now.' The Warp Spiders would know that their interference had consequences.

'As you say. I will see it done,' replied Lhir, bowing again, before turning and striding purposefully out of the room.

Watching him leave, Iden admired the disciplined style of the Guardian. He could see why the Knavir might not be too offended by his presence in the palace, and he was reassured about his decision to appoint him as the head of the palace guards. There was something graceful in his manner that appealed to everyone. It was as though his evident discipline was somehow effortless. In some ways, he reminded Iden of the impeccable Yseult, although he was far less of a warrior than his elegant champion, more of a courtier.

If only there were more Teirtu like Lhir, thought Iden as the young captain disappeared from sight. He looked over to the other side of the chamber where Morfran was reclining in one of the lush couches. Three servants were arrayed around him, one fanning him ostentatiously with the feathers of the long-extinct phaex-firebird while the other two offered a range of foods and liquors. Noticing his father's gaze, Morfran grinned mid-mouthful and gestured to one of the vacant couches.

Iden narrowed his eyes disapprovingly.

'Come father,' scoffed Morfran, mocking Iden's seriousness. 'If we cannot enjoy the luxuries of our position, why did we fight for so long to attain it?'

Without a word, Iden turned back to his window and gazed out over his Sentrium. You did not fight to attain it, he thought, I did.

IN THE CENTRAL quadrangle of the Temple of the Dire Avengers, Yseult sprang and twisted, flourishing her diresword through an elaborate sequence of movements until stopping abruptly. She paused for only an instant. Then she lurched back into motion, dropping low to the ground with her blade held out behind her, and then suddenly sweeping her sword forwards whilst leaping back through its attacking arc. The balanced movements brought her to a halt once again, perched on one foot with the other leg extended behind her to balance the diresword to the front.

She lowered her rear leg very slowly, bringing her blade up vertically and back towards her face in synchronisation.

I see that you have not forgotten your training, Avenger Yseult. The thoughts came from high above, from somewhere around the edge of the hollow central spire of the temple.

She brought her feet together and whipped her sword diagonally across her body, saluting and symbolically cleaning the blade in a single dramatic motion. Then she nodded a deliberate bow in the direction of the sanctum, offering a moment of gratitude for her training and her skills. She owed the Avengers her life, and she would not forget it. It was theirs for the taking, should they ask for it.

She looked up. 'A good teacher leaves a profound impression, quihan,' she called up towards the dimly visible figure on one of the circular balconies that ringed the interior of the spire above the arena. 'My skills, such as they are, are a residue of your own work.'

There was silence, but Yseult could feel the amusement of the exarch. He could not hide it from her.

You always were my favourite pupil, young Yseult. There was a smile in the tone.

Just as the thoughts reached her mind, she saw the figure leap from the balcony above her. It dived out into the centre of the spire, as though streamlined for a dive into liquid. Then it tucked neatly, spreading its arms for stability and turning its head back up over its heels. Then it dropped, feet first with outstretched arms like a descending angel, hitting the ground at speed but catching its weight with perfect timing and the honed elasticity of its legs.

It is good to see you again, daughter of Asurmen. Exarch Lairgnen stood a breath away from her face, his black eyes shining fathomlessly while his long, midnight blue hair writhed around his head, as though animated by its own electrical power.

Yseult folded down onto one knee before him, automatically sweeping her cloak over one shoulder in a mark of respect.

Do you intend to return to us? There was genuine hope in the exarch's mind.

'No, my quihan,' replied Yseult, although her thoughts lingered for a moment on the idea. 'I return from battle in the name of the Teirtu Zhogahn. I come to you for advice.'

On this day of all days, the Zhogahn goes into battle? Lairgnen's thoughts turned to the Passing of Ione.

'Battle came to him. It was the Warp Spiders, quihan. They attempted to gain entry to the Sentrium.'

You stopped them?

'I stopped them,' replied Yseult with a hint of pride. 'I claimed the Arachnir Fiannah in the Rites of Commencement. That victory is yours.'

No, it belongs to the Teirtu now. There was a pause. *So, Aingeal risks the Covenant of the Asurya's Helm? She presses against the wounds of the Teirtu, poking her fingers into their blood. The Aspect Temples had sworn off political affairs – we had agreed – you were right to oppose her.* The exarch fell into thoughtfulness, disturbed by the turn of events.

'The victory was slight, Lairgnen. The Warp Spiders are strong, and the Teirtu Guardians lack the discipline of their training. We were fortunate to have greater numbers.'

Your modesty is well phrased, young Yseult, but your agenda today is transparent. The Dire Avengers cannot and will not stand with the Teirtu, not even against the Warp Spiders. Aingeal's breach of the covenant does not justify our own. The neutrality of the Aspect Temples has been respected for eons on Kaelor, my Yseult, and not without reason. You ask too much.

'You doubt House Teirtu?' Yseult looked up at the exarch, meeting his depthless eyes and gazing into the void within.

This is not about the worthiness of the great houses, Yseult. Iden is a fine warrior, as was Bedwyr. This is a matter of principle. The Temple Guardians agreed long ago not to interfere with the affairs of the Ohlipsean. We made the agreement with Gwrih the Radiant himself.

'But Aingeal disregards that agreement? Should you not avenge this slight?'

Lairgnen smiled a broad, humourless smile and Yseult could not tell where his black eyes were focused. *That is a nice try, Avenger Yseult, but, for now at least, I am the keeper of this temple, not you. The insult is not done to the Dire Avengers, but to the Circular Court. Since we have no affiliation to that Court, there is nothing for which we should seek vengeance. This has nothing to do with the Dire Avengers, Yseult. It is not my concern.*

'You would speak differently if House Teirtu held your respect,' said Yseult, bowing her head again in resignation. She knew that he was correct. The Aspect Temples had to be above the courtly and political fray, despite the clear arrogance of the Knavir eldar who held themselves above the violent methods of the Aspects. On Kaelor, she reflected, everyone is above everyone else.

House Teirtu is a warrior house, Yseult. I have trained many of them myself. This is something that I can respect. There was another pause as the exarch considered whether to go on. *But it is true that there are certain elements of that house that are less worthy of respect. Indeed, there are some that might one day provoke even the Avengers into a breach of our oath.*

* * *

THE GLASS SLIPPED out of Ahearn's hand, clipping the edge of the table and spinning before smashing on the ground. A pool of bubbling blue liquid rushed out between the shards for a moment, but then evaporated, leaving the jagged remains of the glass like a trap on the floor.

'Apologies, my dear Cinnia,' the farseer mumbled with a grin. He was leaning heavily on his staff and swaying slightly. The table already supported an array of glasses, some empty, others half full. 'Let me get you another one.'

'No need, radiance. Allow me,' smiled Cinnia, standing out of her chair and offering it to the inebriated old eldar.

Ahearn nodded seriously, as though acknowledging that this was the proper way to proceed. He lowered himself cautiously into the chair and placed his staff carefully on the table before him, concentrating.

As Cinnia strode over to the tastefully plain, almost featureless cabinet against the wall and gestured it open, Celyddon leaned forwards from his seat and pushed a glass across the table towards the farseer.

'Thank you, my dear,' acknowledged Ahearn, focusing his eyes deliberately and then reaching for the glass. 'Tell me more. What else did that mon'keigh do?'

All three of them laughed at the farseer's choice of insult. It was true that the Teirtu were as unsophisticated as human mon'keigh, but the image was perfect. Still chuckling, Cinnia watched the doors of the cabinet slide apart to reveal an assortment of bottles, carafes and a number of glasses. She peered at them, trying to differentiate between those that were clean and those that were merely empty. After several moments of indecision, she just took the nearest one and then wandered back to the table.

'It was so terrible that the Glimmering Oriana took flight!' declared Cinnia, dropping down into one of the empty chairs. 'She ran out of the shrine as though it were burning down around her. Her eyes were wild and she was clutching the tiny Turi as though desperate to save his very soul.'

The three of them laughed for a moment, but then the laughter trailed into melancholy as the seriousness of the situation slowly and inevitably dawned on them.

'Iden was enraged,' said Celyddon gravely. 'He lashed through the shrine, shattering many of the exquisite wraith-webs. They are irreplaceable.'

'What of that wretch, Morfran?' asked Ahearn, gazing thoughtfully into the mist that hung around the top of his glass. 'Did he not leave with my Oriana?'

'No, radiance. He remained within the shrine, evidently rather excited by the events,' replied Cinnia with obvious disapproval. 'What else would you expect from him?'

'I expected worse,' confessed Ahearn, throwing his drink back and closing his eyes to enjoy the concentrated effect of the burning, volatile liquid in his throat.

There was a long silence as the three Knavir considered the events of the last day. 'Times have

changed on Kaelor,' muttered Celyddon to nobody in
particular. The contemplative silence that
surrounded his lament was enough of a reply.

A movement in the doorway told them that a visitor had arrived, but none of them looked around.
The guards would have stopped anyone distasteful,
or would have at least challenged them. Whoever it
was, they made no sound to interrupt the three at
the table. They waited at the open door, dropped
onto one knee in deference to the presence of the
athesdan and two of the Ohlipsean.

'And Ione?' asked Ahearn with a sudden urgency,
as though he had just remembered the most important issue. 'Was the Ceremony of Passing performed
adequately, at least?'

Cinnia placed her glass carefully onto the table
and then leant forwards earnestly. 'Iden performed
the ceremony himself,' she said, as though revealing a terrible secret. 'The Warp Spider had killed the
shrine-keepers, so Iden performed the ceremony
himself.'

'She had a warrior's Passing,' added Celyddon
sympathetically.

Ahearn said nothing. He picked up his staff and
used it to hook one of the carafes on the table,
dragging it back towards him before pouring himself a fresh glass. His unsteady hands were
suddenly strong and focused, as though all the lev-
ity of the situation had been suddenly drained
away.

'The travesties of the Teirtu are unforgivable,' he said
at last, lifting his glass as though in a toast.

The others raised their glasses and then drained them swiftly. A moment of silence marked their solemnity.

And the Warp Spiders? Our dear and immaculate Lhir informed me that they marched on Sentrium today, and you tell me that Aingeal herself was in the shrine? What was their purpose in this affair? The farseer let his thoughts echo around the chamber, deliberately letting them slip into the mind of Lhir, as he knelt silently just inside the doorway. It was important that the dashing Guardian knew that he was seen as separate from the house to which he was pledged.

'The Zhogahn suspects that they were here for you, radiance,' said Cinnia, swirling the liquid in her glass casually. She could already see where this conversation was going.

'He is concerned that you have resurrected the alliance forged by Kerwyn, radiance,' added Celyddon, his golden eyes gleaming.

Ah yes, my dear lost Kerwyn, responded Ahearn, yet again including Lhir in his gloomy thoughts. *I would dearly love to see him again, but Iden has never revealed to me where he was banished to.* The tone of the thoughts beseeched a response, and Lhir was the only one able to provide one.

The three Knavir toyed with their glasses for a few moments, conspiratorially providing a window for Lhir to interrupt them.

'Radiance,' said Lhir from his position at the doorway, right on cue, 'the Zhogahn has requested that we increase your guard... It is for your own protection at this troubled time,' he explained, clearly unconvinced.

'Ah, Lhir!' said Ahearn, rising to his feet as though surprised to hear his voice. 'Are you at leisure to take a drink with us this time, I wonder?'

The Guardian hesitated, but then rose to his feet and strode into the room. He stopped directly before the farseer and dropped back down onto his knees, grasping Ahearn's hand between his.

Ahearn smiled. 'Please, young Lhir. It is not a relic.'

'Your radiance is too generous with me,' said Lhir, steadfastly staring down into the polished floor. 'I offer my services to take a message to the Glimmering Kerwyn.'

Will not the Zhogahn disapprove of such an act? I would not want to jeopardise your position in House Teirtu, my Lhir. Ahearn grinned in his mind: 'my Lhir' was perfect.

'Lord Iden instructed me to double your guard. That is all. Until I receive further instructions, I see no reason why I cannot be of service to you, athesdan.'

This is generous and dutiful, my dear Lhir. I will not forget this service.

Lhir touched his forehead to the farseer's hand and then rose to his feet. He turned on his heels and strode directly out of the door.

'That was easy,' remarked Celyddon after Lhir was gone, taking a satisfying gulp from his drink.

'He wants to serve. His dhamashir is crying out for something more refined than that brute Iden. He merely required an alternative. Given a choice, most eldar will choose our way. It is our nature,' smiled Ahearn with an edge of sadness. 'I merely gave him that choice.'

'Did you call on the Spiders, radiance?' asked Cinnia, as she watched the complex of emotions pass over the farseer's face. 'Did they come for you?'

Ahearn sat back in his chair and gripped his glass delicately between thumb and forefinger. 'No, my beautiful Cinnia, I made no call. I cannot see why the Spiders marched today, but I can see them in a number of the myriad futures, and I know that Aingeal's soul is full of devotion to Ione; I could feel it even whilst she defiled the shrine.'

'Perhaps this is the time to call on her for aid, radiance?' offered Celyddon, clumsily putting words to the thought that was circulating around the table.

'Perhaps,' replied Ahearn, looking up from his glass and smiling ambiguously.

PREPARE YOURSELF, SAID Aingeal simply, as she leant her weight into the heavy doors and pushed. A jagged crack of light appeared down the centre, crooked like a set of teeth, and then the doors swung open and Scilti found himself staring out into the domains of Ansgar as though for the first time in his life.

He stepped up under the lintel, beside the exarch and surveyed the scene, squinting in the sudden light after years of training in the shadows of the temple. It seemed like a lifetime ago that he had stood out in that green forest zone and listened to Bedwyr rallying House Ansgar for the final battle of the House Wars. Even the youthful Scilti had fallen into line behind the valiant patriarch, as moved by the justice of his words as by the courage of his sword.

The scene had changed since then. The greens seemed somehow less vivid, and the foliage seemed less lush. The trees were thin and their leaves were sparse. The fabled umbhala stood at the centre of the clearing, in front of the temple steps, shrouded in a coruscating energy field, as though to protect it from predators or poachers, and the eldar themselves seemed to slouch and shuffle. There were perhaps a dozen of them at work in the clearing, carving little trinkets out of wood or fashioning them from wraith-bone amidst swirls of potent energy, artisans, wraithsmiths and others.

As the doors of the temple cracked open, all eyes turned up towards them, as though filled for a moment with a spark of hope. Scilti felt the weight of their expectations, but he didn't understand it.

'What do they want?'

Food, perhaps.

The answer was not the one Scilti had been anticipating. He digested it like a shot of strong liquor, shivering involuntarily despite his resolution to seem unaffected.

'They are outcasts?' he asked, trying to fit an explanation to the facts before his eyes. 'Path Finders?'

No. They are regular wayfarers like you. Can you not see the skill that goes into their labour?

Scilti nodded as the eldar in the clearing began to rise to their feet and move towards the base of the steps. Very soon, there was a small crowd assembled, looking up and studying the young Warp Spider and his exarch.

Times have changed on Kaelor since you were last outside the gates of this temple, young Scilti. The eldar of Ansgar suffer the residues of Teirtu's wrath. The House Wars may have ended, but these eldar are still suffering from them. The Teirtu and the Ohlipsean draw a heavy tithe from these lands, heavier than it can service.

Genuine horror gnawed at Scilti's soul. 'Why was I not told?'

You were in training, my young lord. The affairs of Kaelor must not intrude on your training. The way of the Warp Spider is raw and visceral and should have no concern for politics. Remember that.

'This is not politics!' Scilti raised his voice, and regretted it immediately. The gathering crowd below picked up on his tone, as more eldar joined it. 'We are talking about survival here... How could you let this happen?'

What would you have me do?

'Fight!' The answer seemed simple and clear to the young Scilti.

A murmur of recognition pulsed through the crowd below. They could feel the passion and the indignation of the young Warp Spider. Was this the one that they had been waiting for? Was this the one spoken of in Lady Ione's prophecy?

This is not the Warp Spiders' fight, Scilti. The Aspect Temples are sworn to neutrality, you know this.

A figure stepped out of the crowd down below. His grey hair was matted and unkempt, and his clothing was torn and patched, but his eyes gleamed and the hilt of a well-polished sword glinted under his ragged, blue cloak.

'Lord Scilti?' The voice was firm and unwavering, belying the shabby appearance of the eldar who spoke. 'My Lord Scilti, do you not remember us?'

Scilti looked down at the ragged bunch of eldar at the base of steps. He studied them. There was something incomplete about the impression that they gave. There was something hidden in their manner. A simmering defiance seemed to roil and bubble just under the atrophied surface. Despite their broken appearance, a fighting spirit emanated from them.

Looking more closely, Scilti could see the glint of a sword hilt under the dark blue cloak of one, the bulge of a shuriken catapult strapped to the leg of another, the handles of twin witchblades protruded past the shoulders of another, and one leant his weight on a long staff that looked rather like a singing spear.

'These are the Ansgar Guardians?' asked Scilti, turning to Aingeal in disbelief. 'This is what has become of them since the end of the war?' His voice betrayed a mixture of resentment and pain.

These are the survivors, young Scilti. They returned to these lands, and they have been waiting for a leader, for one of the Ansgar to return to them as Lady Ione had prophecied.

Turning back to look down the steps of the temple, Scilti saw the group form itself into a line. Then they dropped to one knee on the bottom step. They swung the torn remnants of their cloaks over one shoulder and touched their fists to the ground in signs of deference to him.

'My Lord Scilti, we have been waiting for you.'

CHAPTER THREE: KERWYN

SOME KIND OF liquid was dripping down from the distant ceiling, making Lhir aware that every level in Kaelor had another level above it, no matter how distant or invisible the ceiling might be. It was one of the special idiosyncrasies of the vast craftworld. Even though it existed as a finite object in three-dimensions, it was almost impossible to find its edges, and it was literally the case that every level had another above it, even those that should have been right at the top. Intellectually, Lhir knew that this had something to do with the fact that the architecture of the craftworld was not restricted to the three material dimensions – it had something to do with tetrahedral design, where the central vertex that defined the dimensions of the space lay in the immaterial realms – but the details of it were beyond him. He remembered hearing that the primitive mon'keigh had once had such a limited understanding of gravity that they had thought that planets were flat, otherwise they could not explain why people didn't fall off them. Despite his unsanitary and messy surroundings, the analogy with the legendary stupidity of the mon'keigh brought a smile to his face.

Besides, most Kaelorians would live their entire lives without giving the matter of craftworld architecture any thought. It was not until they experienced something as bizarre as a leaking roof that anyone was reminded of where they were.

After many long hours of riding to find the location, Lhir climbed off his deep green jetbike and surveyed the matrices of pipes, tubes and conduits that threaded and interwove through the wide, low space. Some of them had ruptured long ago, and reservoirs of oily liquids had pooled under the elevated pipes. The toxicity of the effluent had eaten through the floor in a few places, and Lhir could hear the distant dripping of liquid falling a long distance into the level below, which must either have been evacuated or had never occupied in the first place.

Why would anyone want to live out here? Lhir asked himself, scowling at the smell and the general indignity of the place. He had never heard of anyone choosing to live in the Coolant Wastes, but he was aware that some of the less savoury outcasts were banished into these sectors. Legend had it that the Ranger Vhruar the Hidden spent many years here, self-ostracised from the strictures of Kaelorian society before he had embarked on his epic journey to discover the fabled Black Library. If the rumours were true, then there might still be pockets of Path Finders hidden out here, shunned by the rest of Kaelor, which they shunned in return.

Lhir had been into these sectors before, long ago. He remembered the distastefulness of the experience, but he also remembered the Wastes being smaller and less extensive. He recalled some degradation in the coolant systems that ran through the whole segment, but he didn't remember them being so close to ruination. If memory served him correctly, the Coolant Wastes had sprawled out through these sectors over the last hundred years, growing like a cancer on the fringes of Kaelor. It was as though the Knavir of the Ohlipsean were simply ignoring it.

He couldn't believe that Iden would have banished Kerwyn Rivalin, the farseer's only son, to such a forsaken place. There had to be some kind of mistake. He was duty-bound to check it out; he had promised the farseer.

Leaning over his jetbike, Lhir opened one of the panels on the side and pulled out a long, slender shuriken cannon. It was scarred and battle-marked from previous encounters, but he checked it briefly, making sure that it was still clean and functional; it had been a long time since he had required the use of such a weapon. Not since he had played his part in the House Wars had he needed anything more than his ornate, decorated pistol. The Farseer's Palace was not noted for its large-scale disturbances, and his posting as captain of Ahearn's personal Guardians had given him a virtually ceremonial role.

He tested the weight and the balance of the cannon, holding it comfortably between both hands. It felt good. A flicker of intensity passed through his thoughts, as though something dormant had awoken within him when he picked up the weapon. A voice in his dhamashir whispered bloody thoughts, like the calling of Khaine. Yes, thought Lhir, this is how it should be. He was a Guardian of House Teirtu, not an effete courtier of the Ohlipsean. He had almost forgotten. The Sentrium could have that effect on an eldar.

Movement flashed between the pipes and ventilation shafts ahead of him. It was a glimmer of motion, little more than a disturbance of the light. Instinctively, he looked behind, checking to make sure that it was not a deliberate distraction.

Nothing.

The movement flickered again, in the same place, and Lhir shouldered his cannon, looking along the barrel and through the sighting array. The stabilising gyroscopes whirred faintly next to his ear and his finger automatically touched down on the trigger, a hair's breadth away from firing it.

The motion flashed again, and then again, first to the left and then back to the right. It seemed regular, like a pendulum. Through the optical enhancements of the cannon-sight, Lhir could see a hint of colour in the darkness between several of the ichor-coated pipes.

There was something swinging from one of the over-head shafts.

Lowering his gun, Lhir picked his way forwards through the sludge and debris that was strewn over the ground, ducking under the low-hung pipes and skirting around the edges of those that were ruptured and spilling unknown, toxic effluent onto the slick ground.

As he drew nearer to the pendulum, it gradually became clear what it was. The body of a male eldar was hanging from one of the structural rafters that were supporting the low ceiling. A thin cord had been looped around the hapless eldar's neck and then tied off through a hole in the side of the overhead beam. From where he was standing, it seemed to Lhir that the hole had been drilled or shot out of the rafter with exactly this purpose in mind.

The stench was incredible, and Lhir drew his cloak up around his face, whirling it around his shoulders so that it would act as a mask. On closer inspection, he could see that the flesh of the dead eldar was rotting and flaccid. Skin drooped off his skeleton as though it were several sizes too big for the bone-structure.

Lhir reached up with his cannon and prodded at the body with the tip of the barrel. It rotated slowly under the pressure and swung slightly, bringing the eldar's face around for Lhir to see.

He recoiled in revulsion, withdrawing his gun rapidly, as the tiny jurnaome beetles scurried out of the corpse's vacant eye sockets, disturbed by the sudden motion. The eldar's face was rancid and riddled with sores and bite marks. It was unrecognisable. Looking down at the tip of his gun, Lhir could see that it was coated in a thick, congealed layer of ichor that had simply come away from the body when he had touched it.

Turning away, Lhir inspected the site for clues
about what might have happened and who might
have done this unspeakable deed, but except for the
flesh fragments and bodily waste that had fallen
from the corpse, the area around the hanging body
was clear and clean. In fact, looking around, Lhir
realised that it was unusually clean, as though it had
been specifically cleared by someone. There were
marks on the metallic floor that showed traces of
scrubbing, and an effluent-drenched cloth to one
side suggested that someone had used it to clean the
floor in a circle around the rafter.

Hooking the tip of his shuriken cannon under the
cloth, Lhir lifted it from the ground and let it dangle,
watching the thick sludge drip from it. To his horror
Lhir saw that the cloth was a deep red cloak. Through
the slush and muck that had soaked into it, he could
see the outlines of patterns and icons embroidered
into the fabric, and there, right in the centre of the
material was the golden emblem of the Radiant Star,
the crest of the Rivalin dynasty.

A flash of pain lashed through Lhir's mind as he
realised what this meant. He spun, letting the cloak fall
back to the ground, and gazed back up at the swinging
corpse. There was heavy reddened hair, slightly longer
than he remembered, and the wine-red tunic of the
Rivalin. A collection of ornate blades and trappings
were tucked into the golden belt. A long, elegant chain
hung around the body's neck, decorated at intervals
with jewels that still glinted from under the ichor as the
corpse swung and rotated though occasional beams of
light, and there, on the end of the chain, swinging freely

for anyone to see, was the dull, lifeless waystone of Kerwyn Rivalin, with a clear and perfect crack running through its heart.

In a moment of panic, Lhir swept his eyes frantically around the area. He was searching for signs of a struggle, some kind of fight, anything, but the site was relatively clean and tidy. Aside from the soaked cloak, he found a neatly folded blanket to one side. Stooping to inspect it, he realised that it had been laid on top of a beautiful and ancient shuriken pistol, presumably to keep the weapon clean and properly preserved. The hilt was marked with the Radiant Star. It was Kerwyn's gun.

The realisation hit Lhir like a lance: the farseer's only son had committed suicide. He had been abandoned in the Coolant Wastes by the Teirtu Guardians, presumably on the orders of Iden Teirtu himself, and left to die. They had not killed him, reasoned Lhir, inspecting the evidence, so that Iden could tell Ahearn that he had banished and not executed his son. The farseer would have been able to sense a lie. But this was as good as killing him.

Mercy of Isha! Lhir could hardly stand to be in that disgusting place, but he had a jetbike standing by to take him back to the Sentrium, and his sensibilities were not nearly as refined as those of Kerwyn. How could they have expected Kerwyn to survive in this place? Surrounded by filth and effluent, knowing that his father had become the virtual prisoner of House Teirtu and that his allies, the noble House of Ansgar, had been executed. How could they have expected him to live knowing that his Kaelor was ruined?

They hadn't expected him to live.

Despite the slime and the sludge, Lhir dropped to his knees at the feet of the corpse and hung his head in shame. The heir of the Rivalin throne hung silently before him, with his waystone, cracked, violated, dull and lifeless still hanging around his neck; it was wasted. Only Isha would know the whereabouts of his soul now or how the stone had been broken. It had certainly not enjoyed the sanctity of the Ceremony of Passing into Fluir-haern. Instead, Kerwyn had cleaned his own death-space on his hands and knees, valiantly trying to pass with dignity from these filthy endings. And at some time thereafter, someone had cracked his spirit-stone.

The Knavir were right: Iden Teirtu was a styhx-tann barbarian, unworthy of his position in the Ohlipsean. This ending was a disgrace to Teirtu and a tragedy for the Rivalin line. Political and military expedience, should not take precedence over taste and good moral conduct. In that moment, Lhir was sure that neither Ahearn, Cinnia nor Celyddon would ever sink to these depths of depravity.

Muttering a series of prayers to Isha and Asuryan, Lhir rose to his feet and spread his own cloak on the clean ground. He cut Kerwyn down and laid him on the cloth. Then he gathered up the Rivalin's other belongings and folded them into the cloak, wrapping the corpse in the green and gold emblems of House Teirtu with bitterness and regret in his soul. Hefting the body into his arms, Lhir turned and made his way back to his jetbike.

* * *

THE BANQUET CHAMBER was bustling with life and Morfran was in his element. He sat in the middle of the long side of the head table, displacing Iden who sat a couple of seats to his left. The chair between them had been left unfilled, symbolically empty as though everyone expected Lady Ione to walk in and take her seat at any moment, but every other chair in the room was taken, and a few of the latecomers had been forced to eat and drink on their feet, or to perch on the edges of one of the congested tables.

There was a sudden but gentle sound, like a distant insect. It was perfectly placed to intrigue a developed sensibility, just sufficiently audible to peak the attention of half the eldar in the room, and they were just sufficiently interested to direct the attention of the others. As a wave of quiet washed around the noisy room, the translucent, pearly doors swung slowly open.

All eyes turned, but nothing emerged.

With an abrupt guffaw, as though unable to contain the tension or his excitement, Morfran laughed, spitting a half chewed lump of bloody tureir-iug onto the table and dribbling a trail of sizzling Edreacian down his chin. He felt the eyes in the room drawn to him, and the mixture of disgust and amusement that tickled his psychic senses made him beam.

Today is a glorious day, he began, but then he stopped, allowing a look of theatrical confusion to pass across his face. He peered down onto the table as though suddenly searching for something. Spying the chewed piece of tureir-iug floating in the top of his glass, he pried it out with surprising dexterity and popped it back into his mouth.

Blasts of disgust hit him from all sides at once, and he grinned in pleasure, as though feeding on the revulsion of the others. He could see his lovely Oriana at the very end of the table, her face hidden under a light, veil-like hood. She wasn't even looking at him. In the corner, on the far side of the chamber, standing against the wall slightly apart from the festivities, he could see Yseult. Her cloak was pulled around her as though sheltering her from a terrible storm, and he could see the shape of her sword still strapped into its holster. Her face was like stone and, for just a fraction of a moment, it threatened to disturb Morfran's mood.

'Today is a glorious day,' he repeated, this time out loud as though worried that his thoughts may not have reached everyone. He was still chewing the meat, so his voice was mumbling and only vaguely audible. 'Today we celebrate a great victory for House Teirtu!' he announced, glancing over towards Iden, whose face was a confusion of emotions. 'And!' announced Morfran, as though it was itself an exclamation. 'And... and we commemorate the passing of our dear Lady...' He trailed off, leaving his audience to guess whether this was because he was inebriated or because he couldn't remember Ione's name.

He drained his glass quickly before continuing. *Today, our valiant Yseult Teirtu-ann did battle once again with the cursed Warp Spiders of the domains of Ansgar, and she laid waste to them before the farseer's gates.*

There was a chorus of approval from many, a murmur from some, and silence from Yseult herself.

'And... and our very own Zhogahn, Iden of Teirtu, confronted the exarch in the Shrine of Fluir-haern, frustrating her plans to disrupt the Ceremony of Passing, banishing her back to the styhx-tann regions where she belongs. Thus, my dear patriarch saved the soul of our beloved Lady...'

The chorus of approval was louder this time, as befitted the status of its subject, but there were still murmurs of dissent in the background, and it did not pass unnoticed that Oriana remained utterly unmoved by the speech.

'And... and these things are the perfect excuse for a feast, if ever we needed an excuse!' he cried, slurring his speech and lifting his glass for a moment of solidarity. He realised at the last moment that the glass was already empty, so he leant forwards and grasped the carafe, tipping the whole thing over his head in place of a toast.

There was enough of a response to keep Morfran happy. He could feel the intoxicated amusement of many of the Teirtu present. The Guardians and consorts loved these occasions. They had still not outgrown the novelty of the wealth and power that they had accrued since moving to the Sentrium, and he could feel the disdain of a number of the Knavir courtiers who had deigned to attend the feast.

Hypocrites, he thought. If they detest me so much, why should they come to my table? I detest their duplicity!

But not all of the Knavir appeared repulsed, one or two gazed up at him in amusement from the other side of his table, as though trying to share a moment of understanding with him.

Sit down, Morfran, before you fall down. Iden's thoughts were firm and tinged with disapproval, but they were not without affection. He rose from his own chair, as though to make the point that only one of them should be standing. Morfran teetered for a moment, with frizzing wine bubbling over his face, and then collapsed down into his chair. The Knavir Celyddon Ossian, who was sitting opposite him, quietly reached over and passed him a lush, golden scarf for him to wipe his hands and head on.

It is good of you all to attend this little gathering. Iden cast his eyes around the room, taking in the mixture of Knavir courtiers and the eldar of House Teirtu. It was the kind of mixture that should have warmed his heart, but the differences between the two groups were so clearly evident to him that it made him cringe. He could see why so many of the Knavir wanted to have nothing to do with him or his house, although he found it more than a little irritating that they were more righteous about the ceremony earlier that day than about the feast now. In any case, he was pleased to see the likes of Seer Cinnia of Yuthran and Celyddon of Ossian apparently enjoying themselves at the head table, despite the Morfran's vulgarities. They nodded their acknowledgements as his gaze passed over them.

One or two of the others displayed obvious signs of resentment about their presence, and Iden wondered whether his Guardians had been a little too heavy handed when they had extended his

invitation. Uisnech of Anyon, in particular, seemed
to be seething. His arms were folded tightly across
his chest and he had not touched his drink. Iden was
not surprised to see Oriana's disgust hazing like a
dark aura around her, but he was faintly surprised to
see that the most displeased among the other guests
seemed to be Yseult, who appeared unmoved and
unimpressed.

*It is unfortunate that His Radiance, Farseer Ahearn
Rivalin, could not be with us this evening,* he continued,
realising for the first time that Lhir had not yet
returned from the palace. *Today's events have been most
trying for the farseer, and he is taking some rest. The
antagonism of the Warp Spiders has cost him much energy.
He is old and frail, as you know.*

He wondered how many more times he would have
to make similar excuses about the absence of the
farseer. He thought that he had done it more than
enough already, and, despite its necessity, it displeased him. In spite of all the pomp, ceremony and
ostentation that had entered his life since House
Teirtu had marched in the Sentrium, Iden was still a
warrior in his soul, and he found much of this duplicity and extravagance offensive.

*Nonetheless, in commemoration of our recently passed
Lady Ione, we have a special treat for your delectation.* He
gestured back towards the open, pearlescent doors,
which most of the diners had already forgotten. *May
I present the Harlequins of Arcadia, who intend to perform
the Cycle of the Avatar for our pleasure and edification.*

An excited murmur of anticipation whisked
around the room. Kaelor had become such an

isolated craftworld that the eldar were thrilled merely
to be reminded that there were other Sons of Asuryan
in the galaxy. Harlequins were a rare treat. Besides
which, Iden was pleased to have the opportunity to
expose at least some of the Knavir to the mythic
cycles, which invariably made warriors into the
heroes of eldar history. Anything that supported the
status of warriors was welcomed by Iden. He couldn't
help but think that it was precisely this status that lay
at the root of all his problems in the Ohlipsean.

Military power had been frowned upon for so
many eons before the House Wars, and Knavir had
only reluctantly acknowledged its importance out of
necessity. Necessity breeds hate, and hateful innova-
tion. He knew that he was probably in more danger
now than he had been even at the height of the wars,
facing the magnificent Bedwyr across the lengths of
two great swords. The Farseer's Court held far more
subtle dangers than a blade.

A good natured cheer arose as the first of the multi-
coloured Harlequins shimmered into visibility in the
centre of the room, singing eerily and dancing with
breathtaking grace. Morfran whooped encouragingly,
Celyddon drank deeply from his wine, Oriana lifted
her hood slightly so that she could see the dance, and
Yseult swept straight out the room.

THE NOISE RESOUNDED through the crescent doors,
pulsing like life and driving Naois to distraction. He
stood with his faced pressed up against them, feeling
the vibrancy of the atmosphere beyond. He closed
his eyes and convinced himself that he could see the

events unfolding in grounds of the temple. He could hear the remnants of his father's army chanting their acceptance of Scilti as their new leader, as though they had been waiting for him for all these years. As though Scilti could take up the sword of Ansgar and lead his house back to glory on the ground of battle, as though Scilti could avenge the tragedy done to the great house at the close of the House Wars. As though Scilti could do any of these things!

He couldn't even defeat me in a training bout without breaking the rules, fumed Naois, turning away from the gates and stalking back into the centre of the arena. The sound of the commotion outside dimmed slightly, as though the empty shadows around the arena acted to dampen the noise, but the shadows also closed in around him, wrapping him in a shroud of isolation. For a moment, he felt like the only light in a galaxy of darkness, utterly alone.

It's just because he's older! That's the only reason he has been passed through the Ritual of Tuireann before me... but I'm stronger... I am stronger! His thoughts thundered around the arena like a physical shockwave. *It should be me!*

Sitting in the shadows around the edge of the arena, hidden in the darkness, Ela flinched under the onslaught of fury. There was an anger in her brother that she had not seen before. It was a resentment. It was a violence. It was a passionate sense of injustice. It was like a breath from Khaine.

Reaching down, he gripped the broken shafts of his umbhala staff and ripped them out of the ground, sending showers of sand and shards of metal scattering across the arena. Then he whirled on the spot, spinning the two sticks around his turning body in an intricate pattern that Ela had never seen before. She watched in fascination at the creative destruction that Naois was defining in the arena before her.

He spun and sprang into the air, rotating like a gyroscope as though he had suddenly become the only balanced point in the galaxy. Landing, he drew his broken staff around his body, dragging it through the air with such fury that it seemed to burn against the resistance. As he moved faster and faster, a field of silvering energy started to flicker around him. It was faint at first, but its vague glow gradually grew into an intense halo, as though his skin were burning with passion.

Ela looked on in astonishment. She could feel the energy of the arena being drained, as though it were all been sucked into the centre where Naois danced the furious form of the wolf spider. It was as though Naois himself was a vortex, dragging in the psychic residues that touched everything in the temple, pulling the power around him like a new and luminous skin. As she watched, she realised that the effect was also working on the material realms. She could see the grains of sand on the floor start to tremble and then move, skittering like iron-filings towards a magnet. After a few moments, the sand started to run into little streams, trickling towards the leaping and spinning feet of Naois in the centre of the arena. The intricate runnels shifted and changed direction, breaking into branches and tributaries in attempts to track the motion of the dancing warrior.

After a while, larger things started to move. The posts that defined the perimeter of the arena began to lean towards the middle. Ela could feel the pull being exerted on her in the shadows, and she performed an effort of will to maintain her position. The great crescent doors started to creak, as though being forced back against their hinges.

With a sudden abruptness that shocked Ela, Naois widened his arms in the middle of a spin and released the shafts of his broken staff. They flashed through the arena like lasfire, and ploughed into the back of the web-encrusted crescent doors, punching into them and penetrating nearly all the way through. At the same time, Naois dropped into a crouch in the centre of the arena. His halo blinked out and he was breathing hard after the exertion.

It is not fair. The thought floated freely, like an exhausted, gliding bird.

From her hiding place in the shadows, Ela watched with wide, sapphire eyes. Her amazement was caught partly by the awesome display of power, but mostly because of the aesthetics of the scene before her. The sandy ground had formed into an incredibly intricate pattern, dragged and pulled into trails and gullies by Naois's furious exertions. The floor of the whole arena had been transformed into a giant spider's web, the threads of sand defining the elaborate web from the outer perimeters of the arena and focusing in the centre on Naois's crouching form.

For a moment, Ela thought that she could imagine how the sisterhood of Yuthran had felt as they had watched her pass through the Rite of Alastrinah. For the first time, she thought she could understand the term vaugnh: the abomination. She had always known that the seers of House Yuthran had feared her, but she had never experienced the thrill of that fear. The excitement and terror that had glimmered in Cinnia's sharp, green eyes whenever they had spoken about the future and Ione's prophecy suddenly made sense to her.

She watched Naois get back to his feet in the centre of the web and saw the little rain of spontaneous wraith-crystals crack off his skin and scatter onto the ground like diamond-dust. Was this what Ione had meant when she had spoken of the nascent power of the future that was held in the hands of Bedwyr's heirs? If so, how could Iden of Teirtu have been convinced to show mercy on these Ansgar vaugnh? A new vista of myriad futures suddenly opened up in Ela's mind.

The crescent doors cracked open to reveal the towering form of Aingeal, accompanied by the Arachnir Adsulata. A dim light silhouetted them from behind and a wave of noise from the gathering outside washed inside with them. They peered at the umbhala shafts that were rammed through the structure of the doors, glanced over at Ela, and then stared over towards Naois, who remained standing in the centre of the arena.

Despite herself, Adsulata gasped at the sight. She took in the destruction, the sprinkling of wraith-crystals, and the incredible sand patterns all at once. She could see the exhausted fury burning in Naois's silver eyes as they fixed on her and Aingeal from the shadowy arena.

* * *

THE FARSEER WAS folded into meditation in his tower. His eyes were closed and the atmosphere was heavy with concentrated silence. The air was tinged with incense from a simple bowl full of smouldering umbhala chippings. He let his thoughts pass, feeling them begin to slip out of his conscious control, sliding towards the place of nothingness where farsight resided.

It had been a long time since he had caught more than a glimpse of a possible future. Not since the end of the House Wars and the entrenchment of the Teirtu had his mind found enough peace for its dangerous journey. He had not even been able to see the glimmering trace of his own son amidst the myriad possibilities. It was as though something had clouded his vision or blocked him from the place where he needed to be.

He knew that there were whispers in the Ohlipsean about his waning powers. There had been rumours even before the House Wars that his psychic control was slipping. He had seemed unable to prevent or even foresee the Wars, and he had allowed Kaelor to drift dangerously close to the fringes of the great warp Maelstrom, closer to peril than it had been since its unavoidable encounter with the craftworld of Saim-Hann in the Craftwars so long ago. Even now, the Maelstrom roiled and raged outside and Kaelor seemed unable to move away from it. Some had suggested that the great Rivalin farseer was too preoccupied with other things to focus his mind properly on the paths of the future, as was his hereditary duty. It was not only the austere warriors of the great houses that looked on the Rivalin dynasty as effete and decadent.

Indeed, not everyone had agreed with the old-fashioned Knavir that the rise of the Teirtu had been unwelcome. For some it was at least a measure of meritocracy. At least Iden Teirtu had won his place of power in an open contest. Despite the isolation of the craftworld, it was not unknown that the hereditary system on Kaelor was slightly idiosyncratic and hardly ever employed amongst the eldar of other craftworlds. The eldar were an emotional species, and resentment always simmered just under the surface of their cool exteriors. It was part of what it meant to endure the eldar condition. It was the foundation of the Eldar Path.

A farseer should be beyond such considerations, however, and Ahearn felt his faltering concentration like a dull, painful pounding in his head. There had been a time when he had been able to sit in a trance for days without end, and now he could hardly even manage to get into the place of nothingness. His mind was all over the place, and he stumbled over himself, distracted by noises, thoughts and the faint buzz of intoxication from the Edreacian, which of recent he had been partaking rather more of. The worst of it was that he knew that some of the rumours were correct: he did seem to be losing his gift, and he had never heard of that happening to a farseer before. Never in the uncountable eons of eldar civilisation had a farseer been known to fall back from his sight, plunging back into the partial blindness of the ordinary eldar dhamashir-soul. The

Path of the Farseer, the most immaculate manifestation of the discomforting Path Stalkers, led only
onwards into the future, yet his own path seemed to
have become lost.

Gradually he became aware of the noise that was
rumbling up through the floor, and he struggled to
block it from his mind. He could hear the mumbling
sound of distant voices raised in mirth, and he could
feel the resonance of heightened emotions pulsing
through the conductive structure of the palace.
Instinctively, he knew that Iden Teirtu was holding a
feast, and his mind lurched towards recrimination.
He wanted to blame that styhx-tann warrior for his
own troubles and to lay everything on those broad,
strong shoulders, but he knew that it would not be
fair. His problems had started before the House
Wars. The rise of Teirtu had been contingent upon
them and was merely a symptom of his own fall, not
a cause.

Ahearn felt the tragedy of his own demise more
intensely than ever. If he was honest with himself, he
knew that he didn't really care about the way Iden
had taken over effective control of Kaelor. He had
always found the actual business of ruling rather tire-
some. It had been a useful way to ensure the
continuation of his dynasty, and he had been able to
do many things to increase the affluence and beauty
of the court, but he had never had any real interest in
the concrete business of governance, and the styhx-
tann that comprised the majority of the population
didn't interest him at all. They had repulsed him, and
they repulsed him even more since they had started

to get noticeably dirtier and less cultivated just before the House Wars.

One of the problems with this hereditary system, reflected Ahearn morosely, was that a sense of duty could not be passed on genetically, even if political power, good taste and psychic gifts could be.

Ahearn did resent that his beautiful palace had been desecrated by the dirty, clumsy and artless feet of the Teirtu, and it pained him to the depths of his soul to think of his Oriana caught in the midst of such ugliness. Iden could have the rest of the craft-world, if only he would leave Ahearn's Sentrium alone.

The scent of burning umbhala shavings curled around his body, filling his senses with the hint of forgotten faces and the suggestions of those that might yet be to come. They mingled inchoately, curdling through his thoughts like ghosts in the night.

In the mist behind his closed eyelids, he could see Lady Ione's face floating in the smoky darkness of his mind. Her beautiful, aging face smiled at him weakly, but he saw something patronising in her look, as though she were amused by the bumbling efforts of a loved child. He could see what he had always suspected: that she knew something that he didn't. The realisation was disturbing but it was also distracting. His mind wandered off on a tangent in pursuit of the past, turning his concentration away from the future altogether and towards events that had already been. What had he missed?

Despite his efforts at concentration, Ione's face started to dissipate and shift. The image fragmented and then hazed, fizzling gradually into a new visage that Ahearn recognised immediately. It was Bedwyr. Still the past. He had watched the patriarch of House Ansgar die in the Plaza of Vaul, executed for his treachery during the House Wars.

The connections between the two figures were myriad, and it was not immediately apparent to Ahearn why his mind had conjured them to his attention now. Given the context of the memory – with Bedwyr standing in the centre of the plaza awaiting the signal from Iden for the execution – the connection might well have something to do with the Ansgar heirs, on whose behalf the Lady Ione had begged Iden for mercy.

In fact, Ahearn himself had not been terribly concerned about the fate of the infants, and he was not entirely sure what had happened to them. He had heard reports from Cinnia of Yuthran that the little female had been banished from the Seer House where Ione had placed her in trust, but he had not been interested enough to ask why or where the girl had gone.

He was aware that the male, the young Naois, had been sent back into the ruined and desolate domains of Ansgar, and presumably he was rotting there with the rest of the styhx-tann. It had seemed to him that the warrior house had met with the natural justice that its actions had placed in its future, and he had been beyond caring about the fates of the uncouth progeny of these distasteful thugs.

Rather, that day had been marked by twin tragedies that had struck to the kernel of Ahearn's soul. On that day he had lost Kaelor. Iden Teirtu had marched victoriously into the Sentrium, flying his green and gold banners alongside the claret and gold of House Rivalin, claiming his triumph in the name of the farseer. It had been a clever and even cunning piece of theatre that had guaranteed his acceptance by the Knavir, at least until they started to realise who this styhx-tann warrior was, but by then it was already too late. After many eons of peace and prosperity, it took time for the Knavir to understand the nature of warriors.

On that day he had lost his only son. Kerwyn had stood against him with the Ansgar, giving that traitor Bedwyr the banner of Rivalin to fly alongside the blue and silver colours of House Ansgar. For a while before that, Kerwyn had held his own court, claiming that his father had lost his farsight and accusing him of decadence and inappropriate indulgences. Even worse, not everyone had disbelieved him. Worse still, somewhere in his soul Ahearn also suspected that Kerwyn might not be completely mistaken.

Despite his apparent treachery, Ahearn had not wanted to see his son die with the vulgar warriors in an uncivilised public execution. At the time, he had been most concerned with the vile aesthetics of the spectacle, but in hindsight he realised that keeping Kerwyn alive had been politically useful. With his oldest heir dead, all rights of succession would have passed to Oriana, setting up the nauseating possibilities of a political pairing of Iden's Morfran and his own daughter to produce a Rivalin-Teirtu heir. Such were the vagaries of the hereditary system that had served Rivalin so well since Gwrih the Radiant. In all its long history, the dynasty had never once been forced to bring non-Knavir blood into the family line. Perhaps Iden's decision to banish Kerwyn rather than execute him had been a rare moment of political short-sightedness by the warrior lord.

The spectral face of Kerwyn wisped into Ahearn's mind, morphing out of Bedwyr's steady gaze. His eyes were vacant and staring, like voids through the warp, but there was something different in the quality of the image – it was somehow sharper and more vivid, more present. The ghostly mouth opened slowly, as though about to speak.

'Radiance, I await your leisure.'

The voice seemed heavy and concrete, audible, and it took Ahearn a moment to realise that it was not coming from the smoky vision of his son but from a kneeling figure at the entrance to his chambers.

He opened his eyes slowly, letting his frustration about the inadequacies of his farsight fade into frustration about not having noticed the approach of the young Guardian. He turned his head, looking back towards the doorway, gazing through the smoke that continued to rise out of the bowl of umbhlala. It was Lhir, as he expected, but the Guardian was not alone.

THE CHORUS OF voices was so beautiful that it was painful. Scilti had heard nothing like it for a long time, not since the long down-phases before a great battle or a raid during the House Wars. He could remember sitting in the Ansgar camps, feeling the thrill of anticipation, tasting the promise of blood on

the spirit-breeze of faerulh. He could remember
Bedwyr's seriousness, sitting in quiet contemplation
in advance of the combat, as though playing out its
moves in advance. This time, the choir was sparser
and unspeakably melancholy.

The ragged but once magnificent warrior Khukulyn led the voices, sitting cross-legged before the
others, behind the smoking embers of umbhala. His
eyes were focused somewhere in the past, and Scilti
could see the kaleidoscope of memories cycling
through his open mind. There were visions of blood,
of flashing blades and sprays of shuriken fire. There
was death and the passionate embrace of life, emotions so intense that even their distant echo moved
the listeners beyond their own experiences, as
though the memories were their own.

Down-phase had come and the ambient light was
dim. The embers of umbhala sent a warm, reassur-
ing glow into the air, spitting sparks of light in tiny
bursts of life. Looking around the gathering in the
clearing before the temple, Scilti could recognise
only a few faces from that glorious and tragic time.
Most of them had died in battle, or had been executed after the final defeat. The *Chronicles of the
House Wars* recorded them as traitors, but history
was rarely that simple and such judgements were
usually political rather than truthful. Some had simply disappeared, vanishing into the vast Coolant
Wastes or dropping out of sight in the midst of their
brethren. One or two of the younger ones, like the
prodigy Naois and Scilti himself, had been whisked
away by the Warp Spiders, hidden in the sanctity of

their temples, and trained in the ways of their Aspect to control and shape the blinding thirst for blood that touched the soul of many eldar at some point in their lives.

Meanwhile, the Teirtu had used their dominance in the Sentrium to squeeze the domains of Ansgar, as though slaughtering its sons had not been punishment enough. Iden was a vindictive and shrewd eldar. He knew the danger of hate and the value of fear. More than most, he understood the ways of vengeance. He had established a permanent garrison of Teirtu Guardians in the Reach of Guereal, in the adjoining sectors, effectively blockading the Ansgar into the peripheries. Nobody was permitted into or out of those domains without the Zhogahn's express permission. The Ansgar were effectively banished into their own domain, cut off and excommunicated. Only the Warp Spiders could pass unnoticed across the borders.

The suffering of the eldar of Ansgar had been severe. Just as Iden had intended, some had gradually turned against the ruling house, blaming the actions of Bedwyr and his warriors for bringing the domain to its knees. How quickly those eldar had forgotten the suffering that had led them to rise up in the first place. Despite their long lives and cultivated minds, an eldar's memory was shaped largely by his emotions, hence the past changed shape at least as often as the future did. The past had always been easier to control.

For Scilti the difference in the spirit of Ansgar was shocking.

'Why did you not fight?' he asked, letting his words drift between the eldar like a breeze. 'How could this have happened?'

For a few moments, there was no response. The choir continued their ballad, as though the tragic melody should have been an answer to the question, but then, as the music slowed to a halt, Khukulyn drew his gaze back into the present and turned his eyes on Scilti.

'We did fight, my lord. We fought until this gathering was all that remained of our once glorious army. We fought until our lords were dead and our children were starving. We fought until there was no place on all of Kaelor that would provide us with shelter. We fought until even the ranger outcasts would not look at us for fear that they would be visited by the wrath of the Teirtu.

'We did fight, my lord, until we could fight no more, but without Bedwyr... without any of the Ansgar line still amongst us, there was only ever hope in the past, not in the future. We were defeated, my lord.'

There was a commotion in the darkness, through the trees beyond the clearing. It was the subtle sound of quietly rushing feet. They sounded hurried and careless, as though they had been pushed beyond silence by unusual and urgent haste. Without any sign or word, the eldar in the gathering were on their feet and melting into the darkness. In an instant, the temple steps were empty. The clearing held only the lingering scent of umbhala incense and the faint psychic echo of the choir's song.

Finding himself suddenly alone, Scilti determined to remain in the clearing. Whatever was coming, he was a sire of Ansgar and these were his domains. None had more right than he to be there. He would move for nobody. He would not hide in the heart of his own homelands.

After a few moments, a single figure burst out of the tree line. It was moving at speed, as though being chased by Maugan Ra himself. Even from the middle distance and even in the near darkness of the clearing, Scilti could see that the eldar runner was injured. The figure's gait was uneven, as though it was running merely to prevent itself from collapsing onto its face, and, as it drew rapidly nearer, Scilti could see the slick reflection of blood coating the female's abdomen and leg.

The runner saw Scilti at last, and almost at once her strength deserted her. She angled towards him, stumbling and staggering, tripping forwards and sliding to a halt just in front of him.

He sat, cross-legged where he had been listening to the choir and talking with Khukulyn only moments before, unmoved and unmoving, letting the female's head crash up against his legs. Her eyes were wild and pain was dancing in their depths. Her wounds were deep and severe. Most of the musculature of her left leg had been shredded and there was a chunk of abdomen missing on the same side. The exit wounds were on the front, and Scilti realised immediately that this was a scout that had been shot as she was running away from her enemies.

*They are coming. Guardians from the Reach; they are
coming.*

That was all she managed. Then her eyes opened a
little wider and she died.

As though on cue, the faint noise of dozens of feet
dashing through the forest zone drifted into the clearing. They were close, and closing quickly. Without
looking around, Scilti knew that Khukulyn and the
others were just out of sight. He could not tell
whether they would stand with him, but he could feel
their gazes on him. They wanted to know what he
would do.

Climbing to his feet, Scilti stooped and picked up
the fallen scout. He carried her up the temple steps
and laid her in front of the crescent doors, noticing
for the first time that two umbhala shafts were protruding from them. He unclipped the blue and silver
cloak from the dead body and fastened it over one of
his shoulders, letting it hang next to the blood red
warp-pack that marked him as a Warp Spider. Then,
with determined slowness, he walked back down the
steps and took up position in the very centre of the
clearing, facing the direction of the oncoming attackers.

Standing alone in the crimson armour of the Warp
Spiders, with an Ansgar cloak fluttering at his side,
Scilti waited for them to come.

AS LHIR STEPPED forwards with the body cradled in his
arms, covered in his own cloak, Ahearn could not
help but think of the way that Lady Ione had been
draped in those colours so recently. Behind Lhir came

Uisnech Anyon, one of the elder Knavir of the Ohlipsean, with the aging Yuthran Seer Triptri Paraq at his side.

'Forgive me,' muttered Lhir as he laid Kerwyn on the table at which Ahearn, Cinnia and Celyddon had sat drinking earlier. It had been cleared and cleaned perfectly, so that its surface shone. Then the Guardian stepped back, not wanting to breach the etiquette of the court by standing between the farseer and his son for longer than was absolutely necessary. He left his cloak covering Kerwyn as a shroud, wanting one of the others to make the decision about who was going to remove it.

Very slowly, Ahearn shuffled unsteadily towards the table, clicking his gnarled staff on the polished floor with particular weight, as though unsure of his balance. He paused for a moment, standing next to the head of the table, staring at the cloth as though it were a precious relic. The others stood in silence.

The farseer sighed sadly. With a slow nodding motion, Ahearn blinked his eyes and imagined the shroud being pulled back to reveal Kerwyn's gaunt, rotting and eyeless face. He could see the emaciation of the chest, and the dull, lifeless waystone that still rested against it, attached to the ornate chain that Ahearn had presented to his son after he had passed through the Ritual of Tuireann.

It was bad enough to see the images of his nightmares in his mind, but Ahearn felt a compulsion to look on the ugliness of his son with his real eyes. Something inside him called out for ruination and blood, and there was a part of him that suddenly

found the pristine perfection of his palatial
surroundings offensive. It was as if a ghost of darkness
or a tiny droplet of the blood of Khaine in his veins
had suddenly awakened. With a violent and
concentrated slowness, he reached forwards with his
staff and hooked its tip under the makeshift, blood
soaked shroud. He pushed it back, revealing Kerwyn's
putrid, decaying body fraction by fraction. The fleck
of darkness in his eldar dhamashir-soul thirsted
silently at the horror of the sight.

When you found him... Ahearn began, trying to think
of a suitable question. The conclusions were too obvious to need interrogation. He realised suddenly that
Iden had not been as politically naive as Ahearn had
thought him when he had banished Kerwyn.

'He was in the Coolant Wastes, radiance. He had
been... abandoned,' said Lhir, bowing his head with a
sense of responsibility.

Who?

'Radiance... It seems likely that the Glimmering
Kerwyn took his own life. There was no sign of a
struggle, and he had sanitised his space, despite the
unseemliness of the surroundings.' Lhir paused.
'Radiance, I–'

*You did your duty to your house, honourable Lhir of
Teirtu. The blame is not yours, and I will not forget that
you discovered this horror as a duty to me. Your sense of
duty does you great credit, and your allegiance shows wisdom... and taste. You gave my son your own cloak when
he had nothing.*

Ahearn reached forwards, scooped Kerwyn's waystone out of the decomposing flesh, and then folded

the cloak over the empty body once again. He turned and shuffled back over to the cabinet against the far wall, scraping his staff heavily against the floor and leaving a little trail of his son's tissue.

The others watched him, unsure of how to respond. In the background, they could hear a faint cheer of pleasure coming from Iden's celebrations, which Uisnech had just left. The Harlequins had probably just reached the climax of the *Cycle of the Avatar*, where Khaine, the war god, slays the ancient eldar hero, Eldanesh, whose blood then runs from the bloody-handed god's hands for all eternity.

Radiance. You must not let this pass. Uisnech turned to face the farseer. He watched him carefully clean Kerwyn's waystone, place it into a small cloth bag and then slide it into a compartment in the cabinet. *I have always stood behind you, Ahearn. I was one of the only Knavir to take up arms in the House Wars. I stood under your banner, and commanded your Guardians in your name while you remained in the Sentrium. I did not do this for Iden Teirtu. I did this for the Rivalin Farseer and for Kaelor. Too long have you permitted that styhx-tann to rule your craftworld. Perhaps your son was correct to place his faith elsewhere?*

Ahearn showed no sign of listening. He quietly poured himself a glass of Edreacian from the smoking carafe in the main section of the cabinet, and then took a long mouthful. Turning the glass thoughtfully in his hand, the farseer turned to face the others.

You would have me turn against House Teirtu? There was a pause. *And you would say this in front of this Teirtu Guardian?*

'My radiance, Lord Anyon is right,' said Lhir, dropping to one knee as though making a pledge. 'I cannot
stand for this abomination. Iden has wronged the
Rivalin dynasty, and he has wronged Kaelor. I am no
longer his to command.'

You are too good for this world, Lhir of the Radiant Star,
replied Ahearn with a weak smile.

*Iden already suspects that you are in league with the
Warp Spiders, my radiance,* offered Triptri. *This suggests
that he assumed you had already discovered the truth about
Kerwyn, or, perhaps, that he feared you might see some justice in your son's cause. Perhaps this is the time to bring his
fears out of the realms of conjecture and into the present?*

Looking from the Knavir courtiers, Uisnech and
Triptri, to the kneeling and immaculate Guardian,
Lhir, Ahearn felt a smile creeping across his face. Lhir
was like a breath of fresh air in the foul stench of
House Teirtu. Of course he aspired to more refined
and better things. He had just needed a little guidance.
It never ceased to amaze Ahearn how simply an eldar
soul could be tempted to change its path. Somehow,
events had conspired to make this devoted and dutiful
Teirtu Guardian drop to one knee and beseech the
farseer to call on Teirtu's enemies for aid. A good seer
should have seen this coming.

*You may be right, each of you. Lhir, can I ask you for one
further duty?* Ahearn wondered how far this valiant
young Guardian was willing to go. Perhaps some good
could come out of this after all.

'Of course, my radiance.' Lhir didn't look up.

*Go to the domains of Ansgar and explain what we have
discovered. Ask the Warp Spiders to come to the aid of the*

Rivalin dynasty, as once they thought they assisted our ancient lineage in allegiance to my son. Tell them that we seek to remove the Teirtu from their privileges in the Sentrium.

Lhir flinched visibly at the instructions. The life-long conditioning of hate and distrust towards the Ansgar and the Warp Spiders riddled his thoughts, but he held his will in check.

Give them this, added Ahearn, unclipping his cloak and tossing it over to him.

Lhir looked up and caught the luxurious fabric. He folded it to his chest as though it were a holy relic. 'It will be as you wish, radiance.' He bowed more deeply, touching his forehead to the ground before rising and striding out of the chamber.

THEY WERE DIFFICULT to see at first, emerging from the thick trees in the half-light of the down-phase. Their deep green cloaks served as excellent camouflage, and their movements were naturally in tune with their surroundings, like predatory animals in their native habitat, and they were silent as faerulh.

Scilti simply waited. He stood at the foot of the steps of the Warp Spider Temple in the middle of the clearing, gleaming like a crimson beacon for all to see. His deathspinner was cradled lightly between his hands, like a baby, and beneath his fearsome helmet his eyes shone with excitement.

After a few moments, the attackers realised that they had been seen and that any pretence at stealth was a waste of effort. Instead, they emerged out of the tree line and formed into single file along it, as though they were part of the foliage. There were, perhaps, two dozen of them, each marked out of the shadows by the brief burst of gold from the serpent mark on their chests.

There was no announcement and no battle cry. None of the Guardians stepped forward from the Teirtu line to declare itself to its foe. The Rituals of Commencement were simply ignored, as though they had no place in this fight. Scilti realised immediately that the House of Teirtu would deny that it ever happened, or perhaps the crafty Iden would declare that the Warp Spiders or the residue of the Ansgar had risen up against them and attacked the Guardians unprovoked.

The Warp Spiders should not have moved against Teirtu at the Rivalin Gates. It was a mistake. The vengeance of the Zhogahn will be swift and terrible. The suffering of House Ansgar has not yet begun. Lord Iden has shown great mercy, but that mercy ends here.

Scilti could not identify the source of the thoughts. It was as though they flowed out of the Guardians en masse, rolling over him like a wave. For a few moments he considered a repost. He wanted to tell them that they were mistaken, that Aingeal had meant only to pay her last respects to the beloved Lady Ione, but he knew that these soldiers were neither empowered nor predisposed to negotiate.

Is this really all that is left? One paltry Warp Spider to defend the domain?

This time the mocking thought came from an identifiable source, from an individual in the centre of the line, emboldened by Scilti's apparent reticence.

Unseen inside his helmet, Scilti grinned in response.

Without a moment's hesitation, he clicked his warp-pack, vanishing from the clearing like a suddenly extinguished flame, leaving a wisp of sha'iel like glittering smoke in the shade. There was an instant of confusion amongst the Guardians as they tried to find their bearings. The clatter of shuriken catapults being braced and snatched from side to side rattled through the half-light.

Then there was a shriek. It gurgled sickly and then broke into a shrill scream. It was followed quickly by a dull, heavy sound, like a dead body slumping to the ground.

The Guardians didn't fire a single shot. They saw their comrade fall from his position in the centre of their line. They saw the blood pouring out of the multiple wounds that had suddenly appeared in his chest; but they had not seen anything happen.

There was another cry. This time from one end of the line. It was cut short into a sudden hiss, as though a throat had been slit. Then another Guardian fell forwards into the dirt, blood gushing from a gaping wound across its neck.

The others turned instantly, just in time to see a glimmer of sha'iel dissipate from just inside the tree-line. They turned, opening up with their shuriken catapults and cannons, unleashing a hail of monomolecular projectiles into the shadowy greenery, shredding the plants mercilessly.

At exactly that instant, Scilti jumped back into the material realm, leaping back into the middle of the clearing where he had started. For a moment, he let the blood drip quietly from the tips of the powerblades that ran along his forearms. He inspected them with impressed satisfaction, as though they were new toys that he had been testing. The blood thrilled him.

Looking up at the Guardians, he saw that most of them had turned their aggression into the forest, presumably thinking that he had been attacking their line from behind. The short-sighted fools, he snarled, realising the violent superiority of the multi-dimensional thinking of the Warp Spiders for the first time.

Without hesitation, he lifted his deathspinner and squeezed it into life, unleashing floods of lethal filament in a wide arc, dragging the rapidly discharging weapon across the confused line of Guardians, peppering their armour with clouds of pain. Then, as they snapped their attention back into the clearing, Scilti powered up his warp-pack and blinked out of existence, leaving the Teirtu tracking their weapons uselessly through the empty glade.

A moment later he was among them, standing in the middle of the line as though he were a Guardian himself. In the time it took those next to him to register his presence, he had punched a blade through the neck of one and had cut another in two with a rapid spin from his gun. Dropping suddenly to his knees to break the line of sight, Scilti left his deathspinner firing through the line to his left, shredding the legs of two more Guardians before something struck him from behind, knocking him forwards onto his face.

He rolled instinctively, but he was not used to the presence of the warp-pack and his roll was ineffective, leaving him lying on his back like a stranded spider. He lashed out with his arms, throwing his weight over to the side in an attempt to right himself, but he couldn't do it.

Above him, one of the Guardians crunched his foot down against his chest, pinning him helplessly to the ground. He could hear the others gathering around for the execution, and he cursed his own stupidity. This was his fault. His arrogance had gotten the better of him yet again. Only he would believe that he could take on more than twenty Teirtu Guardians on his own.

The Guardian above him lowered the barrel of his catapult and hooked it under Scilti's helmet, prising it off to reveal the young Warp Spider's face. There was a moment of pause, as though the Guardian wanted to impart a dramatic gesture, and then it placed the barrel of the weapon deliberately between Scilti's eyes.

The Warp Spider determined that he would not flinch. He would not close his eyes. He would die with his eyes fixed on his enemy, so that they might remember his fury for the rest of their days. As he stared up at his executioner, he heard a shout and then a rallying cry. Shots suddenly erupted from all around them, clinking and ricocheting off the Guardians' armour.

He only needed that instant of distraction. Scilti lashed up with his powerblades, hacking through the barrel of his executioner's gun and then following through into his legs. The Guardian's weapon exploded in his hands even as his legs gave way and he started to crumple to the ground. Before the body could slump down on top of Scilti, the Warp Spider blinked away, reappearing on his feet about twenty paces into the forest.

The tree line was alive with fire. Warp Spiders from the temple were everywhere at once, blinking in and out of the materium like flashing lights, hacking at the Guardians with blades and mowing through them with deathspinners. They were not alone. The ragged Guardians of House Ansgar were there too. Khukulyn was a blur of motion as he danced and spun his twin witchblades through intricate and lethal patterns, slicing one of the Guardians into six neat, evenly sized pieces.

He turned and nodded at Scilti, his eyes glinting with the exhilaration of the fight and his unusual blades, which had been awarded to him long ago by the Seer House of Yuthran in special recognition of his prowess at the two-sword style, flashed with the promise of death.

After only a few moments it was over, and the Teirtu Guardians of the Reach lay dead on the edge of the forest of Ansgar. Not a single Warp Spider or son of Ansgar was as much as injured.

A movement in the foliage behind him made Scilti turn, snapping his deathspinner up before him instinctively. There was a heavy shadow in the darkness, standing upright and unafraid, its position exposed completely and deliberately. This was not the stealthy approach of an assassin, nor the frenzied last stand of an embattled foe.

Scilti held his fire as the figure approached, but he did not lower his aim. The approaching eldar was in the colours of Teirtu.

'Warp Spider and son of Ansgar,' said Lhir, dropping down onto one knee when he was close enough to perform a formal greeting. He threw his deep green, Teirtu cloak over one shoulder in a mark of respect, and then he held out the cloak that the farseer had given him, folded neatly into a perfect bundle.

'I have come as swiftly as I could, but I see that the Zhogahn's messengers are fleeter of foot than am I.' There was a tension in his voice that betrayed his anger about the slaughter of his kin. 'I bring word from the radiant farseer, and I bring his colours as a gift. He requests your aid, Warp Spider. He asks that you liberate him from the control of the Zhogahn. He asks that you fight in his name.'

CHAPTER FOUR: BEDWYR

'WHY SHOULD WE believe this traitor?' asked Khuku-lyn as he rose to his feet, giving voice to the misgivings of them all. 'He's just trying to save his own waystone.'

Khukulyn kept his fierce, level gaze focused on Lhir, as though challenging the newcomer to reveal something hidden.

Little Ela sat quietly to one side of the circle of eldar, watching the events unfold. There was open hostility and scepticism amongst the ring of eldar who sat in the wide, blue-black metallic basin – the Sapphire Dell – that had been the seat of office in the domains of Ansgar for many eons. It was hidden in the depths of the Ansgar forest zones, surrounded by a dense tree line that arched over it to form a closed, organic canopy overhead. It was set about an arm's length down into the ground to reflect the patriarch's founding belief that no eldar was above any other and, indeed, that rulers should place themselves below the ruled, since rulers were effectively servants of the masses. Hence, every eldar that won the right to sit in that circle would find his face level with the feet of those he helped to govern. The contrast with the aspiring towers of the Farseer's Palace in the ostentatious Sentrium was obvious and deliberate.

During the course of this down-phase, Ela had watched the Sapphire Dell gradually fill with a seething distrust and revulsion. It was one of the side effects of the design. The artisans had sculpted the basin in such a way as to ensure that the emotions of the councillors could not be hidden from the other members of the council. Instead, they poured out into the middle of the basin and accumulated there until the dell was like a goblet filled with a cocktail of emotion. The purpose had been to ensure truth-telling and to prevent secrecy, and also to promote moderation.

A divided council would rarely find any of its members overrun by hysteria, since the conflicting emotions would gradually balance each other out, producing an atmosphere of calm and rationality. One unforeseen problem, however, was that a unified council could be pushed beyond rationality towards extreme conclusions, since complementary emotions would pool together and reinforce each other, becoming amplified and exponentially more potent. The result could be an atmosphere of hysteria in the Sapphire Dell, particularly in times of obvious and dire need, such as during the House Wars. The Council of Ansgar often found itself as the most literal expression of the emotional nature of the children of Isha.

Even amongst the mix of hostile emotions, Ela could see the particular intensity of Khukulyn's feelings. She could see the suspicion and the deep-seated hatred shimmering out of Khukulyn like an energetic mountain stream. There was something different about his emotions. They were not the generic feelings of mistrust and revulsion that all sons of Ansgar had been trained to hold about the Teirtu; they were sharp and personal. His mind was full of flashbacks. Even as he had climbed to his feet to speak, Ela had seen him replaying battles and slaughter through his mind, as though he was subconsciously fuelling his detestation of the Teirtu Guardian that stood before them. He had fought many battles during the House Wars, and had borne witness to many terrible things. He had done many terrible things too, but there was something else.

Finally, little Ela saw something that surprised her. She saw his recollections of Bedwyr's execution. He had been there in the Plaza of Vaul. He had hidden himself amongst the eldar of the Sentrium, cloaked and anonymous in the crowd. He had seen Lady Ione drop to her knees on the palace balcony. He had seen Kerwyn Rivalin escorted from the plaza, and then Ela and Naois dragged off by their hair. Finally he had watched helplessly as the white-clad warlock had climbed the podium to where Bedwyr stood and placed his fiery hands on either side of the patriarch's head. He had felt the panic-stricken hatred of helpless rage as the warlock's black eyes had erupted into white flames and crackling auras of energy had coruscated down his arms and into his hands. Then, at the last, he had seen the defiant Bedwyr twist his face towards him – isolating his hooded features in the crowd – and bear witness to his cowardly self-preservation. Just as the patriarch's dhamashir was being incinerated in the warlock's psychic inferno, he seemed to accuse Khukulyn of deserting him.

Khukulyn was channelling his own self-reproach into his hatred for this Teirtu Guardian, building him into the representation of his detestation of the Teirtu and his own self-loathing all at once. In that instant, Ela realised that she was seeing a raw death wish for the first time. If he'd had the power, Khukulyn would have killed Lhir and himself at that very instant, thus eradicating their stain from the domain.

'You will do with me as you please, lords of Ansgar,' said Lhir, feeling the aggression whirling around him and realising that he had to speak in order to dissipate the rising emotions. 'I am not concerned with your treatment of me. I have seen the way that you dealt with my unwelcome brethren in your forest, and you would do me no dishonour if you were to deal the same fate to me.'

Is he asking for death, wondered Ela from her vantage point outside the dell? Or does he think that by calling for it, he will escape it? She studied the

Teirtu's upright posture, and found nothing in his manner to suggest that he was affecting a deceit or a plan. He stood ready to die, fully aware of the roiling hatred that the councillors directed at him, fully aware that declaring his willingness to die would not in itself be enough to convince these warriors to let him live. These were all eldar who knew death; they had all seen it before. Some of them had passed through the Rites of Ra during cycles in the Aspect Shrine of the Dark Reapers. Appeals to death meant little here. Lhir seemed to know that, and thus he stood ready to die.

'We will suffer no duplicity here, Teirtu-ann,' spat Khukulyn before any of the others had a chance to respond. 'If this is a ruse to save your soul, you will lose it.'

'It is no ruse, lords of Ansgar.' His manner was immaculate and honourable, worthy of the Knavir themselves.

It's true, realised Ela. She saw that Scilti had also seen the truth of it. His manner was unexpectedly calm, as though his sight were clear of the emotions around him.

'We are not the lords of Ansgar, Lhir of the Teirtu,' said Scilti, rising to his feet. He addressed the Guardian but turned his eyes on Khukulyn, making the older warrior retreat back down to his cushion with unspent fury in his eyes. 'We are their servants.'

Lhir turned to face Scilti, with a look of incomprehension creasing his features. He could feel a shift in the mood of the council, but he didn't understand it. The Warp Spider's words had changed

things in ways he couldn't grasp. Trickles of guilt
and humility curdled into the emulsion of emotions
in the dell.

'You can understand our scepticism, I am sure,'
continued Scilti, gesturing around the ring
inclusively. 'It has been a long time since a Teirtu has
wished us anything but harm, and we have long
learnt to be cautious of the vagaries of the Rivalin.'

'You will not speak ill of the radiant farseer in front
of me,' retorted Lhir swiftly, taking a step towards
Scilti and making the other councillors flinch
towards their weapons.

Ela watched with interest. She could see the genuine affront felt by Lhir. He was sincere in his defence
of the Rivalin Farseer, although he had made no reaction to the slight against his own house. He stamped
his defiance regardless of the jeopardy in which it
placed him. Despite herself, Ela realised that she
liked this Teirtu Guardian; he was transparently and
crisply dutiful.

Standing his ground, Scilti neither flinched nor
moved. He too could see the earnestness of this
Teirtu. 'As you wish,' he said, letting his calmness placate the situation.

'You should believe me when I tell you that I do
not bear this message with a tranquil soul. It has
been a long time since I have wished anything but ill
on the House of Ansgar.' He smiled weakly, wondering whether the Warp Spider was immune to his
charm, 'But none on Kaelor can refuse the call of the
farseer, and thus I stand before you, unafraid for my
soul,' he continued.

He's telling the truth. Ela's thoughts eased unobtrusively but unequivocally into Scilti's mind.

Scilti nodded slowly, as though thoughtful. 'Tell us again why the farseer expects this of us,' he said, sitting back into his cushion and leaving Lhir with the singular honour of being the only eldar on his feet in the Sapphire Dell. 'We will hear you.'

'Farseer Ahearn Rivalin is a virtual prisoner in his palace. Although he is permitted many of the privileges of his position, the Zhogahn will not permit him to leave the Ohlipsean. He was barred even from attending the Ceremony of Passing for Lady Ione. His radiance has suffered this partly because he believed it to be for the good of Kaelor, and partly because he entertained the hope that one day Iden would allow the return of his son – the one-time ally of House Ansgar – Kerwyn Rivalin.

'You will be aware that he was banished from the Sentrium following the House Wars, of course.

'A number of recent events have provoked his radiance into reconsidering his view of Iden and the position of House Teirtu. He asked me to relate to you the disturbing and wholly abhorrent fate of the Glimmering Kerwyn, and to remind you of the allegiance you once swore to him.

'It is for this higher cause – not for your hatred of the Teirtu – that the radiant farseer beseeches you to march against the Teirtu once again.'

There was silence as Lhir's message was gradually absorbed by the councillors of Ansgar. Ela could see that they were touched by his words. Even those that found his story incredible wanted to believe him.

What else could make their painful years of disgrace and suffering worthwhile? The faith of the farseer was a potent force, even amongst the Ansgar: especially for the Ansgar.

'If old Ahearn thinks that we are strong enough to march against Iden, he is as foolish as he is short-sighted,' scoffed Khukulyn without rising. 'From where does he think that we can draw our strength after his pet Teirtu has strangled our domain and slaughtered our children? Why could he not have seen this before the House Wars? That would have saved Kaelor many of its finest souls. I think that your farseer is blind and bumbling like a mon'keigh.'

Lhir's movement was lightning. He spun on his heel and lurched forwards instantly, hurling himself at the veteran warrior. Khukulyn lay pinned under the weight of the Teirtu Guardian with one of his own witchblades pressed to his throat. Meanwhile, the other Ansgar councillors were on their feet with their weapons drawn and trained on the assailant.

'You will not speak ill of the radiant farseer in front of me,' hissed Lhir, applying enough weight to the blade to draw a trickle of blood from Khukulyn's neck.

'He means merely that he doubts our readiness,' explained Scilti, unmoved from his cushion. 'You must forgive our manners, Lhir of Teirtu. We are merely Styhx-tann eldar, and not the cultivated Knavir to whom you have become accustomed.' The mockery teetered between offensiveness and placation. 'We have not shared the good fortune of life in the palace.'

Khukulyn said nothing, but his mouth twisted into a snarl and his eyes narrowed, as though he were daring Lhir to slit his throat. Watching from the sidelines, Ela thought once again that the warrior wanted to die.

'But we are ready, honourable Teirtu. I am a hereditary heir of Ansgar, nephew to Bedwyr, and I will lead us back to the destiny that once was denied to him. The forces of Ansgar and the might of the Warp Spiders have not been so primed for action since Bedwyr's death. If you will stand with us, Lhir of the Golden Serpent, then we will fight beneath the Rivalin banner once again.'

THE JETBIKE SPED between the lines of Guardians that filled the Plaza of Vaul, flashing under the canopy of banners that boasted both the green and gold of House Teirtu and the claret and gold of the farseer's dynasty. Bringing the jetbike to a halt at the rear of the lines, outside the Rivalin Palace, the messenger sprang out of the saddle and strode through the open gates into the grand reception hall at the front of the palace. The chamber was a frenzy of motion and colour. Iden had ordered the conversion of the once luxurious hall into his campaign headquarters and maps and charts hung over the ancient frescoes, and masterpieces of sculpture and artistry had been cleared away in order to make space for strategic models and real-time holographic images.

'Zhogahn. Marshal Yseult,' nodded the messenger, walking directly up to them as they peered over one of the tactical layouts. Morfran sat to one side of the table, lounging casually in a deeply padded chair, apparently bored by the whole furore around him. The messenger simply ignored him and addressed the others. There was nothing ostentatious or stylish in the messenger's manner; it was full of military efficiency. 'The rebels have taken another domain in the styhx-tann sectors. Their progress is swifter than we anticipated.'

'Then our anticipations were not good enough,' snapped Iden in an instant and dismissive response. He was already fuming about the refusal of the Ohlipsean seers to offer counsel in this battle. Even Cinnia of Yuthran had declined to help.

'Where are they now, Nawrad?' asked Yseult. Her tone was gentler but no less serious.

'They have just passed through the domains of Eaochayn on the Innis Straight, marshal,' replied the messenger, swiftly turning his attention from the simmering fury of Iden to Yseult's calmly professional visage. 'They will reach the Styhxlin Perimeter before the commencement of the next down-phase.'

Yseult nodded thoughtfully. She was not unaware of the symbolic significance of the route that the rebels had chosen. 'Numbers?'

'They are few: perhaps twenty old Ansgar Guardians, a single detachment of Warp Spiders and a rag-tag ensemble of other eldar that have rallied to their banners during their march from Ansgar, no more than fifty in all.'

'Banners?' queried Iden, noticing the plural.

'Yes, Zhogahn. They fly the colours of Rivalin alongside the flags of Ansgar.'

There was a long, shocked silence as the significance of this revelation sank in.

'That will be all,' said Yseult, conscious of the rage building in Iden's mind and disinclined to permit the messenger to see the explosion of anger that would undoubtedly follow. Thus dismissed, the messenger turned and strode back out into the plaza.

That cursed old fool! fumed Iden, glowering into Yseult's face in impassioned silence. *I should have executed him along with his son, and done away with the troublesome, decadent and effete Rivalin line altogether.*

Yseult studied him. *You didn't execute Kerwyn, lord?* It was a question. *He was banished.* Her naiveté was suddenly obvious even to her. *Wasn't he?*

Iden remained silent for along moment. His green eyes shifted away from Yseult's face, gazing out of the open gates into the plaza beyond. Yseult could see him controlling his anger and bringing his thoughts under control. It was not the first time that his fury had caused him to step beyond the bounds of propriety.

Kerwyn was banished, Yseult Teirtu-ann, but he died in exile. His death is not on my hands, but I cannot say that I mourn his passing. He was an enemy of Teirtu and a traitor to the Rivalin line. Had he been anyone else, I would have executed him alongside his pet tureir-iug, Bedwyr. Iden's tone seemed honest and open, like a confession.

For how long have you been aware of his death, lord? asked Yseult. She was reluctant to jump to the conclusion that would dishonour her own deeds.

The heir was dead to me from the moment that he turned against Ahearn, replied Iden ambiguously. *I have not thought of him as being amongst the living since the start of the House Wars.*

Yet I fought against him at the Battle of Gelban's Deep. He seemed very much alive at that time, furious with life, recollected Yseult, her thoughts edged with accusation even as her memories were tinged with admiration for Kerwyn's courage.

Well, you need not fight him again, marshal, replied Iden, deliberately misunderstanding Yseult's tone. *For he is now as dead in body as he was once in his soul.*

Yseult was not reassured. *And the farseer himself? Does he know of his son's fate?*

Recent events would suggest that he has learnt of Kerwyn's fate, don't you think? First the attack of the Warp Spiders at the Rivalin Gates, and now the march of the Ansgar bearing the farseer's colours. It seems to me that the sentimental old caradoch is trying to awaken the dead and revive the old alliances. We must crush this uprising before the sons of Ansgar can rally any of the other great houses against us. There are many jealous eyes gazing on our position in the Sentrium, Yseult. Many of the warrior houses of the styhx-tann would crave these luxuries for themselves.

Yseult flinched inwardly, finding Iden's appropriation of the courtier's derogatory term 'styhx-tann' offensive and cheap. Had he so readily forgotten his own origins? There had been a time when he would have used that label as a badge of pride – claiming Kaelor for the styhx-tann – freeing it from the decadence of the corrupt Knavir. She looked at him with altered eyes for a moment, and in her mind's eye she flashed back to the memory of the honourable Warp Spider Arachnir Fiannah, with blood pouring out of her slit throat in front of the Rivalin Gates.

Do we fight in the name of the farseer? asked Yseult, finally putting words to the core of the issue. She turned and looked out into the Plaza of Vaul, where she had assembled two hundred and fifty Guardians under the dual banners of House Teirtu and the Rivalin Court. She knew that a number of the Knavir courtiers were watching the preparations from one of the higher balconies of the palace.

I am the Zhogahn, young Yseult! I was appointed by the Radiant Ahearn Rivalin himself to defend Kaelor against threats to its integrity and security. I am the vanquisher of sin! We fight for the farseer, and we manifest his will on the battlefield... whether or not he remains fully conscious of the content of his own will. We are charged with keeping his intent consistent and his will strong. The banner has not been stolen out of the palace by thieves and then hoisted over our forces as a tactic or deceit. The banner of Rivalin is ours!

There was a hint of hysteria in Iden's tone that made Yseult step back away from him. His long, silver hair had been pulled back into a tight knot, giving his uneven, elliptical face a raw severity that matched his mood. As his thoughts raced, his ancient sword flashed with energy over his shoulder, calling out for blood. The psychic light that coruscated around the blade danced tiny stars into his flashing green eyes.

Yseult could see his passion and his unmoving faith, even as it teetered on the brink of insanity. It was contagious enough for her to be willing to give

her lord the benefit of the doubt. Indeed, doubting
her lord would itself be unbecoming of a servant in
his debt. If the Zhogahn told her that she marched in
the name of the farseer, then she marched in the
name of the farseer. She owed them both at least that
much faith.

'We must make our stand at the Styhxlin Perimeter,'
said Yseult, vocalising properly so that the Guardians
around them would not grow too uncomfortable
about the secrecy of the obviously heated debate
between the two of them. This was not the time for
her troops to doubt the unity of their command.

At the sudden noise, Morfran looked up abruptly
from his stupor, as though startled by an unexpected
interruption. He said nothing, but grinned happily,
his mind elsewhere.

'The Innis Straight meets the Perimeter at the Ula
Pass. Although our greater numbers will count for
less in such restricted territory, that will be the sim-
plest place to arrest the advance of the rebels. They
must cross the pass if their destination is the Sentrium, and we can defend it with overwhelming
strength.' As she spoke, Yseult watched the holographic charts flick through a sequence of images in
time with her explanation, scanning along the Innis
Straight all the way to the narrow, curving Ula Pass
that swept over the great gaping canyon of the Styhxlin Perimeter. There were still a number of
gunnery-emplacements operational on the Sentrium
side of the pass, which were remnants of the expansive defensive ring put in place around the Sentrium
in the closing stages of the House Wars.

What about Lairgnen and his Dire Avengers? asked Iden. *He should come to our aid if I summon him in our time of need.*

Yseult looked up from the charts and saw the maniacal glint still shining in Iden's eyes. His emotions were running away with his thoughts, and he was losing focus on the reality of the problem. Had he been anyone else, Yseult would have slapped him to remind him of the pain of the present.

Not for the first time in her long acquaintance with the patriarch of Teirtu, Yseult found herself wondering how long it had been since he had last endured the discipline of the Path of the Warrior in one of the Aspect Temples. She knew that Iden had been a fine Dire Avenger in his youth, but was not aware of his passing through the dhanir of Khaine after that.

Looking at the delicacy of the thread that seemed to tie him to sanity and keep his mind dangling out of the darkest and most bloody reaches of his soul, Yseult saw clearly that Iden was in need of guidance from one of the Shrines of Asurmen. The demands of political machinations had kept him from heeding the call of his own nature for too long. Whilst he disdained the material decadence of the Knavir, this kind of neglect was also a kind of decadence.

There is no need to call on the Avengers, my lord, replied Yseult in an honest appraisal of the situation. *Our numbers are overwhelming, and the battlefield is of our choosing. Besides, we seek to repel an attack, not launch a programme of extermination. This would be overkill, Zhogahn.*

'You are wrong, child. The Ansgar and those treacherous Warp Spiders need to be taught a lesson. I should have exterminated them ages ago, but my mercy has returned to torture me...' Iden was mumbling audibly, as though talking to himself. 'This is not about repelling them, it's about annihilating them once and for all. It's about finishing what Ione prevented me from completing before.'

The Avengers will not fight for you, my lord. Yseult's thoughts were urgent and pressing, as she tried to prevent Iden from continuing his rambling violence in front of the grinning Morfran and the other Guardians. *Lairgnen will not breach the Covenant of the Asurya's Helm, and nor should he. You know this, Iden of Teirtu. The Aspect Temples must not get involved.*

'They are already involved, you fool!' snapped Iden, drawing suddenly closer to Yseult and drawing the anxious attention of all the eldar in the hall. 'That witch Aingeal has already smashed the covenant. If Lairgnen refuses, he does it because he wishes ill to befall the House of Teirtu. Do you hear me, Avenger Yseult?' He was mocking her. 'Failing to stand with us would be to breach the Helm of Asurya!'

My lord, you are not yourself, counselled Yseult, reeling slightly under the sudden shift in Iden's ire. She stared into his wild, green eyes and saw the paranoia spreading like a disease in his soul. She watched him glance rapidly around the hall, as though searching for invisible or hidden assassins in the shadows. Being in the Sentrium for so long had changed this once magnificent warrior, and Yseult felt the pain of loss. It was clear to her that he needed to step back from his political ambitions, machinations and responsibilities. He needed to return to the outer domains of Teirtu and plunge himself back into the disciplined existence of the Dire Avengers. He needed to rebalance his soul before he became lost to himself. For his sake, as well as for the sake of those around him, Yseult needed to get Iden back to the shrine.

My lord, perhaps you should leave this battle to me. You need your rest. When it is over, we can pay a visit to the Temple of the Dire Avengers together. We can talk with Lairgnen.

'You! Even you would rather be without me!' snarled Iden, firing his accusation at his champion. 'You seek this victory for yourself!'

With an almost impossibly swift motion, Yseult slapped the Teirtu Zhogahn across his face, striking him flatly on his pale, angular cheek. For an instant, an unspeakable violence flared in Iden's eyes, and Yseult thought he was going to strike her back, but then the flames cooled suddenly and his gaze softened.

I am sorry, Yseult. It has been so long since I was last in a battle. I think that I am losing myself in the suspicions and complexities of this place. I was not made for this life, and I exhaust myself in rebellion against it, even as it rebels against me. We will fight together, you and I, side by side. We will be rejuvenated in the flames of combat and given new sustenance by the blood of our enemies. It will be like the old days once again.

Willing to give her lord her faith, as demanded by her sense of duty, Yseult nodded crisply. Perhaps war would be enough of a remedy for what ails him, she thought. Then the two warriors stooped over the holographic charts once again, studying the best way to deploy the Teirtu Guardians. At the same time, Morfran seemed to realise that the entertainment was over. He rose idly to his feet and strolled back towards the interior of the palace, bumping past a number of Guardians as he went and mumbling something about checking whether the Harlequins were still there.

RIDING ON THE open top of the converted Wave Serpent at the head of the Ansgar column, Scilti turned back to view the convoy behind him. It had grown since they had pushed out of the domains of Ansgar with twenty kinsmen and a single squad of Warp Spiders. A number of eldar from the outer realms had rallied to their banners, seeing in the procession a glimmer of hope and the echoes of former glories.

The number of supporters had been small, but some of the veteran warriors that had once fought at Bedwyr's side had emerged from their ramshackle habitation-units with immaculately shining and preserved weapons, as though they had polished and cleaned them in the shadows of every down-phase since the war, waiting. As Scilti's ragtag convoy had passed through their sector, some of the old warriors had seen a chance to escape from the humdrum dhanir of their half-hidden, sedentary and humiliating post-war existence. The call of Khaine had never left them. They had merely suppressed it out of fear of retribution from the Teirtu, and now they finally saw a chance for the cry of battle to rekindle the embers in their withering souls.

Nonetheless, Scilti knew that his army was no more than a pathetic echo of the mighty forces that had marched with Bedwyr into the epic battles of the House Wars. He had been there himself as a young and inexperienced warrior, more passionate than able. He had ridden with the patriarch at the head of great Ansgar forces, feeling the very fabric of Kaelor trembling beneath their might. He knew the spirit of war. He had felt it engulf him like a storm. The clouds of violent defiance that gathered around his convoy were not the stuff of great tempests or raging maelstroms. There was fury and there was the parched thirst for blood, but the epic emotions of the House Wars were simply absent. It was as though there were no mythic heroes marching to battle. It was as though this fight would pass unnoticed, never to be dramatised in a glorious eldar cycle.

In these sectors of Kaelor, the space was wide and open, as though echoing the expansive plains of the home worlds of the Eldar Knights, but here the Faerulh Prairies were barren and metallic. In the peaceful days before the House Wars, these sectors would have been bustling with eldar travelling to and from the Sentrium.

The Innis Straight passed through the prairies before rising several levels to cut through the fabled Styhxlin Perimeter at the Ula Pass. This had been one of the first crossing points to be established after the terrible cataclysm that had cracked Kaelor in two during the Craftwars with the bellicose craftworlders

of Saim-Hann, and it had remained a central artery
through Kaelor ever since. Legend said that the pass
had been held intact by the sheer power of Warlock
Ula Ansgar's will for nearly a year in the last phases
of the Craftwar. It was said that she had held the vast
mass of Kaelor together in her mind, using the
wraithway of the pass to tie the styhx-tann sectors to
the Sentrium. Local folklore claimed that she had
expended so much of her life-force performing this
incredible feat that she had eventually become
utterly absorbed in the wraithpath that finally
formed part of the intricate web of multi-
dimensional bonds that saved Kaelor from cracking
completely into two. The path was built across the
breach as a bridge. Ula's Pass was the pass that had
been made out of Ula.

Over the centuries, a thriving economy had been
sustained along the Innis Straight, with merchants
and rest-keepers sprinkled throughout the plains. It
had been hard to travel without encountering many
fellow travellers, or many lying in wait for them.

It had also been the road on which Bedwyr had
chosen to make his last stand. House Teirtu had
already become firmly ensconced in the Sentrium,
and they had fortified the narrow Ula Pass from their
side. Of the various approaches to the Farseer's Court,
Ula Pass was clearly the most heavily defended, and
Iden had been certain that it was impregnable. The
pass was narrow and sweeping, making it almost
impossible to muster a large force through it, and the
defensive fortifications were elevated along its length,
effectively transforming the restricted corridor into a

slaughter-zone. Bedwyr had known all of this just as well as Iden had, and yet he had personally led his army along the Innis Straight and up into the pass, with the banners of Ansgar and Rivalin flying proudly on either side of his Vyper. The rune-singers of Ansgar tell of how Bedwyr chose that route knowing that it would be his doom. They say that he knew his war was already lost and that a seer of Yuthran had prophesied victory for Ansgar in an honourable death.

But Bedwyr had emerged from the slaughter of the Ula Pass with the bloodied remnants of six of his honour guard. With death pouring from his weapons and seeping from his skin, and with his life dripping away from him, the Ansgar patriarch had fought through hundreds of Teirtu Guardians, penetrating deep into the Sentrium until he had reached the Plaza of Vaul. There he had dropped to his knees before the Palace of the Farseer and accepted his fate.

As Scilti looked across the Faerulh Prairies before him, he could see the glow of the interference-aura that gushed continuously out of the Styhxlin breach. It spread out along the vanishing point on the edge of his vision, defining a line of shimmering, midnight blue like a horizon. The eerie light pulsed through the immaterium, letting the glimmer of sha'iel bleed through from the immaterial dimensions, contaminating the whole area with nightmares.

They are ready for us. The thoughts were calm and unmoving.

Looking down to his side, Scilti saw the small, child-like figure of Ela'Ashbel standing at the front of the Wave Serpent peering ahead into the energy rupture. He had not asked her to accompany him, and he would not have done so. However, she had taken up her position on the leading transport so naturally and calmly that none had thought to oppose her. Her presence was simply inevitable.

The Exarch Aingeal, the Guardian Khukulyn and the Teirtu traitor, Lhir stood with the two of them on the viewing platform on the control vehicle. The five of them had ridden in silence for most of the journey, letting the fluttering banners of Ansgar, Rivalin and the Warp Spiders speak for their common intent. There was little else to be said.

'Can you tell how many?' asked Scilti, following Ela's gaze but unable to see anything in the haze of light and warp energy that curdled along the vanishing point ahead. He supposed that she could not see anything with her eyes either.

Many. The answer was simple and fully anticipated. *But it does not matter. What has begun must be brought to its conclusion. The future rests on this. Victory lies beyond this horizon, not on it.*

They have already taken the pass, added Aingeal. *They must have known of our route significantly in advance to be so well prepared.*

'How could I have known?' countered Lhir, aware of the accusation implied by the exarch. The very presence of the Warp Spider in such close proximity was enough to put the Guardian on edge, and that made him even more sensitive to slights that might have been directed at him. 'I did not know how you would react to his radiance's message, and I could not have known your route.'

'There was no accusation, Teirtu-ann,' said Scilti, although his tone remained edged with disdain. 'Marshal Yseult would have anticipated our route, I am sure.' There was a hint of admiration in his voice when he spoke of Yseult.

Lhir paused for a moment, weighing up the sincerity of his uneasy allies. The mention of the marshal had affected a change in his emotional state. Whilst he was finding it easier and easier to justify the defection of his loyalties from Iden and Morfran to the radiant farseer himself, from Teirtu to Rivalin, the mention of Marshal Yseult gave him cause to reconsider his position once again. Even this Ansgar rebel spoke of her with respect.

Of all the eldar that he was betraying in House Teirtu, Lhir realised that only Yseult would probably understand his reasons, and yet none would confront him more passionately than her. Only she would see the courage and heroic tragedy of this hopeless Ansgar march through the Ula Pass. She would have stood with them, in a different life, but in this life she would fight until every last one of them was dead. For the first time in is life, Lhir saw the tragedy of Kaelor's hereditary system of houses. Yseult should not have been born into the domains of Teirtu. For a people with such a sophisticated sense of destiny and time, it seemed to Lhir that a hereditary system was peculiarly unwise in an eldar society.

'Besides,' added Scilti, seeing the confused emotions in Lhir's eyes, 'these sectors have been running with Teirtu rangers and spies for years.'

'The Zhogahn has been diligent in his ongoing suspicion of the other outer houses, especially of the Ansgar,' added Khukulyn bitterly.

The anti-grav Wave Serpent banked gently as it started a smooth turn, pushing up the slight incline that rose out of the plain and inclined up towards the Ula Pass. Behind them, the other vehicles in the convoy fell into line. In this narrow stretch before the pass, the Innis Straight was barely wide enough for a single-file formation of Wave Serpents or Falcon grav-tanks. Two Vypers could just about squeeze through side by side if necessary, but it would be a precarious manoeuvre. Jetbikes two abreast were possible. The narrowness of the pass was a deliberate defensive device, making it almost impossible to muster a significant assault through the Innis Straight.

The slope rose gently at first, but then it swept into a graceful curve and inclined more steeply, arcing up towards the distant ceiling level. About half way up the ramp, the deck stopped being supported by columns underneath it, holding it up above the Faerulh Prairies, and it began to be suspended by fine, long cables from the ceiling above. The effect was to make the path less stable, allowing it to sway slightly because of the motion on top of it, but it also made the route more restrictive, since the cables overlapped and interwove like giant webs on either side of the ramp, effectively enclosing the incline into a long, curving corridor, flanked on both sides by webbed walls.

'How far to the pass?' asked Lhir, looking around in discomfort. The reality of his situation was gradually sinking in. He was a single Teirtu Guardian in a pathetic convoy of desperate Ansgar rebels heading up into an impregnable, highly fortified, and incredibly restrictive killing zone. He was riding to his death beneath an enemy banner. Yet something in his dhamashir thrilled at the choices he had made. He felt honest and uncomplicated for the first time in his life. Given a choice between life and death, the warrior should choose death every time.

'The Innis Straight curves up another two levels through these webs before it meets the portal of Ula on the fringe of the perimeter,' said Khukulyn. He had been there before.

Scilti nodded seriously, accepting the knowledge of the veteran warrior. He looked through the lattice of webwork briefly, seeing the ramp curving up towards the dark, glittering, immaterial substance of the Sty-hxlin Perimeter ahead of them. Then he looked down over the edge of the decking beneath the Wave Serpent. They had already climbed a hundred metres, and the Faerulh Prairies were rapidly dropping away beneath them, featureless and barren like a great metallic desert.

He had not been along this route since that fateful march of the Ansgar at the close of the House Wars when Bedwyr had drawn his glorious convoy to a halt at precisely the point where the ceiling web reached down to cradle the ramp. Scilti could still remember the great warrior's glittering, silver eyes as Bedwyr had turned to him, placed his hand on his shoulder and told him that he could go no further. The great patriarch had drawn a line and sent all those that had not yet lived through seven dhanir back down to the Prairies below, telling them that this was not their fight, that this was not their time to die. He had told them all that they would have other chances, and that one day they would march through the Ula Pass themselves, triumphant under the banners of Ansgar and Rivalin. He had chosen death, so that his heirs might one day find life on Kaelor.

Like an infant-coward, Scilti had gone back down as he had been ordered. He had not travelled with his lord into the killing-zone of the Pass. He had not witnessed the legendary carnage of that day, and he had not been there when Bedwyr had staggered out of the other side of the pass, defiant and gored, with only six warriors of his once majestic army remaining at his side.

Khukulyn had been there, and he was here again.

Scilti was here now. Bedwyr had told him that he would return, and thus he had returned. Like his lord before him, Scilti had now passed through the Rites of the Warp Spider, and he stood at the head of an Ansgar army under the banner of the farseer. There had been no question about where he would launch his attack. The Ula Pass was the rite of passage, the test of history and it loomed in the future like destiny itself, a single, narrow resolution of the myriad possibilities that stretched out into the temporal distance. He would either emerge as the victorious heir of Ansgar, or he would die in a glorious echo of his lord. Choose death, but be prepared to live.

'Halt here,' said Scilti, directing his command to the pilot in the cockpit below. The Wave Serpent slid

smoothly to a stop and dropped a fraction in height
as the anti-grav impellers shifted down a phase. The
others looked at him expectantly, but he ignored
them and vaulted down off the open command deck
onto the ramp in front of the transport.

He walked to the edge of the ramp and peered
down through the cables at the distant ground, leaning his weight against the wall of webbing. He
looked at the expanse of the Faerulh Prairies, looking
back along the Innis Straight as far as the domains of
Eaochayn. Then he turned his head and looked at the
towering wall of glittering, deep blue energy that was
the Styhxlin Perimeter. It ran forever, like an infinite
and eternal barrier through the very fabric of the
craftworld. He gazed into its depths as though staring
into an ocean. Up ahead, the web-enveloped ramp
plunged into the perimeter like a lance into a water-
fall: the Ula Pass.

'It's incredible, isn't it?' The dulcet voice of Khukulyn was suddenly right at his shoulder. The old
warrior's tone was scented with an artist's appreciation of beauty.

Scilti had not heard or sensed his approach, but he
showed no signs of surprise and left his gaze in the
maelstrom of sha'iel. 'I have never been this close to
it, Khukulyn,' he conceded, 'not here, not in this
place.'

There was an understanding silence. 'It is the same
everywhere you see it, my lord,' said Khukulyn,
addressing Scilti with an honour-title for the first
time, 'and anyway... You are here now, Lord Scilti.
That's what matters.'

Nodding thoughtfully, Scilti gradually realised that he could see stars, planets and swirling nebulae glittering within the perimeter, as though it contained an entire galaxy. He knew that it was an optical and psychic trick, caused by the unusual properties of the sha'iel-rich space, but he also realised that it would please the Knavir eldar of the Sentrium to think that there was a whole galaxy of distance between them and the outer houses on his side of the Styhxlin. He suspected that some of them would have been happier if the cataclysmic rift in the structure of Kaelor had never been repaired at all. Instead, the little Ula Pass existed as a thorn in their sides, like a tiny splinter of webway.

'What happens to those who fall into the breach?' asked Scilti, curious rather than afraid.

'Most fall out into the material space that you can see, although not even the seers of Yuthran have been able to tell us where that is,' replied Khukulyn, watching the heavenly display with profound appreciation.

'And the others?'

'The others are drawn into the sinews of sha'iel that lace the rift. They are lost from time and space. Legend has it that daemons of the Great Enemy lurk within those threads of warp, waiting for the glimmer of an eldar soul on which to feast.'

Scilti shivered at the open mention of Slaanesh, especially on the eve of battle, but there was something perfect about the idea that the Great Enemy would have found a home in the heart of the craftworld: the best place to hide is under the nose of your enemy.

A thought suddenly struck him. 'Khukulyn, how deep is the breach? How long is the Ula Pass?'

'The Ula Pass is two hundred metres in length, from portal to portal, but the Styhxlin Perimeter has no depth at all. If it were not there, you would be able to step across the tectonic crack that split through Kaelor during the Craftwars... except, of course, if the perimeter-field vanished, the craftworld would break in two and fall apart. If you tried to step across now, you would fall into the breach. There is no way around it, and there is no way through it except by using the webway architecture of passages like the Ula Pass. To attempt a crossing at any other point would be to place an infinite and possibly eternal distance between yourself and the other side,' explained Khukulyn, marvelling at the wondrous feat before them.

Taking a last, long look at the oceanic barrier of sha'iel, Scilti turned back to Khukulyn and laid his hand on the veteran warrior's shoulder. He said nothing, but held the other's eyes for a moment, noticing the proud banners that fluttered above the convoy over the warrior's shoulder. Then he nodded and strode back towards the Wave Serpent, vaulting back up onto the command platform on its roof to join the others. They looked at him reassuringly, each with their own hypothesis for why he had drawn them to a halt at that particular point.

Little Ela looked up at him and saw the calm of resolution settling into his demeanour. She had not seen him so well focused since his last training fight against her brother in the Temple. Smiling distantly,

Ela wondered whether her cousin had a part to play in the prophecy after all.

'To the Ula Pass; To death and the future,' he said, feeling the excitement of what was to come beginning to simmer in his thoughts as the Wave Serpent started to move once again.

HE COULDN'T BELIEVE that they had left him behind. First they had promoted that weaker olderling Scilti, just because he had already passed through the Ritual of Tuireann. That arachnir – Adsulata – had not even cared that his cousin had cheated in order to win the bout. It was as though a conspiracy were spiralling around him, aiming to keep him locked away in the temple and out of the battles that roared within his dhamashir. It was a kind of torture, like keeping a warp-beast chained in a gilded cage. Naois felt that it sinned against his nature to be so constrained. The fury of Khaine howled in his mind constantly, just below the surface of his consciousness and it clawed at his thoughts, drawing invisible scars in his mind.

Then the pathetic fools had rallied behind Scilti as though he were the heir to Ansgar! Were they blind as well as foolish? Could they not see the inferiority of his cousin's fighting spirit? He was nothing!

Naois suddenly realised that he should have killed Scilti, instead of letting him loose in his father's domains. Scilti was little better than a selfish oaf, bathing in the reflected glory of the ruling house and seeking to shine in its light. He wanted little more than fame and power, and the return of the glory

days of Ansgar with himself at the helm. He didn't
fight with the taste of blood running over his teeth.
He fought with the promise of rewards glittering in
his mind. He might have been born a Teirtu!

Snarling in the back of his mind, Naois heard a
voice telling him that Scilti had run away. He had
fled from the battle when Bedwyr had needed him
most, leaving the patriarch to stand alone in Ula
Pass, preferring to live to fight another day. When
faced with the choice between life and death, there
should be no choice: life ends, death begins. That is
the way of Khaine. Without war there is no life for
the eldar, there is only the slow, inevitable decay into
decadence, affluence and flabby subsistence.

Why was he the only one who could see that?

Even Ela had gone with them. She should have
known better.

It should have been me! His thoughts echoed out of
the arena and bounced around the corridors of the
temple, searching for a mind that might be open to
them.

He kicked at the sand on the floor, scuffing up the
intricate web-like pattern that Adsulata and Aingeal
had made so much of a fuss about. They had looked
so shocked and thrilled, and he had seen the unspoken questions forming in their minds. Even the
austere and mighty exarch had been affected.

They knew, and yet still they had acted as though
they were blind. They had talked amongst themselves about the significance of the sand patterns and
the wraith-crystals that speckled through them, but
they had said nothing to him, as though he could

not possibly understand what was happening to
him. They were treating him like an infant, like a precious, cursed and pathetic mornah that needed their
protection. They thought he needed protecting from
himself, when it was they who needed protecting
from him.

They treated Ela differently. She scared them. He
could see it in their manner as they skirted around
her, trying to ignore her presence as a body of water
might aspire to ignore the moon. They were drawn to
her and repelled by her in equal measures, but they
did not patronise her. They merely let her act as
though she were nothing to do with them, as though
she were sovereign of her own world, only temporar-
ily or partially present in theirs. In fact, Naois
realised, that was not far from the truth.

They all knew why the Seer House of Yuthran had
been desperate to off load the little female. They had
called her the vaugnh, the abomination, but none in
Ansgar ever gave voice to those reasons. They had
received her without questions and without words;
there were not even any rumours about her. It was
almost as though the eldar of Ansgar had decided to
act as though Ela did not even exist. Her existence
was simply too disturbing. She was amongst them
and beyond them at the same time.

What makes her so special? cursed Naois, letting his
thoughts rattle around the arena like echoing
sounds. In fact, he had never once spoken in audible
sounds, and even the thought of doing so filled him
with a disgust that bordered on nausea. It seemed
degrading and inappropriate for a son of Khaine. He

wasn't even sure anymore whether it was possible for him to vocalise his words.

What makes her so special? he repeated, louder and more powerfully. He was one of the very few who knew the answer, but truth and passion were uneasy comrades, and his mind was full of raw emotion.

Why is she so free? As his mind lashed out, his silver eyes flashed.

He kicked at the sand in frustration, driving his foot through the dust and dragging it into the floor beneath. The metallic ground under the dust glowed for an instant, as though Naois's motion had heated it through sudden and intense friction. Almost instantaneously, something exploded against the back of the crescent doors that barred his way out of the temple. Looking down, he saw a trail of glass crystals defining the line between his foot and the explosion, where the lightning passage of the shard that he had gouged from the floor had superheated the sand and baked it instantly into mica. A low, shimmering thread of flame had ripped through the delicate web-patterns of sand on the arena floor.

Naois threw back his head and yelled a psychic scream into the shadows around the perimeter of the arena, letting his frustration fill the space and saturate the edifice. His inaudible howl was turned back on him by the curving architecture, filling the arena with a mental cacophony and amplifying his aggravation.

As the soundless rage bounced and ricocheted around him, Naois strode over to the sealed crescent doors and pushed against them, leaning his meagre

weight against their ancient and ineffable strength.
The doors had stood for countless eons, since before
the House Wars had been even a hint in the myriad
possible futures of Kaelor. They were studded with
icons of power and runic seals that warded them
from all conceivable intrusion. The crescent doors of
the Warp Spiders could not be opened until their
secrets had been unlocked. In its entire history, none
had ever gained illicit entry to the temple. The seals
also worked from the other side and once a tyro had
been admitted into the temple for training, he would
not be able to leave until he had learnt or been
inducted into the secrets of the crescent doors. One
or two would fail, and would remain within the temple as bound temple priests for the rest of their lives.
Most would either learn the secret or die trying.

As his frustration mounted, Naois could not find
the patience that was expected of a Warp Spider. He
banged his fists against the doors and kicked at them,
trying to force them to part for him. The umbhala
shafts that he had thrown through them in his last
bout of rage were stuck fast, as though fused into
their web-like structure. He gripped the ends of the
shafts and tried to pry them apart, trying to use the
leverage to spring the doors, but nothing moved. He
cursed again, yanking at the umbhala with all his
might until the shafts snapped off in his hands and
he fell back onto the ground, seething.

Springing back to his feet, Naois was about to start
pounding at the doors with the remnants of the staff
when he saw two delicate beams of light penetrating
through the holes that the shafts had left. He peered

at them curiously, noticing the microscopic movements of glittering fragments in the holes. As his
breathing began to stabilise and return to normal, he
leant in closer to inspect the tiny traces of activity.
There were fleets of miniscule little spiders working
their way across the holes in the doors, spinning
thousands of shimmering webs across the cavities in
chaotic coordination until, in only a matter of
moments, the openings had been completely sealed
once again and the light from outside had vanished
utterly.

CHAPTER FIVE: YSEULT

THE RAIN OF fire hadn't started immediately. Instead, there had been an eerie and tense silence as the Ansgar convoy had progressed to the middle of the Ula Pass. Then, without a visible signal, streams of shuriken and laser bolts had started to hail down on them from above. At the same time, the portal behind the convoy at the entrance to the pass had hissed shut, sealing them it. A moment later and the portal at the far end of the pass had slid open to reveal a rank of Teirtu Wraithguard, resplendent in their green and gold psycho-plastic armour. Without hesitation or ceremony, the Wraithguard had levelled their Wraithcannons and unleashed a withering barrage of fire into the prow of Scilti's Wave Serpent.

It was only then that Scilti really understood how lethal the Ula Pass could be. Looking up towards the origin of the hail of lasfire and shuriken, he could see only the void of space, replete with stars and swirling nebulae. The weapons platforms from which the furious tirade of fire was being unleashed were utterly invisible through the singular optical and psychic oddities of the Styhxlin Perimeter, in which they were now trapped. Despite the furious volleys of return fire that arose out of the convoy, the Ansgar had no way of telling whether they were hitting anything, or even whether it was possible to fire up through the void.

Only the road beneath the convoy seemed solid and real, albeit impossibly flimsy and thin. The infinite expanse of deep space stretched to both sides, above, below and behind. The sensation of standing on a paper-thin gangplank in the midst of the galaxy would have been enough to have driven a mon-keigh to insanity.

Aside from the path itself, the only point that seemed fixed in the concrete space of the material realm was the portal at the far end of the pass. It shone like a circular beacon, enticing and real. But arrayed across it, blocking the steady, heavy light of Kaelor, a detachment of wraithguard stood in dramatic silhouette, unleashing continuous pulses of warp-space distortions from their weapons. They stood like colossal gate-keepers, barring the way out of the lost reaches of space as well as the passage from the outer domains of Kaelor into the Sentrium.

Although the twin-linked shuriken cannons and catapults on the pincers at the nose of the Wave Serpent erupted into life as soon as the wraithguard appeared, the gunners seemed to have difficulty fixing their aim through the mire of sha'iel-infused space, and the sheets of shuriken fire rattled past the wraithguard without causing much damage. At the same time, the Wave Serpent was absorbing an incredible amount of damage, not only from the distortion weaponry of the wraithguard but also from the continuous hail of fire from the invisible emplacements above. After only a few moments, the transport started to shudder and quake under the relentless onslaught. Because of the narrowness of the pathway, the vehicle had no room for manoeuvre, making it effectively a static target.

Realising that the Wave Serpent was as good as dead, Scilti and the others vaulted down off its roof and took a moment to shelter behind it while they formulated their plan of attack. Then the pilot opened the throttle and powered the transport through the pass, leaving its cannons clicked to auto-fire as it accelerated towards the wraithguard that blocked the exit. As the distance closed, the Wave Serpent's cannons began to find their marks, and two of the wraithguard suddenly stuttered and broke apart as twin lines of close-range shuriken fire raked through them. The others stood their ground, as though immune to fear.

An instant later, the Wave Serpent convulsed as the onslaught of fire intensified even more. Fiery cracks spread rapidly over its fuselage as its anti-grav units started to detonate inside. Even as the engines failed, its momentum carried it forwards, careening into the wraithguard just as it erupted into a fireball.

The inferno filled the portal at the far end of the pass, engulfing the wraithguard and billowing back along the pathway. Taking advantage of the explosion, Scilti and Khukulyn were already storming along the road in its wake. As they plunged into the blossoming flames, Khukulyn whipped his twin witchblades from over his shoulders, spinning them into readiness. Scilti pumped his deathspinner from side to side as he ran, as though driving himself faster with the rhythmic motion. Both of them raced to be the first into the fray.

Meanwhile, the jetbikes that had been hemmed in behind the Wave Serpent zipped passed Ela, Lhir and Aingeal, flashing past them on both sides in pursuit of the two running warriors up ahead. They were followed by two Vypers, weaving to and fro through the restricted space in single file, with their main cannons angled up into the cosmos, spraying the hidden emplacements overhead with sleets of shuriken. Another Wave Serpent emerged from the rear of the convoy, easing along the pathway with shuriken and las-blasts deflecting off its armour. Ansgar Guardians and Warp Spiders were springing out of its rear doors and hatches, clambering over its roof and then dashing along in front of it, desperate to join the fight up ahead.

Then bringing up the rear, the midnight blue and silver Falcon grav-tank squeezed through the pass. Its turret-mounted star cannon was firing great javelins of plasma up into the invisible heights of the pass, but the line of fire of its prow-mounted shuriken catapults were blocked by the Wave Serpent in front of it. The pilot twitched the tank's prow-scythes in frustration at the restrictive space of the Ula Pass.

HE COULD FEEL the pulse of battle coursing through the Fluir-haern. Death-knells and killing words echoed and whispered on the breeze of faerulh. The icons of Khaine that decorated the walls of the temple sanctum glowed faintly, filling the shrine with an unworldly heat and the scent of blood.

Naois strode through the temple arena and passed through the narrow, gnarled tunnel that led into the sanctum in the heart of the shrine. There, he stood before the Altar of the Spider Exarch, and he knew that war was being waged on Kaelor. He could taste it.

Looking up at the altar, Naois watched the blinking and sparkling runes that were illuminating around the chamber. They seemed to swim into patterns, forming into ancient signatures as though the temple itself were trying to communicate with him. A faint music was dancing through the air, like a chorus of infinite voices singing silently.

On the left side of the Spider Altar was the ceremonial deathmask of the temple seer: the Araconid Warlock. It took a place of honour next to the threaded and interwoven structure of the altar itself, glaring down at him with profoundly lifeless eyes. Above the right side of the altar like a crucified saviour hung the ageless and inexplicable armour of the Lhykosidae – the mythical Wraith Spider of Kaelor. For as long as anyone could remember, the armour had hung lifelessly within the temple sanctum, little

more than a shining, golden symbol of the mystical
origins of the secretive Aspect. On this day, however,
it seemed to glower down at Naois, as though animated with a life-force of its own.

There was a voice just out of hearing. It was like a
whisper of faerulh flickering through the furthest
reaches of the spirit pool, just beyond the detection
of even the most sensitive and open of minds. It was
buried beneath the weight of the incessant gabble of
life on Kaelor, hidden in amongst the chorus of war
that pulsed and chanted through the spirit matrix of
the ancient craftworld. Through some coincidence of
fate, the soundless voice seemed to find a presence in
the armour of the Lhykosidae. The change was
imperceptible, but Naois could sense that the galaxy
had suddenly and instantaneously reoriented itself
around a new future.

He bowed slowly and resentfully to the icons of his
Aspect and then turned away from the altar. The possible significance of the invisible metastasis was
secondary in his mind to the frustration of having
been left behind. He could feel the battle of his generation raging in the distant Ula Pass, but he was
alone and abandoned like a child in the sanctity of
the temple.

Racks of weapons were arranged in preparedness
on either side of the entrance to the passageway that
led back out into the arena. There were rows of
deathspinners and a series of sheaths containing the
powerblade augmentations for Warp Spider
gauntlets. A row of umbhala staffs stood on the
opposite side of the passage mouth, each polished to

such a high sheen that they seemed to be fashioned out of some kind of metallic alloy.

He eyed the weapons carefully and his mind flashed back to his duel with Scilti. The devious cheat had fought him *as though* he had been using the characteristic deathspinner and powerblades of the Warp Spiders, even though he had been nothing more than a tyro with a staff. His victory had been false.

With a sudden resolution, Naois strode forwards and grasped two of the umbhala shafts, one in each hand, and then he breezed through the passageway back into the arena beyond. In battle, he told himself, to ignore reality is to fall into defeat and ignominy. Scilti may have duped the arachnir, but he could not hide his façade from the reaper himself. War makes all eldar honest.

AS THE FIRE died down, Scilti saw the ranks of the Teirtu Guardians marching through the smoke towards them, flames licking at their cloaks and armour like halos of power. The lithe and graceful form of Marshal Yseult was in the lead, several strides ahead of the banners and the other warriors. Her famous diresword remained undrawn at her side, but she swept along before her troops with a calm and inalienable determination. Despite himself, Scilti found a wisp of admiration passing through the flames before his eyes.

Tumbles of smoke rolled across the pathway, blowing over the shattered remains of the Wave Serpent and a number of the ruined wraithguard. Looking to either side, Scilti saw Khukulyn standing ready to fight with his witchblades crossed before his chest. The awesome figure of Aingeal stood on the other side, her deathspinner hanging easily by her leg as though she saw no need to brace it for combat. Behind them, he could feel the pressing presence of the other Guardians of Ansgar and the fleeting, sporadic movements of the squad of Warp Spiders. The jetbikes and Vypers brought up the rear of the vanguard, and the bulk of the tanks still rumbled further back.

Wisps of smoke floated back along the pathway, blurring the advancing line of Teirtu and making the stars of the Styhxlin haze into bursts of light. The scene was suddenly obscure and poorly resolved, but Scilti could see the figure of Yseult come to a stop and wait for her Guardians to pull up on either side of her.

The two forces faced each other through the smoke and the flickering flames for a long moment. The banners of Teirtu, Ansgar and Rivalin fluttered in the convection currents. The star-filled void glittered all around them, and the barrage of fire from the heavens paused, the initial exchanges of the battle having been completed.

There was silence, broken only by the hiss of flames consuming oxygen.

Then all eyes were drawn to the tiny figure of Ela'Ashbel as she walked out of the Ansgar line and into the space between the opposing forces. She was dressed in a simple blue robe, hemmed with golden lace, which billowed in the smoke and rendered her in the image of a ghost.

The others didn't know how to react. Both Ansgar and Teirtu watched the child seer as though transfixed, marvelling at the way the smoke eddied and curled around her as she walked. It was as though her presence had brought time itself to a sudden arrest, and the others were powerless to shatter the stasis that flowed around her like a vortex.

She stopped and turned on the spot, casting her sapphire eyes around the scene, letting them alight on the face of each warrior in the front line of both sides. *This battle is an echo of the unforgotten future. It matters not. Your lives are worth less and more than this. Step aside and let the present through. Give way to what must be.*

Scilti felt the thoughts in his head, just as all the others did. They left an indelible imprint in his mind, like tiny but heavy footprints in snow, but he could make no sense of their meaning, and their imprint melted slowly away to leave his mind feeling empty and pristine, as though it had been suddenly purified. He turned to Aingeal and looked up into her golden mask.

The truth is often spoken in languages that we cannot understand, responded the exarch without looking down, but keeping her eyes fixed on the infant seer before them. *Failing to understand it, however, is no excuse for mistaking it for falsehood.*

'You are not welcome here, Sons of Ansgar and Spiders of the Warp. You will turn back, or we will turn you back,' called Yseult from her line beyond Ela. It was as though she hadn't heard the child seer's words, or was simply ignoring them.

A tumbling cloud of smoke passed over Ela, obscuring her from sight. Almost immediately, the adversaries seemed to forget about her completely, as though the smoke had erased her from time.

Who are you to refuse us welcome, servant of Teirtu? replied Aingeal, in an obvious and ritualistic repeat of their last encounter.

'I am Yseult Teirtu-an,' announced Yseult, taking a step forward of her own lines so that she could be seen clearly by both sides, 'and I am duly empowered to welcome our friends, just as I am more than capable of repelling our enemies. Are you prepared to fight me on this day, Exarch of Khaine?'

Scilti stepped forward of his comrades, pre-empting the response of his exarch. 'I will fight you on this day,' he called, letting his voice resonate with confidence. 'I am Scilti Ansgar-ann, Warp Spider of the Temple of the Lhykosidae. Is this good enough for your blood, daughter of Teirtu?'

Instead of words, Yseult responded with a bow, flourishing her cloak into a whirl that culminated in its discard, leaving her standing forwards in a low combat stance with her hand touched to the hilt of her magnificent sword.

At the same moment, Scilti folded his arms across his chest and vanished from his position at the head of the Ansgar forces. He reappeared only a few paces in front of Yseult, where he returned the bow in an ostentatious show of respect for the famed Teirtu Guardian.

Just as they were about to lurch into combat, another voice arose from the Ansgar lines, stopping

them in their tracks. This was not how it was supposed to happen.

'I will not suffer to wait another moment for the
blood of a Teirtu!' The voice boomed with emotion.
'The wait has been more than long enough already.'

Khukulyn was striding out into the space between
the frontlines. His witchblades were already drawn
and poised, in dramatic disregard for the normal etiquette of the commencement of battle.

'Is there not one of you who will stand forth and
fight me? Or would you all hide behind the female
Avenger?'

His voice seethed with passion and violence, as
though his sense of decorum had been completely
obliterated by his lust for blood. Images of Bedwyr's
eyes flashed through the heavens around him, and
he knew what he had to do to return peace to his
soul. When faced with the choice, he had chosen
death.

None of the Teirtu Guardians moved, even as the
striding warrior broke into a run towards them, lashing his twin blades across his body and down to his
sides as he stalked at them.

Then a voice made Khukulyn stop.

'I will fight you, Khukulyn, valiant son of Ansgar!'
It was Lhir.

The Teirtu Guardian stared across at the assembled
forces of House Teirtu, and he felt the conflict of
emotion bunch into a heavy weight in his abdomen.
He could see the banner of Rivalin fluttering
proudly above the heads of his kinsmen, and he
knew that the same banner flew over the paltry

forces of Ansgar behind him. His hands had presented the farseer's cloak to the rebel house; he had brought this battle into being, pulling it out of the mists of the possible futures and giving it weight in the present. Not even the farseer had been able to bring this about on his own; Lhir had become the agent of war. He could see nothing but death in his future, no matter which way he turned.

As Khukulyn turned slowly to face his own kinsmen, Lhir took a couple of steps clear of the Ansgar lines. At that moment, it might have appeared to all present that the warriors had both changed allegiances, that the old Ansgar veteran stood at the fore of the Teirtu, and that the immaculate, young Teirtuann stood ready to defend the honour of the Ansgar.

A murmur of unease whispered through the Teirtu Guardians as some of them recognised Lhir amongst the enemy. For a moment, Yseult's composure faltered as a number of the missing pieces suddenly fell into place: Lhir must have been responsible for taking the Rivalin banner to the domains of Ansgar; he was one of the farseer's personal guards, but what could have shaken the faith and the loyalty of a Guardian as immaculate and honourable as Lhir? She could not believe that he had been corrupted by greed or ambition, and his current stand proved that he had not. In the back of her mind, she knew that this must have something to do with Kerwyn's fate, but she repressed the disruptive thoughts to focus on the matter at hand. The matter of Iden's treatment of the farseer's heir would wait until the battle was won.

As he started to pace back towards his own kinsmen, the flash of rage on Khukulyn's face suddenly
gave way to satisfaction. He had never trusted the
intentions of the stranger from Sentrium, and he
had always trusted his own instincts. This was the
perfect opponent for him to regain a measure of his
lost honour.

STANDING IN THE centre of the arena once again, the
youthful Naois held his arms out by his sides as
though revealing himself to the gods. He balanced
the umbhala staffs in his open palms as he rolled his
head back and gazed up towards the domed ceiling.
High up above him, the veins through the ceiling
started to glow, as though a breath of life had passed
over a cluster of smouldering embers. The veins
smouldered and then burned, revealing the hidden
pattern of webwork that laced the inner face of the
dome, lighting it up like passion.

At the same time, Naois started to move. He could
feel the compulsion of the shrine wrap around him
as his eyes fixed on the spiralling design above. Ten-
tatively at first, but then growing in confidence and
speed, he began to trace the reflection of the burning
veins of the wolf spider above into the sand that lay
in a thin layer over the floor at his feet. He spun the
staffs in his hands as though they were extensions of
his arms, dragging them through the dirt and scraping them into intricate designs that his limbs could
not have managed on their own. The shafts seemed
to pivot around his hands, as though each tip were
somehow separate and alive in its own right, giving

him the appearance of an eight-legged arachnid as he skittered and danced over the arena.

He moved faster and faster, performing the dance-like patterns of the combat forms that he had learnt from Adsulata and the Exarch Aingeal, as his motions blurred more smoothly and less rhythmically into those of a spider. The tips of the umbhala staffs gouged into the floor, scattering fistfuls of sand and flecks of burning ground around the arena.

As he moved, he could feel the shrine talking to him. It was sharing its knowledge with him, feeding him with the whispers of the myriad dhamashir-souls that swam ineffably through the matrix of Fluir-haern, into which the Temple of the Warp Spiders was partially submerged. The Warp Spiders were singularly well attuned to the spirit of Kaelor, drawing their nature from the tiny crystalline creatures that roamed the highways and byways of the infinity circuit eliminating all psychic contaminations.

He spun and leapt, spiralling through the air and then dragging the umbhala through impossible contortions in the fabric of the floor, wrenching webs and matrices into the metallic structure, and leaving them riddled with flames.

He could feel his anger and frustration teetering on the edge of his control. The voices of Kaelor told him that Aingeal and Ela were already in the Ula Pass. For a moment he could see them in his mind. A vision of galaxies and stars flashed through his consciousness, showing the Warp Spider and the ehveline standing unmolested in the void. Then there was Scilti doing battle with a graceful Teirtu

Guardian, and he caught a glimpse of his father's staunchest guard, Khukulyn, prowling around a foe that he could not name.

There was a burst of darkness and then the scene shifted. He saw Aingeal lying dead with her armour engulfed in daemonic fire. He saw Scilti sitting cross-legged next to the corpse, gazing down at his own bloody hands and weeping. He saw Khukulyn's mutilated body, dismembered, ruined and neglected, tumbling through the infinite void, and he saw Ela's porcelain face, running red with rivers of blood that poured out of her eyes like tears. A hand reached for her face, wiping away the blood. It was the hand of Ahearn Rivalin. He was smiling oddly, in a way that Naois had never seen before and could not understand.

It was as though the movements of war that Naois was rehearsing in a frenzy of frustrated rage in the arena somehow formed a connection with the spirit pool and its untapped potential for vision through-out Kaelor and throughout time.

The vision did not placate him. Rather it fed his anger.

It should have been me! He couldn't believe that they had left him behind while they marched to their doom in the Ula Pass. Even he knew that they could not triumph in the territory that had almost been the end of Bedwyr himself. If they had marched without any visions or aspirations of victory – if they had marched with heroic doom in their souls, like Maugan Ra – then why leave him behind to rattle and shake in the sanctity of the temple. It made no sense. It was almost as though Aingeal had wanted to make him angry and leave him alone with his frustrations.

He lashed out with the staffs, spinning tightly in the middle of the arena, focusing his fury along the lengths of their organic shafts and sending chains of wraith-thread whipping out of their tips. After a moment, he released them and let them flip and flash through the thickening webs around him until they punched into the dome of the ceiling, penetrating all the way through to their trailing tips. Then he slumped onto the mica-strewn burning ground, exhausted and spent.

Blood calls! I hear it. It should have been me... They wrong me, keeping me a prisoner in my own lair.

SCILTI TURNED BACK to face Yseult, letting the question of how to proceed float between them. The Ceremony of Commencement was supposed to include only one representative from each side, but the impatience of Khukulyn and the vagaries of Lhir had already ruined the established process. They could each feel the discomfort of their troops, who hesitated with their weapons, unsure of whether to wait for their marshals to complete their duel or to storm into the fray after the other two. The situation seemed suddenly frozen in time, like a priceless vase on the point of smashing to the ground.

From her position in the midst of the Ansgar, Exarch Aingeal studied the complexities of the scene. She wondered why Ela's intervention had been ignored, but then instantly dismissed the question. There was no way that the others could understand the little abomination. Part of her wondered whether anyone would even remember the incongruous figure of the child wandering out into the warzone, alone and apparently unprotected, speaking in a silent tongue that everyone could hear.

Besides, she realised, this fight was no longer about Kaelor or even about the Ansgar and the Teirtu. This was a battle for the private, unspoken passions that raged within Scilti, Khukulyn and Lhir. Only Yseult seemed innocent and pure of intention.

As Yseult and Scilti nodded their understanding to each other, Lhir unclipped his shuriken pistol and levelled it at the charging form of Khukulyn, whose twin witchblades glinted with menace and the thirst for death.

There was a brief moment before the parallel duels were joined. It hung in the air with a significance that was not wasted on any of those present, but was shattered almost instantly as Yseult lurched forwards. She unsheathed her diresword and swept it into a smooth killing arc in one seamless motion. At precisely the same time, but twenty paces away, Khukulyn whipped his blades out to his sides as he closed on Lhir and then spun them back across himself, hacking in towards the Guardian.

The blood came from everywhere at once.

Scilti ducked to one side to avoid the diresword, bringing his deathspinner around and squeezing off a spray of discharge in counter-attack. The gush of monofilament wires riddled into Yseult's armour even as her blade hacked straight through the Warp Spider's gun and struck solidly into his forearm. Both of them fell back, bleeding and stunned by the immediate ferocity of the other.

Meanwhile, Lhir held his ground in front of the charging Khukulyn. His pistol was levelled directly between the eyes of the veteran Ansgar Guardian, and he seemed to smile faintly as though his aim was perfect and true, but he did not take the shot. Instead, he simply stood with his gun outstretched in readiness as Khukulyn's blades sliced into both sides of his abdomen at once, screaming in an echo of the psychic force of his weapons.

There was another finely balanced silence as Yseult and Scilti disengaged and renegotiated their positions, prowling around each other to hide their wounds and present only their strengths. They were searching for glitches or gaps in the stance of the other.

At the same time, Khukulyn froze in horror: Lhir had not even raised a fight. The Teirtu Guardian still stood with his pistol raised and with a faint, fading smile on his face. Two fatal gashes had opened up diagonally through his abdomen, cutting him through from both sides at once. He had been sliced into thirds by Khukulyn's raging blades, even before the old warrior had realised that the young Teirtu-ann had no intention of fighting back.

Lhir nodded into Khukulyn's appalled face as though thanking him for the release. Then a trickle of blood appeared in the corner of his mouth and his eyes glazed over. A moment later his body simply fell apart, sliding and slumping into three bloody sections on the ground at Khukulyn's feet.

Aingeal could feel genuine horror spreading through Khukulyn's soul. The veteran Guardian had expected to find his own death in this fight. He wanted it. He craved it, and Aingeal could see the frustrated rage building in his mind, as though he felt cheated by Lhir's self-sacrifice. He wanted nothing more than to make recompense for his own guilt by laying down his life for the Ansgar. When faced with the choice between life and death, he had chosen death, but his choice had been taken from him. Lhir's desire for death had been even more extreme than his own. He had not even felt himself worthy of dying in the throes of combat. Death had been enough, even the ignoble death of utter, pointless surrender.

Khukulyn, on the other hand, needed to die trying. His horror turned quickly into rage, and he spun on his heel to face the lines of Teirtu Guardians. He yelled incoherently at them, lashing his blades in fury and sending droplets of Lhir's blood speckling over the ground. Then he started to charge again, slowly at first but accelerating steadily, just wanting to throw himself into the mire of enemies and fall whilst fighting without hope. However, following his inspiration, the other Ansgar Guardians stormed into the charge behind him, yelling, crying and brandishing the dual banners of Ansgar and Rivalin.

Aingeal watched motionless. This was not her fight, but it would have its uses. She waited while the charge skirted around the duel of Scilti and Yseult and then parted around the almost absurd figure of Ela, rushing past her like an insentient river flooding around a rock. She held the child's tragic, sapphire gaze for a moment and then signalled to the other Warp Spiders, who remained in formation behind her. There was an instant's delay, and then they blinked out of existence, one after another in rapid succession.

LOOKING DOWN AT his hands, Naois realised that he was still attached to the umbhala shafts that he had buried in the roof by thin lengths of wraithweb that seemed to have seeped out of his body. There was a mess of glittering scales coating his body like the outer layer of a caecilian's skin, but the tiny, crystalline scales had somehow formed into long, delicate chains.

Holding up his arms, Naois lifted himself into the air, using the tensile strength of the criss-crossing webs around him. He pulled himself up into the middle of the elaborate and complicated array of webs that laced and interwove throughout the space above the temple arena.

After a few moments, he found himself suspended in the heart of the glittering wraithweb, which reached from the web-cut ground up into the glowing veins of webbing in the domed ceiling. It was as though the interior of the temple had been transformed into a giant lair.

A feeling of calm embraced him for the first time since he could remember. He felt suddenly at home, as though he were in touch with the whole of Kaelor. His resentment at having been left behind by his cousin and sister gradually dissipated, and he reclined in the interweave beneath him.

The threads of his gigantic, otherworldly web seemed to tremble and quiver as he lay in them. Tiny vibrations pulsed along them and oscillated against his skin where strands touched his crystal-speckled body. At the same time, a whispered cacophony of voices whirled around him, as though each of the threads was speaking to him.

Quieting his mind, Naois listened to the myriad souls that coursed through the strands, and he realised that his web had reached into the infinity circuit itself, like a series of precise spider bites into the veins of a massive body. The web pulsed with energy, like a matrix of capillaries drawn out in the material realm.

In that moment, a vision of the shattered and ruined webs of the interior of the Shrine of Fluirhaern flashed before his eyes, filling his mind with anger once again. In the ghostly echoes of the immediate past, he could see Iden of Teirtu ripping through the ancient and delicate structures with his alien sword, unleashing his own fury at the spiders of the warp and venting his rage against the soul of Kaelor itself. He could feel the violence of opposition swelling through the arteries of the craftworld and pulsing in his mind. It was as though Kaelor itself wanted this eldar stopped. It was as though the Fluirhaern was searching for an agent to express its will.

The image was followed by a barrage of other pictures and voices, flickering one after the other and pouring into his mind with relentless force. Fragments of Kaelor's past intermingled with whispers thrown back from the future until Naois's mind reeled under the cascade. He saw the starving masses in the outer realms of Kaelor, deprived and suffering after years of oppression and neglect by the court. He saw the glittering radiance of the Sentrium and the decadent, oblivious splendour of the Knavir. He saw the Exarch Aingeal, dripping with blood, suddenly grasping at the slumped and age-ruined form of the farseer in his tower. He saw Ela standing unmolested and untouched in the middle of a battlefield with her sapphire eyes ablaze in red flame, while shuriken and lasfire lashed past her on all sides.

Then the detailed scenes shrank into points of light, spinning into a spiralling galaxy through the darkness until they exploded into a picture of Kaelor itself. The craftworld hung in the murky depths of the void, massive and incredible as only the architecture of the ancients could be. But it teetered on the brink of an abyss, like an ocean-ship on the point of falling over the edge of the world. The screams of daemons emerged from the abyss and great lashing tendrils of bloodlust reached up to claw at the majestic form of the craftworld, dragging it closer and sucking on its armoured shell as though drawing out its marrow.

The maelstrom, Naois realised, his eyes snapping open and widening unnaturally. *Kaelor is heading for the roiling warp-wastes of the maelstrom, and Ahearn is too blind to notice, or too wrapped in the decadence of the moment to care.*

THE ULA PASS was ripped through by lasfire and sleeting volleys of shuriken. They rained down from the hidden gun emplacements high above the pass, apparently obscured amongst the stars and nebulae that glittered within the Styhxlin Perimeter. Lashes of fire also tore along the pathway, exploding out of the tanks that faced each other from either end of the narrow corridor, flashing around and over the heads of the dozens of eldar warriors that hacked and danced in combat between them.

Only the child seer, Ela'Ashbel, wandered unphased, untouched and unperturbed by the dense mire of violence that filled the pass. She shuffled through the smoke and the flames, pushing past the battling warriors and sliding in between the streaking lines of munitions fire. It was as though neither the Ansgar nor the Teirtu even noticed her presence. Or, if they did, they simply could not bring themselves to lay hands on her.

At the rear of the Teirtu lines, Ela could see the ostentatious Falcon of Iden. It was decorated wildly in the house colours of Teirtu, with an awesome golden serpent snaking around its dark jade hull, its fanged mouth wide open across the prow. With slow, delicate determination, little Ela started to make her way through the raging battlefield towards it.

After only a few steps, she emerged into a small clearing in the battle. The Guardians of both sides had instinctively left the area clear, as though it were reserved for some higher purpose. No fire rained into it from above, and the vicious crossfire that sliced through the rest of the pass seemed to slide around it. In it, Ela saw the prowling forms of Yseult and Scilti, still locked in their duel.

Scilti's deathspinner lay in pieces on the floor, and great chunks of his warp-pack had been hacked clear away from his back, its smoking remains crackling with unleashed and uncontrolled energies. His arms ran with blood from the various gashes that Yseult's blade had ripped through his thick armour and his flesh, and a number of the powerblades on his gauntlets had broken off, but he still moved with sure-footed focus.

For her part, Yseult moved with a rare delicacy. Her diresword was a blur of elegant motion around her, defining a sphere of energy that crackled with menace. She seemed light on her feet and almost unaffected by the exertions of the duel. A number of thin cuts had been sliced across her face by Scilti's blades, and trickles of blood ran down her neck. A long spike protruded from her shoulder, where one of Scilti's powerblades had penetrated straight through and then snapped off in her armour.

With a sudden movement, Scilti feinted to his right and then spun back to his left, bringing the bladed back of his right hand around in a sweeping arc towards the side of Yseult's head, but the Teirtu Guardian was faster. She swayed back, letting the blow pass harmlessly but fractionally in front of her face. As its motion continued, she brought her blade up into a vertical arc, driving its live edge into the underside of Scilti's arm. There was a moment of resistance, but then Scilti's forearm flew clear, spraying a bloody arc as it tumbled to the ground.

The Warp Spider wailed and spun, bringing his other arm around instinctively, trying to protect himself, but Yseult stepped smoothly inside the flailing arm, blocking it with the hilt of her sword even as she jammed her shoulder forcefully into Scilti's chest, lifting him off his feet for an instant and then sending him crashing to the ground at Ela's feet. Before he could find his feet again, Yseult was upon him, straddling his abdomen and pinning his remaining arm under her knee.

The Teirtu Guardian lifted her diresword above her head, flipping it around ready for a downwards thrust into the Warp Spider's neck. Just at that moment, her eyes caught the blue and gold waft of the hem of Ela's robes in front of her. She hesitated for an instant, glancing up at the incongruous and calm face of the child who stood alone, ghostly and apparently unfazed by the battle raging around her. For a fraction of an instant, she tried to rationalise the presence of the childling. In that moment, she looked into Ela's radiant sapphire eyes and she felt something shift inside her, like clouds suddenly blowing clear of the moon.

THERE WAS A ripple in space and then Exarch Aingeal burst silently into the corridor. A moment later five more Warp Spiders erupted into existence behind her. This was as close as they could get to the farseer's chamber. The chamber itself was powerfully shielded against any and all psychic infringements, no matter how small, and the passage of a detachment of Warp Spiders through the warp would hardly constitute a small disturbance. Indeed, it was only thanks to the incredible disruption in the sha'iel fields throughout

Kaelor caused by the battle that was raging within the Styhxlin Perimeter that the squad had managed to penetrate so far into the Sentrium without detection.

Detection was now inevitable.

Stalking to the end of the ostentatiously decorated corridor, Aingeal peered around the final corner. Four Teirtu Guardians stood guard in front of the heavy doors at the end of the immaculately polished passageway. They held shuriken catapults diagonally across their chests, braced and ready. Aingeal ducked back into the corridor with her squad.

How many? asked Adsulata.

Four.

There will be others on this level.

Yes. This should be done quietly, agreed Aingeal. *The rest of you will stay here. Others will come, but let nobody pass.*

The exarch and her Arachnir nodded silently to each other and then vanished.

An instant later, they reappeared before the doorway into the farseer's chambers, standing in-between the two pairs of Guardians. Before the Teirtu even had chance to shift the balance of their weapons, Aingeal punched out with both hands simultaneously, driving them through the chest plates of two of the Guardians, shattering their spines under the force of her burning fists. At the same time, Adsulata spun her powerblades across the throat of one while she swept the feet out from under the other. Even as the falling Guardian hit the ground, she was already unloading clouds of shimmering monofilaments from her deathspinner into his face.

As one, the two Warp Spiders turned to face the doors. They scanned around its frame, searching for signs of runic seals that would frustrate the entry of the unauthorised, but they could see nothing. Exchanging glances, they pushed the doors experimentally, not expecting them to open.

The doors creaked and then cracked open, folding slowly into the room beyond.

An abrupt silence flowed back out of the room, as though everyone inside had suddenly stopped talking. Ahearn was standing next to the long table, leaning on his staff as though exhausted. A number of the Knavir sat around the table, reclining and comfortable. A half-drained carafe of Edreacian wine stood in pride of place in the centre of the table, and a number of glasses in various states of emptiness were arranged over the surface. The Iden heir, Morfran, was sitting at the head of the table in place of the farseer, with his feet propped up on the tabletop.

With varying speeds, determined by their levels of intoxication and sense of superiority, the Knavir turned to see who was disturbing them. Ahearn reacted first, lifting his gaze to meet Aingeal's almost before the doors had opened. A flash of emotion passed between them, making the exarch hesitate on the threshold for an instant. There was something unexpected in the farseer's eyes.

After a lingering moment of slow comprehension, Morfran dropped his feet to the ground and stood up, reaching for the shuriken pistol that he kept ceremonially bound to his thigh. He fumbled at the catch on the holster until he had to look down and unclip it with both hands. Meanwhile, two of the other courtiers at the table rushed over to the farseer, placing themselves between him and the Warp Spiders in the doorway. Two more remained in their seats, watching the events with an unusually detached interest.

We mean the farseer no harm, said Aingeal, letting her thoughts touch every mind in the room. She simply ignored the bumbling attempts at aggression from Morfran. *We come at his request. Release him to us, and we will leave you unharmed.*

Cinnia and Celyddon, the two courtiers standing in front of the farseer as a living barrier, looked suddenly uncertain, but there was a dramatic quality to their hesitancy that made Aingeal uncomfortable. They were not as surprised by her announcement as they pretended, but the exarch had no time to worry about the intricacies of Ohlipsean politics. These twisted contortions of emotion and intellect were some of the principal reasons why the Aspect Temples had sworn not to intervene in the political affairs of Kaelor.

Meanwhile, Uisnech Anyon and Triptri Paraq merely nodded from their seats at the table, showing that they understood. Only Morfran showed any sign of aggression. He had finally managed to produce his pearly pistol, and he had levelled it unsteadily across the chamber in the general direction of the Warp Spiders.

'I cannot permit you to commit this outrage,' he said. His voice trembled slightly, but slurred more.

'We will protect the radiant farseer from your styhx-tann barbarism, as we have done for years, warp spawn.' He swayed slightly.

The exarch ignored him. *Stand aside, Councillors of the Ohlipsean. We have no dispute with you.* Aingeal's tone was flat and direct. The Knavir were feeble, effete and utterly harmless once deprived of the political authority that the presence of the farseer gave to them. For hundreds of generations they had known nothing of the sword or of the dhanir of the warrior. The Sentrium and all of Kaelor had subsisted in an easy peace. It was only in the last generation that things had changed so markedly. There was no need to damage these living anachronisms, unless they decided to cause problems.

There was the faint click-whine of a pistol firing. Then again. A tiny shuriken buried itself into Adsulata's chest armour, and another hissed past Aingeal's head and impacted against the wall behind them. Instantly, Adsulata vanished and reappeared directly behind Morfran's swaying figure. He seemed to sense her presence, because he tried to turn to confront her. However, the sudden motion upset his already inebriated balance, and he twisted his body without lifting his feet. In one clumsy, heavy motion, Morfran of Teirtu tripped and fell flat on his face on the tabletop, where he passed out.

Do not think that we are unaware of what we gain from this, Exarch of Khaine. The thoughts came from Cinnia of Yuthran as she stepped aside, revealing the hunched and aging form of Ahearn Rivalin, who

shuffled past her towards the Warp Spiders with his
staff clicking unsteadily against the polished floor.

ON THE HOLOGRAPHIC optic-enhancer in the stomach
of his Falcon tank just outside the Ula Pass, Iden saw
it happen, as though in slow motion. He had filtered
out the melee that had raged throughout the narrow
corridor of the pass, and had focused tightly on the
duel between his perfect Yseult and the warpling
Scilti, spawn of the Ansgar. He had watched his
champion prowling around her prey like a raptor,
keeping her distance until the choice moment and
then swooping in with her blade and leaving her
mark. He could see that Scilti was scarred and bleeding copiously. It should have been only a matter of
time.

Just as Yseult had made her final move, dismem-
bering the Ansgar and stepping inside his pathetic
counter, knocking him to the ground and pinning
him like a hopeless wretch, Iden had watched in confusion as a girl child had wandered onto the screen
of his viewer. The stranger was little more than a
childling, shaven-headed like a tyro of Yuthran, but
dressed in the flowing, sumptuous and simple blues
of Ansgar. She was like a ghost of something long forgotten, and she drew his eyes like a black-hole draws
light. She was a disarming moment of peace in the
storm.

Ela? The name came to him like a repressed fear.
He had not seen the abomination since Bedwyr's execution in the Plaza of Vaul, but his certainty grew
with each of her tiny, shuffling steps. What was she

doing there? Why wasn't she dead? Why wouldn't one of the Guardians just snap the tiny aberration in two and rid him of her?

Then it happened. Yseult had raised her diresword for the deathblow, aiming its point directly into the neck of the fallen and pinned Scilti, but just at the last moment, Iden's champion had seen little Ela. She had paused for too long, somehow transfixed by the infant abomination. The hesitation had given Scilti just enough time to wrest his remaining arm free and plunge its blades up into Yseult's stomach.

Although he couldn't hear Yseult's cry, Iden himself screamed. He watched her rock back under the treacherous thrust and then drop her magnificent diresword. It fell slowly from her hands, as though reluctant to be parted from the grip of such a worthy warrior, but then it clattered down onto the deck next to Scilti.

The Warp Spider ripped his gauntlet out of the marshal's gut, pulling long trails of tissue and blood out with it, until Yseult simply collapsed on top of him. She was dead.

Iden screamed and wailed in disbelief. The last time he had fought in the Ula Pass he had lost more warriors than he had thought possible, and Bedwyr had somehow managed to emerge out of the other side of the maelstrom that he had unleashed in that supernatural corridor. He would not witness a repeat of that failure.

All gun emplacements open fire. His thoughts flashed instantaneously into the minds of the gunners in his Falcon, but also up to the Guardians that occupied the elevated gun platforms above the pass. They had been under the orders of Marshal Yseult to contain the engagement so that it could be fought with appropriate honour, but they possessed the means to end it once and for all if necessary.

Zhogahn, your own Guardians are still in the pass.

Leave nothing alive. His fury overcame his reason. *Nothing.* The etiquette of the engagement meant nothing. The glory of a skilfully won victory meant nothing. All that mattered was blood and death. *Kill them all.*

As he stared in furious, maniacal disbelief at the holographic projection of the optic-enhancer, he saw the little abomination Ela'Ashbel turn from Yseult's corpse and look up at him, as though suddenly aware that he was looking down at them from elsewhere. For an instant, he looked into her radiant sapphire eyes and saw horror itself.

Why had Ione saved that sleehr-child?

PART TWO : METASTASIS

CHAPTER SIX: NAOIS

IT LOOKED AS though the Temple of the Warp Spiders had been bombed. The ornate, carved walls were cracked and crumbling. Lumps of masonry had slumped into piles around the base, crushing foliage and covering much of the surrounding greenery in dust. The central spire that had once risen out of the polygonal edifice was riddled with rifts and cracks, and it appeared to be on the point of collapsing. A thick, scaly layer of crystals clung to the spire, as though keeping it together. Beneath them, the legendary crescent doors of the Lhykosidae hung open and unguarded. They pivoted on their broken hinges, like little more than barn doors.

Even the steps that ran down into the clearing in front of the temple were lined with fractures and fissures. Gouges had been taken out of the metallic decking, and shards lay strewn throughout the clearing.

Is this Iden's work? The farseer was genuinely shocked. _I had no idea._

Ahearn Rivalin emerged out of the sleek, low transport with difficulty, hanging his weight off Adsulata on one side and another of the Warp Spiders on the other. Exarch Aingeal was already ahead of them, standing out in the clearing and staring up at her decimated temple. For the briefest of moments, she wondered whether the Zhogahn really had the power to do this, so deep into the outer realms and so far from the Styhxlin Perimeter.

No, farseer, she replied at last. _We cannot lay this at Iden's feet… at least not directly._

Without waiting for the farseer, the exarch sprang up the ruined steps and rushed through the crescent doors. She could feel that something had changed. It was as though the temple had done this to itself. The atmosphere was charged with power, fizzling between the molecules and atoms in the air, giving the whole scene an electric thrill that filled the exarch with anxiety. She realised suddenly that her ancient temple had exploded from the inside out, as though something inside had expanded beyond its confines and burst through the edifice like a spider fighting its way out of a cocoon.

It felt as though something had been transformed. The energy of the temple itself had been assimilated into a metastasis, leaving something other than the shrine in the place where the shrine should be.

As she passed through the wrecked doors, Aingeal slid to an abrupt halt. In the light-streaked shadows inside, a vast complex of glittering, crystal threads were spread into a series of concentric spirals that rose towards the centre of the once immaculate domed ceiling. They formed a breathtaking funnel-web that made the famous threads of the Shrine of Fluir-haern appear random, paltry and flimsy. The huge expanse of shimmering wraithweb encompassed the entire arena, blocking access to all the other corridors into the interior of the temple, and opening up into a massive funnel-mouth just inside the threshold of the shattered crescent doors. It drew the eye naturally up to the narrow focus of the funnel, where the body of an eldar warrior was held suspended like the captured prey of some monstrous spider. Beyond the outstretched body, Aingeal could just see the veins of the dome glowing with energy and life.

For many long years, the Exarch of the Warp Spiders had felt no fear. Indeed, immunity to fear of enemies was one of the effects of her ascension to the position of an Exarch of Khaine. Death no longer held any mysteries for her. However, staring up into the incredible web, Aingeal felt an uncomfortable and destabilising mixture of emotions. She was in awe of her own Aspect, as she saw what her temple had generated with its own essential and unbridled will. There was a flicker of resentment as she realised that it had never done anything like this for her, its chosen agent on Kaelor, its dedicated exarch. There was also the unfamiliar and frosty touch of fear, wisping around her waystone like an icy breeze. What creature of the warp had been given life in this realm?

The Arachnir Adsulata appeared at Aingeal's shoulder, supporting the farseer's weight as he shuffled up the steps. They were curious to see what had brought the impressive figure of the exarch to such an abrupt halt on the threshold of her temple.

Adsulata gasped. *The Lhykosidae?*

Aingeal offered no response, for the question had been turning over and over in her own mind, tumbling like a hot coal through snow. She didn't want to touch it.

For a long moment, Ahearn said nothing at all. He surveyed the ruination of the temple and inspected the bizarre wraith-crystal webs that coated everything within, like a delicate layer of frost. Then he turned and looked back out over the steps, through the clearing outside and into the dwindling forest beyond. There were stains on the ground and in the foliage where blood had been spilt recently, and the greenery was already crisping into toxic browns.

He had expected blooms and unusually beautiful creatures speckled through heavenly glades, mirroring the natural splendour of the lost domains of the Eldar Knights, the Knavir of legend.

Despite himself, his mouth curled into a snarl of displeasure. *Why have you brought me to this?* he asked. *I cannot live in this... mess.*

The Warp Spiders ignored him. They were staring up into the funnel-web, watching the suspended and intertwined body in the eye begin to move. They could only see its back as its arms and legs flexed slowly. It turned on an axis, rotating as though free of the effects of gravity, and then it bent its neck back so that its face pointed down towards the doors. Its silver eyes flashed down from amongst the glittering scales.

Naois. Aingeal put a name to the creature suspended in the dome of the temple. The comfort of putting a name to the unknown was cold. There was a horror in the recognition that she hadn't known since she had felt the inexorable calling of Khaine.

We should not have left him alone. It was a confession, as though she had known what would happen.

Adsulata was struck with awe. *Naois? Naois is the Lhykosidae?*

There was a long silence as Naois glowered down at them from his position in the eye of his funnel-web. All the light in the crumbling temple seemed to emanate from his silver eyes, as though all other sources had been extinguished or were somehow irrelevant. He drew in their gazes as though he were drawing prey to bait. He held them.

The farseer pushed back between them, easing through into the interior of the temple and following the gazes of the Warp Spiders up into the heart of the chaotic array of threads and wraith crystals. He tilted his head, as though the angle would help him to see more clearly.

The Ansgar heir, he nodded, unphased and calm as though merely impressed by the logic of what he saw. *It seems that Ione was right about this one. The Lhykosidae? I can recall an early cycle from the days*

*before the coming of war to Kaelor. Perhaps it was even
Bedwyr who shared the tale with me, although it may
have been the long-passed Kaswallan.*

He paused, as though recollecting the story, apparently unaware of the magnitude of the event
unfolding around him. *The Lhykosidae is some kind of
exarch, isn't it? It is said to manifest the bellicose force of
sha'iel itself, in the form of a Warp Spider?*

Ahearn looked from Adsulata to Aingeal, as though
expecting one of them to confirm or rebuff his memories, but they were ignoring him utterly, as though
hardly even aware of his presence between them.
Their eyes were fixed on the figure of the spider-like
Naois, who held them in his silver gaze as he stalked
closer through the web.

'I thought that this was just a myth,' said Ahearn
out loud, feeling like a child being ignored on a
momentous occasion. 'It's a story told to frighten
childlings when they act disrespectfully towards the
Fuir-haern. The Lhykosidae is supposed to be the
Guardian of the spirit pool of Kaelor!'

It is no myth, Farseer Rivalin, as you can see, replied
Aingeal without shifting her gaze. *The Lhykosidae –
the Wraith Spider – appears to us at the time of our
greatest need. Its armour lies enshrined in the sanctum of
this very temple. It is said that it fought at the side of
Gwrih the Radiant during the Craftwars, your radiance,
but it has not been seen over the long eons since that time.*

'Where has it been?' mocked Ahearn, as though
deliberately refusing to believe what he could see
with his own eyes. His whole life had been spent in
the refined isolation of the Sentrium, and he was not

willing to sacrifice his sanitised sense of reality so quickly. It was bad enough that he had been forced to come to this vulgar and brutal outer realm, but he did not have to accept its violent and uncultivated cosmology.

It awaits the appropriate time, explained Aingeal, conscious of her duty as the Guardian and keeper of the temple and yet still transfixed by Naois's eyes, *and the appropriate host.*

'It has come to help in the fight to rid me of the disgusting Teirtu!' announced Ahearn conclusively, instantly appropriating the imagery of the legend for his own purposes.

'Perhaps,' said Aingeal, turning reluctantly from the horror-infused sight as she heard the approach of vehicles through the forest outside.

Following the exarch's gaze, Adsulata also turned in time to see the Falcon grav-tank emerge from the battered and tattered tree line. It was pocked and scarred, as though it had suffered a severe bombardment. The sleek, midnight-blue fuselage was dented and bent out of shape, and the gun turret had been blown away, leaving the tank open roofed and ruined. Its engines spluttered rheumatically, and whips of smoke rose from the exhaust arrays. As it eased to a halt at the bottom of the temple steps, pulling up along side the Warp Spider's transport, it lurched and trembled erratically, like an animal on the point of death.

The hatch on the rear of the Falcon fell open, crashing to the ground like an uncontrolled ramp. After a few seconds, the tiny figure of Ela'Ashbel walked

down the ramp into the clearing, turning her sapphire gaze immediately up towards the farseer and
the terrible sight of the ruined temple. Behind her
came a motley procession of eldar warriors. A bloodied Scilti limped down the ramp, hanging off
Khukulyn's shoulder, but there were only three others behind them. All of them were slumped and
exhausted, as though they had faced the wrath of
Kaelis Ra, the Bringer of Death.

Seeing the small numbers, Adsulata looked out
over the Falcon's wrecked roof towards the tree line
and waited for the Ansgar Vypers and jetbikes to
appear, but nothing came. The Falcon was the only
vehicle to return from the Ula Pass.

FROM THE KNAVIR balcony of the Farseer's Palace, Cinnia watched the procession of Teirtu warriors as they
marched down the wide boulevard of the Tributary
of Baharroth that fed into the Plaza of Vaul. A
squadron of deep jade and gold Falcon grav-tanks
were followed by a small fleet of Vypers and jetbikes.
They were shining and bright, as though freshly prepared for a parade of strength, and the light that
reflected off them filled the grandiose Tributary of
Baharroth with an emerald atmosphere of luxurious
colour.

Two squads of towering wraithguard marched at
the head of the convoy, each loping along with an
organic fluidity that belied their artificial construction. Their sophisticated sensor arrays glowed across
their teardrop helmets, and the spirit stones of once
great Teirtu warriors sheened on their chests. Each of

the giant Soulguard of Teirtu bore a massive victory
standard, bearing either the serpent crest of Teirtu or
the radiant star of Rivalin. Nearly twenty such banners fluttered impressively over the head of the
convoy, filling the boulevard with a fabricated wash
of pride and majesty.

Iden Teirtu rode between the two detachments of
his Soulguard, on an open-topped gun deck, soaking
in the dulled enthusiasm of the crowds that had been
primed and ushered into the street to welcome their
returning Zhogahn.

Watching from her balcony with the other Knavir,
Cinnia realised that Iden had not yet been informed
about the loss of the farseer. It seemed that none had
dared to share the news with the great and terrible
Zhogahn. He was returning as the Rivalin – decreed
Vanquisher of Sin, and yet he was returning to a Sentrium devoid of the Radiant Rivalin himself.

Even from the height and distance of the balcony,
Cinnia could see Iden's frustration with the luke-
warm and forced reception. His pain and indignance
was clearly heightened by the fact that the procession
was also the funeral cortege of the much loved Yseult
Teirtu-ann. If the truth were known, it was only
because of this last fact that any of the Knavir had
deigned to attend the homecoming. After the passing
of Ione, Yseult had been the last member of House
Teirtu viewed with anything like admiration or
respect by the courtiers of the Ohlipsean. Her loss
was felt as a genuine tragedy by most of the eldar of
the Sentrium, although the manner of her death
would mean that many would blame Iden rather

than sympathise with him. Such an immaculate and disciplined soul should not have been shredded in a pointless show of military dominance. There had been no need for the elaborate and almost ceremonial combat in the Ula Pass, since the Styhxlin Perimeter had been more than sufficiently fortified to repel such a small force.

The Knavir whispered that Iden had grown so forlorn after the onset of peace following his triumph in the House Wars that he was desperate for any chance to unleash the violence that roiled in his dhamashirsoul. They said that he was growing unbalanced, forced to live a sedentary life in the Sentrium. The Battle of Ula Pass was seen by some as nothing more than an indulgence. Iden was merely playing at being the great warrior. He was flexing his muscles in a vulgar, theatrical display of power, risking the lives of his eldar, including that of the valiant and much-loved Yseult. It was ostentatious and counterproductive, like using a brightlance to carve a mornah. It had been vengeful beyond reason, like the wrath of Asurmen, who was said to have trapped the soul of his brother Tethesis in the first ever diresword in order to inflict greater pain on his enemies.

Beloved though Lady Ione had been, none could believe that Iden's actions were inspired merely by the Warp Spider's interruption of Ione's Ceremony of Passing. Iden's hatred of Bedwyr and the Ansgar had made him into a monster of Khaine, and it had cost him the soul of his champion.

If they had been asked, a number of the Knavir eldar on the balcony of the Farseer's Palace would have voiced some sympathy and admiration for the paltry force of Ansgar warriors who had stood their ground in the face of vastly superior firepower, defiant to the last. They had marched into the Ula Pass knowing that it was the march to their deaths. They had chosen to die rather than live in the conditions to which the Teirtu had condemned them. The account of how Yseult had attempted to fight them honourably in the conventional fashion, doing justice to their stature and showing due appreciation of the precious value of all eldar souls, had already spread around the Sentrium like a gust of faerulh. Everyone knew that Iden had ordered the massive bombardment, disregarding the ceremonies of battle because of the terrible loss of Yseult, disregarding the cultivated and disciplined aesthetics of war because of personal loss.

Uisnech Anyon watched from the balcony as the parade advanced into the Plaza of Vaul, undisguised disgust on his face. His simple grey cloak belied the sophistication of his mind, but it also spoke of the austerity of one who had once been a warrior himself. Many dhanirs before, Uisnech had turned a cycle in the Aspect Temple of the Swooping Hawks, one of the most exclusive and ancient of the Aspect Shrines on Kaelor. Perhaps because of the natural elegance of the Winged Phoenix, Baharroth, who founded the Aspect, the Swooping Hawks had always been the most respectable and admired of the Aspects amongst the Knavir of Kaelor. Initiation into the temple, which lay within the bounds of the Sentrium, was restricted to members of the Knavir, on the rare occasion that any of them should ever feel the draw of Khaine. Whilst Uisnech was aware that this kind of social control over access to a warrior aspect was one of the idiosyncrasies of Kaelor, he also approved of the way that it ensured that the cultivated Knavir would be able to pass a dhanir as a warrior without losing their sophistication and well-developed aesthetic values.

Training in the Temple of the Swooping Hawks was carefully monitored and controlled by a special committee of the Ohlipsean, and Uisnech was the senior counsellor of this so-called Phoenix Wing. An unfortunate side effect of this exclusivity, however, was that the other Aspect Shrines on Kaelor viewed the Swooping Hawks with a level of suspicion that sometimes bordered on ridicule. In particular, the Dire Avengers – by far the largest of the Aspect Shrines on Kaelor, as on many other of the craftworlds – were open about their disdain for the gentrification of Khaine that they perceived in the Swooping Hawks of Kaelor.

Uisnech had once stood at the head of the farseer's army at the height of the House Wars. Unique amongst the Knavir of Kaelor, he understood the imperatives and emotions of battle. He had been one of the few Knavir to recognise the inexorable rise of military power on Kaelor during the ending of the Era of Radiance, and had been one of the few that had sought to construct his own army of Guardians in his home domains of Anyon. He had been almost the only Knavir to lay his own life and those of his own Guardians at the feet of the farseer when the

House Wars had begun. After the initial skirmishes, the farseer had allied with House Teirtu, and Uisnech had dutifully fought alongside Iden.

He knew the capacities of the Zhogahn. He knew that Iden was an impressive warrior, but he also knew that the Teirtu patriarch did not have the constitution for politics or for life in the Sentrium. He knew that the great warrior's soul was conflicted between an ambition for power and respect on the one hand, and a craving for blood on the other. He had not been trained to resolve the tension between the two, and he had not been gifted with the natural capacities to do so. Perhaps he had been born onto the wrong craftworld. Iden would have made the perfect leader of a Wild Rider Clan on Saim-Hann. On Kaelor, in the Sentrium amongst the Knavir, he seemed like a beast.

The thing that disgusted Uisnech more than Iden's vulgarity, however, was the fact that the Zhogahn – the so-called Vanquisher of Sin – had been tricked by a cheap distraction. He had been so caught up in the drama of the Battle of Ula Pass and in his hatred for the Ansgar that he had not even stopped to think that Ula and the Ansgar might merely be a sideshow.

With the benefit of hindsight, it seemed incredible that Iden had believed even for a moment that Scilti Ansgar-ann would have walked willingly and wilfully into the Ula Pass, knowing that it was a battle that he could not possibly win, without having an ulterior motive. Iden had made the classic mistake of thinking that his enemy had the same emotions and passions as him. The Ula Pass was the most emotive possible site for a battle between the Teirtu and the Ansgar, and young Scilti would have known that Iden would not refuse the challenge. It was a matter of fighting spirit. It was a question of a warrior's honour. For Scilti, the death of Iden's finest warrior must simply have been a bonus.

Iden had been set up. Not only did he look vulgar and uncouth to the Knavir because of his uncontrolled violence, but he also looked like a fool. While he was flexing and posturing in the Ula Pass, the Warp Spider Exarch Aingeal had been flitting through the Sentrium and abducting the farseer. Even though Uisnech was secretly pleased about this outcome, he couldn't help but despise the Teirtu for his short-sighted stupidity. In fact, it served him right, he thought. The fool had even left his disgusting son, Morfran, in charge of securing the palace.

Uisnech considered his hypothesis for a moment and he realised that he might be giving the young Scilti too much credit. For the plan to have worked, there was no reason why the youthful tyro needed to be aware of what was going on. Indeed, the emotional effectiveness of the plan rather relied on Scilti's sincerity. It was suddenly clear to Uisnech that the whole enterprise had been conceived by the devious mind of the Warp Spider Exarch herself.

She had encouraged the same simple warrior ethic in Scilti that Uisnech had been bemoaning in Iden. They had both gone into the Battle of Ula Pass thinking that they were reliving the last epic battle between the Teirtu and the Ansgar and they had both been prepared to throw everything they had into the

fray. Scilti had chosen to die for this ridiculous honour. Meanwhile, Aingeal had the perfect diversion.

His suspicions and interest aroused, Uisnech wondered whether the exarch had planned anything else
to happen at that time.

Down below in the Plaza of Vaul, Uisnech and Cinnia could see the ceremonial platform of Morfran and
Oriana ease out of the gates of the palace and angle
towards Iden's advancing platform. The Radiant Oriana held little Turi in her arms as usual, as though
they were inseparable.

He's got some nerve, muttered Cinnia, as though to
herself. *He's going out to meet his father.* She wondered
how Morfran was going to explain the loss of the
farseer to his already fuming and distraught father.

Perhaps he is wise to share the news in a public place,
offered Uisnech in return, keeping his eyes on Morfran.

He's certainly made a big deal of his injury. Cinnia was
peering down at the medical-packing around
Morfran's right leg. It was clearly fresh, but was already
marked with a creeping stain of blood. *I suppose that
he's assuming that Iden is a father before he is a leader.*

Uisnech nodded silently. Then they both realised at
the same time: *He wasn't injured during the abduction!
The Warp Spiders didn't touch him! He's shot himself in
the leg to make it look as though he fought to defend the
farseer!*

The Knavir on the balcony could hardly restrain
their disgust at the conduct of the styhx-tann Teirtu
in their midst. They watched Morfran's platform
approach that of Iden, and they could see the ritual

exchange of greetings for a public ceremony, but they were too far away to hear what was being said. After a few moments, they saw Iden's already gaunt and distressed face turn white with rage. Then he struck out, slapping his son and heir across the face in the middle of the crowded Plaza of Vaul, making the whole of the Sentrium gasp in shock at the terrible breach of decorum.

THE SANCTUM OF the Warp Spider Temple had survived the damage to the rest of the shrine almost untouched. The runes and icons that speckled the walls were blazing with a thrill of life that Aingeal had never before seen in her temple. The webbing on the altar was as though on fire, glowing with passionate intensity and the relics were transformed, beyond recognition.

The deathmask of the Araconid Warlock gazed forth from the left of the altar, its eyes glimmering with distant majesty and power, as though the mask had suddenly found a life of its own. On the other side of the altar, held above it in cruciform glory, the golden armour of the Lhykosidae shimmered with an ineffable and inalienable radiance. It was a beacon. It was calling out and drawing its agent near. It was as though the Fluir-haern were reaching through the ancient psycho-plastic form and beckoning for a new body to give it life.

'The temple is alive,' muttered Aingeal, giving her thoughts a whispered volume as though to anchor them in reality. She gazed around the sanctum in wonder, feeling as though she had entered into the

very heart of her Aspect. For the first time since her
ascension, she felt a tinge of alienation from the
shrine that she had tended for all those years. She
could not explain what was happening, and she
wasn't sure why it had never happened for her. She
had not experienced feelings of jealously for longer
than she could remember – since before she had
become an Exarch of Khaine – and her normal eldar
existence had been brought to an end. Yet something
resembling bitterness was curdled into her sense of
awe.

Why wasn't it me? She kept the question to herself.

The farseer and Arachnir Adsulata were busy
around the altar, laying Naois's oddly transformed
body onto its glowing, web-lined surface, like an
offering to Khaine or to the Fluir-haern, whichever
was watching. The young tyro had lost consciousness
and fallen out of the massive funnel-web above the
arena. He was exhausted and spent, as though his
exertions while the others had been away had used
up all of his energy. There was something unnaturally ceramic about his skin, as though a layer of
delicate crystals had formed just below it, and he
seemed unable to close his silver eyes, which were
run through with flecks of black, like a matrix or web
of shadows in his soul. He stared up at the golden
armour above the altar, his eyes transfixed and yet
unfocused.

Scilti stood with Khukulyn in the mouth of the
passageway that fed into the sanctum, still leaning
on the older warrior for support. They watched the
proceedings in disbelief. It had been only hours since

they had been fighting desperately for the honour of Ansgar in the Ula Pass, and now they were in the sanctum of the Warp Spider Temple with the Radiant Farseer, and the heir of Ansgar teetering on the brink of a sinister metastasis. Somewhere in Scilti's mind, he wondered whether this had been the purpose of the events of the last day: his own elevation from the status of tyro before that of Naois – something of which he had been so proud – and then the hopeless battle against the Teirtu. Had these events been stage-managed to produce a transformation in Naois. Had this all been about Naois, and not about him after all? Despite the evident suffering of his cousin on the altar, Scilti could not repress the wave of personal bitterness that trickled through his soul. Would he always be in Naois's shadow?

Even from the passageway, they could see Naois's convulsions. His body was suddenly rigid and then limp, as though all of his muscles were spasming in succession. His body was changing before their eyes, but his eyes seemed to scream with an irrepressible and terrible pain, as though his very soul was being tortured and transformed.

While Aingeal dashed forwards to help Adsulata hold the youth down, the farseer stepped back from the altar and began a whispered chant. He touched his fingers together in a complicated sequence of patterns and contortions, generating delicate wisps of sha'iel that wafted out of his hands and over Naois's struggling body, covering him in an intricate lattice of threads that seemed to both sooth and restrain his turmoil.

At the same time, little Ela pushed past Scilti and Khukulyn into the sanctum. She walked deliberately up to the farseer and stood at his side, watching his interventions with earnest interest. She seemed unphased and unsurprised by her brother's condition, and appeared completely at ease standing next to the Rivalin Farseer, as though that was were she belonged. For his part, Ahearn spared a brief sideways glance at the child seer before turning back to the matter at hand, with the faintest suggestion of a smile on his face.

After a few moments, Naois's convulsions eased and then stopped, leaving him lying on the altar in peace, shrouded in a dense web of sha'iel. Aingeal and Adsulata released his limbs and stepped back, letting a breath of relief ease through the sanctum. Things seemed to be under control.

Very slowly, Naois's body started glowing. The light traced the threads of the net of sha'iel that lay over the top of him, as though thickening them and feeding them with energy from some invisible source. Soon, he was bathed in light, and the web that covered him had become a shroud, wrapping him like a chrysalis.

Meanwhile, Ahearn continued to chant, and wispy tendrils of energy continued to flow from his hands. After a few moments, the field around Naois started to pulse, as though becoming unstable, and then delicate vines started to creep upwards, questing towards the armour of the Lhykosidae, which was already alight with golden force.

Very quickly, the reaching vines coalesced into a glittering trunk of energy, connecting the withering

body of Naois with the ever brighter form of the
golden armour above. It pulsed and flashed with an
organic rhythm, as though the process of life itself
were being laid bare in the sanctum of the Warp Spiders. The runes and icons around the walls burnt even
brighter as massive currents of sha'iel swirled around
the capillaries of the infinity circuit in the region, as
though the spirit of Kaelor were at work in the temple, even while Naois's body grew visibly weaker and
increasingly translucent.

There was a flash like an explosion, and then all
light was suddenly sucked out of the sacred chamber.
When the runes flickered back into life, Naois's body
had vanished from the altar, leaving only a pile of
wraith-threads fluttering in the gentle gusts of faerulh
that breathed coolly through the sanctum. It seemed
as though the youth's energy had been bled dry.

Cautiously, as though bringing a delicate process to
a close, Ahearn stopped chanting and unclasped his
hands. Even before he looked up at the splendour of
the golden armour above them, he looked down at
the tiny figure of Ela'Ashbel at his side. As though
suddenly full of fatherly pride and concern he
reached out his hand and rested it on her smooth
shoulder.

The others were staring up at the golden armour
with undisguised awe. Slowly, it flexed its shoulders
and rolled its neck, as though it were awakening from
a long sleep with aching joints and stiff muscles.
Then, with effortless ease, it shrugged itself free of the
rig that held it cruciform and resplendent above the
altar, and dropped down to the floor.

It was shorter than the others had expected, perhaps a full head shorter than Scilti. It was magnificently simple in design, resembling the armour of a Warp Spider, albeit without the cumbersome bulk of a warp-pack on its back. Long, elegantly curving blades protruded like fangs from its forearms, and its limbs were coated in tiny, toxic hair-like bristles, little more than a couple of microns in diameter, but the attendant eldar's attention was drawn completely by its eyes. Although the armour's helmet was entirely sealed into its shoulders, its eyes seemed to shine with organic life. There was no suggestion of a visor or augmentations. The armour itself seemed to have eyes, and they shone with a silver light that held everyone in their thrall. They were laced with black webs, like lethal traps for anything unwary that strayed into them.

Only Ela seemed to be unaffected by the presence of the terrible creature. She shrugged off Ahearn's hand and walked directly towards the Lhykosidae, reaching out her arms and wrapping them around the armour's golden waist, as though she were hugging a relative. In response, it placed a gauntlet on her head without a word, touching her gently.

Ela nodded and waved her hand at the altar, which trembled for an instant and then slid down into the ground, as though being lowered by some kind of mechanical device. Behind it, three thrones were revealed in an alcove in the wall at the back of the sanctum. The one in the centre was the Fanged Throne of the Wraith Spider, glorious and golden in its majesty. The one on the left, behind the deathmask, was smaller and set lower into the ground, the throne of the Araconid Warlock. The final throne, set a little lower than the other two, bore the mark of the exarch.

Without a word, Naois ascended the pedestal of the Fanged Throne and took his place as the legendary Wraith Spider, with little Ela perched neatly on the seat of the warlock's throne next to him. They stared down at the farseer and exarch, their startling sapphire and silver eyes burning with the fury of Ansgar. A crackle of warp lightning flashed through the temple, as though a terrible storm was coming. Adsulata bowed deeply and Khukulyn sank to his knees, taking Scilti down with him.

THE INTERIOR OF the Shrine of Fluir-haern was utterly transformed. Iden had ordered it purged of all taints of the presence of the Warp Spiders, and a detachment of Aspect Warriors from the Temple of the Fire Dragons had been sent to cleanse the space through their sacred flames. Exarch Fuarghan had hesitated for a moment before acceding to the request, pondering the implications of a ritual purification for the Covenant of the Asurya's Helm. He was fully aware that Aingeal had already breached the accord, but he was equally aware that the other exarchs remained united in their opposition to the Warp Spider's cavalier actions. He did not want to take her conduct as the precedent for his own.

In the end, Fuarghan had resolved that a purification was a purely ceremonial duty rather than a political intervention, and he had felt compelled to provide the righteous flames of his Aspect as a fittingly auspicious way to cleanse the most sacred site of Kaelor. It was better that the Fire Dragons did it properly than allow it to be bungled by the Teirtu Guardians. The fact that the cleansing was focused mainly on the eradication of the exquisite, eons-old wraith-webs that once riddled the shadows of the shrine was incidental, or so he told himself.

The shrine-keepers that Aingeal had killed had been replaced from the shrine's school of tyros, and a bank of six hooded and robed eldar stood before the famed Tetrahedral Altar at the end of the main aisle. Their practiced stillness made them appear like little more than perfect statues as they waited for Iden and his cortege to advance along the aisle.

The Zhoghan of Kaelor strode purposefully up the aisle, holding the faintly glowing jewel of Yseult's spirit stone before him like a tear of Isha. He was flanked on one side by Exarch Lairgnen of the Dire Avengers, who had come to pay his last respects to a fallen daughter of vengeance, and on the other side by Oriana, who bore her son like an offering to the gods. Behind them came the husk of Yseult, borne on the same flat, anti-grav palanquin on which she had been rushed from the Ula Pass. It was a simple and crude device, etched and scarred from use, and edged with droplets of spilt blood, hardly appropriate for a high ceremony in the Shrine of Fluir-haern.

Yseult's honour guard marched behind the palanquin. They had their cloaks draped respectfully over their shoulders, despite the seared and scratched state of their battlefield armour. None had been given the opportunity to change into ceremonial dress. Iden had been so incensed by the loss of the farseer and so grief-stricken by Yseult's passing that he had proceeded directly into the shrine once the victory parade had reached the Plaza of Vaul.

Because of his unseemly haste, he had not given the Knavir any opportunity to join the cortege, and so none of them were in attendance. Unlike the case of Lady Ione's Ceremony of Passing, Iden did not even stop to think about the possible, political repercussions of such exclusions.

Finally, at the back of the procession came Morfran. He hobbled on his shuriken-shredded leg, struggling to keep up with the others, the mark of his father's hand still raw and red across the side of his face.

Iden climbed the steps to the Tetrahedral Altar in silence and dropped to his knees. Four of the shrine-keepers accompanied him, two on each side, chanting quiet and potent incantations to purify his way and to prepare the Fluir-hearn for the passing of Yseult. With a simple, austere lack of ceremony born of his warrior heritage, Iden placed Yseult's spirit stone in the little tear-shaped slot on the altar and nodded a bow of respectful parting. He muttered a vow of vengeance and then rose slowly to his feet. Even the shrine-keepers seemed surprised by the terse and abrupt manner of his conduct, normally a Ceremony of Passing for such a distinguished eldar would take several hours, not a mere instant. It was supposed to be a ceremony, a rite of passage for those left behind as much as for those departing. For Iden, it seemed, it was simply a functional activity: Yseult's dhamashir must be committed to the sanctity of the Fluir-hearn.

Turning to face the rest of the cortege, he signalled that the shrine-keepers should retreat back down the steps and leave him to stand alone. Then he peered towards the back of the aisle over the heads of the exarch, Oriana and the honour guard, picking out the reddened eyes of Morfran and holding them in determined disgust. He could still remember the drooling excitement that his son had shown the last time that they had been in the shrine, and he snarled involuntarily at the thought that this was his own heir.

What had he done wrong? Had Morfran always been such a decadent and self-indulgent tureir-iug, or had he changed since the Teirtu had made the Sentrium into their home? For a moment, Iden realised that many things had changed in House Teirtu since they had come to the court, and those changes were not necessarily for the better. They were richer and more comfortable, of course. They had more time for the finer, artistic and sensuous pursuits that had so gratified and characterised the Knavir for eons of Kaelorian history, but they were losing the disciplined austerity of the Warrior Way; he could feel it slipping from his fingers like melted ice. In that instant of clarity, he realised that a type of hysteria was lurking in his mind. An unhinged and suddenly undisciplined lust for war was beginning to devour his soul. He still had enough self-control, but he could feel it slipping, and he was reflective enough to

wonder whether the fulfilment of his ambitions to
become the farseer's Zhogahn was simultaneously
the seed of his own insanity.

'Today we have witnessed a great change on Kaelor,
the likes of which we have not known since the glorious and terrible days of the House Wars,' he
announced, letting his voice resonate and echo
though the shrine and out into the Plaza of Vaul
beyond. He kept his eyes locked fiercely on Morfran.

'Today we lost a great warrior and a powerful soul.
Yseult Teirtu-ann, daughter of vengeance, was an
immaculate and worthy eldar, the likes of which we
have rarely been privileged to see. I regret...' He
paused, glowering at his son in front of everyone. 'I
regret that she pledged herself to my house and that
I did not adopt her into my own line, so that I might
have called her my heir.

'Although today was a great victory for the House
of Teirtu and for the Radiant Court of the Ohlipsean
in whose name we vanquish the sins of Kaelor,
today we also lost...' He wasn't sure how to put it.
The gravity of the loss went beyond his ability at
words.

'We also lost our farseer.' He had always found
simplicity the best way for warriors and, although he
was aware that the Knavir would find this vulgar, he
had no other tools at his disposal.

As the whispers of suppressed shock rippled
through the cortege and out into the crowds outside,
Iden proceeded with the practicalities of the situation in which they now found themselves. 'The
Radiant Rivalin, in whose name I have been

appointed as the Zhogahn of Kaelor, has not passed out of this realm, but is merely lost to this domain. He was forcefully abducted,' he continued, glaring an accusation at Morfran, 'by the treacherous Warp Spiders from the domain of Ansgar. I vow to you that he will be recovered from the sinners, and that the sinners will be vanquished by my own blade.

'In the mean time, to demonstrate our piety and devotion to the Rivalin dynasty and the glorious institution of the farseer, we will confer upon our own heir the title of farseer, so that we might continue to march in his name in the battle to come.'

There was another ripple of shock, louder this time and more hostile. Meanwhile, Morfran's eyes bulged with stunned delight. He could hardly believe how well things had worked out. He had thought that his father was genuinely mad at him for losing the farseer, but it seemed that it had been a pretence for the crowds and that he was to be rewarded with the greatest of all possible prizes. After all, how could Iden really object to the removal of the last obstacle to the absolute power of the Teirtu on Kaelor. First they had dealt with Kerwyn, and now with old Ahearn. He had done his father a favour! He started to push his way through Yseult's honour guard, stumbling and bumping his way along the aisle towards the altar.

'In this sacred Shrine of Fluir-haern, in the sacred name of the Radiant Rivalin, of which I am now the ranking representative in the Sentrium,' announced Iden, signalling the shrine-keepers into action, 'I hereby confer on young Turi the title and privileges of farseer, and I vow to serve as his Zhogahn for as long as Asuryan deems it fateful.'

Like the Knavir, Iden knew that he could not keep control of Kaelor without the name and symbolism of the House of Rivalin behind him. One member of that house must always be the patron of the Teirtu, just as Ahearn himself had been during the House Wars. Now that Kerwyn was gone, perhaps his own bumbling and stupid son had actually opened the doors for Turi to take the throne: a Teirtu of the Rivalin line. Even if he could not recover Ahearn alive, Iden might have the cards he needed to win this game.

Morfran stopped in his tracks and looked up at his father's thin, calculating smile with humiliated hatred in his eyes. Meanwhile, the rush of rumour, whisper and conspiracy spread through the Sentrium like water through oil.

CHAPTER SEVEN: KHUKULYN

STANDING AT THE bottom of the cracked steps of the Spider Temple looking up at the broken crescent doors, Khukulyn waited with trepidation in his heart. The injured and unsteady weight of Scilti still hung from his shoulder, and other eldar of the domain were already beginning to gather around them. Rumours of the arrival of the farseer had spread quickly through the forests, and many had heard the violence that had shaken the temple. Dozens of eldar from different dhanir had gathered in the clearing below the crumbling temple, and more were joining them all the time. The atmosphere was thick with anticipation, as though the crowd knew that something momentous was about to happen.

Like the others, Khukulyn had been told the stories of the Wraith Spider – the fabled Lhykosidae – in his youth. He knew the myths about the fantastical origins and the fatefulness of the appearance of the strange entity, but he had never really believed them. He had always preferred to trust in the real, material strength of his own witchblades. He had followed Bedwyr into uncountable battles without the need for anything mythical or supernatural to strengthen his arm. Devotion to one's lord and his house was a reward in itself, and to place one's faith elsewhere was either a mistake of vanity or fear. Loyalty was earned by valour and action, not merely by the appearance of shimmering golden armour. The youthful Scilti had earned his place at the head of the house in his battle with the Guardians of the Reach. The infantile Naois had proven nothing, and this was not the time for chasing ghosts, no matter whose ghosts they were.

He was not sure what had happened to Bedwyr's son in the sanctum, but he was not about to bow to a fiction just because of the compelling aesthetic of the legend. He would require some kind of proof. He chastised his own weakness when he realised that he had dropped to his knees when Naois had taken his place on the throne. He had been awed by the spectacle, but he was not one of the effete Knavir that would dote merely because of beauty or the emotional resonance of a tale. Truth was to be found at the tip of a sword, not scraped out of a mythical history with an artisan's chisel.

A hush descended on the crowd as Naois and Ela walked out of the ruined gates. The inspiring figure of Exarch Aingeal emerged from the interior of the temple behind them, and beside him, leaning heavily on his staff as though on the point of collapsing, shuffled the farseer. In a triumph of theatre, the four figures halted on the top step, bathed in the scene before them.

Khukulyn could feel the will of the assembled eldar; they *wanted* to believe that these childlings were their saviours. There was desperation in the air, born of years of deprivation and a new panic caused by the ruination of the Spider Temple and the sudden arrival of the farseer. Emotions were high, and they were searching for direction. The eruption of hope flooded out into the clearing, mixing into a potent force that sought to swamp the minds of all. It was the kind of crowd hysteria of which only the eldar were capable, their emotions having such intensity that they could affect a shift in the fabric of reality. Given a significant number of sufficiently focused eldar souls, they could change the galaxy, as they had done once before, at the time of the Fall. Tragically and fortunately, there were no longer enough of the children of Isha remaining to affect change on such a scale, although the Fluir-haern contained a potent force for one able to wield it.

Naois said nothing as he surveyed the mass of eldar that had assembled before the steps. This was the first time that he had passed out through the crescent doors since he had been brought from the Sentrium following his father's execution. The domain looked different, but his eyes were different too.

He stepped forwards, leaving Ela alone with Aingeal and Ahearn, and placed his armoured boot slowly down onto the next step. As he did so, the

crowd that had assembled before the shrine dropped
down onto its knees. A low, almost silent chant arose
from the clearing, wafting up towards the shrine like
a tide drawn by the moon. It was the spirit of dedi-
cation. Only Khukulyn and Scilti remained on their
feet, staring up at the terrible, golden figure.

Ignoring the adoration of the remnants of the Ansgar eldar, Naois's attention was drawn immediately to
the fringes of the clearing. He swept his silvered eyes
around the perimeter, as though he had seen flickers
of movement on all sides. Tiny reflective bursts
flashed from the shadows of the thin forest, showing
the presence of eldar who preferred not to be seen.
The glint of polished weapons and the faint sheen of
aged but well-kept armour pricked the shade.

For a long moment, nobody moved. The devoted
crowd was waiting for a sign or a word from their
messiah. They craved it, and their minds cried out in
the silence, begging Naois to admit that he had come
to lead them to salvation. Naois showed no signs of
having heard their calls, and no sign of concern for
their show of devotion. His eyes continued to scan
the forest, searching for the shimmering threats that
lurked in the shadows.

In the lull, Scilti struggled free of Khukulyn's shoulder and climbed three steps towards the crescent
doors, studiously avoiding lifting his gaze from his
own feet. He stood, bleeding freely into the stairs of
the temple from which he had emerged so recently,
with his armour cracked and broken. The contrast
with the gleaming golden myth above him could not
have been more stark, and not for the first time Scilti

found his heart simmering with resentment towards the prodigal son of Bedwyr. Turning back towards the crowd, he struggled to contain his emotions.

'Your eyes are your judges,' he said, only vaguely audible. 'The farseer has returned his blessing to the House of Ansgar, and the heir of Bedwyr has found himself in the temple of his forebears. Once, not that long ago, Lady Ione of the Hidden Joy made a prophecy that saved the lives of Naois and Ela. We must assume that this prophecy is coming to pass.' He paused, suddenly aware that something didn't make sense. How could Ione's prophecy have saved Naois and Ela from Iden's vengeful wrath if it had spoken of the resurgence of Ansgar under their leadership?

'I kneel before the rightful heir,' he continued, putting the thought aside as though it had been a contrivance planted in his mind to deliberately skew his purpose. As he spoke, he turned back to the temple, lifting his eyes up at the golden armour that stood magnificently above him, and flinched when he realised that Naois wasn't even looking at him. It was as though Naois had not even noticed him. He was gazing out into the forest like a sailor viewing the horizon.

There was a murmur through the crowd as the eldar appreciated the weight of Scilti's concession, giving up his recently awarded position of house leadership to his younger kinsman. It was a bold and honourable act.

'I do not recognise this vulgar pup!' The low voice rang out with confidence and defiance. 'I will not follow this childling just because he has such pretty armour! He must prove himself, as Lord Scilti has done, and as his father did before him. We are not the Rivalin; we are a house that rests on strength and merit, not on elaborate shows and rituals.'

Naois turned his head slowly, finally looking away from the trees and bringing his silver eyes around to face the defiant and proud figure of Khukulyn, around whom the other eldar had parted to leave him standing alone in a circle of space.

Silence descended like a sudden snowfall, blanketing the scene with baited breath as the crowd tried to anticipate how the challenge would be received. Most of them knew Khukulyn. They knew that he did nothing without good reason, and that his defiance could not be without purpose. He was a warrior of honour. An air of disbelief settled quickly over the crowd, for if Khukulyn had a reason, they could not tell what it was.

From his position on the steps, Scilti spun to check that his ears where not deceiving him. He could not believe that Khukulyn had spoken in such a way, especially after his own public capitulation. Khukulyn had been with them in the sanctum of the temple when the metastasis had occurred. He had seen Naois's transformation. What could his purpose possibly be? Was there really any room for doubts?

He will be killed, Scilti thought, as though the conclusion were already foregone. In a moment of panic, he scanned around the edges of the clearing from his elevated position, looking over the heads of the crowd to see whether there was some way to extricate this honourable warrior from the situation. There was nothing, but in the shadows of the tree line he saw the glint of metallic equipment: weapons in trained hands. He squinted, trying to make out more detail, and then realised that the eldar in the trees wore the tattered colours of Ansgar. There were dozens of them. Perhaps hundreds more were hidden in the forest beyond sight.

What are you doing? he asked, returning his attention urgently to Khukulyn. *How can you hope to survive?*

If I survive, there is nothing worth living for. If I die, I will have shown the Ansgar how to live, replied Khukulyn, his eyes flashing with the promise of death.

Suddenly, Naois sprang from the top of the stairs, turning a slow, spinning summersault as he arced over the steps and landed in the clearing amongst rapidly scattering eldar. He face Khukulyn and nodded a curt bow, giving the veteran the respect due to his years. Their eyes met for a moment, and Khukulyn saw the horror that lurked in the heart of the black webs in Naois's gaze.

WITH THE ANCIENT diresword held horizontally before him like a precious relic, Iden stood in the middle of the central quadrangle of the Temple of the Dire Avengers. The space was dark with faint purple light, and Iden breathed in the atmosphere like a withered plant soaks in water. For the first time in many years, he felt alone and at peace. His ridiculous son was back at the Farseer's Palace and his honour guard had left him at the temple's main gates, knowing that there were few places more secure anywhere on Kaelor than the Shrine of Vengeance.

It is a beautiful blade, is it not? The thoughts came from nowhere and everywhere at once.

Iden smiled, but he did not turn or look around. It had been a long time since he had been at the mercy of Exarch Lairgnen, and he savoured the helplessness of prey for a moment. Lairgnen had a special talent for humbling even the most exalted of visitors to his shrine, in which he was the undisputed master, and Iden felt his own vulnerability like a bracing blast of arctic air. It thrilled him. The stodgy, luxurious safety of the Sentrium had almost made him forget what it felt like to fear death. He had almost forgotten what it meant to be alive.

It was a gift to my finest student.

'It was a rare gift indeed, quihan,' replied Iden, addressing his former master as a pupil.

There was a delicate but definite sound behind him, and Iden knew that Lairgnen had just dropped down from one of the balconies that ran around the inside of the hollow spire above the quadrangle. It was one of his characteristic greetings, and it never failed to impress.

It's been a long time since last you graced these halls.

'I have come to return the blade to you,' continued Iden, turning to face the exarch. 'The diresword is an emblem of your Aspect, and it belongs here with you.'

Without a word, Lairgnen reached out and took the sword from Iden, inspecting it lovingly, as though it were a lost childling. *I am grateful that you would make such a journey at such a time as this just to return a sword.* The exarch's tone bordered on incredulity. He had nothing to fear from this Zhogahn, and his direct manner was tinged with only the most minimal and formulaic of honorifics.

It is a beautiful blade, he conceded, as though that explained Iden's motives. *It once belonged to your father, Iden, and it is said that it contains the soul of Naem-zar, one of the Wild Rider chieftains of Saim-Hann captured during the Craftwars. It certainly has the unbridled fury of such a wild warrior, and it required a wielder of unusual discipline and skill.*

In any case, I am pleased to have a memento of my lost Yseult. I confess that I had hoped that she might return to the Avengers in due time. She would have made a formidable and righteous Exarch of Khaine, but the Lady Ione had warned me that it might not come to pass...

'I did not come here only to return the sword, quihan,' confessed Iden, more abruptly than he would have liked. 'I came to ask for your assistance.'

You want the Avengers to fight at your side. You want us to turn our vengeance against the Ansgar and against the Warp Spiders of their realm. Lairgnen looked up from the sword and stared at Iden. *You are transparent, my lord. You were always an emotional warrior, Iden; this is both your most intoxicating strength and your most debilitating weakness. It makes you powerful in battle, but it also makes you predictable.*

'They must pay for what they have done, quihan. You cannot deny the value or power of vengeance in this case. I was taught its use in this very chamber.

They have sinned against Teirtu and they have sinned against Kaelor, and I am the Vanquisher of Sin. They have also deprived us of a star in the darkness of these times, and we must avenge Yseult's passing.'

She came to me before the end, replied Lairgnen slowly, as though not hearing Iden's words, *and she asked me to breach the covenant to stand with her at your side. I refused, Iden. There are bigger issues than the fate of Yseult or House Teirtu in this story, and the Covenant of the Asurya's Helm has a role to play in Kaelor's future. Have you not seen what is happening in the Sentrium? Have you been so obsessed with vengeance and the affairs of the broken House of Ansgar that you have neglected what lies right under your nose? Have you not seen the crackling energy of the Maelstrom coursing through the veins of Kaelor? The craftworld is in peril, Iden of Teirtu, Zhogahn of the Rivalin Court. There are sinners in need of vanquishing, and you must steel your resolve to see it done.*

'Will you stand with me or not, Exarch Lairgnen?' asked Iden flatly. He did not need to be lectured by this Exarch of Khaine. It was bad enough that he had to endure the whispered, duplicitous criticism of the Knavir. He was the lord of the Sentrium, not them. He was the Zhogahn.

'I do not ask you to march to war with House Teirtu, since I know that you are sworn not to, despite the Aingeal's treachery. I ask only for a raiding force to avenge the murder of Yseult and to recover the farseer. Both are functions worthy of the Avengers, quihan.'

You do not intend to invade the domains of Ansgar?

Iden bit down on his teeth. 'I understand that you would not be able to participate in such an action, exarch, and I do not ask you to do so.'

You have not answered my question, Lord Iden.

'You do not want me to answer your question, Lairgnen! You want to avenge the death of your protégé, and what I have said permits you to do it with a clear conscience and without abrogating the covenant. If the idiot Morfran decides to launch an invasion at the same time, that will be merely an unfortunate coincidence caused by a bungling fool. I am asking only for a strike of vengeance, not support in a political war. What we do in ignorance we do without sin.' Iden smiled.

You have become quite the politician since your move to the Sentrium, Iden, nodded the exarch. *You will have your Avengers.*

IN THE ABSENCE of the farseer, Morfran sat at this place at the table. His bandaged and aching leg was propped up on the edge, giving the impression of relaxation instead of pain. He had an almost empty carafe of Edreacian wine in his hand, which had doubtlessly helped to alleviate the self-inflicted agony of his shredded limb. Sitting opposite him was the delightful Cinnia, bedecked in the delicate red court chiffon of the Yuthran sisterhood. It was worn loosely and without self-consciousness. Next to her sat the handsome figure of Celyddon Ossian, whose sumptuous robes and golden eyes made the others think of luxury every time they looked at him. It was the first time that any of them had been in the farseer's chambers, high up in the tower, without Ahearn shuffling around on his staff, fetching drinks and making sure that his guests were comfortable.

'I can't believe that you shot yourself in the leg!' laughed Cinnia, lying back in her chair as though it were a couch. 'It was so transparent. Even that sober-minded prude Uisnech saw through you!'

'It hurts,' moaned Morfran, as though that should be enough for some sympathy.

'Serves you right, you clumsy tureir-iug,' countered Celyddon.

'Perhaps I should have shot you?' laughed Morfran, draining the carafe and then hurling it across the table towards Celyddon.

'Why did you have to shoot anyone?' asked Cinnia. 'Did you really think that Iden would believe that you fought with the Warp Spiders and that they shot you in the leg as you stood between them and Ahearn?'

'What does it matter what he believes?' replied Morfran. 'It is almost too late for him to change anything, anyway.'

'Almost, but not quite,' said Cinnia, suddenly serious. She leant forwards onto the table. 'The prophecy has not yet come to pass. We must retain our vigilance, otherwise all of this will be lost.' She cast a relaxed arm around the room to indicate what she meant.

The others fell into silence, as though they had suddenly understood the gravity of the situation, and Cinnia rose to her feet. She swept her arm over the tabletop, clearing the glasses and empty carafes, which clattered to the ground and smashed into pools of smoking liquid. Then she climbed up onto the table and sat cross-legged in the middle, composing her robes around her in an incongruous display of decorum.

Closing her eyes and interlacing her fingers in her lap, the Yuthran seer started a whispered, resonating chant that quickly filled the chamber with trembling vibrations. The others looked up towards the ceiling where an oily image was beginning to sheen into visibility. It was faint at first, but quickly grew in density and coherence, revealing a vision of the startling depths of space in which the massive structure of Kaelor was sailing. The stars shifted in a complicated parallax, showing the movement of the huge craft-world, but there was something unusual about the pattern of the movement, as though Kaelor's path was somehow circuitous or contorted. The stars seemed to twist in a slow arc, as though the craft-world were turning gradually in a wide spiral.

As the scene shifted, a fringe of purpling colour infused the edge of the picture. It grew brighter and more intense as a vast, roiling cloud of warp energy bled into view. It was punctuated by gashes of dark light and scars of sickly brightness, which seemed to roil and curdle into nauseatingly chaotic patterns. On the cusps of the massive warp storm, the space-time fabric of the material realm seemed to twist and bleed, as though the void of deep space were pouring into the boiling Maelstrom.

Morfran looked up into the moving image and smiled broadly. 'Not much further to go,' he said,

letting his excitement bubble in his throat as he
spoke. 'We're almost there.'

'You're sure that this is going to work, Morfran?'
asked Celyddon. The sight of the Maelstrom made
him suddenly doubt their plan. It did not look like
the heaven of sensual and artistic pleasures that had
been promised to them. It looked like hell.

Cinnia gasped with a sudden thrill and opened her
eyes, which glowed bloody red with concentration.
'It will work, Celyddon of Ossian. We have made a
bargain, and it will be kept.' The voice had an
unusual edge to it, as though it wasn't Cinnia's at all.
It sounded as though something was speaking
through her. 'Everything is moving in the right direction, and soon there will be more souls to feed our
lust.'

Morfran grinned at the prospect, but an involun-
tary shiver pulsed through his body, as though his
flesh rebelled against the unbridled decadence of his
mind. He stared at the serenely daemonic figure of
Cinnia for a moment, letting his thoughts touch her
skin as it flickered in and out of view beneath her
chiffon robes, and then he lifted his eyes into the
swirling Maelstrom above. He couldn't believe that
Kaelor had strayed so close to that warp-cauldron
without anyone noticing or protesting. After all, the
sons of Asuryan had spent all these long eons since
the Fall trying to escape from the lascivious fingers of
the Great Enemy, and now Kaelor found itself teetering so close to an inferno of lust. It was as though the
Rivalin Farseer had engineered it, encouraged it, or at
least permitted it.

In the back of his mind, Morfran even wondered whether the indulgent souls of the Knavir had created the roiling storm as a manifestation of their communal extravagance. The idea was simply too delightful, and it made him squirm in his seat.

Cinnia blinked, closing her burning eyes and then reopening them in their normal sharply drawn green.

'We need only a few more souls,' she said, lying back along the table between the other two, as though physically exhausted from unseen and otherworldly exertions. She sighed, feeling the last tingling touches of pleasure breath between her porcelain skin and her weightless robes.

RETURNING NAOIS'S BOW, Khukulyn whipped his witchblades over his shoulders and spun them loosely in his hands, flexing his shoulders and warming his muscles. Meanwhile the crowd of eldar before the Spider Temple pushed back from the challengers, leaving a wide clearing, like an arena for the combat.

Without further ceremony, Khukulyn charged forwards, lashing his blades in figures of eight as he ran. A couple of strides short of Naois, he thrust his weapons forwards and then lunged, diving like a thrown lance towards his foe.

For Naois, it was as though the whole thing was moving in slow motion. He watched the veteran warrior rush towards him and then throw his weight into a lethal strike, but he watched with disinterest, as though the action did not really concern him. A moment before the tip of Khukulyn's blades were about to pierce into his armour, he stepped aside, letting the other warrior's momentum carry him right past, stumbling and falling onto his face.

It was ridiculous.

He watched Khukulyn climb back to his feet and dash back in to attack, swiping his glimmering witch-blades in a complicated form, hacking down diagonally from above and below at the same time, with his face set in concentrated fury.

Naois watched with more curiosity this time. The form of the attack was imaginative and interesting, and he could see the passion flowing out of Khukulyn, but there was no malice in the attack, and Naois felt no danger. He took a step back and let the blades lash past his face, just fractions from his mask, tilting his head to one side quizzically.

Khukulyn pressed his drive, flourishing his flashing blades in increasingly furious and rapid formations, slicing them around the impossibly fast figure of Naois, who simply stepped aside each time, as though unimpressed.

It was infuriating. Naois had not even parried a single strike, let alone struck out with a counter-attack. He had just moved around all of Khukulyn's swipes as though trying to avoid fighting altogether. For a moment, Khukulyn wondered whether the son of Bedwyr merely thought that he was an unworthy challenger. Was he being mocked?

It didn't matter. What mattered was that he was putting his life on the line for the good of the House of Ansgar. If Naois really was the Wraith Spider of legend, then Khukulyn would gladly lay down his life in order to prove it to those who would doubt it. The Ansgar would need its full strength if it was ever to challenge the Teirtu again, and that strength could never be mustered if there was doubt about the leadership of the house. Even Scilti had not been enough to bring the warriors out of their hideouts in the forest.

If he were not the Lhykosidae, then Khukulyn would lay him low and save Ansgar from the fate of marching hopelessly into battle behind a pretender to the throne. If he killed Naois, son of Bedwyr, he would be doing it for the good of the Ansgar, although he knew that the house would never forgive him for it.

Either way, Khukulyn's life was over, but he had chosen death long ago. He had chosen it when he had seen the recrimination in Bedwyr's eyes as he had died in the Plaza of Vaul. He had chosen it in the Ula Pass, when he had charged into battle with only his blades, but he had been cheated of an honourable death of deliverance. Or perhaps he had been spared so that he could die in a last act of devotion to Bedwyr. He was dead already, and death held no more mysteries or fears for him.

He thrust out with his right hand and then spun back around to his left, trying to anticipate Naois's evasions, but both blows missed their marks as the golden armour danced clear of the strikes.

'Fight me!' yelled Khukulyn as he realised that Naois had not even drawn a weapon. 'I will not be mocked.' At the least, he thought that he was owed an honourable and serious end, not the death of a bumbling fool.

I deserve better than this mockery, he thought, as he dropped low and swung both blades in parallel towards Naois's legs.

The next few moments passed in slow motion for Khukulyn. He saw the golden boots of Naois's armour spring into the air, jumping cleanly over his swinging witchblades. Then he watched as Naois's weight dropped again with impossible speed, crunching the soles of his boots down onto the flat sides of his twin swords and snapping them out of his hands. In automatic response, Khukulyn sprang forwards, launching himself bodily into the golden warrior before him. This time not even Naois could move aside quickly enough to avoid the collision, and Khukulyn slammed into him with his full force.

Naois didn't move. He was a full head shorter than the veteran Guardian that smashed into him, but it was as if Khukulyn had thrown himself at an immovable pillar. He crunched into Naois's abdomen and wrapped his arms around his waist, trying to wrestle the youth to the ground, but it was futile.

Instead, Naois reached across and gripped Khukulyn by the neck, yanking the Guardian away from his waist and snapping his powerful neck like a straw. It was almost as though it was an accident.

For a moment, Naois stood erect, his arm outstretched, with Khukulyn dangling limply from his grip like a rag doll. He looked up into the fading light in Khukulyn's eyes and saw a glint of gratitude flash back at him. His own black-webbed, silver eyes stared back blankly and without comprehension, and then he dropped the dead Guardian of Ansgar into a heap at his feet.

There was silence throughout the clearing in front of the temple as the assembled eldar tried to understand what had happened. Khukulyn Ansgarann lay dead at the feet of the heir of Ansgar, who turned away from the most devoted of his father's warriors as though he were nothing. There seemed to be no emotion within that majestic golden form, no remorse, no pain, no anger and no compassion. What did this mean?

As Naois climbed the first few steps, heading past the stunned Scilti and back up towards little Ela, whose calm face was running with tears, and the horrified figure of the farseer, he paused suddenly. He saw the exarch turn away and stride back through the gates into the crumbling interior of the temple. But there was something else. Slowly, he turned back towards the crowd and cast his eyes around the open space, scanning the tree line like a sensor array.

On the far side of the clearing, there was a rustling in the foliage and a solitary figure emerged. It stood upright and proud on the cusp between the forest and the open ground. It held a long ranger rifle in one hand, while the other hand lingered over the hilt of a pistol in a holster that was strapped to the side of its chest. It was shrouded in a long, hooded cloak that may once have been a rich, dark blue, hemmed in silver thread, but the material was ragged and dirty, as though it had not been repaired or replaced in many years.

After a moment, about a quarter of the way around the curving tree line, another similarly cloaked figure emerged. It held a long bladed, executioner glaive in both hands, braced diagonally across its chest. Whilst the cloak and garments of the eldar were in a poor state of repair, the elegant blade of the executioner shone immaculately, as though it had been polished and sharpened every day.

Then another figure stepped out of the foliage, this time with a bulky shuriken cannon braced in both hands. Then another with an ornate firepike and another with what looked like a singing spear. Then another and another until there must have been sixty or seventy eldar warriors in a crescent before the Temple of the Warp Spiders.

As though at an agreed but invisible signal, dozens more warriors that were hidden amongst the crowd that had assembled earlier threw off their ragged, matted and colourless cloaks to reveal the blues of Ansgar and strode out to join their brethren around the tree line.

As one, more than a hundred Ansgar Guardians threw their once magnificent midnight-blue cloaks over one shoulder and sank to one knee, punching their fists into the ground in a sign of reverence and devotion to their new leader.

Naois stood on the steps of the temple, and beside him, Scilti's eyes widened in amazement at the number of Guardians that had survived in the forest zones for all these years. Then his eyes narrowed again as he realised that they had remained in hiding when he had tried to assemble a force to march on the Teirtu only days before. They had emerged for Naois and his golden armour. They had emerged because of Khukulyn, but they had offered him nothing.

Naois swept his eyes around the kneeling warriors for a moment, without a word, as though in appreciation of the scene. Then he turned once again and strode up the steps of the temple, breezing past Ahearn and Ela and disappearing into the shadows within, leaving the crowd and the Guardians unsure about how to proceed.

CHAPTER EIGHT: AINGEAL

THERE HAD NOT been a Convocation of the Exarchs for untold ages. The Aspect Temples had agreed long ago that their power must not be put to political use on Kaelor. They were fully aware that one or other of the shrines had complete power over various of the other craftworlds, and that some of the mightiest of the majestic vessels, such as the legendary Biel-Tan, were ruled by a warrior council in which all of the exarchs sat together. It had been a conscious decision on Kaelor, back in the days of peace following the terrible Craftwars, which had so nearly torn the entire world in two. Gwrih the Radiant had convened the Convocation, summoning each of the exarchs to the chambers of the Ohlipsean and laying his vision of the loss of Kaelor before them.

The Craftwars had pushed the Aspect Temples and
the great houses of the outer realms into the centres
of power, and all of Kaelor had relied on them for
security and survival. They had accumulated vast
reserves of resources, bleeding the artificial world dry
of its mineral and psychic reservoirs in the quest to
build more and better armies. At the end of the Craftwars, as Saim-Hann was finally repelled and Kaelor
tumbled, free-falling through the vastness of deep
space, the exarchs and house patriarchs had stood
hovering on the brink of civil war. They had magnificent armies poised and waiting for merely a single
word from them. They waited, ready to unleash their
passion for blood against any enemy that their leaders defined. The years of war-readiness and constant
battle had pushed the breath of Khaine deeply into
the souls of many Kaelorians, leaving them primed
and ready, and thirsty for battle.

The fate of Kaelor was balanced on the edge of a
knife. Push it in one direction and the craftworld
would spiral into an existence of eternal war, as
though blending the bellicosity of Biel-Tan with the
furious intramural conflicts of Saim-Hann. One push
in the other direction, and the paths of the future
held eons of peace and prosperity. To the first of the
Rivalin Farseers, the choice had seemed as obvious as
the choice between death and life. He had chosen
life.

Gwrih the Radiant had summoned the Exarchs of
Khaine to the crumbling remains of the Ohlipsean
and had asked them to swear an oath to him, to the
Rivalin dynasty, and to the maintenance of peace on

Kaelor. He had drawn up the Covenant of the Asurya's Helm, and watched each of the exarchs place their hands on the helm and speak their vow, never to interfere in the political concerns of the craftworld. It was a guarantee for the future, and with it the future seemed guaranteed.

On that day, the crumbling, cracked and ruined remains of Kaelor had been placed in trust into the hands of the Rivalin. Those who could have opposed the future stood aside and let it happen, either war-weary or simply blind to the other possible consequences of what was being done. Kaelor became a feudal domain, ruled by the hand of a single dynasty in the name of peace and prosperity. All the major challengers to power were bound in impotence by their own vows, but also by their concern for the very survival of the craftworld on which they lived.

The stage was set for decadence as much as for peace.

As Aingeal sat in meditation in the sanctum of her Spider Temple, setting the beacon to summon the second Convocation of the Exarchs, she could not help but wonder whether Kaelor would have been better served had they refused to seal the helm all those eons ago. She had been there. She had pledged her vow with the others. She had been one of those who had spoken in defence of the radiant farseer's vision. She had been one of the first exarchs to wrestle free of the raging, compulsive voice of Khaine that had thundered in her mind for the previous years of relentless battle, driving her as though she were an

aspect of the war god himself. She had been one of
the first to realise that the Way of the Eldar was not
comprised entirely by war, just as the Way of the Warrior was not encapsulated entirely by the Path of the
Warp Spider. It needed variation and the disciplined
cycles of the Ihnyoh, just as Asurmen and the Eldar
Knights had predicted after the Fall. It was the rare
dhamashir that could sustain a single dhanir forever,
stuck as a Path Stalker for all time. The eldar
dhamashir-soul was not equipped or prepared for
eternal war. It needed peace in which to grow and
flourish. The eldar were a wayfaring people. They
needed to move from dhanir to dhanir as their soul's
needs dictated. Even the Exarchs of Khaine should be
able to see that about those over whom they stood
sentinel.

Just as an eldar soul cannot live with eternal war,
reflected Aingeal wistfully, so it cannot live with perpetual peace. The tendency towards extremes that
marked the eldar character meant that the only persistent state that could be healthy was one of
persistent change. Dangers lurked in all extremes. For
the eldar, decadence in any pursuit might lead to
futures worse than death.

As the exarch muttered her invocation, pushing her
thoughts through the myriad highways of the infinity
circuit in pursuit of the other exarchs, she let part of
her mind wander. She held a vague image of the cosmos in her mind's eye, seeing it as though through
the eyes of another. Someone somewhere on Kaelor
was monitoring the course of the craftworld through
space.

The image was smouldering and infernal, shot through with storms of sha'iel and billowing warp clouds. Kaelor was skirting the edges of a maelstrom, but Aingeal found no surprise in this. She had been watching the proximity closely for the last several years. It had been a long slow process. It was not the case that the craftworld had made a sudden leap through the webway only to emerge so close to this terrible conflagration. It had been within distance for longer than Aingeal cared to remember. Perhaps it had even been there at the time of Gwrih the Radiant. Perhaps, pondered the exarch cynically, it was at the time of the last Convocation that the maelstrom had first appeared in the visible distance, unseen by the unwilling eyes of the Kaelorians.

Others must have seen it. The exarchs and their war-locks must know, just as she did, but the Helm of Asurya kept them from interfering with the farseer's directives in the Ohlipsean. Surely the seers of Yuthran could see it? They should be able to see it even better than her, so why had they done nothing? Had nothing been done?

Given the unusual spatial and temporal properties of the warp, Aingeal had often wondered whether it was possible to gauge the correct distance of the craft-world from the firestorm outside. Although it was partly in material space, much of it was simply unreal and immaterial, merely the raw projections of the warp, infused and seeping into material space through a horrible process of osmosis. The warp dripped and then poured through into the seen dimensions through ever widening perforations in the fabric of space and time. It pushed and raged to get in, but there had to be a reason for why it had appeared so close to the craftworld. For every push, Aingeal wondered whether there had also been some kind of pull.

Coincidence was an ancient and forbidden word on Kaelor. The eldar had outgrown it ages before.

If distance was difficult to gauge, Aingeal had realised long ago that she could not be certain whether Kaelor had been slowly drawing closer to a distant maelstrom, or whether a small breach in space-time in the foreground had been slowly growing into the infernal storm that raged just out of reach. Was it the case that Kaelor had not been steadily advancing towards a distant horror, but rather the horror had been gradually forming on its doorstep and keeping pace with the craftworld's attempts to flee?

Either option contained terrible implications, either way, it seemed clear to Aingeal that it was already well past the time when something had to be done. The exarchs could no longer stand aside, hidden behind their anachronistic vows, and do nothing. They had already ignored the rise of the great houses in the outer realms. They had watched the periphery of Kaelor grow poor and embittered as Gwrih's radiance had become increasingly focused in the Sentrium, leaving the outer realms with nothing. They had watched the warrior heroes of Teirtu and Ansgar rise up against the inequities of the feudal, hereditary system and bring battle back into the perpetual peace of the Rivalin's plans, inevitably returning some balance to Kaelor's soul.

The craftworld had changed, and Aingeal could see that it resembled the war-torn and precarious state that it had been in at the end of the Craftwars. Just like the eldar soul, the spirit of Kaelor moved in cycles, no matter what the Ohlipsean tried to do to prevent it. It could not exist in perpetual peace; that was as much of an aberration as perpetual war. Only cycles of change could last forever.

As it had done all those eons before, Kaelor was again balanced on the edge of a knife, teetering on the brink of its own destruction. The exarchs could no longer pretend that they had no influence on the paths that the craftworld chose to navigate into the future. However, just as the souls of the Kaelorians had once been so steeped in blood that they had found it hard to conceive of a world at peace, so now they had become so wrapped in the pleasures of peace that they would find it hard to embrace war once again. The rule of the Knavir had turned Kaelor against the values of the exarchs, and their only hope lay in the warrior houses of the outer realms.

War must return to Kaelor. The eldar must know what it means to bleed again.

Finally, Aingeal's mind located the last of the exarchs, Waendre of the Swooping Hawks, and she issued her summons, requesting that they all meet in the Temple of the Warp Spiders for a second Convocation of the Exarchs.

IT WAS A scene that had not been witnessed in the Sentrium since the last days of the House Wars, when Iden Teirtu had marched his army along the Tributary of Baharroth and up to the gates of the Farseer's Palace to claim his honours. Since then, the military power of the Teirtu had been implied rather than asserted, since the Knavir and other eldar of the Sentrium had found the presence of warriors so offensive and abhorrent. Aside from the minimum necessary security to service his ongoing paranoia, Iden had attempted to permit life in the Sentrium to continue at its previous pace, even if that meant sending much of his glorious army back to the domains of Teirtu.

Kaelor had changed once again, and Iden could no longer afford the luxury of pandering to the effete decorum of the Knavir. The Plaza of Vaul was filled with Guardians, five hundred, maybe more. Their emerald cloaks and gold-etched armour shone and their banners fluttered proudly above their heads. Falcons, weapons platforms, Vypers and jetbikes were interspersed throughout the formation. There were three Fire Prism tanks and an entire squadron of Wave Serpents. The infamous Soulguard of Teirtu was arranged to one side: the Wraithguard squadrons that Iden had constructed during the course of the House Wars, using the spirit stones of his finest fallen warriors to animate their souls. The inorganic, artificial constructs were magnificent and terrible in equal measure, as they stood with implacable, mechanical calm waiting for orders. They brought the unerring and fearless determination of the dead back onto the battlefield.

From his balcony in the Farseer's Palace, Iden inspected his army with pride swelling his chest. It was like a homecoming. In that moment, seeing the

Sentrium riddled with deep green armour and the glittering gold of the serpent of Teirtu, Iden felt a forgotten calm return to his soul. The power and the threat of violence that his army represented was like a tonic for his tortured mind. He had spent too long attempting to suppress his passion for battle and his thirst for war, just to please the farseer and his disgustingly decadent courtiers. He had suffered years of being made to feel inferior and barbaric, merely because he had been enchanted by the affluence and sensuous grandeur of the Ohlipsean. Now, looking down at the most powerful military force that Kaelor had seen during the time of peace, Iden realised who he was once again. Once again he understood that the power of his sword was no less abhorrent than the devious, political machinations of the Knavir. Indeed, he saw that his sword was more honest, more direct, and ultimately more compelling than the moralising of impotent, decadent fools.

'My children!' he yelled from the balcony, using vocalised tones to bolster his defiance of the culture of the Knavir, who found such audible volume uncouth.

As one, five hundred Teirtu Guardians turned on their heels and looked up towards the balcony.

'My children! Long have you suffered the ignominy of silence and invisibility. Where once you had raised flames that were seen by the gods themselves, you were then hidden under the sackcloth of the prejudice of others, but no more! You are hereby returned to the light once again. Your swords gleam with the eye of Khaine and the swift cunning of the Serpent of Teirtu. You are called upon to forge your souls through the strength of your bodies. Once again you are given the opportunity to live: choose death!

'You have been wronged in this time of peace. You have not been rewarded as you should have been for the heroic deeds of the House Wars. Together we brought the enemies of Teirtu to its knees, and we took the Sentrium for our own. Yet the Sentrium did not accept us...

'Once again, you are the proud and glorious army of Teirtu. You are my army!'

A loud, thunderous, cheer roared out of five hundred throats, making the Plaza of Vaul tremble, and Iden grinned maliciously at the thought of the appalled Knavir on their balcony higher in the palace. He thought of the affected outrage of the witch Cinnia and of the prudish, fragile mother of the new farseer, Oriana. Most of all, he thought of the pathetically earnest Uisnech of Anyon, who had refused to summon his own army to stand beside the Teirtu, as they had stood together in the name of the farseer in the past.

'On this day, you will march against the old enemy once again. On this day, we march against the Ansgar!

'They have stolen our prize and insulted our standing, sneaking into the Sentrium and abducting the farseer, after we had left our defences low out of trust in the new peace.

'On this day, we finish the war that we permitted mercy to leave incomplete. Now we bring the House Wars to an end!'

Another great cheer rose from the warriors in the plaza, thunderous and resonant like a powerful engine. The eldar started to stamp their feet and pummel the hilts of their weapons against the ground, making the area pulse with the violence of life and the lust for death. At that moment of frenzy, the gates of the Farseer's Palace cracked open and a phalanx of warriors emerged into the plaza. They wore the robes of the Rivalin and flew the twin banners of the Farseer's House and House Teirtu. Morfran marched at the head of the group, striding with uncomfortable determination and doing his best to affect the aloof charisma of leadership.

The Teirtu Guardians parted to permit Iden's son and heir passage to the front of the army. Despite the contagious euphoria that echoed and throbbed in the emotional dhamashirs of the assembled warriors, Iden could feel a ripple of doubt suddenly pass through the crowd. Had he not done enough to whip them into an irrevocable passion? Would enough of them retain sufficient reason to reject the leadership of his bumbling son?

The ripple of uncertainty passed. It was overwhelmed by the tide of passion and barely restrained violence that had been pent up for years and then given a vent by Iden's words. Nothing short of death or defeat would turn this army from its purpose now, Iden realised with satisfaction. Not even his fool of a son could mess this up, he thought, and if he did mess it up, he would be dead, so the future held only the best possible outcomes. Meanwhile, Iden had another battle to fight.

* * *

ONLY LAIRGNEN OF the Dire Avengers had refused the summons, but this had not surprised any of the others. It was well known that Iden and many of the Teirtu had been trained in the Shrine of Vengeance and, whilst none would dare to call the integrity of Lairgnen into question, it would have been almost unthinkable for him to attend a convocation in the current circumstances. Aingeal had made her own position very clear, long before, and her position seemed to sit in opposition to that of the Avenger in nearly every conceivable way.

The sanctum of the Spider Temple remained shrouded in shadow, and the darkness was accentuated rather than diminished by the fiercely glowing runes and icons on the walls, as well as by the ghostly apparition-projections of the seven exarchs that had appeared for the convocation.

What would you have us do, Aingeal of the warp? The image of Waendre stood out of his holographic, winged and taloned throne. *The Swooping Hawks have witnessed the gradual decline in the martial spirit of the Knavir from close at hand. We have fewer and fewer tyro from the knightly families. Only the Anyon retain their devotional corvee. Our numbers grow small and our energy weakens. There is only one who might one day replace me on the Raptor's Throne, but even he is as yet ignorant of this possible future.*

The Knavir have never been warriors, Hawk Waendre, replied the image of Morenn-kar of the Howling Banshees. She did not rise from the ancient and beautiful Storm Throne, but spoke instead with the authority of casual disdain. *They have always viewed the dhanir of Khaine as vulgar and without sophistication. They are as ignorant as they are weak. You waste your time with them. We defend the tears of Isha, not them.*

The Howling Morenn is right, offered Fuarghan, standing sharply from the Flaming Throne of the Fire Dragons. His image burned brighter than all the others, as though the flames of his Aspect gave his dhamashir-image an unusual and special intensity. He stood with the dignity and pride that had once been associated with the Eldar Knights of old. *The Knavir have emasculated Kaelor and left it weak in the face of the evils that we must face.*

It is worse than that, hissed the vague and almost invisible presence of Kuarwar, the sinister and shadowy Exarch of the Dark Reapers. His image shifted slightly, as though to indicate that he was standing, but the apparition was too subtle to be seen clearly, and it looked merely like a rippling of oil. *The unchecked indulgences of the court have generated those very evils. The future is darkened by the brightness of their present decadence.* He paused, knowing that the others could not fail to understand his meaning. *I am not the only one here who has seen the maelstrom outside. It is not there by coincidence.*

You believe that the vision of the Radiant Gwrih was flawed? asked the glittering, silver shape of Andraste, the slender and elegant Exarch of the Shining Spears. *You think that Kaelor would have been better off had it degenerated into another age of relentless war?*

War is my master, death my mistress, intoned Kuarwar.

I believe that what has happened has brought us to the present, and that this is a time neither of peace nor of prosperity for any but the Knavir themselves. Moina of the Striking Scorpions spoke with gentle force, as though accustomed to taking others by surprise. *Kaelor was never meant to become a floating pleasure palace. It was from such monstrosities that the craftworlds were first built to flee. Kaelor moves into the dimness of the distant past, not into the future. Gwrih's vision was incomplete. It was his understanding that was flawed.*

And what of the great houses? What of Iden Teirtu? Has he not driven Kaelor even closer to the brink? Aingeal spoke from her own throne, sitting beside the vacant thrones of the Lhykosidae and the Araconid Warlock. *We should have stood against him before to protect the Ansgar. Had Bedwyr survived, balance would have remained on this craftworld. Iden is too weak. He was intoxicated by the Ohlipsean. Now matters are worse.*

Extremes give birth to extremes. Kuarwar's thoughts slid like oil. *You speak of your pet Lhykosidae? The Wraith Spider? You blame his metastasis on the rule of the Teirtu?*

The Zhogahn has set the stage for the prophecy. It is his own doing, replied Aingeal simply.

Ah, the prophecy, exclaimed Kuarwar. *You speak of the vision of Lady Ione?* An unearthly laugh crackled around the chamber. *Do you really understand her motives, I wonder? Subtle and intricate was the mind of that Yuthran Seer. The future is not a simple place, even for a warrior; how much more complex must it be for the visionary?*

She sought to maintain balance! insisted Aingeal. *Preserving the heirs of Ansgar ensured that the decadent peace of the time from before the House Wars could not return. She told Iden that the survival of his greatest enemies would mean the salvation of his soul and the entrenchment of his power. Had all of the Ansgar been slaughtered, like Bedwyr, then even the House of Teirtu would have collapsed into the decadence of the Sentrium! Without a foe, what need is there for a Vanquisher of Sin or his army?*

Whilst Iden listened to her pleas for mercy, he did not understand her reasons, and his soul has grown flabby. He has lost himself in the pleasures of the court and he has driven the Ansgar to the point of annihilation, while his repulsive son has indulged himself to an unprecedented degree. He has created greater foes that even Ione could not have foreseen.

The other exarchs listened carefully to Aingeal's impassioned speech. They could see the possibilities of truth that it contained.

There is much truth in what you have said, Spider of the Warp, said Kuarwar eventually, *but I think that Ione was not so blind that she could not see how Iden would interpret and act upon her prophecy. Her farsight was powerful. In another place she may have become the farseer. You neglect the possibility of the subtlety of her mind, and of the independence of her soul. She was a seer of House Yuthran, not a Spider Warrior of Khaine. Her motivations lie elsewhere than yours.*

You suggest that the Lady of the Hidden Joy meant for the end of days to befall us? challenged Aingeal, with passionate incredulity tingeing her thoughts.

You believe that we are facing the end of days? asked
Andraste in disbelief. *That is precisely what Gwrih set
out to avoid. He foresaw it in the endless wars of our kin,
not in the creative peace of the Knavir.*

His bias made him blind! snapped Aingeal. *Both of
his routes into the future were imaginary and flawed.
There is no hope of a utopia, of eternal peace for the sons
of Asuryan. There is no dystopia of perpetual war and
bloodshed for the children of Isha. It was a false choice!
It ignores the most important thing about Kaelor: it
ignored the fact that we are eldar! Even the most pious
of shrine-keepers cannot avoid battle forever, but even
the exarchs of Khaine cannot fight all the time; how
much less so can the normal wayfarers of Kaelor?*

*Gwrih was a politician, not a messiah. Can't you see
that his greatest achievement was to make us all confuse
one for the other. He made use of the turmoil and uncertainty at the end of the House Wars to consolidate his
grip on power and to recreate his image for posterity. We
all believed him at the time, but it is not heresy to say
that he was wrong!*

*Are you saying that the Covenant of the Asurya's Helm
was a trick?* asked Waendre.

Not a trick, a political device.

*And now you want us to shatter the Helm in order to
stand with you against House Teirtu. Is that correct?*
Moina's thoughts were deceptive in their softness.

Iden must not be permitted to regain the farseer,
answered Aingeal, feeling the indecision in the
chamber. It was not a simple or trivial thing that she
was asking of the exarchs, and she knew that she
was asking for more faith than she had earned from

them. Her various recent interventions in alliance
with the Ansgar made her seem partisan and unreli-
able. Her argument was malformed and incoherent,
and she was relying on the emotional resonance of
her conclusions. *The tyranny must end before it creates
a foe too terrible for us to confront.*

THE ANSGAR FORCE moved smoothly and silently
along the Innis Straight, pushing through the
Faerulh Prairies like an army of ghost riders on
phantom steeds. There were two squadrons of silver
jetbikes, each edged in touches of midnight-blue. A
clutch of aging Wave Serpents occupied the core of
the convoy, their paintwork blistered and scored as
though they hadn't received any attention for years.
The remnants of foliage still clung to the armour,
betraying the fact that the transports had been hidden in the forest since last they were used. Two
shining Falcons flanked the open-topped gun deck
that held the vanguard of the convoy, immaculate
in the reds and golds of the Warp Spiders. The gun
deck itself supported an improbable alliance of figures: the abominable infant Ela, the bandaged and
bleeding Scilti, the polished and alert Arachnir
Adsulata, and the eerily magnificent, golden-
armoured Naois.

The banners of Ansgar, of Rivalin and of the Warp
Spiders flew above the unlikely convoy, each
fluttering splendidly in the breeze of motion. There
was also an additional banner, held high at the
front of the column as though attempting to cast its
shadow over each of the others. It was made of a

shimmering fabric that looked like liquid gold,
rippling in the gusts of faerulh, and its face was
marked with a black web of such impossible and
painful intricacy that it brought tears to the eyes of
those who looked at it. It was the banner of the
Lhykosidae, and he held it aloft with the kind of
implacable certainly that left no mistake in whose
name he marched into battle. The Wraith Spider
was fighting under his own colours. His comrades
just happened to be marching at the same time.

In the distance, over the vast, barren and metallic
expanse of the Faerulh Prairies, the huge vertical
wall of warp energy that marked the Styhxlin
Perimeter could just be seen, like the burning line
of a sunrise over an ocean. The blood-soaked Ula
Pass was still some distance away when Naois
vaulted down from the gun platform and planted
his standard in the ground, thrusting its umbhala
staff through the decking as though it were soil. He
looked towards the horizon with a fixed stare, holding the Styhxlin Perimeter in his gaze as though he
could control it with his eyes.

The rest of the convoy came to a halt behind him,
confused and anxious because of the interruption
to their journey. They had all assumed that their
march would end at the Farseer's Gates on the bor-
der of the Sentrium. Scilti stared down at his
incorrigible cousin from the platform, unable to
understand why he did not push on towards the
Sentrium.

'Do you intend to make your stand here?' called
Scilti, climbing down to stand with Naois. He did

not know how to address his cousin any more. He could not bring himself to call this golden creature Naois, so he simply omitted a name altogether. 'You do not wish to take the pass?'

Naois turned his gaze from the distance and inspected the bloody figure of Scilti. For the first time since Scilti had defeated him in his last dual as a tyro of the Warp Spiders, he acknowledged his cousin's presence.

The pass will fall.

Turning his attention back to the horizon, Naois lifted his hand and pointed up towards the highest reaches of the perimeter, where the Innis Straight curved up towards the Ula Pass. Even from that distance, Scilti could see a sudden flash of darkness appear in the blue flames of the Styhxlin barrier as the portal to the pass opened and tiny movements of greens and gold started to pour out onto the elevated sections of the path of Innis.

The battle for the pass will be fought before it is breached.

Naois leant forwards slightly, as though he had caught sight of something unexpected and distant. For a moment, he thought that he had seen a series of purple flecks amongst the flood of Teirtu green as the stream of Guardians and vehicles flowed down towards the prairies, but then the purple was gone, and Naois dismissed it from his mind. His concern was for the realities of battle, not for flights of fantasy or paranoia. If those distant flecks of purple turned out to be Aspect Warriors of the Dire Avengers, it would become evident soon enough.

As the Teirtu forces reached the level of the
prairies, they started to fan out, spreading over the
wide, expansive plain like a wave of oozing, green
effluent. They had probably sighted the Ansgar column from the portal of the pass, and they were
already beginning to deploy into their attack formation.

It was a premature move, and the tactics of the
Teirtu commander were instantly telegraphed across
the flat unobstructed plain. The squadrons of jetbikes moved out to the flanks while the Falcons and
Fire Prism tanks dropped to the rear to provide ordi-
nance, leaving the loping wraithguard and the Wave
Serpents to push through the middle.

The Teirtu set out their forces to defend the pass
when they had the superior numbers needed for an
overwhelming attack. Had they wanted merely to
block the advance of the Ansgar, it could have been
done less expensively in the pass itself, just as the
talented Yseult had shown against Scilti. It was an
army assembled for the annihilation of the Ansgar,
but it was being commanded by a coward.

With a series of brisk signals, Naois indicated that
the Ansgar forces and the Warp Spiders should
spread into an offensive spearhead on his mark. The
line was to be drawn exactly at the point where the
banner of the Lhykosidae had been planted. The
dusty echo of the once magnificent army of Ansgar
fell quickly into formation behind Naois, making
him into the advanced point of an attacking wedge.
The Wraith Spider was to be driven into the very
heart of the Teirtu line.

It was here in the Faerulh Prairies on the Path of Innis that the first great battle of the Prophecy Wars would be fought.

IDEN HAD SEEN the assembled army of Ansgar with his own eyes as he had emerged from the Ula Pass amongst the detachment of Dire Avengers that Lairgnen had placed at his disposal, and he had felt a thrill of excitement pass through him. It had been so long since he had last looked out onto a battle-field worthy of the name. He had hesitated for a moment to take in the scene before dashing off with his raiding party, splintering away from the main Teirtu force. Not since that last, fateful stand of the Ansgar in that very sector had he felt the burning fire of Khaine in his blood. Not since Bedwyr had he felt the presence of an opponent that made him lust after his own death in mortal combat.

Rushing out of the Ula Pass, he had looked out over the Faerulh Prairies and seen the startling golden form of the leader of the Ansgar. It was not the youth Scilti, who had stolen the life of his pre-cious, beautiful Yseult, and it was not the little abomination Ela'Ashbel, although he could feel her presence like a poisonous gas in the air. The golden warrior was someone new.

It had hit Iden like a blunt, dull, mon'keigh bullet: it was Naois, Bedwyr's heir. How glorious he looked, and how transformed! For a moment, Iden found himself wishing that he could abandon his mission of vengeance against Aingeal. He wished that he could forget the enfeebled political imperative of recovering the farseer to legitimise his rule. In that moment, for the first time since he had faced Bedwyr, Iden felt his dhamashir-soul cry out for its own death. To meet his end at the hands of Naois would be a glory unattainable in the decadent court of the Ohlipsean, no matter how long he might live and rule.

The Dire Avengers around him ushered him quickly from the Innis Straight, leaving that moment of clarity to die slowly in Iden's memory, like the slow fading of the image of a bright light on his retina. They rushed down the suspended section of the path, and then bailed off the lower section, sliding and leaping down the blind side of the sheer embankment to hide themselves from the eyes of the Ansgar.

The squad made rapid progress over the plains towards the domains of Eaochayn, where there was a sub-temple of the Dire Avengers waiting to provide them with transportation and reinforcements. By the time they approached the edges of the forest zones of Ansgar, skirting around the precincts of the Spider Temple, their numbers had swollen to twenty, and they rode in two purple and green Wave Serpents.

As the formations of the two forces settled, Scilti looked back over the blue and silver Guardians, the silver jetbikes and transports, and the shining red grav-tanks. It was a proud army, far superior to the small force that he had led into the pass, but it was little more than a memory of Bedwyr's glorious army. The numbers were significant, but they were less than a quarter of those that they faced. The weapons were formidable, but they were old and untested in years.

He could see victory, though, in the confident posture of his kinsmen. He could see the thrill of finding life again in the way that their weapons were braced and their feet were planted. He could see death gleaming in the eyes of each Guardian, as though they had lived all those years in hiding solely so that they could die in glorious carnage on this field of battle. He could see power flowing through their souls, as they fed off the sheer presence of Naois, as though he gave them succour in their passion.

Naois himself appeared unmoved and unmoving. He stood with one hand clasped around the staff of his banner and gazed across the diminished space at the Teirtu lines. In his other hand he held another, simple staff of umbhala wood. It was as though he were waiting for them to come to him, daring their defensive formation into an attack.

'Are you going to issue a challenge?' asked Scilti, wondering whether this new Naois would honour the rites of commencement.

None will fight me. The answer was unequivocal and patently true.

Scilti inspected Naois, trying to work out whether this meant that he would attack without a challenge, or whether he would wait for a challenge to be issued to him. Then, as he looked at the golden armour, he realised that Naois had armed himself with Khukulyn's twin witchblades, strapping one to the thigh of each leg.

'Naois,' he said, suddenly recognising something of his cousin in the warrior at his side. The small sign of honour to the deceased veteran showed that he was some kind of eldar after all, although what kind of eldar he was remained a mystery.

Here it comes. Ela's thoughts pushed into both their minds as she walked up from the gun platform behind them, easing between them to stand next to her brother at the head of the army.

Scilti looked over towards the Teirtu lines, expecting to see one of their warriors stepping forwards to issue the challenge of commencement, but there was nothing. The lines were unbroken and tightly organised. There was no sign of a champion or marshal moving to the fore. In that moment, Scilti actually wished that Yseult was still alive so that he could confront her once again.

A sudden eruption drew his attention to one of the Falcon tanks in the middle of the Teirtu front line. Its gun barrel barked with flame and the tank shuddered visibly as it spat a missile in a steep parabola. The trail of fire arced up into the air above the battlefield and then tipped its nose down towards the Ansgar formation.

So it begins, hissed Naois with disdain for the manner of the first shot of the war.

He shifted the umbhala staff from his right hand into his left, gripping it at its point of balance like a javelin. He took a quick step back from his banner as he felt the weighting of the shaft, and then darted forwards again, hurling the length of umbhala into the air like a spear.

It flashed through a straight trajectory, leaving a glowing air-friction trail behind it until it pierced straight into the nose of the plummeting missile, which had just begun its descent towards them. The staff penetrated the warhead and detonated the plasma charge inside. A miniature red star exploded into existence above their heads, sending concentric rings of blinding light pulsing over the plains in all directions and rippling into the Styhxlin barrier behind the Teirtu. After a couple of moments of dazzling brightness, the star collapsed into a rain of superheated plasma globules that splashed down to the ground between the two armies, hissing and bubbling furiously against the metallic deck.

A stunned silence settled over the Faerulh Prairies as the warriors of both houses realised what had just happened. The first, ceremonial exchange of the Prophecy Wars had been between a tank and a single warrior, and the warrior had won.

With a victory cry already formed in their throats, the Guardians of Ansgar and the Warp Spiders charged forwards, flooding around and past Naois and Ela, pressing their wedge formation in the centre of the Teirtu line with Scilti and Adsulata at the spearhead, driving it onwards with inspired self-belief.

NONE OF THEM had come. Aingeal stood in the arena of her temple, sheltered under the gradually fading remains of the wraith-webs, facing the ruined but once breathtaking crescent doors. She was in full armour and held her treasured deathspinner braced and primed in both hands. Behind her, in the relative safety of the sanctum, Farseer Ahearn Rivalin was seated in meditation, searching the myriad futures for one in which Kaelor was not consumed by its own daemons. The rest of her Warp Spiders had departed with Naois, hailing him as the Wraith Spider and falling in behind him without question. She had not tried to stop them, and she knew that they would be needed in the coming war.

She had remained behind to stand guard over the temple and its precious guest. She had known that Iden would come for the farseer. There was no conceivable future in which he would permit the Radiance of Rivalin to reside in the domains of the Ansgar. His raid was inevitable.

So she had called on the other exarchs for aid. She had summoned a convocation and challenged them to reconsider their vows of non-interference. It had seemed to her that they had listened to her and taken her seriously. They had said that they would support her, that they would come to her aid. They had promised Aspect Warriors to stand at her side.

None had come, and Aingeal stood alone in the crumbling remains of her once glorious temple. In the halcyon days of House Ansgar, before the House Wars, the Warp Spiders had been as numerous as even the Dire Avengers, with shrines and sub-temples in many domains across Kaelor. Since then, Aingeal had overseen the decline of her order. She had watched it wither and shrivel in tandem with the fortunes of the Ansgar themselves, whilst the Avengers had flourished alongside their patrons, the Teirtu. Lairgnen had been the only one of the exarchs that had not responded to her call, but it seemed that his absence had been enough.

Now she stood alone between Iden, the Dire Avengers and the final destruction of the last Spider Temple on Kaelor. She stood alone, knowing that this was the end, and knowing that a new future was opening to others elsewhere.

As she listened to the deepening whine of Wave Serpents powering down in the clearing outside and saw that she had been abandoned to her fate, she felt death creep into her soul. The thrill of fire started to burn through her veins, and flames of thirst licked at her thoughts. For the first time in countless years, she heard the whisperings of Khaine in her mind, vivid and real as though he had descended from the unseen realms to stand beside her when all his exarchs had abandoned her.

She chose death.

Feet clattered on the steps outside as warriors ascended towards the broken doors. She could hear others dashing around to flank the temple buildings in case there were other routes of escape. She could hear the servos in the shuriken cannons on the Wave Serpents rotating to face the doors in order to cut her down if she showed her face, and she could feel the heavy impacts of Iden's boots as he trod the ground in front of the temple for the first time in his life.

Iden has come, she smiled, perceiving an end worthy of her last stand.

She chose death.

The first Dire Avenger was dead before he'd even crossed the threshold. Aingeal lingered just long enough in the centre of the arena for the first wave to see her there. Then she blinked out of existence at the moment they opened fire with their shuriken catapults. She hissed back into the materium just as the leading Avenger crested the final step of the stairs outside, and she simply decapitated him with a swipe of the powerblades on her right arm. With the same motion, she spun and drove her other hand into the side of the next warrior's helmet, punching through and mulching his skull.

Taking a moment to look down the cracked and crumbling steps, she saw at least six other Aspect Warriors charging up towards her, and then she warped back into the temple.

The second wave was better organised than the first. They approached the doors in two teams, one on each side, covering each other as they advanced. Aingeal watched them in amusement, hidden in the shadows around the edge of the arena. She could sense their concentration on the space just inside the doors, as though they were already convinced that she would be there, waiting for them.

She smiled evilly and warped back out onto the steps, facing the backs of the two teams as they cautiously advanced into the doorway. With casual abandon, she lifted her deathspinner and unleashed a hail into their backs, strafing her fire from one side the doorway to the other to ensure that she covered them all.

There was a faint click as the gunners in the Wave Serpents behind her in the clearing charged the accelerators for the shuriken canons, but just as they opened fire at the step on which Aingeal was standing, she vanished again, leaving the rain of monomolecular projectiles to ricochet harmlessly off the masonry.

From his position between the Wave Serpents, Iden cursed the incompetence of the Avengers' gunners. Then he heard their screams from inside the Wave Serpents, and he cursed the exarch as well, as he realised that she was in there tearing them apart with her hands.

He flicked a signal to the team of Avengers that had taken up position on the side of the shrine to block off one of the possible escape routes, indicating that the exarch was not in the temple and that they should move in to find the farseer. To the team on the other side, he made the sign that they should enter the shrine and plant their plasma charges.

Meanwhile, there was an electric fizz and a hiss behind him. It was a sound that he had grown to recognise, and his first instinct was to dive to the ground. His instincts served him well as a volley of fire from Aingeal's deathspinner whined over his back, shredding the material of his cloak as it billowed up behind him.

He hit the ground too heavily and Aingeal was on his back before he could roll over. A piercing pain lanced through his shoulder as she thrust a powerblade down through it, pinning him to the ground. He snapped his head back abruptly and smashed the back of his head into the exarch's face-mask, making her lurch backwards. As her weight shifted, he rolled over, tearing his shoulder free of her loosened blade and kicking out with both legs.

The kick lifted Aingeal into the air and sent her crashing onto her back on the ground. By the time she had found her feet, Iden was also upright. He had drawn his famous sword in both hands and held it horizontally through the space that separated him from the exarch. A stream of blood ran down his arm from the puncture wound in his shoulder, and it fizzled as it touched the hilt of his alien blade.

There was a shout from the entrance to the temple above them as the two teams of Avengers reappeared, jobs done. The farseer shuffled along in the middle of them, leaning heavily on his gnarled staff and putting up no visible fight.

Aingeal looked from Iden to the Aspect Warriors and back again, momentarily uncertain about which posed the greatest threat or presented the greatest challenge. She squeezed the trigger of her death-spinner, unleashing a half-hearted volley towards the Avengers, but Iden used the opportunity to lunge forwards with Soul-Slayer and hack towards the exarch's head.

She dropped low and brought the deathspinner up to block the attack, but the exquisite blade crashed straight through the weapon, shattering it into explosive fragments as the ammunition detonated inside.

Iden followed through, leaping into the attack as Aingeal staggered back. He sidestepped and brought his crackling, sinuous blade around in a horizontal arc, driving it into Aingeal's warp-pack as she tried to evade the strike.

She fell as the warp-pack spluttered and burst into flames, hitting the ground hard. For a moment she seemed unable to move, and Iden stood over her with his blade poised, waiting for the moment of drama to grip him. His eyes gleamed with excitement as the thrill of Khaine coursed through his veins.

Then Aingeal started to flicker. She seemed to jump in and out of existence without moving from her position on the ground, as though her sparking and burning warp-pack were malfunctioning in some way, but she couldn't move.

After a few moments, the remaining Avengers descended the steps and joined Iden to watch the freak show, bringing the farseer in tow. They leered over her, enjoying the bizarre and sadistic suffering of the exarch of Khaine.

You should see this before you pass, exarch, said Iden, pointing past Ahearn and up at her crumbling and ruined temple. A moment passed with nothing happening, and then the plasma charges inside detonated, instantly transforming the temple into a sphere of plasma, a raging inferno of atomic fire. The silhouette of the temple showed black in the heart of the firestorm for a fraction of a moment, and then it was incinerated utterly.

Now you can pass happily, smiled Iden sarcastically, raising his alien blade above his head for the death blow. He let out a cry of focus as he brought Soul-Slayer down with all his strength onto the prone target, closing his eyes to better feel the moment of death.

A cold, burning pain ripped through his back and out of his stomach.

Now I can pass happily, replied Aingeal as the Dire Avengers shredded her with their shuriken catapults. She had managed one final warp jump, appearing immediately behind Iden and punching her powerblades through his abdomen before collapsing down on top of him.

She had chosen death.

THE BATTLE WAS an anticlimax. Naois stood in the heart of the action but felt more like a spectator than a warrior fighting for his life. He saw Scilti engaged in one contest after another, hacking through his opponents at close range with his powerblades or spraying them with his deathspinner from greater distances. Adsulata blinked and flashed through the melee, slicing a throat here and punching through a skull there, moving with a graceful ease that Naois could appreciate. The plains were beginning to run slick with blood. Occasionally he caught glimpses of little Ela wandering the battlefield like a ghost, untouched and unmolested by the weapons and hands of both sides. It was as though none of the combatants could see her at all, or that it simply did not occur to them to attempt to do her harm. She moved in an aura of inexorable safety.

None had yet challenged Naois. He had not even drawn Khukulyn's witchblades. A lone wraithguard had advanced on him a while ago, as though unaware of what it was doing, but Naois had dismantled it before it had even fired a shot at him. The Teirtu Guardians passed by him as though they couldn't even see him. He searched their ranks for a marshal or a leader of some kind, anyone that might consider themselves worthy, but there was no one. Their commander was hidden away at the very back of their force, cowering behind the Fire Prism tanks and a full squad of wraithguard. He was not even worthy of command, let alone of combat with Naois. This was not the War of the Ages that Naois had wanted.

Then an icy shockwave blasted across the plains, rippling out from the outer realms in the direction of Ansgar and crashing into the Styhxlin barrier. It covered the Faerulh Prairies in screams of agony and chilled the souls of all the warriors on the battlefield. For a brief surreal moment, all the combatants stopped, some of them in the middle of a strike, others already impaled on a lance or a spear. There was a pristine moment of silence, as though sound itself had suddenly become impossible.

Then everything erupted back into fury once again, as though nothing had happened. Only Naois understood. He could feel the rage of violation beginning to build inside him. He could feel Khaine etching fire through his veins with the tip of his shining spear, and he could feel the terror of a hundred thousand eldar souls screaming in the labyrinth of infinity circuit.

In that moment, he knew that his temple was gone.

With slow deliberation, Naois unsheathed the witchblades and held them out at his sides like a

cross, reaching out and opening his chest in a grand
declaration of his presence and intent. He was issu-
ing a challenge to the entire Teirtu army.

The first Guardian to die was almost an accident.
Duelling with one of the Warp Spiders, the hapless
Teirtu had retreated right onto the point of one of
Naois's blades, impaling himself. With a brisk, irritated motion, Naois lifted the blade and swept the
dead Guardian off onto the floor, as though merely
cleaning his sword.

Then he started to run. His burning eyes were
focused solely on the command unit at the back of
the Teirtu force, and he ploughed his way through
the fray in grim determination to get there. He was
like a ball of golden flame, roaring through the las-
riddled quagmire of battle.

He parried swords, ducked shuriken and evaded
lasfire, leaping and rolling with breathtaking grace.
His own blades flashed in coruscating patterns of
psychic fire, leaving a trail of the mutilated and the
dead in his wake.

The Teirtu could no longer ignore this manifestation of war as it rampaged and raged through their
ranks, but it seemed as though Naois was engaging
them and ignoring them at the same time. He
showed no signs of attachment or investment in any
of the combats, and his eyes never deviated from the
command post. Even when he dropped and spun
under a volley of cannon fire, springing up again to
decapitate the gunner with a single swipe, it was as
though the movements were simply part of his run.
He was just clearing obstacles, like a hurdler clearing

the gates to get to the finishing line. The obstacles themselves had no meaning to him; they could have been anything, or nothing, it didn't matter.

Eventually, the Teirtu Guardians began to scatter out his path, clearly aware that there was nothing they could do to stop this force of the gods. So the field of battle parted before him as he charged onwards, but this seemed only to drive Naois to greater rage, as he was deprived of a vent for the violence that roared untamed in his soul.

'WE MUST RETREAT!' gasped Morfran, staring at the holo-projection of the battlefield from within his armoured transport at the back of the field. The battle was not going as planned. The smaller Ansgar force seemed to be well organised and inspired. It had pushed up into the heart of the Teirtu lines and broken their formation, shattering the battle plan into a free-for-all of close combat.

There was something else. He couldn't tell what it was, but a burning image on the projection was ploughing forwards through the battlefield towards his own position. Perhaps it was a tank or a giant war walker? Whatever it was, Morfran could see that his own forces were weary of engaging it, and he was sure that this meant that he didn't want it to reach him.

'We may never be able to muster a force of this size again, Lord Morfran,' answered the rugged old Guardian at his side. Iden had left the veteran Turyae to counsel his inept son in case of need. 'To retreat now may not be wise.'

'Look!' cried Morfran, pointing at the ever closing burning image on the projector. 'If we don't retreat, we'll be dead!'

'There are worse things than death, my lord,' countered Turyae, whispering the warrior's truism.

'You think I'm a coward?' Morfran's eyes narrowed with hatred as he faced his accuser. 'I did not ask to be here, Guardian. I was sent. I have other things to do, more important things!'

'As was I, my lord. That is the fate of the warrior: to be sent to his death.'

Morfran snarled, his panic shifting easily into contempt. 'You fool! You blind and misguided fool! Death may come to us all one day – it may not – but you should not accept it on the whim of another. You should not lay down your life for my ridiculous father and his pathetic warrior codes. You should live while you are alive!'

Turyae slapped him abruptly across the face.

'Sound the retreat, Turyae,' said Morfran with calculated calm.

'As you wish. I will command the rear guard action myself, my lord. Do I have your permission to take one of the Soulguard squads?' Turyae spoke through gritted teeth, refusing to let the Morfran's cowardice ruin a lifetime of honour and devotion.

'Fine, whatever you like,' said Morfran, waving a dismissal. 'Just get this vehicle back through the Ula Pass as quickly as possible.'

NAOIS SAW THE commander's tank peel away from the rear of the Teirtu lines and accelerate back up the curving ramp that led into the Ula Pass. A trail of Guardians, vehicles and weapons platforms followed suit, falling into retreat, and he knew that the battle was won, but his soul was unsatisfied and he threw back his head to scream his frustration across the blood-slicked battlefield.

As the Teirtu army's retreat degenerated into a rout, Naois scanned the decimation that surrounded him. Emerging out of the smoke and flame ahead of him was a single figure, a Guardian of Teirtu who announced himself in the manner of the old custom, declaring himself to be Turyae Teirtu-ann. As he bowed, a full squadron of wraithguard emerged from the smoke behind him and opened fire at Naois.

Yes, hissed the Wraith Spider as he felt death calling once again.

PART THREE: THE INEXORABLE

CHAPTER NINE: DEFIANCE

THE PLAZA OF Vaul had hosted so many great events over the last few days that the eldar of the Sentrium could have been forgiven for reaching the point of numbness or emotional saturation, incapable of feeling the grand emotions of regal ceremony. For the eldar, emotions were a cumulative phenomenon, each one stacking up on top of the last until they exploded into a fury of expression or were fundamentally confronted, contradicted and deflated. Hence, a sequence of great victories would bring ever higher tidal waves of euphoria crashing over society, but a number of consecutive tragedies would rapidly push whole communities to the verge of virtual suicide. They called it emotional contagion, and it was the natural affliction of a psychic race.

The atmosphere in the Plaza of Vaul was dark, and the light-phase of the sector seemed to dim in dramatic sympathy as though the Fluir-haern could feel the sinking mood. There had been so much death, and so many of the brightest lights of the court had been extinguished. It had started with the fair Lady Ione herself, but then there had been the valiant young Marshal Yseult. The courtiers in the Farseer's Palace also remembered the gallant Guardian Lhir, but recent reports suggested that he had been slaughtered in battle.

Then Morfran had returned from battle, unscathed but bathed in the ignominy of defeat. The irony was not lost on many.

For many of the most refined eldar of the Sentrium it felt that the best and the most beautiful were gradually being taken from them, leaving only the crude and vulgar dross of the Teirtu to pollute the stately boulevards. It was bad enough that the styhx-tann warrior house had to be there in the first place, but it was even worse to see the most acceptable of them gradually perish in such barbaric ways, and to see the most vulgar survive through it all.

Now it seemed that even the Zhogahn would join the ranks of the passed. News had got back to the Ohlipsean in advance of the party of Dire Avengers that escorted the wounded patriarch. Exarch Lairgnen had delivered the message to Uisnech Anyon of the Circular Court, explaining that Iden had been injured in a battle with Aingeal of the Warp Spiders during his attempt to recover the farseer from his imprisonment. He said that the wounds were serious, and that the Warp Spider's blades had been laced with a psycho-toxic venom that had made the patriarch of Teirtu delusional and fevered. The Aspect Warriors that were with him suspected that he would not last through the next down-phase of dharknys, if he made it back to the Sentrium at all.

When Morfran had heard the news, he had battled to control his sense of relief. Had there been some way for him to ensure that his father would die on the road before re-entering the Sentrium, he would have done his best to make it happen. He simply could not face the prospect of his father's fury when he returned to discover that not only had he failed to crush the Ansgar before they could reach the Ula Pass, but that he had also fled from the battlefield to save his own life. Iden would tell him that Yseult would never have acted so shamefully, and he would be right.

Turyae had not acted so shamefully.

Morfran had never claimed to be a warrior. It was a mere accident of fate that he had been born into the Teirtu line. It was the worst of all possible things: a coincidence. So, it was bad enough to have been forced to march into battle in the first place, not to mention to have to return to the already gloomy Sentrium with more depressing news for the Knavir, but then to have his overbearing father berate him for his cowardice was more than he could stomach. It was almost enough to make him grasp his courage in his hands and attempt to organise an assassination. It couldn't be too hard to arrange an accident to befall the injured and feverish Zhogahn as he travelled through the increasingly unstable sectors outside the Sentrium.

The effort, small as it might have been, and the risk defeated his will.

Instead, he contented himself with a show of concern and a public display of preparation for the return of the Zhogahn. He organised a summoning, drawing in all the eldar of the sector and crowding the Plaza of Vaul in anticipation, filling the domain with a pervasive sense of doom and foreboding. If Iden was not already dead by the time he arrived, the atmosphere itself would probably be enough to kill him.

In full armour, with the emerald and gold cloak of Teirtu draped over his shoulder as smartly as he could manage, Morfran took up his position on the pedestal next to the ceremonial, silver anvil that occupied the centre of the plaza and marked the geometric heart of Kaelor itself. He had attempted to press a number of the Knavir into joining him in the plaza, but only Cinnia and Celyddon had bowed to his pressure.

The others, led by Uisnech Anyon, had decided to boycott the reception. Instead, they stood aloof and separate from the silent crowd on their customary balcony overlooking the piazza. From a sense of duty that was buoyed by the presence of Cinnia and Celyddon, Oriana had reluctantly agreed to accompany Morfran, bringing the infant Farseer Turi in her arms, and for a moment Morfran had wondered what would happen to his own son if Ahearn returned with his father. The concern flickered fleetingly in his mind as he realised that he should be more worried about what was going to happen to him.

A powerful swell of silence rolled down the Tributary of Baharroth. It was oppressive and heavy, rolling like a dense and viscous liquid over the press of eldar that lined the boulevard, pushing just ahead of the solitary purple and green Wave Serpent as it slowly eased towards the palace. All of the onlookers knew the identity of the incumbent, and they bowed their heads out of a sullen mixture of respect, relief and dread.

The banners of Teirtu were held horizontally by the periodic Guardians along the route in a mark of mourning and respect. Morfran hoped that Iden would not be coherent enough to notice how few the Guardians were.

Despite the gravity of the sinking feeling that pressed down on Morfran, he found himself straining to see down the boulevard. He realised that there was a contrasting thrill of excited anticipation in his abdomen; this was potentially the moment that he had been waiting for. The premature death of Iden would open up a whole new range of futures for him, just as Cinnia had told him, and, if it was handled correctly, it could also open up new possibilities for Kaelor, once the old warrior's spirit stone was safely enshrined in the infinity circuit.

This might be the moment at which the future became clear to them all.

The Wave Serpent slid with deliberate slowness, dragging its morbid presence into the Plaza of Vaul. It passed through the corridor that had been kept

clear by the crowd and drew to a standstill in front of
Morfran's podium. The hatch on the back of the
transport hissed open, folding down to the ground to
form a ramp.

After a long and silent pause, two Dire Avengers
strode down the ramp. Behind them came a small,
self-guiding anti-grav stretcher bearing the cloak-
shrouded body of Iden. The golden serpent was
curled on his chest, as though nestled into dormancy,
but its lustre was dimmed and, despite the efforts of
the Avengers to arrange the cloak tastefully for the
benefit of delicate Knavir, it was speckled and stained
with blood. Two more Aspect Warriors marched
behind the stretcher, making an honour guard of
only four for the farseer's first and last Zhogahn.

Finally, hobbling noticeably and supported by his
staff, the farseer himself shuffled down the ramp on
his own. Before he reached the ground, he looked up
at the group on the podium and nodded a weary
greeting. There was a spark of something else in his
eyes, which may have been gratitude, hope, or even
resentment.

The Dire Avengers led the stretcher around the
edge of the Wave Serpent and past the front of Morfran's podium. They paused for a moment beneath
the son of Teirtu, forcing Morfran to look down at his
father's face, letting him see that his father's green
eyes were open and staring, as though fixed on a distant horizon. Then they manoeuvred the stretcher so
that it covered the silver anvil, cutting its power so
that Iden's body lowered gently down onto the
ancient, ceremonial monument, where once had lain

the bodies of each of the Rivalin Farseers since Gwrih.

Bracing himself, Morfran descended from the podium and approached the body. He looked down at the pain wracked face and saw the unfocused and massively dilated eyes, and the unnaturally white skin, drained by blood loss. A feeling of relief washed over him. There was no way that Iden was going to survive. Indeed, he realised quickly, there was not really any reason to wait for his death before performing the Ceremony of Passing.

The thrill of victory buzzed through his mind at last.

He peered down into his father's face and smiled. 'Now you are under my control,' he muttered, letting a droplet of saliva fall unseen into Iden's eye.

Even in his deathly state, Morfran could see his father's rage build. He could see the realisation that Morfran had lost the battle with the Ansgar and that his own efforts to recover the farseer were now in vain. His death would be for nothing. Nobody would know about the duel with Aingeal. They would merely remember the broken and bleeding old warrior lying like a corpse on the silver anvil of Vaul, waiting for death to take him.

Ione had prophesied that he would die after a heroic victory. She had said that he would pass into the spirit pool of Kaelor in the Shrine of Fluir-haern, in a great and stately public ceremony. She had said that he would become the sire of the next farseer and that the Teirtu and Rivalin lines would blend. That was why he had spared the abomination, Ela of

Ashbel, and the hateful runt, Naois Ansagr. That was why he had permitted Kerwyn Rivalin to live in exile.

Unable to speak or even to make his dwindling thoughts heard by another, Iden glared up at his son's gloating and bloated face. His green eyes flashed with hatred. He hated Morfran for his incompetence, his repulsive decadence, and for the very fact that he was still alive. He hated that Morfran would take over House Teirtu when he died. He hated himself for being so blinded by emotion and hungry for glory that he had not properly considered all the possible meanings of Ione's prophecy.

He hated Ione for leading him into a future that contained his doom. Why would she betray him so profoundly? Did she see something in the future that was more important, or was she simply in league with the Ansgar? He had heard the rumours at court about her relationship with Bedwyr, but had paid them no heed. He hated Kaelor: the twisted emotional politics, the duplicitous commitment to eternal peace under the perpetual threat of war, the shocking and destructive disparities between the life styles of the Knavir and the rest of the craftworld, and the incredible, short-sighted obliviousness of the Ohlipsean, which continued as though the system was working perfectly. The whole set-up seemed to be deliberately designed to support and heighten the indulgences of the courtiers, as though they were some kind of hideous, anachronistic pleasure cult.

As he stared up at the hateful and obnoxious face of Morfran, he realised for the first time what he should have been doing with his power. Just as he had been duped by the beloved Lady Ione, so too, he had been duped by Kaelor. Rather than expending his life, energy and warriors in the name of the corrupt and decadent institutions of Kaelor, rather than attempting to bolster the ancient regime of the Rivalin and to rule as their legitimate champions, he should have been trying to overthrow the Rivalin and its Ohlipsean altogether.

Instead of fighting against the Ansgar, he should have formed an alliance with the honourable Bedwyr and transformed Kaelor into a warrior society, disciplined and glorious like the legendary Biel-Tan. For the first time, he realised that he had permitted the pompous Knavir to divide the warrior houses of the outer realms, making him feel inferior, making him feel as though he should crave and be grateful for the patronage of the farseer, as though Kaelor itself was inconceivable without the Rivalin dynasty at the helm.

He had thought that the Knavir were naive and incapable of understanding the power of the sword, when in fact they had been shrewd and conniving, harnessing the bloodlust of others to fight their battles for them so that they could remain in undiminished luxury. They did genuinely disdain the warriors, but Iden had been wrong to think that the Knavir had failed to understand their importance.

It had all been a trick, and with his last moments of lucidity Iden raged against the atrocities that he had committed in the name of the farseer. With his last breath, he saw Bedwyr's face flicker through his mind, and he realised that the patriarch of Ansgar had been

the finest eldar that he had ever known. Then he
looked up at the drooling and thrilled face of Morfran
and saw the shape of the future that he had forged for
Kaelor.

All he could feel was hatred.

THE RIVALIN GATES that barred the main route into the
Sentrium were closed. Beyond them, through their
mysteriously translucent structure, Naois could see the
glittering lights and splendour of the Farseer's Court. It
was as though light itself resided on the other side of
those gates. In the dimness of the distant past, Naois
had been led to believe that the whole of Kaelor had
looked like that: radiant and glorious, like a living
icon to the majesty of the galaxy-spanning eldar
empire. Now, the contrast with the territories through
which the Ansgar had marched to get there was stark.

The domains of Ansgar were atrophied and decaying
after years of hardship and oppression, and even the
less disfavoured and more central domain of
Eaochayn showed signs of the same haemorrhaging of
wealth and prosperity. Kaelor was gradually being
bled dry.

The Sentrium glittered like a diamond in the heart
of Kaelor, radiant and pristine as though untouched
by the turmoil and suffering that had wracked the
craftworld since before the onset of the House Wars.
Somehow it had managed to preserve its stately
grandiosity, despite the blood-soaked ruination that
riddled the rest of the craftworld.

As Naois drew his army to a standstill about a hundred metres from the gates, holding up his fist to

indicate the halt as he stood proudly under his banner on the gun platform at the head of the force, he could imagine how other eldar had become intoxicated by that sight: the vision of beauty and perfection, of cultivation and civilisation. There was a sense in which it might seem so vastly superior to the lifestyle and living conditions of the outer realms, and he understood intuitively that part of the eldar dhamashir craved those things.

Somewhere in his species-memory, he knew that the very first eldar to reach for the stars, at the very birth of the galaxy, had done so out of faith that the stars would bring them affluence and comfort in the future. The first eldar to plunge into the warp and start the construction of the webway had thought mostly about the material affluence that would be brought by instantaneous travel through space. They had thought about the possibilities for leisure that were offered by such monumental advances. They had thought about the pleasures in which they could indulge their tastes with all the saved time, and all the delicacies that could be summoned from the new parts of the galaxy that would suddenly be within their reach.

There was a certain propensity for intoxication lurking in the eldar psyche that made them weak in the face of temptation. That was why they had fallen in the first place. The Fall was historical proof of his hypothesis, as though proof were necessary. The Sentrium spoke of the same afflictions, but on a rather more minor scale. There Naois saw the decadence of a sub-cultural group – he might even call it a cult – and not of an entire craftworld or an entire species.

Its repulsiveness was manifest to him. It represented the collapse of all the disciplinarian values of
the Aspect Temples and even of the Ihnyoh Eldar
Path. It was anathema to him. It was an aberration. It
made him feel unclean.

Looking across at the gates, he could see the sentinel gun emplacements near the top, where the edge
of the gates met the underside of the floor of the level
above. In fact, the Sentrium was one of the few places
in all of Kaelor that had no levels above it. It was
somehow excluded from the odd spatial effects of
the construction method that made it almost impossible to find an outer layer of the craftworld, which
meant that all the various levels above and below the
Rivalin Gates simply ended in an abrupt and impenetrable wall when they reached the space occupied by
the Sentrium. One of the most famous artisans in
Kaelorian history, Nurior the Sound, had once gone
insane trying to locate and map those walls. He had
never managed to do it, and it remained the case that
nobody knew for sure where the other levels bordered against the great, radiant dome of the
Sentrium, or even whether there were any such borders.

Making the boundaries of your domain utterly
incomprehensible to nearly anyone who might be
interested in entering it was a brilliant and effective
way of keeping people out, better than any gun, cannon or blade.

Nonetheless, two bright lances were mounted into
emplacements at the top of the gates along with an
old-fashioned   distort   cannon,   which   was

presumably one of the additions made to the defences by Iden. It was certainly not elegant enough to have been installed by the Knavir. The gate was speckled with auto-tracking shuriken cannons, disguised artfully as parts of the intricate carvings that graced the surface.

He could just about make out the jittering movements of eldar in the gun boxes, and he could feel their nervousness. They knew that Naois, the Ansgar and the Warp Spiders had dismantled Morfran's army and penetrated through the Ula Pass in pursuit of the retreating Teirtu army. They knew that the Rivalin Gates offered little resistance to them, and that the hundred-strong army of the Wraith Spider could take the gates at any time. The impressive gunnery was more show than substance.

The forces of the Ansgar were arrayed in a spearhead behind Naois's platform. The armour on the Warp Spiders' tanks and the Ansgar transports was laser scored and riddled with the indentations of shuriken fire. The silver and blue jetbikes were dented and scratched, and the Guardians looked even scruffier than they had when they had set out, but the tanks had been decorated with the trophies of war: green helmets and armoured plates hung from every fixing. The Teirtu serpent adorned the side one of the Wave Serpents, where it had been ripped off an enemy transport; and a Teritu banner was displayed from an antenna on the back of one of the jetbikes. It was engulfed in flames and was burning slowly and eternally in a cool, psychic fire. Finally, laid across the front of Naois's weapons platform like

an elaborate fender was the armoured shell of one of
the Soulguard, one of Iden's own prized wraithguard.

The overall impression of the army was that of a
ragtag band of merciless and barbaric mercenaries.
They might have been darkling pirates from the
hideous reaches of Cormaragh. It was not at all
impressive in any of the terms that the Knavir of the
Sentrium would understand, and that was why Naois
knew that it would fill the court with dread. He came
as an uncultivated and unapologetic warrior soul,
and he brought with him death, unsanitised and
unadorned.

It was just death.

Satisfied with the atmosphere of fear that his presence was generating amongst those that peered out
of the Sentrium at his army, Naois vaulted down off
the anti-grav platform that he shared with Ela, Scilti
and Adsulata, and then thrust the umbhlala shaft of
his own Lhykosidae banner into the deck.

He marked his territory.

'You're not going to attack the gates?' asked Scilti,
jumping down to stand at Naois's shoulder. He was
bloodied from the battle with the Teirtu, and he
could feel the fire of Khaine still burning in his veins.
He was impatient for more death, and he couldn't
believe that Naois had stopped before reaching the
tower of the farseer.

For a moment Naois did not even look at his
cousin, but kept his eyes fixed on the glamorous
vision before them. Then he turned his silver and
black eyes on Scilti, letting him see the horror that
lurked within him.

What purpose would it serve? In there we will find nothing but the end of our times. There are no battles to be won, only prizes to be taken.

'We have come so far, Naois! How can we stop now, when we could take the Sentrium for our own? Look at it, Naois! Look at it. Isn't this what your father fought for? Wouldn't he have wanted you to take the extra step? Imagine that glittering prize for the House of Ansgar!'

Yes, he would have attacked the gates, you are right. The reply was flat and blunt, like a hammer. *But I am not Bedwyr, and you are not his heir, Scilti Ansgar-ann. There are more important matters to be attended to than the sacking of the Sentrium.*

Exasperated and stung, Scilti turned and looked up at Adsulata and Ela, who stared blankly back at him.

'Then I shall attack the gates for you, son of Bedwyr,' he replied. 'I will need two squads of Guardians and one of the Falcons.'

There will be no attack on this day, replied Naois in a tone that brooked no argument. It was as though he had looked into the future and knew for a fact that neither he nor Scilti would attack before the next up-phase of laetnys. It was not an order, it was merely a fact.

'We did not come all this way only to falter at the last,' said Scilti, hardly able to contain his frustration. 'I did not come here to look at those radiant gates and not to touch them!'

Naois looked at him for a moment and then turned away without another word. It was a patronising glance, as though he were disgusted. Then he strode back past the anti-grav platform on which Ela and Adsulata were still standing, without looking up. The Guardians behind the platform parted quickly to let him through, and he strode briskly through their ranks as though with a purpose, pushing out of the other side of the formation behind the lines.

The others watched him go without a word, but each of them had the same question on their minds.

ELA'ASHBEL WATCHED her brother thunder his banner into the ground before the Rivalin Gates, claiming the main tributary to the Sentrium for the Wraith Spider. She noted that he used his own golden banner, shot through with black webbing, rather than planting the colours of Ansgar or those of the Warp Spiders. There was something unspeakable about his manner that made her uneasy. He seemed somehow unnaturally pure of purpose, as though he was no longer exercising the faculty of free will but was rather incarnating the judgements of some higher force. He emitted no aura of consciousness. There were no decisions.

As her brother turned and walked away, brushing past her and moving towards the back of the lines, Ela realised that he was not focused on the Sentrium at all. It was of almost no concern to him. Instead, his thoughts were elsewhere, back at the ruined Temple of the Warp Spiders and with the broken Exarch Aingeal.

Like all the other eldar that had fought in the battle before the Ula Pass, Ela had felt the shockwave of the temple's destruction. Unlike most of them, she had known what it was, and she had felt the aftershocks resounding in Naois's mind. She had seen his fury rise and watched him crash into a rampage through the Teirtu.

But the Wraith Spider was no Dire Avenger. The legends say that it returns to Kaelor in moments of great peril as the incarnation of the Fluir-haern. It does not fight for itself or for vengeance. There is no room in its will for the petty impulses of revenge.

Ela could see the battle raging in Naois's dhamashir, as he fought to reconcile his own personal desires for the greatness of his father's house against the overwhelming force of inexorable destiny. She could see that it was a battle he was losing. Even before his outrage in the arena of the temple, when Scilti had finally bested him, even before his fury at being left behind in Scilti's battle against the Guardians of the Reach, even before the wraith-tendrils of Fluir-haern had captured his soul in their tightly woven web, Naois had struggled against his nature and his fate. It was as though he had been the reluctant participant in a gradual process of metastasis since the moment he was born. The Wraith Spider's host was given no choice, he was chosen.

Lady Ione had seen it, just as she had seen Ela's own unusual path. The seers of Yuthran had seen the dangers right at the start, and they had expelled little Ela from their sisterhood, calling her the vaughn – the abomination, but they had done nothing more than to cast her from their sight, as though scared of the possible consequences of action against her, as though the future held too many contending hells and they could not decide between them. In the end, they had simply opted for refusing to accept responsibility for the little aberration in their midst, and they had thrown her out to fend for herself. They must have known that this would send her back to the domains of Ansgar, and back to Naois.

'Where is he going?' called Scilti. His gaze followed Naois's back, but his words were addressed to Ela.

He goes to perform the Rituals of Remembrance, answered Adsulata. *He offers honour to the fallen exarch of his temple.*

Ela simply nodded. She could feel the calling, like a vacuum drawing in the thoughts of the Warp Spiders. They were all watching Naois with the desperation of those watching the last flame flickering in the darkness of a subterranean cavern. With their exarch and their temple gone, he represented the dhamashir of the Warp Spiders on Kaelor, and they watched him in awe, as though he were a walking god amongst them.

I must assist him. She was my exarch too, continued Adsulata. Instinctively, she moved to the edge of the platform and poised for the jump.

Wait, said Ela, staring after her brother but directing her thoughts to the arachnir. *There is a more important need.*

Adsulata paused.

Iden is about to die. Aingeal wounded him mortally, and his son will do nothing to save him.

Good. The arachnir's response was blunt and aggressive.

Perhaps, but don't you see what this will mean? Iden's spirit stone will be mingled into the Fluir-haern, injecting a new thread of hatred into the soul of Kaelor.

Surely the spirit pool can absorb the emotions of any eldar, no matter what their disposition? Adsulata seemed doubtful.

Your question is wrong, arachnir. Of course, the Fluir-haern can absorb Iden's energy. The question, rather, is what effect that energy will have on the direction of Kaelor. Already this craftworld teeters precariously on the brink of its own doom, the very end of days. It skirts the fringes of a roiling warp maelstrom of its own making, and the atmosphere within the craftworld fluctuates between gloom and fury in the Outer Reaches, with indulgence and deca-dence rooted in the Sentrium. The future of Kaelor is finely balanced, so delicately that a single, powerful soul like that of Iden might tip it over the edge.

You can see this, Ela of Ashbel? asked Adsulata.

It is clear to see, replied Ela, realising at that moment just how obvious it was. It was almost as though Kaelor had been driven directly towards this moment of choice, as though it had been manipulated into reaching a delicate pivot. The maelstrom, the return of war to Kaelor after long ages of peace and then the appearance of the Wraith Spider, all spoke of a well-planned trajectory. It could not be merely coincidence, not under the guidance of such a line of visionary farseers. Had Gwrih seen this in the future? Was this abyss playing in the mind of Lady Ione when she gave voice to the prophecy? Could Ahearn really not see the patterns and threads of the future being pulled into the present? *This is the time of fate.*

What would you have me do? asked Adsulata, return-ing to little Ela's side and presenting herself, as though being summoned for duty by the exarch.

Perhaps there is nothing to be done, mused Ela thoughtfully. *Perhaps it has all already happened, and we are just here to bear witness to the playing out of the end of days?*

I do not believe that there is nothing to be done, with the Lhykoisidae and the Ehveline standing amongst us at this time of destiny. Adsulata pulled herself to her full height, suddenly filled with pride.

Your faith is short-sighted, arachnir of the lost Spider Temple. Naois's role in this is unclear even to me. He does not act out of the desires of his soul, so the futures contain no echoes of his will. He is unmoulded and unformed. His resolution is shaped neither by us nor by him, but rather by the Fluir-haern. He is an agent, not an actor in this.

What of Iden's spirit stone? If we could prevent the Ceremony of Passing, would that alleviate the problem?

Ela paused and turned back to the glittering Sen-trium, considering the question. The bright lights seemed to dim, as though a thick curtain had sud-denly been dropped over the glorious, central domes of Kaelor. Dharknys fell unnaturally early. *It may, for a time, but I suspect that things have already moved beyond such simple solutions. If it is not Iden's soul, it will be the collected souls of the dead Guardians or the Dire Avengers. I am sure that these battles have produced a stockpile of spirit stones that have yet to pass through the ceremony. Not since the House Wars them-selves have we seen such bloodshed in the heart of Kaelor.*

Iden's spirit stone may be more symbolic than pivotal at this point. Whoever is behind this has played a subtle and certain game.

Perhaps a detachment of Warp Spiders could infiltrate the Sentrium and disrupt the ceremony? We might even be able to steal the spirit stone of the Zhogahn.

Perhaps, replied Ela, unconvinced and unimpressed, *but it will make no difference.* Finally, she could see that there was nothing that could be done to derail Kaelor's journey into the future. It had been fashioned with such skill over such a long time that there was almost no room for manoeuvre in the present. They needed a miracle, an inexorable force to confront the massive, rolling weight of history as it followed its course into the future.

OUTSIDE THE SHRINE, the Sentrium was veiled in a heavy and pervasive darkness. It had fallen like a sudden, silent storm. The Kaelorian down-phase of dharknys had arrived earlier than normal, falling over the glittering sector like a shroud. The eldar in the Plaza of Vaul and the Tributary of Baharroth were sullen and sombre, as though manifesting the dark mood that suffused the domain.

The interior of the shrine was all but deserted. None of the crowd from the darkness of the plaza outside had been permitted entrance. Oriana had swept back into the palace with little Turi, turning her back in horror on the conclusion of affairs that were unravelling before her. She had seen the maniacal glint in Morfran's eyes, and had wanted no part in what was to come.

Followed by the shuffling figure of the aged Rivalin Farseer, the shrine-keepers escorted Iden's stretcher down the echoing central aisle of the Shrine of Fluir-haern. They were kept under close observation by Morfran, in case they decided to cause problems because of the unusual condition of their charge. Iden was clearly still alive.

Cinnia and Celyddon stood at Morfran's side on the podium before the Tetrahedral Altar. Before Iden died, Morfran wanted his father to see that he had been accepted by a segment of the Knavir that had never taken Iden to their hearts. Iden had always thought that he had been disdained because he was a warrior, and this was certainly the reason why a great many of the Knavir disliked him and his house. Morfran, however, had quickly learnt that at least one group of the courtiers did not care at all about the death or violence on the hands of the warrior houses. They merely wanted to enjoy the pleasures that had always been afforded to the Knavir of the Sentrium.

As long as nothing interfered in their cultivation of pleasure, they would accept anyone. These were the Knavir that were after his own heart. They accepted him for all the same reasons that they rejected his stoic father. They accepted him for all the same reasons that his father had despised him.

As the stretcher was brought to a halt before the altar, Morfran slowly descended the steps to stand over his father. The shrine-keepers looked from the prone, wide-eyed body of Iden to Morfran and then to the farseer, whose wrinkled and aged face betrayed no emotion at all. Sharing panicked glances with each other, the shrine-keepers did not know how to proceed. The waystone of a living dhamashir should never be removed from its body. It was monstrous. It was the kind of deed that was retold in the horror-fables of the darklings. It was a kind of torture that cried out to the daemons of the warp like an offering or a sacrifice. The shrine-keepers could not even think about performing the deed, and the prospect of placing the living soul of an eldar who had suffered such a monstrous outrage into the Fluir-haern filled them with terror. They could not even begin to understand what the effects might be, or what kind of horrors would be unleashed into the spirit pool of Kaelor.

Get out. The powerful, unequivocal thoughts rolled over the shrine-keepers from the podium, emanating from the red-robed Yuthran seer as she strode down the steps to join Morfran next to Iden's stunned face.

The shrine-keepers seemed frozen to the spot, as though immobilised by fear or disbelief.

Out! Cinnia's command jolted their minds and made them move, shocking them back into the immediacy of the shrine. They hesitated for an instant, unsure whether to take orders from the Yuthran seer in the presence of the farseer and the dying Zhogahn and his son. Then they bowed swiftly, relieved simply to be released from the scene, and hurried back down the aisle and out into the plaza beyond, moving with the haste of perpetrators escaping from a crime-scene.

As the shrine-keepers vanished, Morfran looked over at Cinnia and grinned. He checked back over his shoulder at the handsome figure of Celyddon, who had remained standing before the altar, and he grinned again.

Turning back to the prone body of his father, Morfran lifted his eyes into those of the farseer, the wide grin still cracked across his face. Ahearn offered no response, knowing that there was nothing that could be done. He merely lowered his own eyes onto the face of his Zhogahn, who lay helplessly between them.

Very slowly, Morfran inclined his body so that he was stooped over Iden, bringing his face within fractions of his father's so that their eyes filled each other's gazes. At the same time, he reached under the folds of the cloak that had been draped over Iden's body to hide the hideous wounds that had been inflicted by the Warp Spider. He felt the shiny, polished gem of a waystone attached to a chain around Iden's neck. It was still warm to the touch, as though radiating life. As his fingers closed around it, he saw his father's eyes flare with panic and fear.

There was movement in his pupils, as though he was fighting against his own immobility with all of his strength, battling to empower a last flicker of movement from an arm or a leg that might prevent the terrible violation. His lips moved fractionally, but the old warrior did not even have enough strength to form a single word. After a long life of glorious battles and power, at the last, Iden lay in utter helplessness before the indulgent malice of his own son.

Mustering his pride for a final moment of dignity, Iden accepted that this was his end. His eyes welled with resilient pride, hatred and venom, but as Morfran's grip closed on his soul-stone, even Iden's formidable will collapsed into horror.

His eyes flared for an instant, and then they suddenly fell into darkness, as though the light of his life had been sucked out into a vacuum. At the same time, Morfran withdrew his hand, clutched around Iden's faintly glowing and blood-slicked waystone. He lifted it over his father's body and opened his fist so that the others could see what he had done, and then he turned and sprang up the steps towards the Tetrahedral Altar.

Without ceremony and in excited, undignified haste, he pushed the waystone into the little socket in the side of the altar. For a moment, nothing happened, and Morfran looked back down at Cinnia with confused dissatisfaction written across his face. A glimmer of recrimination flickered in his eyes, as though he was blaming her for promises unfulfilled.

As he looked away, sparks of sha'iel arced through the substance of the altar, as though some kind of reaction had been triggered. Threads of light flashed through the floor of the shrine, riddling the walls and then running back together in the middle of the ceiling, as though collecting into a pool. After a moment, the pool started to pour down from the ceiling in a rushing, liquid column of warp energy, plunging down into the middle of the aisle.

The Knavir, farseer and Morfran looked around the radiant and blazing interior of the shrine with

appalled wonder. They could see that the ancient
structure of the edifice at the very heart of Kaelor
could not withstand the intensity of the energy discharge. It was as though the Fluir-haern were
rebelling against the violation done to it, as though
hundreds of thousands of passed eldar souls were
raging all at once. The shrine blazed like a brilliant
beacon in the warp, crying out to the thirsting and
lascivious energies and daemons that quested
towards it from the maelstrom outside, making the
material realms quake and shudder. The dharknys of
the Sentrium was suddenly rent asunder as tendrils
of purpling warpfire lashed through its structure. All
over Kaelor, eldar stopped in stunned and unexpected fear.

As the four eldar in the shrine spun and gazed in
awe, the Tetrahedral Altar seemed to crack from
within, as though an incredible pressure of light was
trying to escape from its ancient and impregnable
form. The unearthly and unreal pressure from the
unseen dimensions expanded suddenly and
abruptly, exploding the altar into a fountain of
sha'iel-drenched shards that rained down
throughout the shrine like the fires of heaven.

CHAPTER TEN: REVOLUTION

SCILTI COULDN'T BELIEVE what was happening. They had fought their way from the Outer Reaches and through the Ula Pass, chasing the retreating Teirtu army in a drive that would have made Bedwyr proud. The diminished but victorious army of Ansgar was poised on the point of taking the Sentrium, positioned just outside the Rivalin Gates with a powerful force and with the thrill of superior morale still coursing through it. The glittering jewels of the Farseer's Court were within their grasp, radiant and shimmering with temptation. It would take only the utterance of a single word, and the Ansgar would storm into the crystal domains, recapture the farseer and claim the statuesque grandiosity of the Sentrium. Vengeance and justice could be theirs at last.

For some reason, Naois did not seem to understand their position. He had drawn the army to a halt, just as he had before the battle of Ula Pass. The Ansgar had stopped short of the final destination, teetering on the brink of their victory like a rock on the point of falling from a cliff. Despite the violence of his initial frustration, Scilti had gradually convinced himself that Bedwyr's son had stolen a glimpse of the future, and that he knew that the Teirtu would ride out to meet them if they held their ground. He presumed that Naois would prefer to fight the deciding battle out in the open ground before the great gates rather than inside the labyrinthine and restrictive crystal streets of the courtly sectors. This would be an echo of his tactics at the Styhxlin Perimeter, where he had waited for the foolish Teirtu commander to rush out of the pass and engage the Ansgar in the open ground of the Faerulh Prairies.

However, after nearly a day of silence and meditation amongst his fellow Warp Spiders, Naois showed no sign of preparing for an assault of any kind. Even when the sudden crackling explosion of warp energy had pulsed inexplicably and terribly through the structure of the craftworld, shattering the pristine light of the Sentrium into myriad shards of purple darkness, Naois had not moved to exploit the disarray that followed. He had simply continued to sit with his eyes closed, motionless and calm, keeping the Ansgar army lingering on the edge of readiness and its will to die.

He had sat for a day in silent meditation within sight of the Rivalin Gates, in the middle of a ring of quietly chanting Warp Spiders. His fierce silver eyes had remained closed and his mouth had worked through the shapes and sounds of the ritual chant that swirled around him. The Aspect Warriors had separated themselves from the main Ansgar force, but only symbolically. They had remained within a few dozen paces of the ranks at the rear of the spear-head.

Suddenly, Naois's eyes had flicked open. For a moment he had looked around the circle, taking in the figures of each of the Aspect Warriors that surrounded him, lending him their strength for his remembrance of the fallen exarch, but high above them, in the distant ceiling, they had all felt another type of energy rippling through the structure of Kaelor. Naois could see it crackling and coruscating like a concentrated storm.

Something had been unleashed.

Then Naois had risen slowly to his feet and bowed respectfully to the warriors around him.

We should return to the temple. His thoughts had contained no violence and no coercion, but they had been undeniable. *There is nothing more for us here, and the armour of the exarch must be properly enshrined. The Temple of the Warp Spiders must not be permitted to lie in rubble.*

The Aspect Warriors had risen and then dropped back down onto their knees, pushing their fists to the ground in a show of deference and duty to the Wraith Spider in their midst. With the exarch dead, Naois was the unambiguous emblem of their shrine. His word was their law, and if he said that they should turn away from the Rivalin Gates and return to the forest zones of Ansgar, then that was what they would do.

That is precisely what they had done.

To Scilti's amazement and horror, Naois had simply ushered the Warp Spiders back into their Falcons and then left, taking Adsulata and little Ela with him. They had merely nodded and followed him, as though his choice made immediate and natural sense, or as though it didn't really represent a choice at all. They had made no attempt to convince Scilti to join them, and Naois had left the impression that Scilti should remain in front of the Rivalin Gates to police the route and to prevent the Teirtu from pursuing him as he returned home to the outer realms. It seemed that he had no ambitions to occupy the glittering prize, only to ensure that the Teirtu could not inflict any further ills on the eldar of Kaelor.

As he watched the contingent of Warp Spiders disappear into the distance along the wide Boulevard of Koldo – the legendary and wide throughpath that led from the centre of civilisation out into the retrograde styhx-tann provinces – Scilti shook his head in dismay. He could not believe that the long-hidden Ansgar warriors had emerged from the depths of the forest zones to fight for this cousin, just because he was Bedwyr's son. Look at the heir now, walking away from the battle that would define their times.

He would not walk away. He would show the Ansgar Guardians and the whole of Kaelor that he was the rightful patriarch of this great house. He would show them that Khukulyn had been right to accept his leadership without question, but to challenge that of Naois. The merciless way in which his cousin had dealt with the honourable challenge of the veteran warrior should have been enough for all the eldar of the Ansgar to judge his worth, and yet still they poured out of the forests to follow him.

Now, the so-called Wraith Spider was fleeing the battlefield. His taste for blood and death were diminished, and the touch of Khaine had deserted him. Instead, it was Scilti who stood before the Rivalin Gates at the head of the Ansgar army. It was Scilti who held the fate of the Sentrium in his grasp. It was Scilti who felt the seductive whispers in his mind, drawing him on into the glittering, crystal sectors of the court. Although he could not identify the source of the tempting and sensuous voices, he found them almost irresistible. They spoke to something deep within his dhamashir, moving him at a level that was essential and beyond rational control.

Scilti knew the word of Khaine, and that word was war.

When Scilti and Naois had faced each other in combat in the arena of the Spider Temple, Scilti, not Naois, had emerged victorious. So, as Naois was vanishing back into the cursed, filthy and oppressed domains of the styhx-tann, leaving Scilti with the glittering glory of the cultivated heart of Kaelor, things were merely returning to their correct order.

Scilti turned away from the diminishing shape of the Warp Spider convoy as it neared the distant horizon and stared at the grandeur of the Rivalin Gates as though with freshly awoken eyes. Great sheets of warp energy arced and crackled through the ceiling and the floor under his feet, as though underlining the drama of the moment. Something had changed in the atmosphere of the Sentrium. To Scilti it felt as though the balance of power had shifted.

How could any eldar stand so close to such glory and not feel the righteousness of grasping it in their hands? To turn away would be to deny his essential nature.

He could feel the eyes of the Ansgar Guardians pressing into his back. They were wondering what he was going to do. There was a wave of anticipation, as though the house warriors expected him to turn around and lead the army back to Ansgar, following in the footsteps of Naois. He could sense the expectation, as though it was somehow unthinkable to them that he would do anything independently of his mysterious cousin.

In that moment, he hated Naois. He realised that he had always hated him. Everyone had always thought that his cousin was special. They had whispered about a prophecy that laid out a dark and powerful future for the little sleehr-child. They were frightened of him, just as they were of his abominable and unnatural sister, but it was all because of his father's execution. It was the stuff of legends, but that didn't mean that the legends were anything more than rumours or fictions invented by the idle minds of the Knavir or the rune-singers. Everyone made such a fuss about the intervention of Lady Ione to save the Ansgar heirs, as though that in itself were proof of a great and mysterious destiny. Well, it wasn't.

Even in the temple of the Warp Spiders, the shrine-keepers and the Aspect Warriors had all treated Naois differently from him. The arachnirs had granted him special privileges and singled him out for praise, even when Scilti had performed in a superior manner. That was why he had been so pleased when, at the last, he had bested Naois in their final combat before he had ascended from the apprentice rank of tyro to take on the full armour of a Warp Spider. As far as he knew, Naois had still not passed the tests to become an Aspect Warrior. He was still too young. Whatever had happened to him, or whatever he had managed to convince everyone had happened to him, Scilti was certain that Naois had never found a victory in an ascension match in the arena. He was just a tyro in fancy, golden armour.

Technically, Scilti should still be the patriarch of the House of Ansgar, not that precocious and spoilt little runt. How typical that the eldar of Ansgar and the Aspect Warriors of the Warp Spiders could not see the difference between the glitter of golden armour and the substance of real fighting spirit. Emotional creatures were easily duped by show rather than substance. Could they not see that Naois had turned away at the vital moment? That even now he was heading back to the crumbling remains of a ruined temple in the decimated domain of Ansgar rather than claiming the glittering prize for his own house.

The Sentrium glittered like a trophy before him, and Scilti realised that this was his opportunity to show the Ansgar and all of Kaelor what he was made of. Before the up-phase of laetnys returned in a few hours, he vowed that he would be feasting in the splendid decadence of the Farseer's Court, and that the farseer would serve him a glass of steaming Edreacian wine.

Lifting his hand, he gave the signal to start the assault on the gates.

THE JOURNEY BACK to the domains of Ansgar was fast and uneventful. The route had already been pacified during the crusade to the Sentrium, and the eldar of the intervening domains had welcomed the Ansgar forces as liberators, even if they had retained a measure of suspicion about the Warp Spiders. Hence, the return route was simple. A number of settlements along the way had tried to extend warm welcomes to the returning warriors – they too had been told the legends of the Lhykosidae in their childling days, just like the eldar of Ansgar – but Naois had simply swept past them as though he hadn't even noticed their hands of hospitality. They left a trail of confused and disappointed Kaelorians in the domains of Eaochayn and Rhouearn, before they finally plunged back into the forests of Ansgar.

When they emerged from the tree line into the clearing around the once proud temple of the Warp Spiders, the Falcons trickled to a halt, as though staggering with shock. The temple lay in ruins, with masonry scattered all over the glade. The walls had been blown out by some kind of explosion from inside, and the spires had collapsed down onto themselves, leaving piles of rubbles to mark their original positions.

Lying in amongst the debris and masonry, just before the broken and cracked remains of the steps that had once led up to the fabled crescent doors, a patch of shimmering red marked the location of Exarch Aingeal. Her waystone was missing from her chestplate, and her armour was all that was left of her, as though her body had drained away into the ground or infused into the psycho-plastic, armoured shell that she had not removed for so many years. Only her head retained any organic matter and, although her face was stretched into a grimace of pain, her mouth betrayed the crease of a grin, as though she had experienced an instant of satisfaction amidst the agonies of her death.

Vaulting down out of one of the Falcons, Naois looked down at the fallen exarch and then up at the ruined temple. A flicker of outrage burned coldly in his silver eyes, and then he clambered up the remains of the steps to inspect the extent of the damage within the depths of the interior of the shrine.

He reached down and lifted a couple of chunks of masonry, casting them easily aside as he sifted through the ruins. Eventually, after a few moments of searching, he located a large, heavy, horizontal slab of sha'ielbhr that was still undamaged and fixed in place against the ground, where the floor of the temple had once been. He found several unbroken shafts of umbhala wood amongst the rubble and, spinning one in his hands, he thrust its tip under the edge of the wraithbone slab to use as a lever. With a single, smooth movement, he prised the slab out of the ground to reveal a dark passageway with a stairwell underneath. It led down under the ruined sanctum that had once housed the webbed altar, where the ancient Spider Thrones had lain hidden for eons.

Pushing the slab aside, Naois flicked a hand signal to Adsulata, who had already descended out of one of the Falcons and was stooping at the side of the deceased exarch. The arachnir gathered the body of Aingeal into her arms and then walked slowly up the steps to join Naois. As she clambered carefully through the rubble, Naois nodded crisply at her and then vanished down through the opening into the vaults under the shrine.

The cave under the temple was wide and high, with a series of arches and pillars speckled through it, holding up the structure of the temple above. It was like a cavernous catacomb, and the staircase spiralled down out of the ceiling like an elegant helix, touching down onto the shimmering, liquid surface of the floor. The darkly reflective, oil-sheened pool that covered the ground was run through with a network of narrow, white walkways each of them appearing to run a vaguely concentric but interconnected pattern around a central point, in which the liquid bubbled with barely suppressed energy. Flecks of darkly flashing light arced through the fluid, like electricity running through water. From the stairwell, the floor resembled a giant, intricate web, radiating out from a funnel-trap in the middle, which simmered with a hidden, sinister and lurking life.

Naois waited at the bottom of the carved steps for Adsulata to join him, and then led the way through the labyrinth of pathways, criss-crossing his way sure-footedly towards the centre, as though the path was hardwired into his brain.

Once they reached the pool in the centre, Naois muttered a few inaudible words and moved his hand slowly over the bubbling liquid. For a moment, nothing seemed to happen, but then the bubbling grew more intense and the thick liquid began to seep gradually over the lip of the walkways around it, as though the level of the pool was steadily rising.

Adsulata stepped back instinctively, springing from one pathway to the next concentric ring out from the centre, but Naois stood unmoving, letting the strange liquid lap around his golden boots, as though he drew some kind of comfort from it. As its level rose, it oozed around his feet, viscous and thick, and then it started to creep up his boots, drawing dark shimmering tendrils of liquid out of the pool. It was as though the liquid wanted to absorb the lustre of the golden armour.

Naois half turned and held out his arms to Adsulata, nodding to encourage her to pass Aingeal's body over to him. He gripped the exarch's armour and turned easily, holding it in his arms as if it were an infant.

Meanwhile, the simmering, oily liquid had risen to a boil, sending waves of viscous fluid gushing over the inner walkways and over Naois's feet. As he watched, Naois saw the tips of spikes begin to protrude from the roiling turmoil. The tips rapidly became eight long, inwardly curving shafts arranged like a circular, open-topped cage. After a few moments, the base of the cage emerged out of the rush of liquid, and it became immediately clear that the object was a kind of throne. It resembled an inverted spider, with its legs pushed up into the air to form the back and sides, and its stomach was the seat. At the front of the throne, wide fangs protruded from a gaping mouth, out of which poured an oozing torrent of fluid.

Turning Aingeal's body as though it were weightless in his arms, Naois carefully lowered her onto the seat and laid her back into the Exarch's Throne of Enshrinement. After a short delay, a series of glittering wraith-threads started to solidify out of the dark, bloody liquid, questing over the enthroned armour, quickly covering it in an elaborate, sparkling web, cocooning it in the throne's clutches

An instant later, Aingeal was gone. The throne sank almost instantaneous back into the pool, leaving a momentary vortex to indicate the abruptness of the motion. There was silence, and then Naois muttered a few words of closing, sealing the passage to the subterranean throne chamber in which the armour of the exarch would remain until summoned once again by the calling of the next Warp Spider soul to be lost to Khaine.

As the level of the strange liquid gradually subsided, Naois knelt down on one knee and inspected the fluid. He poked an experimental finger into its gooey substance and then withdrew it, letting a long, sticky tendril draw up after his hand, as though the liquid were reluctant to release him.

What is it? asked Adsulata.

It is the Fluir-haern, replied Naois absently. The knowledge was lodged deep in his species-memory, as though it were merely part of his mind. *It is the blood*

of Kaelor, the conductive wraith-fluid that rushes through the arteries and veins of the craftworld. This reservoir beneath the Temple of the Lhykosidae was discovered at the time of the First Incarnation. It manifests the intimate connection between the Warp Spiders and the spirit pool of Kaelor. It reminds us of our duty to keep the craftworld pure. In return for our devotion, it holds our exarch in trust, enshrining it in the raw energy of Fluir-haern until it is called once again.

As Naois's thoughts eased into Adsulata's mind, the pool in the centre of the great web started to simmer once again. Jagged lines of purple light sparked and flashed suddenly, and the pool bubbled and rippled with a new energy, as though animated from beneath. The sickly, viscous fluid curdled and moved, swirling with the currents and ineffable tides far beneath.

Naois rose quickly to his feet, instinctively recoiling from the sudden change in the mood of the conductive liquid. Then he saw something familiar begin to form in the pool. The ripples began to morph and settle, as though the liquid were becoming increasingly dense and rubberised. The contours of a giant face began to push up through the pool.

The farseer! Adsulata's thoughts were alarmed and surprised.

The dark, oozing face of Ahearn Rivalin took an approximate form in the pool, and its mouth moved slowly, as though struggling to form words through a time-lag. The liquid continued to pour into the cavity formed by the open mouth, flooding the words into gurgles.

'Warp Spiders of Ansgar... Naois, son of Bedwyr...
Scilti Ansgar-ann has slaughtered the court... palace
runs with blood... out of control... lost souls.'

Suddenly, the image seemed to lose all coherence
and the face simply collapsed, slumping back into
the pool and leaving no evidence that it had ever
been there in the first place.

THE COURTIERS SAT in stunned silence as Scilti drank
glass after glass of Edreacian wine. He sat back in the
farseer's ornate seat at the table, with his feet kicked
up on the tabletop in a manner that reminded some
of Morfran. Cinnia sat primly at his side, grimacing
with a thrilled mixture of fear and disgust, hardly
knowing how to react to the orgiastic transformation
that had suddenly gripped the Sentrium. Intricate
crackles of sha'iel flashed through the wraithbone
elements in the room, revealing the shifting and
inconstant mood of the craftworld. Meanwhile, the
other courtiers sat in stunned awe, unable to react
properly to anything. Whilst they had despised Morfran for his slovenly decadence and his vile lack of
cultivation, they had never feared him, except
because of his association with Iden. They looked at
the Warp Spider with an altogether different attitude.
He frightened them as much as he repulsed them.

He had breached the Rivalin Gates without so
much as an opening exchange. There had been no
ceremonies of commencement, and no bandying of
insults or ambitions. The gates had been simply
blown apart by a constant and relentless tirade of
fire, splintering them into little more than shredded

curtains, and annihilating the Guardians who had sat in the gun boxes, unable to dent the fury. There had been no chance for surrender, despite the crushing victory that the Ansgar had won against Morfran in the Faerulh Prairies, and despite the fact that the Guardians of the Gates had no hope of standing before the assault and no honour code that would have called on them to die in a futile last stand. Scilti had offered them nothing but death.

Once inside the Sentrium, the fury of the Warp Spider had not diminished, but rather it had soared. As the structure of the courtly sector had flashed and cracked with the furious warp-storms that continued to rage within the material edifice of the craftworld, it was as though Scilti was suddenly infected by a contagious rage, and he had led the once honourable and immaculate army of Ansgar Guardians into a frenzy of violence. As the army advanced through the streets and boulevards of the Sentrium, pushing closer and closer to the Farseer's Palace, they had become less and less restrained, as though their inhibitions were being gradually eroded. Their famed discipline and self-control seemed to collapse, as though their wills had been compromised by luscious temptations. There was a lust for blood coursing through the streets.

By the time that the Ansgar had reached the Plaza of Vaul, where the remaining Teirtu Guardians had mustered for a last stand, Scilti had lost all control over both himself and his warriors. It had been more of a slaughter than a battle, as the Ansgar had carved through the defenders as though possessed by the

force of Slaanesh, thrilling with the ecstasy of blood,
death and spilt souls that swirled around them in a
tempest of violence. Never before had the streets of
the Sentrium run with the blood of eldar. Not during
the Craftwars and not even during the worst excesses
of the House Wars had the violence clawed so closely
at the Farseer's Palace. The Knavir had never had to
witness it before.

Only a handful of Teirtu had escaped the slaughter,
and some had even turned against their own, as
though caught up in the contagion of Scilti's rampage, turning their blades and shuriken catapults
against kinsmen or even against themselves. It was a
frenzy of killing, an orgy of violence. It was as though
the combatants fought merely for the thrill of feeling
the blood of another speckling against their skin. All
thoughts of goals and higher purposes seemed to
have vanished.

A clutch of the Knavir had watched the bloodbath
from their balcony, high above the frenzied scene.
Whilst many had turned away in horror or disgust, a
number had remained at the railing, staring down in
gruesome fascination, feeling the thrill of voyeurism
caressing their souls. Some of those that had rushed
away in a show of revulsion gradually seeped back to
the balcony until it was nearly full. As they looked
up, they could see the lightning arcs of sha'iel coruscating through the buildings and structures of the
Sentrium as the Fluir-haern seemed to rail against the
violations done to it by the deeds of Morfran and by
the incursions of the Maelstrom outside. As they
looked down, they could see the blood-slicked Plaza

of Vaul reflecting the crackling damnation back up at them, as the Ansgar and Teirtu warriors hacked into each other with passionate abandon.

Scilti had found the cowardly Morfran cowering in the farseer's personal chambers, hiding behind the proud, fair Oriana and the innocent infant Turi. Even the frail old Rivalin Farseer himself had tried to stand between the maniacal Scilti and the cowering son of Iden. Morfran had not gone out with the Guardians to confront the attack of the Ansgar, but had watched the events from the farseer's balcony. There was the glitter of excitement in his eyes, and his thin lips were wet, as though he had been drooling.

Without even pausing for thought, Scilti had marched across the room, pushed the farseer aside and punched his powerblades into Morfran's abdomen. Evidently satisfied that the Teirtu heir was as good as dead, Scilti had then turned and left as abruptly as he had come. However, whether by coincidence or design, Scilti had missed all the vital organs, and Morfran had lain in a growing pool of his own blood for a long time before two Ansgar Guardians had appeared and dragged him down to the banquet chamber with Oriana and Turi, leaving a slick trail of blood along the polished and pristine floors of the palatial corridors.

All three of them were strung up over the table. Beautiful silken ropes had been tied around their necks and they had been hoisted one after the other. They had been suspended from the high chandeliers. One member of the little family group hung from each of the three chandeliers that lit the ends and middle of the head table. Morfran had not even put up a fight. He had already lost too much blood and had never been strong enough to confront a Guardian in any case. He simply swung limply from the cord around his neck, dripping a steady trickle of blood from the wound in his abdomen as his face grew paler and paler. The Glimmering Oriana had also failed to offer any resistance. She had stared Scilti in the face with the composure and dignity that marked the very best of the Knavir. When the rope had been tied and drawn tight, just before she was lifted off her feet, she had spat her contempt for the Warp Spider into his face, in a rheumatic globule.

Little Turi had screamed. They had left him until last, so that he could watch Morfran and Oriana's suffering. They had let him scream and thrash and fight helplessly. Then they had simply strung him up next to them, letting him kick and swing until the last of his childish rebellion was spent.

Scilti had watched the suffering of the Teirtu heir with particular pleasure, imagining that this should have been the fate of Naois and cursing the weakness of Iden's will that he had allowed the little abominations to live. Aside from the political naivety, it suddenly seemed incredible to Scilti that Iden had been able to deprive himself of the unspeakable pleasure of doing such violence to the helplessly innocent and the helplessly corrupted all at once. It was like a poem, and Scilti could feel the vile, sickly, sensual pleasure of the irony coagulating in his soul as he drained another glass of Edreacian wine and kicked at Morfran's feet to make him swing.

Cinnia and Celyddon exchanged glances as they sat opposite each other at the table, overflowing with foodstuffs and drinks. They could hardly believe the transformation that had ravaged the Sentrium. They had worked so hard and for so long to protect the pleasures and privileges of the Knavir, shunning the crude, over-disciplined violence of the warrior houses, that they had never even considered the possibility that violence could be a kind of pleasure.

For long years, they had kept themselves somewhat separate from the other courtiers, indulging themselves in the refined, cultivated and delicate pleasures of the Sentrium as profoundly as their natures demanded. Together with a small group of like-minded Knavir, they had lived in the species-honesty that was denied and frustrated by the Eldar Path of Ihnyoh. They called themselves the Isha-ann, the seekers of truth. In his uncouth and repulsive way, Morfran had been a fellow traveller on that path, but none of them would mourn his passing. Despite their decadence, they were still Knavir and they still had standards of sophistication to uphold.

Iden had been the real enemy: disciplined, stoic and bellicose all at once. He had been a concentrated and dedicated opponent of the indulgence that the so-called Isha-ann had pursued. Although he had admired the grandeur of the court and had craved its approval, the Zhogahn had never been able to free himself of the discipline of his warrior dhanir. No matter how much he may have wanted to immerse himself in the pleasures of artistry and intoxication, combat remained his only indulgence.

Scilti was entirely different. There was a scintillating cocktail of disciplined violence and a wreckless abandon in him. Battle was not about honour or victory or worthiness or even politics, it was a matter of blood and ecstasy. It was an indulgence in itself, like a symphony or a poem. Pain was not a side effect of a strike, but rather it was its purpose. Different types of pain might combine and harmonise into whole new experiences of pleasure. The pain of others was exquisite, but the pain of self was an ineffable joy.

Scilti was neither a bumbling, hedonistic fool like Morfran nor a stoic, joyless warrior like Iden. He was a genuine sadist, and this realisation sent a thrill of excitement pulsing through the stunned Cinnia and Celyddon. A whole new world of pleasures had suddenly opened up to them, and it was a world as perfectly suited to the new, chaotic and corrupt atmosphere of the Sentrium, as the lashes of the warp Maelstrom outside Kaelor, mingled with the appalled violence of the Fluir-haern.

The bound and gagged farseer had been discarded on the floor at the foot of the table, beyond the shocked, silent and austere figure of the aging Yuthran Seer Triptri Paraq, whose skin pallor had begun to turn green with horror at the proceedings. A pool of Edreacian wine had spilt around him and was soaking into his cloak as he lay immobile.

As she watched, Cinnia realised that the humiliation and suffering of the Radiant Farseer made her soul flare with delight. Scilti was a genius of diabolical decadence. Then she noticed that old Ahearn was licking at the wine on the floor, and she wondered for a moment whether he was enjoying it.

CHAPTER ELEVEN: PURGATION

HAVING LAID THEIR exarch to rest in the liquid embrace of the Fluir-haern, the Warp Spiders returned to the Rivalin Gates. Their numbers were few – little more than two squads ensconced in two Falcon grav-tanks – but their spirits were dark and firm with intent. As they approached the gates, they could see the destruction that Scilti and wrought. The delicate and beautiful structure of the famed gates was cracked, shredded and ruined, and the bodies of the gate's defenders still lay dead on the ground or amidst the remnants of their gun boxes.

Yet again, Naois drew his force to a halt outside the Sentrium. He clambered out of the Falcon and strode towards the gates on foot, but when he reached the threshold of the court sector, he stopped on the line as though unable or unwilling to take the next step.

He looked down the section of the Boulevard of Koldo that ran into the heart of the Sentrium from the gates. Just as the myths and legends had said, its streets were paved with wraithbone and the buildings were fashioned of glistening crystal. Unlike anywhere else in Kaelor, except perhaps for the forest domes of Ansgar, the ceilings were almost invisibly distant, but on this day, high up in the aspiring dome, cracks of sha'iel flashed like bolts of lightning, lighting up sections of the ceiling for him to see.

It was not difficult to imagine the effect that such a place could have on the sensitive dhamashir of the children of Isha, and the intimate connections between architecture and power were not lost on Naois. On an instinctive level, he could see that the Sentrium had been designed deliberately to seduce the soul, and for the first time he wondered whether that had been Gwrih the Radiant's intention. Was it possible that the gradually increasing decadence of the countless eons since the Craftwars had been foreseen and anticipated, and even encouraged? The divide between the Knavir and the great houses of the outer realms had been a design feature? But to what end?

Looking more carefully down the street, but still refusing to take the step into the Sentrium, Naois saw the blood. It ran in thin trickles along the side of the pathway. It was smeared against the windows and splattered against the crystal walls. He could see hands reaching lifelessly from shattered doorways, and there were even a few bodies left lying in the gutters, as though they had been pushed aside to clear the road.

As the Maelstrom flickered and lashed through the psycho-conductive structure of Kaelor, filling the Sentrium with eerie, purpling light, Naois could feel the lazy corruption of the Knavir shifting into a terrible violence. The seductive perfume of the Great Enemy blew through the street, where once the delicate scent of the faerulh had wafted. It was as though he could feel his own dhamashir changing.

This war was no longer about the Teirtu or the Ansgar, or the ancient feuds of great houses. This war was about the collective dhamashir-soul of Kaelor. The insidious corruption and decadence had been allowed to prosper in the heart of the craftworld for too long. Just as last time, the Lhykosidae had returned to purge the system. The Sentrium had to fall.

Naois took another long look down the bloodied road and then turned back towards his own force. The Warp Spiders were spent. On the whole of Kaelor, there remained only two squads, collected into the hulls of two Falcon tanks and assembled outside the Rivalin Gates. There were, perhaps, only twelve Aspect Warriors standing ready to take on Scilti, the once honourable Ansgar army, and whatever else lay in wait in the distorted and barely recognisable Sentrium. Even for the Wraith Spider, the odds looked slim.

As he gazed at the tanks with despair scraping at his mind, a hatch jettisoned and little Ela climbed out onto the top of the hull. Her blue and silver robes were the colours of Ansgar, and her sapphire eyes shone with undimmed radiance. She looked

over at Naois, staring evenly into his silvering eyes,
and then she smiled faintly.

*This is why we are here, brother. Choice lies only along
the paths of others. For us there is only this. There was
only ever going to be this.*

As the darkness descended over the Sentrium, the
solitary, golden figure of Naois standing before the
ruined Rivalin Gates was like an icon of war; a pure,
unsullied force of destruction.

THE SILK BANNER of Anyon fluttered proudly on the
horizon. It was black like the void, but edged with
the palest blue. Just out of the centre, a single,
stylised wing curled into a crescent, and it glittered as
though studded with sapphires.

The army was small, little more than a detachment,
but it shone like the embodiment of pride as it
marched in Uisnech Anyon's wake. There were a few
jetbikes and a couple of Vypers, but no heavy
weapons. It was the remnant of the force that had
confronted the Ansgar at Iden's side during the
House Wars, and it had neither had the cause nor the
opportunity to rebuild since that victory.

At the head of the abrupt column, Uisnech wore
the sumptuous, ceremonial battledress of Anyon. A
great, pale plume rose out of his helmet and a long,
shimmering black cloak fell from his shoulders. In
his hands he gripped a lasblaster, and a series of
glints from his belt revealed that he was carrying a
chain of plasma grenades. Behind him was an honour guard of Swooping Hawks with their majestic
wings spread out in an ostentatious display. Then

came the Anyon Guardians, marching on foot and skimming on their rapid strike vehicles.

As they emerged out of the Vine of Maugan and turned onto the Boulevard of Koldo to exit the Sentrium, Uisnech saw the figure of a golden warrior standing in the middle of the shattered Rivalin Gates, as though barring the way out of the Sentrium. For a moment, he thought that the young eldar warrior was standing alone – the crystal light of the Sentrium burst off his golden armour and obscured Uisnech's view of the Warp Spider Falcons behind him – but as his eyes adjusted to the brilliant reflections, he realised who the startling warrior must be.

The two small forces stood facing each other for a moment, on either side of the threshold to the Sentrium. Having witnessed the atrocities of the Teirtu and then the Ansgar, the Anyon were leaving the court to consume itself, preferring to have nothing to do with it. However, the Warp Spiders were poised on the brink of their own annihilation, ready to storm into the Sentrium with death on the tips of their blades and spilling from their guns.

The childling Ela stepped out into the space between the two, emerging like a childling ghost out of the obscure darkness behind her brother.

Uisnech of Anyon. She knew who he was without asking. *This is not the time to flee from the corruption of the court. That time passed long ago, and yet you stayed. That choice has been lost to us. This is the time for boldness, not cowardice.*

Despite the slight to his honour, the old warrior Uisnech found that he could not feel affronted by the childling. She was transfixing, like a darkling wych. He held out his hand to stop his meagre but proud army, and came to a standstill opposite Naois, with Ela equidistant between them.

The farseer had fallen into the hands of your abominable kinsman, aberration of Ansgar, and the time is not long past since I stood against your father.

The past is not our concern on this day, Lord Anyon of the Veiled Blade, except in so far as it has brought us here into this present. It is the path to the future that determines our wills and our worth, replied Ela, her words belying her youth. *We stand on the precipice, and Kaelor is poised ready to fall.*

There was a long pause as Uisnech considered the unlikely figures of Ela and Naois. He looked past them at the shining but battle-scarred Falcon gravtanks and took note of the banner of the Lhykosidae that flew confidently above them. He had heard the legends of the Wraith Spider, just like all the other eldar on Kaelor, but he had also heard the prophecy of Lady Ione, and he found it too incredible to believe that the youthful Naois could really be such a powerful agent of change. It was simply too great a coincidence. There was nothing cruder and more vulgar than a coincidence. It was merely a destiny that lazy minds had failed to understand.

As he swept his gaze around the blood-soaked streets, Uisnech saw that he could not leave the Sentrium in this condition, no matter how much its recent occupants had disgusted him. As a descendent of the original Knavir, the eldar knights that had first set out for the stars aboard the epic craftworlds, his obligation was to Kaelor and the eldar souls that it contained. That was why he had stood with the farseer and then with Iden during the House Wars, not for his personal pleasure or benefit, but because he had been convinced of their honourable and righteous intentions. It was clear that the fall of Iden had changed everything.

I will stand with you against Scilti and the ugliness of the court, he replied at last, sweeping his arm into an elegant bow.

Make no mistake, Uisnech of Anyon, we do not stand against ugliness. We bring it with us.

FOR THE FIRST time in his life, Scilti's first thought was to flee. When he heard the opening shots of the first exchange in the Plaza of Vaul outside the palace, he looked around the banqueting chamber and realised that Naois was coming to take it all away from him. Throughout his whole life Scilti had contended with his younger cousin arriving later than him and stealing the limelight away. Exactly the same thing had just happened in the domains of Ansgar, after all.

Now, after Scilti had led the Ansgar to their moment of greatest power and privilege on Kaelor – after he had usurped the throne of the farseer and left the aging Ahearn crawling around the floor in pools of wine – Naois came charging along to steal it all away. It wasn't fair. It was as though the son of Bedwyr simply could not stand to see his cousin's success.

A series of explosions shook the banqueting chamber, making a number of bottles on the table tip over.

They rolled inevitably towards the edge and then fell, smashing onto the floor. Crackling lines of energy arced through the walls, around the room, fizzling and hissing with mysterious potency.

'You must defend the palace!' yelled Scilti suddenly. He dropped his feet off the table edge and swept his glance around the room, swaying slightly with intoxication. He could see a number of the Ansgar Guardians with their heads down on their tables, and a number of others who were deliberately avoiding his eyes. One or two clambered languorously to their feet, as though preparing to depart for the Plaza of Vaul.

'It is your duty to defend this palace!' he yelled again, struggling to find any words to inspire his drowsy and sated warriors. All discipline appeared to have collapsed. While they had been rampaging through the Sentrium, taking what was there, the lapse in concentration had meant little to Scilti – he was happy to see his warriors indulged after so many years of deprivation – but now, when everything was on the line, he needed them to recover themselves.

'It is your duty to defend me!' he shouted, realising that this was the most important and pressing problem. There was real emotion in his voice, and he was full of a ridiculous, self-centred certainty that this passion would be enough to reawaken his Guardians. At that moment, he could think of no cause more lofty or honourable than the defence of his own person: he had chosen life.

A few of the Guardians nodded in ascent, pushing back from their drinks and food and staggering to their feet. They swayed unsteadily and their eyes were blurry. Then they bowed slowly, as though the action required an unusual amount of concentration, before turning and wandering out of the room, bumping into each other and the doorframe as they went.

At the same time, a number of the Knavir courtiers that had joined the banquet cautiously climbed out of their seats and began to file out of the room. Scilti noticed that they were surprisingly steady on their feet, as though not intoxicated at all and, for a moment, he wondered how they could sit in the presence of such delectable delights and yet refuse to indulge.

He chuckled at them, feeling his sense of ridicule rising. He didn't need them. The least accepting of the Knavir could run off back to their private chambers in the palace if they wanted to. They were no fun, and they were certainly of no help. They just lowered the mood of indulgence that had settled over the hall. They spoilt things. Besides, enough of the Knavir had remained in their seats, smiling with wild eyes. Right next to him, Cinnia reached up and touched his arm, as though encouraging him to forget about the others and to rejoin her at the table.

Watching them go, distracted by Cinnia's touch, Scilti's thoughts started to race. Despite the fact that his Guardians were standing ready to defend him, he suspected that they might not be enough. Naois had an unnerving tendency of winning, and he had even appropriated the myth of the Lhykosidae in order to make himself appear more important and inspiring. It was typical.

Scilti hated him.

After a moment of tension and fury, Scilti slumped back down in his chair as though exhausted. He leant forwards and picked up a random glass, downing the smoking blue liquid in one shot. Kicking his feet back up onto the table, he prodded at one of the platters of tureir-iug, picking at the sumptuous and delicious flesh absent-mindedly, as though he had spontaneously forgotten what all the fuss had been about. At that moment, all he could think about was the fact that he had been deprived of such wonderful delicacies for so many years during his time in the Temple of the Warp Spiders. He couldn't believe that he had managed to endure the poverty and hardship of life in the Outer Reaches.

Kicking out, he sent the platter skidding across the wine-slicked table, scattering glasses and carafes as it went, and he watched with a gleeful smile as it teetered on the edge before clattering to the ground next to the bound farseer. The old eldar flinched visibly and let out a moan.

THE TRIBUTARY OF Baharroth was even worse than the Boulevard of Koldo. There were bodies strewn over the floor, and blood trickled down from the statues that flanked the once stately avenue, forming sticky coagulating pools. The elaborate wraithbone carvings that ran along both sides of the main thoroughfare were laced with crackling arcs of energy, and they flashed as though pulsing with the dark embers of forbidden life. Some of the icons seemed to shift and move as the Warp Spiders

passed by with the Anyon Guardians. It was as
though the monuments were watching. It was as
though distant, unnatural eyes were using the structures as lenses and watching through them.

The great statues of the Winged Phoenix and Uran-
tar-jain, the first Exarch of the Swooping Hawks on
Kaelor stood about half way along the tributary each
side of the boulevard, like magisterial pillars with
the tips of their wings touching in a grand arch,
under which all traffic on the way to the Plaza of
Vaul and the Farseer's Palace passed. Looking up
from the back of the Falcon towards their distant
and proud faces, Ela could see that they appeared to
be crying. Thick trickles of dark, bloody liquid were
seeping out of their eyes and running down their
smoothly carved features. For a moment, Ela saw the
flickering image of a past vision, with her own eyes
weeping with blood, and she remembered the scene
of fire and devastation that she had seen in Naois's
eyes when he had been defeated by Scilti in the Spider Temple.

*The Fluir-haern. Kaelor is weeping its own blood into
the streets*, murmured Ela, letting her powerful,
infantile thoughts infect all those around her. *This is
the end of days.* She sat cross-legged on the roof of
one of the Falcons, while Naois and the other Warp
Spiders rode inside the two grav-tanks. She appeared
like a mascot or emblem, utterly unphased by the
turmoil that tortured the domains around her.

As the ruby and gold Falcons and the black and
sapphire Guardians of Anyon advanced in a single
convoy towards the winged arch, it became clear that

the passage beneath it was blocked. It was slick with
the crackling and coagulating liquid that had oozed
out of the Winged Phoenix's eyes and coursed down
into the avenue, but there also seemed to be a group
of eldar warriors standing to bar the way. For some
reason, it was difficult to tell how many of them
there were, as though they represented more warriors than were actually present. There were echoes
of others surrounding each of them. Auras of violence and power flowed out of them like halos, as
though they were simply unable to contain the
abundance of power that resided within their
restricted armoured forms. They were armies in
themselves and they stood without moving or
flinching in the path of Ela and Uisnech, who
marched at the head of his force next to the child
seer's grav-tank.

Beyond their formidable and unyielding shapes,
Ela could see the swirling energy patterns that
marked a discharge of violence and blood in the
Plaza of Vaul. Even from that distance, which made
her normal vision useless, she could recognise the
signatures of Guardians and Aspect Warriors doing
battle with each other and spilling their souls into
the streets with their lifeblood.

In the inaudible realms of sound, she could hear
the wailing of pain and the whoops of pleasure that
marked out the daemonic from the natural inclina-
tions of the eldar warriors. It seemed that the
uncontrollable urges for gratification that had prodded and poked at the Sentrium for long eons had
finally broken through its reserves and the remnants

of its discipline, and the eldar of the court fought amongst themselves as though possessed by a terrible thirst. Other than the drive for the ecstasy of violence and death, Ela could feel little sense of purpose in the ongoing fighting.

You will not pass without confronting us, ehveline. The thinker knew who she was.

Do you seek anything other than death in the heart of Kaelor?

There is nothing but pain here, little ehveline. Can you really see what's ahead?

The thoughts boomed and resonated with power, pounding from different sources and forcing their way up to Ela from the warriors beneath the arch. They were accusatory and tinged with fury, as though the thinkers were on the brink of rage.

Exarchs of Khaine, replied Ela, recognising the group for who they were. *My brother brings only his swords, and expects to find only death in this forsaken place. I can see only that his expectations are not wilful. They are not his.*

As her mind spoke, sheets of warp-lightning flashed through the distant ceiling and crackled down through the winged arch, revealing the figures of six exarchs in the middle of the boulevard, blocking the route. Only Lairgnen of the Dire Avengers was absent. They glimmered menacingly, like an undeniable reality.

Do you mean to bar our progress, quihan? asked Uisnech, stepping forward of the others to address Waendre, the Exarch of the Swooping Hawks under whom he had once trained. *Do you mean to set your*

*talons against us and to leave the frenzied fools to bring
this craftworld to its end of days? Do you mean to do this
under the great arch of our forebears?*

*We cannot interfere in the political affairs of the
Ohlipsean, Hawk Uisnech. You know this better than
most.* Waendre's wings unfolded slightly, as though he
were discomforted by the situation.

If you block our path, then you are interfering, countered Uisnech plausibly.

*And what if it is our intention to intervene, Hawk of
Anyon?* The thoughts were cold like mountain water.
It was the glittering Andraste of the Shining Spears.
She was playing with him. *What if events have driven
us beyond the restrictions of the Helm?*

*Would you encourage us merely to step aside without a
thought for violence?* The dark and brooding thoughts
of Kuarwar, the Exarch of the Dark Reapers, rumbled
like falling rocks.

Would you ask us to forego our duty? challenged the
proud and shining figure of Fuarghan, the Fire
Dragon.

I would not ask anything of you. The thoughts were
coarse and burning, like roughly chipped coals or
burning glass. They tore into the minds of the exarchs
like an assault. As they reordered their minds to ease
the pain, they saw Naois pop one of the hatches of
Ela's Falcon and climb out. Without hesitation, he
sprang down from the grav-tank and strode out to
meet them. *You will do what you will. It is not for me or
Ela or even for you to determine. What must be, will be.*

*Your reticence has been an intervention for all these
eons,* added Ela, as though stacking weight onto her

brother's words. *By abiding by the visions of Gwrih and refusing to abrogate the Asurya's Helm, you have played a role in all this. On your shoulders rests some of the weight of the end of days.*

The exarchs did not move, and they showed no signs of having been affected by the words of the infant seer, but they stared at Naois with undisguised curiosity, as though he were the ghost of a long-dead friend. He was a full head shorter than any of them, but as he stepped closer to them they stepped back in unison, as though instinctively trying to keep a safe distance from the gold-armoured childling.

You are the Lhykosidae? hissed Moina the dark green figure of the Scorpion Queen. She pointed the barrel of her Scorpion's Claw gauntlet at his chest as though trying to keep him at a distance. *You have returned to us, just as the prophecy foretold.*

He returns to the Sentrium... whispered the hesitant thoughts of Morenn-kar, letting her chain of thought fade as though unsure of whether to pursue it.

You will step aside, challenged Naois, *or you will join us in this fight. We come only for death, not for the riches and pleasures of this court. The future holds only blood and fire. Death is the most favourable outcome for us all. You will step aside, or you will join us in death.*

We are the exarchs of Khaine, Wraith Spider. There is already nothing but death in our souls. Kuarwar's thoughts were subtly emphatic.

And yet they come alone, without their Aspect Warriors, noted Ela with interest. Perhaps it was the case that the terms of the Asurya's Helm explicitly forbade the political involvement of the Aspect Shrines, but not of the exarchs? But, such a creative loophole smacked of the kind of political machinations that the exarchs were supposed to avoid. It seemed more likely, she reflected, that the exarchs simply did not trust the discipline of their own warriors in this climate. They were probably being kept securely in the interiors of the temples, sealed away from the temptations and turmoils that were overwhelming the Sentrium. They were probably right to protect their warriors in this way. This was no ordinary confrontation with a visible foe.

THE PLAZA OF Vaul was teeming with action as the unlikely convoy advanced out of the Tributary of Baharroth. Sheets of warp-energy flashed through the air above the plaza, giving the scene the oppressive force of a storm. Tiny shards of wraith-crystals speckled down like toxic rain. On one side, the Shrine of Fluir-haern appeared to be under attack by a large and varied group of eldar. On the other side, a detachment of Ansgar Guardians stood vigil in front of the Farseer's Palace, disciplined enough to hold their lines amidst the turmoil, but apparently unconcerned by or oblivious to the hideous acts that were going on around them. In the centre of the plaza, the fabled silver anvil was surrounded by a mob that appeared to be engaged in some kind of ritual or sacrifice. It was the kind of scene not seen since the Fall, with the children of Isha turned against themselves in a quest for greater levels of violence and pleasure.

Naois's warriors paused on the brink for a moment to collect their thoughts and to compose their minds against the onslaught of images and emotions that flooded out of the plaza. Then, as though suddenly resolved to a common purpose, they charged forwards into the fray. Only Ela remained standing on the threshold of the plaza. She stood alone, as though transfixed by the horror of the scene, and little crystalline tears began to form in her sapphire eyes. She knew that she was staring into the abyss, and that the only way out would be the purging of the fallen souls. The only hope for Kaelor was to spill the blood of its children.

THE ELDAR IN front of the main gates to the Shrine of Fluir-haern were little more than a violent rabble of Knavir. They had an assortment of weapons, but there was no organisation. They banged and pounded against the gates with the butts of cannons and the hilts of blades, trying to shake the structural integrity of the ancient gates. Something unspoken in the back of their collective, contagious mind drove them to try to gain entrance to the shrine, as though they were thirsting after the shining beacon of the Tetrahedral Altar.

Waendre was the first of the exarchs to engage, swooping down from high above the crowd. His glittering white wings rendered him into the image of Baharroth as he loosed a chain of plasma grenades from his belt, letting them free-fall into the mire below.

Three explosions of fire and light ripped through the crowd in rapid succession, pluming instantaneously into orbs of superheated plasma and

incinerating sections of the crowd. However, the rest
of the throng carried on as though failing to notice
the onslaught from the Swooping Hawk. It was as
though their minds were clouded and intoxicated
with a single obsession.

Circling above the fray, Waendre unclipped two
more grenades. Just as he was about to release them
he saw the radiant, golden form of Fuarghan charge
into the crowd below, spraying a vicious melta-beam
from his firepike and thrashing with his burning fist.

The dark green menace of Moina was not far
behind. She was darting through the crowd with
practiced precision, slicing and hacking with her biting blade whilst rattling shuriken out of the barrel of
her scorpion's claw.

From his vantage point in the air above the fray,
Waendre watched the rowdy crowd collapse into carnage. The disorganised attack against the Shrine of
Fluir-haern was abandoned as the eldar slowly
realised their mortal peril. Despite the large numbers
in the crowd, Fuarghan and Moina were blazing and
untouchable moments of death, like beacons of light
in a rough and tumultuous sea.

Reholstering his grenades, Waendre swooped
down out at the crowd, lunging out with his talons
and strafing lines of lasfire through the panicking
mob.

LITTLE ELA'ASHBEL wandered forwards into the Plaza
of Vaul as though in a dream. She could see
Waendre's shining figure swooping and diving out of
the sky in front of the Shrine of Fluir-haern, like a

burning angel against the lightning-scarred ceiling, raining death down onto his own Kaelorian kinsmen. Beneath him, the flames of Fuarghan bathed the unruly mob of fallen Knavir in fiery death, and Moina's flashing blades glinted in the reflected fury of the flames.

In the centre of the plaza, Andraste's laser lance was cutting a swathe through the throng around the silver anvil as she charged into the fray. Meanwhile, the sinister figure of Kuarwar had planted his feet some distance away from the rabble and was unleashing an inferno of fire from his reaper launcher, shredding the cultists even as they persisted in their attempts at a ritual sacrifice on the Anvil of Vaul. At the same time, the lithe and acrobatic figure of Morenn-kar vaulted and leapt through the crowd, spinning into intricate patterns of death with her two-handed executioner sword, slicing through limbs and taking off heads with breathtaking grace and apparent ease.

Ela was in a daze. She could see the multifarious aspects of Khaine unleashed before her in a frenzy of death, turned against the children of Isha, just as Khaine had once laid waste to the ancient eldar heroes.

It was all unavoidable. It had been made inevitable so many eons before, perhaps even by Gwrih the Radiant's vision. Perhaps it was merely an inevitable aspect of the eldar dhamashir? It was a sleehr soul, unbalanced, precarious and in need of discipline. The challenge was to keep the souls of the fallen from the clutches of the thirsting Great Enemy, even

if that meant slaughtering their fellow eldar. Kaelor
was willing them to do it. It had given form to the
merciless Lhykosidae as a way to bring balance to the
craftworld's decadent heart. It was a force that
wanted for nothing other than death. For the self, it
wanted nothing.

As the maelstrom crackled and flashed through the
conductive structure of the craftworld, Ela could see
everything clearly. The warp-storm outside had been
conjured by the cumulative decadence of the Knavir,
and it was drawing in the whole of Kaelor. Tendrils of
lusting and lascivious energy were already questing
out from it and riddling the craftworld, infecting the
souls of the weakening Kaelorians and dragging it
closer to the clutches of Slaanesh, who waited in the
tempest beyond, always waiting impatiently for the
dhamashir of the children of Isha. As the souls of her
brethren collapsed into their own decadence, they
willed Kaelor closer and closer to the brink. A ritual
sacrifice to Slaanesh was being performed on the Anvil
of Vaul.

The decadent and the fallen had to be killed before
the combined force of their wills could provide the
roiling maelstrom with more energy – perhaps energy
enough to engulf Kaelor entirely – or before the lust of
the Knavir could thrust Kaelor into the warp-storm, as
though drawn in by an immense gravitational force.

Death was the only solution. Only in slaughter
could Kaelor find its salvation.

With tears pouring from her brilliant sapphire eyes,
Ela wandered aimlessly through the carnage in the
Plaza of Vaul, watching the exarchs rain butchery and

terrible death onto their kin. On the far side of the plaza she could see Uisnech's tiny Anyon force together with the golden armour of her brother approaching the Ansgar Guardians that blocked his way into the palace. Without pausing for even a moment, Naois broke into a charge, pulling the twin Witchblades of Khukulyn from their scabbards and slashing them out to his sides. At the same time, Uisnech took to the air, hurling a string of plasma grenades into the midst of the Ansgar just as they levelled their shuriken cannons and lasblasters.

In the radiance of the plasma blasts, Ela could see Naois as a dancing silhouette, spinning and vaulting through the Guardians of his own house, slicing and hacking with the blades that he had taken from the last Ansgar Guardian to oppose him. He moved without hesitation and without mercy, dispensing slaughter on all sides as he cut his way towards the gates of the palace. The Ansgar Guardians were merely obstacles in his path. It was as though all of Naois's personal pride and devotion had vanished, to be replaced by a wordless and inexorable will to death and purgation. He was no longer the son of Bedwyr, he was the Lhykosidae.

As the glimmering, golden armour of the Wraith Spider vanished through the defensive lines and flashed into the palace, Uisnech and his Anyon Guardians fell into combat with the disoriented remnants of the Ansgar Guardians.

THE DOORS TO the banqueting chamber were closed and locked, barred from the inside. Without a moment's hesitation, Naois lowered his shoulder and charged at the doors, shattering them and throwing them off their hinges. Shards and fragments sprayed into the chamber beyond, and the remnants of the doors skidded into the room along the floor, leaving Naois framed in the doorway.

A volley of shuriken fire clattered against his golden armour, but the tiny projectiles ricocheted harmlessly, as though bouncing off an impenetrable field. Looking over to one side of the room, Naois saw the overturned table and the squad of Guardians that were cowering behind it. The barrels of their shuriken catapults rested on the edge of the table. He turned his silver and black eyes on them for a moment, as though considering whether they were worth his time, but then a movement on the other side of the room caught his attention.

Turning, he saw a knot of Knavir courtiers standing in a line in front of Scilti, blocking his way. A female in flowing red robes held out her hands as though to plead for mercy. A golden-eyed male in sumptuous, rich garments dropped instantly to his knees in supplication and fear. In trembling hands, two others levelled pretty shuriken pistols at Naois and squeezed the triggers.

Naois paused to let the shurikens bounce off his armour, watching them with uncomprehending curiosity. Why would these eldar attempt to harm him with such paltry weapons?

He crossed the space between them in a couple of strides, cutting the two gunmen in half with his blades and kicking the pathetic figures of Cinnia and

Celyddon aside. They tumbled to the ground and crashed against the bound and gagged figure of Ahearn, who lay curled in a protective ball under the high table.

Scilti stood alone in front of Naois.

The two cousins stared at each other for a moment, as though sharing a moment of recognition, but they could not possibly recognise each other. Neither of them was the same as they had been the last time that they had confronted each other in combat, when they had both been tyros in the Spider Temple. One had been transformed by the gleaming riches and sensuous pleasures of the Sentrium and the corrupting truths of the maelstrom. The other had undergone a metastasis, fuelled by the spirit of Kaelor.

Outside in the Plaza of Vaul, they could hear the battle raging. Screams and wails of pain were punctuated by the exchange of gunfire and the exclamations of explosions. At the same time, warp-lightning cracked through the wraithbone elements of the palace structure, making the banqueting chamber tremble.

Suddenly, Scilti vanished. His warp-pack had been repaired and was functional again. Reappearing abruptly behind Naois, he thrust towards his cousin's golden back with his own powerblades, but Naois was not taken by surprise. He turned instantly, as though he had been able to watch Scilti's path through the warp. Parrying the thrust, Naois cut down with Khukulyn's blade and hacked off Scilti's arm at the elbow.

Wailing with pain, Scilti instinctively punched with his other hand. Without moving, Naois blocked the strike and trapped Scilti's arm. Then, with slow deliberation, he drew one of his own blades across the Warp Spider's ruby armour and took his other arm.

Once again, the two cousins stared into each other's eyes for a moment, as though sharing a final instant of understanding or searching for a last vestige of familial compassion. Armless and bleeding, Scilti saw no glimmer of mercy in the horrible silvering eyes of the Wraith Spider. His own eyes widened slightly in terror at what he saw, and then Naois cut him twice more, once bisecting him through the abdomen, and once parting his head from his shoulders an instant before the first cut could kill him.

Turning from the dismembered remains of his cousin's corpse, Naois swept his gaze around the room one final time. He saw Cinnia, Celyddon and the farseer cowering harmlessly and pathetically under the table. He considered them for a moment, and then another rattle of shuriken fire strafed into his armour from the bank of Guardians on the other side of the room. Slowly and without any apparent urgency, Naois turned and strode towards them. One tried to run, another stood ready to fight, and a couple simply dropped their weapons in terror and stood rooted to the spot. The Wraith Spider carved them into pieces one after the other, and then simply turned and strode out of the chamber, breezing past the bound farseer as though he wasn't even there.

EPILOGUE: PROPHECY

As the Lhykosidae vanished out the ruined doors, Cinnia turned to Celyddon and smiled. It was a complicated smile, containing a mixture of emotions. She was relieved that the abominable Wraith Spider had left her alive, but she was also happy. There was a real swell of elation in her smile.

With a casual gesture, she reached over and unfastened the bonds that held the farseer. He uncurled and rubbed his wrists, looking gratefully at Cinnia as she untied his gag.

The three of them sat under the high table for a long moment, in silence, sharing a pristine moment of relief, as though they had just been reborn. Then, spontaneously, they burst into laughter.

Could we have asked for anything to have gone differently? asked Ahearn as he swept his gaze around the

room and took in the bloody mess that Naois had
left behind.

No, it has all gone perfectly, my lord, replied Cinnia,
smiling broadly and then clambering out from under
the table. She wandered over to the segmented
remains of Scilti and fished around in his corpse for
a moment before producing his spirit stone. *We will
be able to harvest so many of these after all the slaughter,
more than enough to persuade our sensuous patron to
grant us greater pleasures, perhaps even enough to push
Kaelor into the maelstrom.*

I can't believe that Ione's plan worked so well, inter-
jected Celyddon. *She managed to perpetuate the House
Wars long past the victory of the Teirtu with her silly
prophecy.*

Yes, we owe the old witch a debt of gratitude, agreed
Cinnia. *She even managed to arrange for me to sculpt the
little ehveline. Her plan was flawless.*

You should not forget the vision of Gwirh in all this,
added Ahearn, as though defending his family's honour. *It was his model of Kaelor that set the scene for all
this. Without him, none of this would have been possible,
and we would still be deprived of the kinds of pleasures
that our dhamashirs crave. We would still be living the
half-lives of the wayfarers.*

The three companions walked joyfully through the
corridors of the palace, collecting the spirit stones of
the warriors and other eldar that Naois had slain on
his way to the banqueting chamber. By the time they
reached the main gates of the palace, the raging
battle in the Plaza of Vaul had diminished to a
simmer. The exarchs were still there, mopping up the

remnants of the fanatics, but they had broken the back of the disorganised and inchoate foes, and the ground lay thick with blood and corpses as testament to their furious achievements.

Look at this harvest, whispered Cinnia to Ahearn, trying to suppress her excitement. *Can you imagine what kind of experiences we will be rewarded with in exchange for all these souls?*

The farseer nodded briefly, letting the satisfied smile fall from his face as the others in the plaza began to notice his presence. He stooped over into a hunch and leant more heavily on his old, gnarled staff. Then he shuffled out into the plaza, limping and struggling as though buried under the weight of a terrible ordeal.

Ahearn saw the diminutive figure of Ela'Ashbel, wandering through the flames and the corpses like a little angel of death. Her face was dirty with blood, but it ran with pristine tears as she stopped and looked over towards the farseer with her startling sapphire eyes.

It is not over, is it? she asked him, without accusation or anger. She just wanted to know the answer. For an instant, her eyes flickered over to Cinnia, and a spark of appalled recognition died almost immediately into indifference. Her old mentor was nothing.

It is over for now, my little mornah, replied Ahearn, shuffling over to her and kneeling down before her. He placed one hand on her shoulder and looked into her eyes, as though searching for something hidden deep within. He thrilled with excitement at the power of the soul within. Even he could not have expected to be presented with such a gift. *Where is your brother? Has he abandoned you?*

He has returned to Ansgar, she responded while her fixed eyes still gazed around at the devastation. *His role here was finished. He brought death to those who needed it, but he has no desire to stay in this Sentrium. He has seen what it has done to others. He will rebuild the Spider Temple and remain in the outer realms.*

Very good, said Ahearn, smiling faintly. Leaning his weight on Ela's slender shoulder, he climbed back to his feet. *Come, my little mornah. We have much to attend to if we are to return Kaelor to its former honour and glory. We must start to rebuild the Ohlipsean, but first we must conduct the appropriate rites with the poor, lost souls of the fallen. Things will be different from now on, you have my word.*

Appendix

*An introduction to Craftworld Kaelor, and
glossary of associated terms.*

AFTER THE FALL, Kaelor lost all contact with the other
fleeing craftworlds, as it flashed out into the darkness
of intergalactic space, falling into the very fringes of the
galaxy. For long ages, it was thought lost and it fell into
misremembrance by the other eldar. It was utterly isolated, and it seems that it cherished this isolation as its
security; in this its motivation is somewhat different
from that of the peripatetic Alaitoc.

It took many eons of searching to re-establish contact
with Kaelor, since it had drifted past the furthest
reaches of the webway. As a result of this isolation, its
organisation is atypical compared with the other craftworlds. The first file here outlines those features.

It also seems that the extended period of introspec-
tion and lack of contact even with the various
Harlequin troupes that prowl the webway has caused
corruption (or evolution?) in the collective memory of
the mythic cycles of the eldar. The second of these files
provides an account of local terms, phrases and names,
together with brief explanations of the local variances
in terms that should seem familiar to all eldar.

Organisation of Kaelor

Farseer – On other craftworlds this is often a position gained by merit, after a long and arduous struggle along the Path of the Seer. On Kaelor, the title has become almost completely institutionalised. It is the ritual and ceremonial title given to the ruler of the craftworld. In practice, this title has been handed down through the line of a single family (the Rivalin dynasty) for thousands of years, passing from father to son. The family is gifted with farsight, and all members of it have evidently been seers for as long as records and memory exist.

However, there are many other seers on Kaelor, and many other families, some of which would covet this exclusive title and power for themselves. This 'imperial arrangement' has permitted the Rivalin to construct a lavish court, the so-called Ohlipsean (and it is rumoured, not unreasonably, that the lavishness of the court is also why the Rivalin family will not give up their claims to the title), but it has also bred increasing discontent, particularly as the lavishness of the court increased and started to send the peripheries of Kaelor slumping into poverty and atrophy.

Rivalin Farseer's Court – Comprised of the so-called Knavir Eldar of Kaelor, that is, eldar from families closely connected to House Rivalin. They have no independent domains of their own, and they live entirely at leisure, enjoying courtly privileges and political authority.

Great Houses – A number of families broke away from (or were broken away from) the Rivalin in the distant past. They took new names and established semi-independent domains in the outreaches of Kaelor, where the hands of the court could barely reach. Their life styles are simpler, more austere and more violent than those of the Knavir eldar. Violence and battle is not unknown, and it is not viewed with such disgust. It is a natural part of existence in the less decadent zones. These houses pay tithe to the court in return for the farseer's blessing, occasional advice, and ongoing endorsement of their ruling privileges.

Aspect Temples – The Aspect Temples are independent of the court and (technically) of the great houses, although they have precincts and shrines built within the areas of control of a number of the great houses, and some have close connections because of this. Because of their emphasis on the violent aspects of the eldar soul, they are viewed with fear and disgust (mostly disgust) by the court and by any of the great houses who aspire to be considered Knavir eldar. However, a number of the great houses have come to see the Aspect Temples as a useful source of training and see them also as potential power resources. The apolitical status of the Aspect Temples is in stark contrast with their powerful, institutionalised position on craft-worlds such as Biel-Tan.

Seer Houses – Like the Aspect Temples, the Seer Houses are technically independent places of pilgrimage and study. In them, eldar can learn the ways of the seer or can consult oracles with greater power than their own.

The Seer Houses are an unusual feature of Kaelor society, and they came into existence partly as a result of the institutionalisation of the position of farseer.

Powerful seers (often more powerful than the farseer) needed independence from the court. They endangered the position of the farseer and, consequently, were in danger. By depoliticising and institutionalising their function, the seers were saved. The court suffers their existence and calls on their services from time to time, particularly to train their offspring.

Like the Aspect Temples, Seer Houses have a regular turnover of members, as eldar pass through their seer-cycle, but they also have a sizeable permanent membership (the 'family' of the Seer House) comprised of those seers who are fully committed to the seer way – so-called dhanir-seers, or sometimes path-stalking seers. Seer Houses typically may have any number of such dedicated seers (those who would usually be considered 'farseers' on other craftworlds), making them a powerful force on Kaelor. From time to time, the Seer Houses will send their own family members out to join the great houses as consorts, partners or oracles. Hence, the Seer Houses of Kaelor have long reaches, and their fingers pull many strings.

Religious Cults – There are a number of independent religious cults active on Kaelor, outside and beyond the Aspect Temples and Seer Houses. In fact, records suggest that there was an alarming rise in pleasure cults during the later years of the Rivalin Dynasty, when the craftworld drew nearer and nearer to the maelstrom. A number of these cults (and certainly the most spectacular of them) is alleged to exist within the court. Such cults are virtually unknown on other craftworlds (or perhaps they are simply better hidden?).

Glossary:
Names, Places, and Terms of Kaelor

Adsulata (Arachnir) – Senior Aspect Warrior in the Temple of the Warp Spiders, harking from the domain of the Ansgar.

Aereb-beetle – A tiny, red insectoid creature that is reputed to have been one of the first life forms to evolve uniquely within the biosystem of Kaelor after the craftworld fled into deep space following the Fall. Colonies of the creatures cluster around the moisture-vents of the forest zones, where they survive in a peculiar yet persistent ecosystem, flittering and darting on their incredibly rapid wings. Because of its qualities and history, the little creature is considered with some affection amongst the more sentimental Kaelorians, and its name has entered common usage to indicate a range of meanings: unexpected resilience, purposeful industry and determined speed.

Ahearn Rivalin (Farseer) – Oldest surviving seer of the grand Rivalin lineage, the line that has overseen Kaelor since the Fall. His family has witnessed (and designed) the glorious grandiosity of the court and of Kaelor's Radiant Age. Ahearn claims direct descent from Gwrih the Radiant, but the tastes of the Sons of Rivalin are rumoured to be unusually extravagant. Discontented eldar in the provinces whisper that Ahearn's farsight is failing him and that he can no longer see beyond his own death.

Aingeal (Exarch) – The ageless Exarch of the Warp Spider Aspect Temple. The temple has an ancestral connection with the House of Ansgar, since a number of the Aspect's temples are found in the home sectors of the Ansgar and are thus supported by Ansgar tithes. A number of Ansgar have trained in those temples. Aingeal is the mentor of Naois Ansgar and of Scilti.

Alastrinah Yuthran – The founder of the Seer House of Yuthran. She was a compassionate, beautiful and powerful psyker with a gift for farsight. As the consort of the first Rivalin Farseer – Gwrih the Radiant – she established a glorious lineage and a tradition of service in the Farseer's Court. The symbol of House Yuthran – an eye filled with an ocean of water – is said to reflect Alastrinah's soul.

When she died, the ring from the third finger of her left hand was placed on an altar in the sanctum of the great house, and the sanctum was refashioned to mirror its perfect form; this is the so-called Ring of Alastrinah in which young wyches are initiated into the house. Yuthran wyches of high standing or exceptional power will be granted a duplicate of the ring, fashioned out of psycho-reactive wraithbone, which they wear on their third finger as a sign of their sisterhood.

Arachnir – A term used amongst the Warp Spiders of Kaelor to indicate a command-rank, junior to the exarch but senior to the other Aspect Warriors.

Aspect Warrior – *Asureah* – Warriors trained in the Aspect Temples. Although the eldar of Kaelor readily concede that Khaine was a God of contradictory blessings, the Aspect Temples are still viewed with fear, suspicion and awe by most. As on other craftworlds, however, many eldar pass through a period in their long lives when they hear the calling of Khaine. Hence, as part of their journey along the Eldar Path, many Kaelorians receive training as Aspect Warriors.

One of the unusual features of the Aspect Temples on Kaelor is that many of the Aspects have developed hereditary links with specific great houses, in whose domains they build their temples and from whose domains the majority of their warriors are drawn. Most of the largest Aspects are represented on Kaelor. The Dire Avengers have a number of large temples, supported by the patronage of the powerful House of Teirtu. The Warp Spiders were once as numerous as the Avengers, but their fortunes have ebbed and flowed along with those of their patrons, House Ansgar.

Kaelorians appear to subscribe to a conventional version of the story of the origins of the Aspect Temples. In keeping with the wider traditions, the storytellers of Kaelor explain that each of the Aspects draws its nature from one of the myriad aspects of Khaine. Each represents one of the violent predilections inherent in the eldar soul. Rather than presenting the Aspect Temples as theatres for the indulgence of these predilections, the storytellers present the temples as places of spiritual meditation and physical training, where Kaelorians can learn to harness, control and benefit from their unfortunate natures. This functional view does not appear to be shared by everyone, and the Knavir eldar are well known for their disdain of the temples.

Like other craftworlds, Kaelor supports the conventional origination of the Aspect Temples in the enigmatic person of Asurmen, who is reputed to have started the Path of the Warrior shortly after the Fall, believing that the newly nomadic children of Isha would need to learn military discipline to survive in an increasingly hostile galaxy.

The methods of practice he established were designed to condition the eldar soul to embrace the violence within without permitting it to consume or pollute the purity of the soul. This was the Path of the Warrior. To this end, Asurmen established the first of the Aspect Temples, the legendary Shrine of Asur (which Kaelorians identify as coterminous with the Aspect of the Dire Avengers), from whence his finest students [later identified as the Asurya or Phoenix Lords] spread throughout the fragmented and nomadic sons of Asuryan, carrying with them the teachings of this great warrior. Yet each of the students embraced a different style of combat, reflecting the different ways in which Khaine had whispered into their souls.

So it was that Jain Zar established the Howling Banshees, Fuegan moulded the Fire Dragons, Baharroth incepted the Swooping Hawks, Ahra (also known as Karandras on some craftworlds) created the Striking Scorpions, and the sinister Maugan Ra birthed the Dark Reapers.

On Kaelor, these legendary progenitors are called the Asurya, and one version of the mythic cycle tells of the way in which they fled the destruction of the Shrine of Asur when one of their own – the so-called Fallen Phoenix – turned against them. Surprisingly, given the history and power of the Aspect on Kaelor, there are no extant records concerning the progenitor of the Warp Spiders, which has led some to conjecture a connection with the Fallen Phoenix. An intriguing local legend speaks of the so-called Lhykosidae (Wraith Spider), which appears to be an unorthodox re-imagining of the concept of the Asurya. It is conceivable that

Kaelorian folklore is building towards the conclusion that the Lhykosidae was the Fallen Phoenix, although this hypothesise has never heard or seen explicitly.

Asureah – See Aspect Warrior.

Asurya – *Phoenix Lord* – On Kaelor and a number of the other craftworlds, the mythical Asurya are identified with the persona and armour of the first exarch of each Aspect – those originally trained by Asurmen in the Shrine of Asur at the time of the Fall. It is usually maintained that this glorious armour remains animated by the spirit of the Asurya and continues to fight as the incarnation of an aspect of Khaine forever.

An interesting and indigenous idiosyncrasy on Kaelor is the Kaelorians' mythic solution to the problem of not knowing the identity of the first exarch of the Warp Spiders. The Wraith Spider (Lhykosidae) is evidently a de-material conception of the originator. Rather than seeking to identify the Asurya as a historical or legendary warrior, the Warp Spiders of Kaelor seem to believe that it is an expression of the energy of the little crystalline creatures that guard the purity of the craftworld's infinity circuit. They suggest that the Wraith Spider is somehow an incarnation of that essential energy – an intriguing interpretation of the meaning of the Asurya [see also Aspect Warrior, Exarch].

Asuryan – *the Phoenix King* – The greatest of all eldar gods. Except for the genesis myths about the way that Asuryan separated the gods from the mortal eldar at the beginning of time, few of the mythic cycles relating to Asuryan appear to have been preserved on Kaelor. This has serious implications for adherence to Ihnyoh.

The Kaelorian wraithsmiths seem to preserve a version of the legend of the *Tears of Isha*, in which Vaul (the smith god) caught the tears shed by Isha (the mother goddess) when she heard that her children had been banished by Asuryan. Then Vaul fashioned those tears into spirit stones, which would permit the children of Isha to remain forever in contact with her. Despite the ostensibly unsympathetic portrayal of this great god, the eldar of Kaelor, like other eldar, often refer to themselves as the 'sons of Asuryan.'

Athesdan – Farseer or High Warlock – It appears that this is an archaic term for the Farseer of Kaelor, from the eons during which the office of farseer carried with it military responsibilities. The word has almost vanished from common parlance, but it is occasionally used by members of the great houses to express ironic disdain for the alleged weakness of the Rivalin farseers.

Bedwyr Ansgar – Deceased patriarch of House Ansgar, executed by Iden Teirtu at the end of the House Wars. Like the Teirtu, the Ansgar can trace their family line back to the blood of the Rivalin. The Ansgar have close ancestral connections with the Aspect Temple of the Warp Spiders, and a number of the sons (and daughters) of Ansgar have trained in the temple. Bedwyr is the progenitor of Naois and Ela'Ashbel.

Bonesinger – See Wraithbone for details.

Bricriu Seosahm – Head of House Seosahm and councillor on the Ohlipsean.

Black Library – In keeping with most of the craftworld eldar, the Kaelorians retain a number of myths and legends about the fabled Black Library. One such story tells of how the legendary (and original) Kaelorian Ranger, Vhruar the Hidden, spent a thousand years searching for the library vowing never to return to Kaelor until he had found it. Various versions of the tale suggest that he is still searching the webway in pursuit of his goal, banished from his society in self-imposed isolation. As far as anyone is aware, no Harlequins have ever encountered this heroic ranger. Note that Kaelor's slightly idiosyncratic conception of the Black Library (and the webway) might be partially explained by the lack of reliable or consistent contact by the Harlequins for the past several eons.

Caradoch – A furry quadruped originally native to the planet known as Lsathranil's Shield. The animal became extinct even before the desertification (and eventual destruction) of the planet because it lacked the faculty of suspicion. It became an affectionate name for an aging eldar amongst the Exodite colonists, many of whom fled to Kaelor when the Great Conflagration consumed the planet.

Cegorach – the Laughing God – The Great Harlequin. The eldar of Kaelor retain knowledge of one (contested) story of Cegorach during the War in Heaven, in which the Laughing God apparently tricked star god Kaelis Ra – the bringer of death – into turning against his own silvering hordes of Yngir [a more common version of this myth on other craftworlds replaces Kaelis Ra with the mythical foe of Cegorach, the so-called Outsider (Khamus).

This version tallies well with the Harlequin prophecy of the *Return of Khamus*, in which the Outsider returns to visit its revenge on the children of the Laughing

God]. A more popular myth surrounding Cegorach on Kaelor is that he escaped the effects of the Fall even without turning to the disciplined life of Ihnyoh. The Esdainn (rune-singers) of the Farseer's Court tell of how the Great Harlequin's mocking and irreverent nature distanced him from the decadence, hedonism and corruption that had enticed Slaanesh into existence.

The fact that the Harlequins do not wear waystones has not escaped the attention of the Knavir Eldar, who appear to interpret the *Song of Cegorach* as a parable that condones an indulgent lifestyle for as long as it is indulged in self-mockery. During the so-called *Age of Anguish*, it appears that Cegorach became something of an icon for those Kaelorians who sought to abandon the Ihnyoh altogether.

Celyddon Ossian – Head of House Ossian, one of the great houses of Kaelor, and councillor on the Ohlipsean. He is famous for unusually dark skin, golden eyes and his richly ostentatious robes.

Cinnia Yuthran (Seer) – Also known as Maeveh of the Hidden Joy – one of the senior seers in the House Yuthran. She is also a representative of that house at the Farseer's Court. She is heir to the functions and responsibilities of Lady Ione, and is mentor to Ela'Ashbel.

Circular Court – The Ohlipsean – the Circle of Rivalin – the Rivalin Court – The highest consultative assembly on Kaelor since the time of Gwrih the Radiant, who established it as a means of unifying the various great houses in a central council. The houses represented on it have tended to be those with some kind of familial or strategic connection with the Rivalin dynasty, leading to some dissatisfaction and unrest amongst the heads of the other houses.

Craftwar – An ancient war between Kaelor and another craftworld. Even the rune-singers of Kaelor appear to preserve very little information about why this war was fought, where it took place, and what happened during it. A number of works of poetry (such as the *Tragedy of Ghurius*) and several military epics (such as the *Arc of Destiny*) that claim to depict events from this war exist in the most comprehensive libraries of Kaelor.

A copy of the *Arc of Destiny* that is kept in the House Library of Ansgar claims that the Craftwar was won by Kaelor because of the timely intervention of the so-called Lhykosidae or Wraith Spider [see Asurya, Exarch]. However, the authenticity of all of these documents is highly questionable and for eons they have been declared forbidden by the Rivalin Court.

Dharknys – See down-phase.

Dhanir – *stage, path, way* – The term used as a category for the particular social role that a Kaelorian eldar is currently occupying, be it the dhanir of the warrior, seer, artist or whatever. It is to be distinguished from the more elaborate term Ihnyoh (Way or Path), which refers to the cyclical Eldar Way itself. For most eldar on Kaelor, Ihnyoh consists of a series of specific dhanir [see Wayfarer], although some do become stuck in a single dhanir [see Path Stalker].

Dhamashir – Soul.

Down-phase – Dharknys – A period of darkness that cycles through each sector of Kaelor, providing an artificial night on the massive craftworld. It is, in fact, a naturally occurring phenomenon (or, at least, the Kaelorians have no technical understanding of how or why it occurs). A plausible theory suggests that it has something to do the ebb and flow of the tidal currents within the infinity circuit, which would make it an intriguing indicator of the life cycle of the craftworld. Dharknys passes into a period of laetnys (up-phase) in a regular cycle, everywhere except within the Shrine of Fluir-haern, where it is always light.

Edreacian Wine – An unusual, blue, intoxicating beverage that is unique to Craftworld Kaelor, despite the relatively simple Eldreacian technology used to manufacture it. Many Kaelor eldar assert that it is actually toxic and poisonous to eldar from off-Kaelor; this has proved to be so for some, but certainly not all. It is usually served chilled, but even at reduced temperatures it lingers on the point of vaporisation, sending out a constant mist of blue. Consequently, the wine is as much inhaled as drunk.

Ela'Ashbel – Sister of Naois Ansgar and daughter of Bedwyr (allegedly by a different, unnamed mother – rumours suggest a tryst with the beautiful Lady Ione). A child-seer of incredible power. She is ostensibly under the tutelage of Cinnia in the Seer House of Yuthran. She is famed for her unusual and startling sapphire-blue eyes.

Eldar Path – See Ihnyoh.

Esdainn – Warlock, also Rune-singer – In common parlance on Kaelor this has come to mean any psyker with tendencies towards (and Aspect training in the arts of) war and violence. The evaluative force of the word appears somewhat negative. Interestingly, the Kaelorians appear to have conflated this term with the label given to story tellers or rune-singers, particularly those who relate the great mythic cycles that contain tales of heroism, war and combat.

The most famous of these is the young Deoch Epona who, despite her youth, is already a master of her craft. It appears that dedicating one's mind to combat (even to stories of combat) is frowned upon in Kaelorian culture. The unusual non-dualism between acting violently and relating violence might warrant further meditation.

Ehveline – There is a Kaelorian myth called *The Lost Daughter*, which is kept alive in a number of Seer Houses, including the House of Yuthran. It is a variation on the classic mythic cycle of the *Tears of Isha*. In this version, Isha manages to keep one of her most cherished daughters hidden from the Phoenix Lord when Asuryan banishes Isha's children from the heavens.

The myth tells the story of how this child was raised in secret by Isha, who taught her the secrets of the universe, until her powers grew so great that it became impossible to keep her hidden from Asuryan any longer. At that time, Isha transported her ehveline down into the mortal realms, placing her amongst the isolated and well-hidden eldar of Kaelor for her own protection from the wrath of Khaine and the suspicion of Asuryan.

It is said that the ehveline's immortal soul then commenced a process of cycling through reincarnations in mortal eldar forms, always in the shape of a beautiful female with startling sapphire eyes. The legend suggests that the incarnation of ehveline will never appear to grow beyond childhood, since the daughter of Isha descended from heaven before becoming fully grown. This is an interesting and unique Kaelorian myth.

Exarch – The keeper of an Aspect Temple. As on other craftworlds, exarchs on Kaelor are those Aspect Warriors that have become consumed by their violent nature and unable to suppress their love of combat. Hence they become unable to pass out of the Path of the Warrior, remaining stranded in that aspect of their existence until their deaths. Exarchs come to personify the qualities that are expressive of their chosen Aspect, and it is to them that the temple looks for leadership and guidance.

Most will never remove their armour, and Kaelorian legend is full of stories of exarchs that became so infused with the psycho-plastic substance of their armour that they were literally absorbed into it, leaving a psychic echo of their souls to guide and assist the next exarch who dons the armour [other craftworlds share similar stories, but the secrecy of the Aspect Temples makes it hard to verify them].

Kaelorians also tell of a rogue exarch – the so-called Lhykosidae or Wraith Spider. This legendary warrior appears once every few millennia to bring justice and peace to Kaelor. He will rise out of the ranks of the Warp Spider Temple, but his powers will transcend even those of the exarch. Amongst various other theories, it is conjectured that he is a kind of Asurya (or Phoenix Lord), but since Kaelorian lore is ignorant of the origination of that Aspect [see Aspect Warrior], this Wraith Spider is said to take on the essential soul of the Warp Spiders, and this is done through a kind of spiritual awakening rather than by finding and donning the armour of a fallen Phoenix Lord, as described by the other main Aspect Temples.

The Warp Spiders of Kaelor believe that they draw their name and power from the tiny crystalline creatures that roam the webway and the craftworld's own infinity circuit, purging them of all non-eldar psychic energy. Hence, the Wraith Spider is held to be a monumental force of purification, returning to Kaelor at its moment of greatest pollution and atrophy. The mighty Kaelorian wraithsmith, Vhaalum the Silver, posited an interesting interpretation of this myth, suggesting that the Wraith Spider was the personification of wraithbone. Both are entities that directly manifest the energy of sha'iel in material form, albeit one becomes organic and the other mineral.

Like the Aspect Temples themselves, exarchs are viewed by the Knavir Eldar of Kaelor as primitive and vulgar representations of the unsavoury side of the eldar soul. However, no Kaelorian appears to lack a sense of fear and awe when confronted with one.

Exodine Knovah – Eldar Knights – The mythical nobles who led the fist exodites to salvation before the Fall. Some Kaelorian scholars attribute the origins of the term Knavir to this phrase.

Externis – Eldar not from Kaelor.

Faerulh – the breath of the lost – A mythic breeze said to emanate from the very soul of Kaelor. The most sensitive minds are said to be able to hear the voices of their ancient ancestors carried on the whispering wind.

Fluir-haern – See Infinity Circuit.

Fall (the Fall) – The eldar of Kaelor have preserved a number of stories relating to this event, although the craftworld's history is punctuated with periods in which memory of this most formative and cataclysmic event appears to have been lost. Consider in particular the so-called *Age of Anguish*, during which a number of the practices designed to protect the eldar from their own natures [see Ihnyoh] as well as from the Great Enemy were either abandoned or questioned. Amongst some of the Knavir eldar, there appears to remain some scepticism about the historical legitimacy of the various stories of the Fall. On this issue, it might be lamentable that Kaelor has had such scarce contact with the Harlequins throughout its long, isolated history.

According to the most common versions of the stories (typically those told by the rune-singers of the great houses), the Fall occurred dozens of eons into the ancient period, before the coming of Gwrih the Radiant. It happened at a time when the eldar civilisation had reached its zenith, when it spanned the vastnesses of the galaxy. Its confidence – and its arrogance – knew no bounds. It was at this time that the tendency of the eldar soul towards extremes of emotion and intellect finally gave rise to the Great Cataclysm.

Feeding on their unrestrained hedonism and fuelled by the exotic cults that flourished throughout the breathtaking empire, the great daemonic form of Slaanesh was birthed into the mire of Sha'iel. Hence, according to this story, the Great Enemy is the unholy child of the children of Isha, produced by the uncontrolled nature of the eldar.

As hysterical and insane indulgence gripped the eldar, causing the civilisation to collapse under its own decadence and orgiastic violence, those who retained their senses fled. At the same time, the Great Enemy worked its magic in the warp, tearing the fabric of the materium and producing immense maelstroms of Sha'iel that started to consume the eldar empire. Some – known as the Exodine Knovah (the Eldar Knights) – led populations to new, virgin planets in the furthest reaches of the known galaxy, seeking to hide their souls from the thirsting clutches of Slaanesh. Others fled to the stars aboard massive craftworlds – huge, self-contained, space-faring bio-systems like Kaelor.

Those who remained behind were no longer recognisable as the sons of Asuryan. It was on these craftworlds that the Eldar Path (Ihnyoh) was developed as a way of protecting the souls of the eldar from the temptations of their own extreme natures and hence as a way of keeping them from the clutches of Slaanesh, who constantly thirsts and quests after the slightest flicker of the extremist souls of those who first gave it birth.

Great Enemy – See Slaanesh.

Gwrih the Radiant – The first Rivalin Farseer and the founder of the Circular Court of Kaelor. Legend has it that Gwrih was a great poet and wraithsmith, bringing peace and unity to his people through the power of his aesthetic glory. At least one version of the story of Gwrih depicts him as one of the original Exodine Knovah – the Eldar Knights – who first led sons of Asuryan away from their decaying and degenerate civilisation before the Fall.

Very few legends depict Gwrih as a warrior of any kind, and the rune-singers of the great houses tend to pay him little respect in their histories of Kaelor. In fact, it seems that he came to prominence on the back of a massive war between Kaelor and the craftworld of Saim-Hann, although the details and motivation of this so-called Craftwar appear to have been lost.

Harlequin – Riellietann – The children of Cegorach. In common parlance on Kaelor this has come to mean an eldar with an opaque or mysterious nature. The eldar of Kaelor appear more than usually suspicious of them. One can only assume that this is because of the low frequency of contact between the Harlequins and Kaelor, although there is probably also an element of the opposite causality.

House Wars – The epic wars that shaped Kaelor. The term refers to a complicated series of political and military battles for primacy between the great houses of Teirtu and Ansgar, with the Farseer's House of Rivalin caught in the middle. House Teirtu won this war under the leadership of Iden, who promptly had the patriarch of Ansgar (Bedwyr) executed. For undocumented reasons, Iden's consort, the Lady Ione of the Seer House Yuthran, pleaded for mercy on behalf of Bedwyr's infant son (Naois) and baby daughter (Ela). Rumours and legends have grown up around these surviving heirs, fuelling the suspicions and paranoia of Iden.

Iden Teirtu – Warrior lord and patriarch of the great and powerful provincial House Teirtu, able to trace his family bloodline back into the ancient House of

Rivalin, many eons earlier. Iden was the victor in the House Wars against House Ansgar and he is the slayer of their patriarch, Bedwyr.

Infinity Circuit – Fluir-haern – Spirit Pool – To some extent the significance of this hallowed and sacred repository appears not to be fully appreciated by sections of the population of Kaelor. In particular, the so-called Knavir eldar seem to treat it as a chiefly ceremonial or ritual entity, with little functional or substantial importance. That said, the rituals surrounding the passing of an elevated soul into the Fluir-haern are amongst the grandest and most elaborate in the court.

Outside the circle of the Knavir, in the great houses, the importance of the matrix appears to be understood in more conventional terms. The rune-singers of House Ansgar, for example, are clear that the Fluir-haern is a repository for the souls of deceased eldar, where they are kept safe from the clutches of the Great Enemy, and from whence they can be summoned for purposes of advice and wisdom by the living.

According to this interpretation, the Fluir-haern is also apt to whisper its own messages to eldar with minds sufficiently open to hear it – this 'breath of the lost' is sometimes known as faerulh. One version of the Ansgar myth also suggests that the Fluir-haern will eventually become a psychic force powerful enough to confront the might of Slaanesh with the combined power of millions of Kaelorian souls. This incredible force will be led by the mythical Lhykosidae (the Wraith Spider) in the battle of the End of Days. Hence, Kaelor must remain hidden long enough to build up this psychic arsenal.

Ihnyoh – the Eldar Path – Like the eldar of other craftworlds, those of Kaelor enjoy a naturally long life, especially when compared with the other mortal species in the galaxy. Unlike the other craftworlds, however, Kaelorians (particularly the so-called Knavir eldar) do not seem to adhere very rigorously to Ihnyoh. Indeed, it seems that the storytellers have either forgotten the story of Asuryan or have been forbidden to relate it.

Amongst the Aspect Temples, the exarchs and their rune-singers (Esdainn) do seem to retain this knowledge, and a number of the great houses are consequently better informed than the Knavir. The basic shape of the story is conventional: the Path is conceived as a solution to the passionate and volatile nature of the eldar soul, which, left unchecked in the form of unrestrained self-gratification and decadence, resulted in the Fall. It is a cyclical path that sees the Kaelor eldar dramatically changing their social role at irregular intervals – the most high profile being the paths of the seer and the warrior, although the Knavir are renowned for avoiding the latter and for lingering in the more artistic paths.

The basic concept (that a healthy mix of variety and discipline will resolve the innate tendency towards excess in the eldar soul) appears to be widely accepted on Kaelor. However, as on other isolated craftworlds, a small community of outcasts – known as rangers – have turned their back on this Path, believing that it is too restrictive and that the dangers of abandoning it have been exaggerated by eons of mythic embroidery. The rangers of Kaelor have developed a rich mythic tradition of their own, largely centred around the heroic figure of Vhruar the Hidden, who was apparently the first of the Kaelorians to throw off the discipline of Ihnyoh in pursuit of something more essential and natural to the eldar spirit.

Kaelor is, however, almost unique amongst the craft-world eldar in so far as its adherence to Ihnyoh often appears to be more formal than substantial, especially amongst the so-called Knavir. It seems that unusually feudal circumstances combined with isolation and distance from other craftworlds may have led to a gradual decline in species-memory about Ihnyoh on Kaelor, particularly in the highest echelons of court society.

Consciousness of the Path appears strongest amongst the Seer Houses and the great houses, who maintain close ties with the Aspect Temples.

Ione (Lady) – Senior seer of the Seer House of Yuthran and consort to the Teirtu patriarch Iden. A powerful and popular Knavir Eldar of the old school. Despite some rumours about the precise nature of her relationship with Bedwyr Ansgar, whose children she saved from the wrath of Iden at the end of the House Wars, her reputation remains immaculate.

Isha – the Mother Goddess – Goddess of the Harvest – the Seeing Eye – The eldar of Kaelor, particularly the Seer Houses, preserve a number of the central myths about Isha. They appear to be aware of at least one of the versions of the story of *Lileath's Dream*, in which Lileath the Graceful [more commonly known as Lileath the Maiden on other craftworlds] told Khaine about a vision of him being ripped asunder by one of the mortal offspring of Isha and Kurnous, the God of the Hunt.

According to the Kaelorian version of this myth, the mortal in question is Eldanesh, one of the first great eldar heroes. However, this addition to the story is probably the result of confusing the later *Ballad of Eldanesh*, in which he attempts to avenge the suffering of Isha by killing Khaine, only to be ripped apart by the Bloody-Handed God.

Similar events are related in the *Cycle of the Avatar* [see Khaine]. Nonetheless, in response to this warning from Lileath, Khaine resolved to hunt down the mortal children of Isha – the eldar. He slaughtered many of them before his bloodlust was arrested by Asuryan, the Phoenix King, who took pity on Isha when he saw the glittering beauty of her tears – one shed for each of her hunted children. Hence, Asuryan separated the heavenly and the mortal realms, forbidding any contact between the two. This saved the children of Isha from Khaine's wrath but doomed them never to see their mother again.

In sympathy, it is said that Vaul, the Smith God, fashioned Isha's tears into Spirit Stones so that she could retain some contact with her cherished children.

Ishyrea – Seer – Gifted of Isha.

Kaswallan Ansgar – The long-passed father of Bedwyr.

Kerwyn Rivalin – Son of Ahearn and direct heir to the farseer's throne.

Khaine, Kaela Mensha – the Bloody-Handed God – War God. The eldar of Kaelor have managed to maintain a number of the central myths surrounding Khaine. However, it appears that some of the details have been lost or embroidered throughout the eons. The rune-singers of Kaelor sing of Khaine as the vanquisher of Kaelis Ra – the Yngir star-god that raged a war through the heavens.

In that cycle (the *Birth of Fear*), Khaine fights alongside the great eldar hero Eldanesh and wields the immortal Blade Wraiths fashioned for him by Vaul, the Smith God. Yet the rune-singers also sing the (more reliable?) *Cycle of the Avatar*, in which Khaine wages war against the Children of Isha, defying Asuryan, the greatest of the eldar gods, chaining Vaul to his anvil, and joining forces with the Yngir.

According to this cycle, it was Khaine that slew the heroic Eldanesh and condemned the eldar to mortality. Horrified by the violence of Khaine, Asuryan cursed him, making his hands drip with Eldanesh's blood for all eternity – hence, Khaine the Bloody-Handed God.

The storytellers of the Farseer's Court of Kaelor often relate only the *Cycle of the Avatar*, which explains why the War God's name is muttered with disgust by the Knavir eldar. Elsewhere on Kaelor, these myths are usually told in immediate succession, presumably to emphasise the unpredictability of the dual natured god of war and of the eldar soul.

In House Ansgar, the *Cycle of the Avatar* ends with Khaine's demise in his futile battle with the Great Enemy, Slaanesh. It is said that when confronted with this daemonic threat to his people, Khaine threw himself into the battle without hope of victory, but buying the eldar time to flee from their own Fall into the abyss. It is said that Khaine's ruined body was shattered into pristine fragments of bellicosity and scattered throughout the galaxy, awaiting reinvigoration as an Avatar.

From these two myths, it seems that the great houses of Kaelor are keenly aware of the contradictory, heroic and tragic nature of the Bloody-Handed God. Unlike the Farseer's Court, the great houses appear to maintain connections with various Aspect Temples, wherein young eldar learn to draw their strength from Khaine. [See Aspect Warriors]

Knavir – one of the many names used on Kaelor to describe the terrestrial eldar before the Fall. It has come to have connotations of ancient respectability mixed with naive anachronism.

The term is rarely affectionate and has become somewhat abusive. A contested and highly politicised version of the origins of this term suggests that it is a distortion of the ancient class of Exodine Knovah – the fabled Eldar Knights who were reputed to have been the heads of great noble houses that led the Exodite eldar away from the declining eldar civilisation before the Fall, establishing a second generation of civilisations in other parts of the galaxy.

Laetnys – *Up-phase*. See also down-phase.

Lairgnen – Exarch of the Temple of the Dire Avengers.

Lhykosidae – *Wraith Spider* – A mythical warrior from the legends of the Warp Spider Aspect, allegedly a kind of exarch or even Asurya that is somehow constituted from the warp essence of the tiny crystalline creatures that purify the infinity circuit of Kaelor. [See Asurya, Craftwar, Exarch]

Menmon – *the Soul Taker* – The name of a (probably fictional) Kaelorian eldar of the Seer House of Yuthran who supposedly learned the secret and forbidden arts of necromantism from a vagabond ranger who made contact with the craftworld during the so-called Age of Anguish.

According to legends, the ranger was once a Spiritseer from the craftworld of Iyanden, and he gifted Menmon with the ability to capture the souls of her fellow eldar, enabling her to use them in the construction of so-called Wraithguard warriors.

Whether or not this legend is based on truth is hard to discern – its subject matter is so offensive to the sensibilities of the Kaelorians that it has all but vanished from public memory.

In House Yuthran, Menmon gives her name to one of the most arduous and terrifying of the various rites of passage through which an initiate must pass in order to gain access to the inner sanctums of the great Seer House. Although the details of the rite are known only to those who have passed through it, it appears to be concerned with defences of the soul.

Mhyrune – An extinct family line of famed fabric manufacturers from the Mhyrineq Nebula. In Kaelorian parlance, the word has come to be associated with any type of fabric or thread of extraordinary quality. In particular, the local legends suggest that the ancient weavers used to inscribe runes of power into each thread that they used in a weave, producing cloth with incredible and peerless psychic qualities.

Mon'keigh – This term refers to a race of sub-intelligent beasts that lived in the twilight world of Koldo. In acient times, these beasts invaded the eldar lands and subjugated them for many years. The mon'keigh of legend were cannibalistic, misshapen monstrosities, eventually cleansed from the galaxy by the hero Elronhir.

This term is used by the eldar of Craftworld Kaelor to refer to a number of non-eldar species that the eldar deem inferior, in need of extermination.

Morfran Teirtu – The son of Iden and approximate contemporary of the Ansgar heir, Naois. His consort is the fair Oriana Rivalin.

Mornah – The name given to the tiny wraithbone carvings made by the master wraithsmiths in the Trials of Vaul, during which the smith demonstrates his mastery of the art. The intricate objects are little larger than a finger nail, but they contain many years' worth of craftsmanship and detail. The word has also come to be an affectionate term for a talented or promising infant.

Mrofth – A small, winged insectoid with no digestive apparatus. Hence, it never eats. Instead, it draws its energy directly in the form of heat from fire. They can often be seen in small groups, circling and swooping through flames.

Naois Ansgar – Son of Bedwyr, heir to the House of Ansgar, and closely connected with the Temple of the Warp Spiders. He is the younger cousin of Scilti and elder brother of Ela Ashbel.

Ohlipsean – See Circular Court.

Oriana Rivalin (Seer) – The daughter of Ahearn and (slightly) younger sister of Kerwyn. She is the consort of Morfran, the bumbling son of Iden of House Teirtu, and mother of Turi.

Path (the Path) – See Ihnyoh.

Path Finder – *outcast* – *ranger* – The most famous of the historical rangers on Kaelor is Vhruar the Hidden, who reputedly spent a thousand years searching for the Black Library. [See also Path Stalker, Ihnyoh].

Path Stalker – The term that Kaelorian eldar use to describe an eldar that has become stuck on one specific dhanir or path, hence escaping from the cyclical nature of the Ihnyoh. The most obvious examples are exarchs, but on Kaelor bonesingers are also placed in this category. Interestingly, unlike on other craftworlds (where equivalent terms often do not exist), the farseer is sometimes not regarded as a Path Stalker on Kaelor, since his status is a result of hereditary social position rather than necessarily a result of his having become stuck in the dhanir of the seer.

A related term is Path Finder, which is sometimes used to describe the function of rangers on other craftwords. On Kaelor, however, the term has come to take on a broader significance. Whilst it remains a category that encompasses the rangers on Kaelor, the reason for this is two-fold: first, it is because of the obvious fact that the rangers are engaged in reconnaissance (ie, finding paths), but second, it is because they are self-consciously free of the strictures of the Ihnyoh and thus they are forging a life path of their own. They are not stuck on a single dhanir like a Path Stalker, but they are outside the structure altogether – attempting to find their own path that feels closer to authenticity [for more on rangers, see Ihnyoh].

This second rationale contains a darker side on Kaelor, since it also appears to have become appropriated as a self-definition by those Kaelorians who are sceptical about the value of Ihnyoh in the first place. These are hedonists, not rangers. The term entered common usage amongst the so-called Knavir eldar during the *Age of Anguish* [see Waystone].

Phoenix Lord – See Asurya.

Quihan – Teacher, or master.

Rillietann – See Harlequin.

Ritual of Tuireann – The coming of age ceremony initiated in the Farseer's Court of Kaelor by Fedelm Tuireann (also known as Tuireann the Ancient). Fedelm was an old Harlequin abandoned by her troupe on Kaelor as the craftworld fled the chaos of the Great Fall. Despite being so old, her manner was always youthful, and her appellation has come to be used ironically to indicate an eldar behaving younger than their age.

Rune-singer – See Esdainn.

Sapphire Dell – The circular council-area of the domains of Ansgar. It is a circular, blue-metallic pit, lowered into the ground to ensure that the councillors themselves are always on a level lower than those over whom they rule. Its structure is supposed to reflect the political commitments of the ruling House of Ansgar.

Sentrium – The name given to the sector in the heart of Kaelor in which the Circular Court is located.

Scilti – Elder cousin of Naois Ansgar and Ela Ashbel. In the House Wars, he fought alongside his uncle, Bedwyr, but as a young and inexperienced warrior. He was trained in the Temple of the Warp Spiders in the domain of the Ansgar.

Sha'iel – The energy of the warp.

Sha'ielbhr – See Wraithbone.

Slaanesh – *the Great Enemy* – *The Devourer of Souls*. Like the eldar of other craftworlds, the Kaelorians retain at least parts of the mythic cycles of the Fall, in which Slaanesh is depicted as having been birthed by the combined, unrestrained hedonistic energies of eldar souls. In common with the majority of other craftworld eldar [for an exception see *Vol.IX – The Errant Son: Heranghra*], most Kaelorians (particularly in the great houses) see Slaanesh as an ever present danger and threat. They embrace the Ihnyoh as a defence against its clutches.

Sleehr – A technical term used by seers and wraithsmiths to describe an imbalance between the material and immaterial energies of an entity. In common parlance it has become a term of derision to indicate a polluted, unbalanced, flawed or offensive personality – eg. Sleehr-child.

Spirit Pool – See Infinity Circuit.

Spirit Stone – See Waystone.

Styhxlin Perimeter – The great tectonic divide that was cracked into a chasm through the structure of Kaelor during the so-called Craftwars between Kaelor and Saim-Hann in the period immediately preceding the Radiant Age of Gwrih. The chasm was never materially repaired, but rather it was psychically bonded. Hence, because of a quirk in the properties of Sha'iel-infused space, the long, jagged canyon appears to drop straight through Kaelor and out into the vacuum of space, no matter where you stand to look at it. Since Gwrih the Radiant established the Circular Court, the Styhxlin

Perimeter has traditionally been seen as the line of division between the domains of the Knavir eldar and those of the provincial great houses – the so-called Outer Houses. One Ansgar legend suggests that it was the result of an abortive but deliberate attempt by the farseer to rid Kaelor of the (warlords of the) great houses altogether.

Styhx-tann – A derogatory term used by the Knavir to refer to eldar from the far side of the Styhxlin Perimeter.

Tureir-iug – lumbering sloth – The slightly disingenuous name given to the Waercats of Poupriah, which were domesticated by a group of prospectors from Kaelor several eons ago and then farmed within a number of the eco-domes that are speckled throughout the craftworld. Despite the clumsiness and disdain implied in the name, the Knavir of Kaelor appear to be very partial to the meat of these creatures – and their farming is virtually monopolised by the House of Ossian. This is an odd deviation from the norm on Kaelor, where most eldar appear to avoid eating animal flesh for reasons of ritual purity.

Turi Rivalin – The son of Oriana and Morfran, hence the grandson of both Ahearn Rivalin and Iden Teirtu.

Tyro – The term used to label an apprentice or trainee warrior in an Aspect Temple. It indicates the status of one who has not yet been inducted into the temple's secret teachings, or one who has not yet attained sufficient mastery of its arts to be called an Aspect Warrior.

Uisnech Anyon – Head of House Anyon, one of the great houses of Kaelor, and one of the leading councillors on the Ohlipsean.

Ula Pass – A permanent, narrow corridor through the Styhxlin Perimeter along the famous Innis Straight. It approximates the technology of the webway, although on an infinitely smaller scale. It is one of the most heavily fortified access routes in the Sentrium and was the site of the last great battle of the House Wars, where the forces of the Ansgar were virtually wiped out following a suicidal drive through the Pass by Bedwyr Ansgar.

Local legend suggests that Ula was a warlock from the domains of Ansgar, trained in the Temple of the Warp Spiders. It is said that she expended her entire life-force in order to prevent Kaelor from cracking apart during the Craftwars by constructing the corridor as a bridge to bind the two sides together with the sheer power of her will. Some of rune-singers suggest that she became so infused with her creation that her soul provides the structural integrity of the pass.

Umbhala – A rare tree found only in two locations on Kaelor, both of which are protected within defensive eco-shields. One is within the Sentrium, and the other is under the protection of the Temple of the Warp Spiders in the domain of Ansgar. They flower once every two hundred years, and it is said that the blooms are of such beauty that simply gazing upon them can heal any affliction. The wood from the tree is so hard that Kaelorian folklore declares it to be indestructible. In practice, it is so rare that it is never used for construction, although the Warp Spiders have been known to fashion it into combat staffs. It is also rumoured that the bark of the umbhala has psycho-toxic qualities that are sometimes employed by seers in the form of incense.

Up-phase – *Laetnys*. See also down-phase.

Vaugnh – Abomination. The origin of this rune is contested on Kaelor. The most contested (but popular) philological studies suggest that it was first inscribed on the hilt of each of the one hundred mythical blades of Vaul, which (according to Kaelorian myth) were fashioned by the smith god as a gift for Khaine in his fight against the Yngir, the Ancient Enemy.

A more conventional version of this myth suggests that Vaul forged one thousand of these enchanted blades as a ransom payment to Khaine for the release of Kurnous and Isha, whom the War God had taken captive after Asuryan discovered the existence of the Tears of Isha (see Isha). It is reputed that Vaul attempted to trick Khaine by including a normal blade amongst the others; his trick failed.

Although it is rumoured that at least one of these blades survived the terrible War in Heaven, allegedly in the care of the Harlequins of Arcadia, no eldar of Kaelor has ever been able to verify the truth of this.

Vaul – the Smith God – Acclaimed as a craftsman without peer and famed as the creator of the legendary Blade Wraiths wielded by the ancient eldar heroes: Ulthanesh, Eldanesh and Lanthrilaq the Swift. It is said that Vaul was without morality and that his single purpose was beauty rather than truth. The wraithsmiths of Kaelor hold Vaul as their most potent patron, and Gwrih the Radiant built many monuments to honour his name.

Warlock – See Esdainn.

War in Heaven – Isha, the Mother Goddess, and Kurnous. the God of the Hunt, were imprisoned for countless years in the fires of the wrath of Khaine.

Bound with bonds of flame and scorching iron, the god and goddess were cast into a burning pit out of the sight of mortals and gods. Of all the gods only Vaul the Smith pleaded for them, and eventually he swore an oath to Khaine that he would make a hundred swords in exchange for their release, for Vaul was the greatest swordsmith of all eternity and a single blade forged by his hand was of incalculable value.

A date was fixed one year hence for the completion of the bargain. When the time came for Vaul to deliver the weapons, he had still one unfinished blade. To conceal the shortfall, Vaul took an ordinary mortal blade and mixed it amongst his own work. At first Khaine was so pleased with the weapons that he failed to spot the deception.

Only when Isha, Kurnous and Vaul were far away did he discover the forgery. He roared with anger, calling Vaul a cheat and crying out for vengeance. This was the beginning of the long struggle between Khaine and Vaul, which is called the War in Heaven. [See also Isha, Vaugnh.]

Wayfarer – This term appears to have no equivalent on any of the other craftworlds that I have visited. It appears to refer to eldar who follow the normal progress of Ihnyoh, moving from one Dhanir to the next in a cycle throughout their lives.

Waystone – the Tears of Isha – Like all craftworld eldar, the Kaelorians commit their souls to the sanctity of a waystone to keep their immortal spirits out of the hands of the Great Enemy, Slaanesh, at the point of their deaths.

Indeed, in a period of strife on Kaelor known as the *Age of Anguish*, which followed the so-called *Radiant Age* of Gwrih, groups of Knavir eldar began to question the validity of the practice. The Kaelorian *Age of Anguish* was marked by an unprecedented disrespect for tradition, myth and legend, which perhaps explains why so many of the great mythic cycles have fallen out of memory on Kaelor.

In a manner typical of many craftworlds, the Kaelorians wear their waystones around their necks, either on ornamental chains or fused into the chest plates of their armour.

Webway – Kaelor is unusually reluctant to enter the webway, perhaps because of its tendency towards isolation and solitude, even from the rest of the craftworld eldar. The rune-singers of Kaelor depict the webway as being a construction of the Old Ones, who fashioned it when they originally took to the stars in the immeasurably distant past. To some extent, the vast network of passages through the immaterial dimensions that permits such rapid travel throughout the galaxy has become associated with the War in Heaven and with war in general.

Legend suggests that the last time Kaelor made a major journey through the webway, it encountered the bellicose craftworld of Saim-Hann, resulting in the so-called Craftwars. A number of other stories (such as the *Demise of Altansar*) appear to have been modified throughout Kaelorian history. They now suggest that travel in the webway constituted a serious risk of exposure to the ever-lusting eye of Slaanesh.

Perhaps because of these narrative quirks, the Knavir eldar are ambivalent about the webway, preferring to keep the vast craftworld in the thicker dimensions of real space, hidden in the furthest reaches of the galaxy.

There are two obvious deductions that can be drawn from these unusual aspects of Kaelorian social lore. The first is that there may be some connection between this attitude towards the webway and the disdain with which the Knavir eldar have tended to view the Aspect Temple of the Warp Spiders, which maintains a sophisticated portal into the webway. The second is that there is a clear connection between this attitude and the lack of contact between Kaelor and the Harlequins.

Wraithbone – Sha'ielbhr – As on a number of other craftworlds, the essence of wraithbone is drawn out of the warp and fashioned into material substance by a category of wraithsmiths called the bonesingers. The material is incredibly tough and resilient (and therefore hard to manipulate), and it always retains its connection with the warp, which makes it a perfectly efficient psychic conductor.

Wraith Spider – See Lhykosidae.

Yngir – Against whom the Old Ones and the eldar waged wars. According to Kaelor myth, the greatest of the Yngir, Kaelis Ra – the bringer of death and darkness – was slain for the first time by Kaela Mensha Khaine and his lightning-spear in the epic battle that left his own body riddled with shards of silvered poison, forever transforming his own visage into that of the reaper, but Kaelis Ra can never truly die, for it is death incarnate. The Kaelor version of the mythic cycle of the *Birth of Fear* tells how the howling and raging essence of Kaelis Ra, freed from its physical form by the death-blow of Khaine, swept through the materium and infiltrated the very fabric of the eldar race, infecting them with an inalienable fear of the grave. For some, this infection is a kind of Sleehr.

Yseult – A renowned warrior who is not part of the Teirtu family line, but is pledged to the Great House of Teirtu. She is the same age as the house heir, Morfran. She was trained in the Aspect Temple of the Dire Avengers.

Zhogahn – The Vanquisher of Vice. A politico-military title awarded by the farseer to military leaders who represent the interests of the court in battle. The title fell into disuse following the establishment of the Rivalin Court, since incidents of battle on Kaelor dropped off to almost nothing. Iden Teirtu was appointed to the rank of Zhogahn following his victory over the Ansgar in the House Wars. He appears to have interpreted this title to mean that he has effectively been given the powers of a regent, ruling in the name of the farseer. Iden was the first Kaelorian to receive this title since the Craftwars.

ABOUT THE AUTHOR

C S Goto has published short fiction in *Inferno!* and elsewhere. His work for the Black Library includes the Warhammer 40,000 *Dawn of War* novels, the Deathwatch series and the Necromunda novel *Salvation*.

WARHAMMER
40,000

CHAPTER WAR

Don't miss

CHAPTER WAR

Coming soon from Black Library:
The storming new instalment
in the Soul Drinkers series
by Ben Counter

CHAPTER MASTER SARPEDON of the Soul Drinkers took to the centre of the auditorium, watched by the hundreds of fellow Soul Drinkers. He was a horrendous sight. From the waist up he was a Space Marine, a psychic Librarian, with his purple power armour worked into a high collar containing the protective Aegis circuit and the golden chalice symbol of the Chapter worked into every surface. He was an old man by human standards and his shaven head was scarred by war and sunken-eyed with the things he had seen. From the waist down, however, he was a monster – eight arachnid legs, tipped in long talons, jutted from his waist where human legs should have been. One of his front legs was bionic, the original having been ripped off what felt like a lifetime ago.

'Brothers of the Chapter,' he began, his voice carrying throughout the auditorium. 'We have come so far it is difficult to imagine what we once were. And I am glad, because it shows how far we have left that time behind.

Some of you, of course, have never known the Chapter other than as it is now. And I am glad of that, too, because it shows that in spite of everything the galaxy has thrown at us we can still recruit others to our cause. We have never given up, and we never will. The new initiates, and those who have now earned their armour, are proof of that.'

Sarpedon looked around at the assembled Soul Drinkers. There were faces he had known for as long as he could remember, back into the earliest days of his service in the Chapter before he had led it away from the tyranny of the Imperium. Others were new, recruited by the Chapter in the days since the schism. The auditorium itself currently served as the bridge of the *Brokenback* and it had once been a xenobiology lecture theatre on an Explorator ship that had become lost in the warp. Large dusty jars containing the preserved bodies of strange alien creatures were mounted on the walls and Sarpedon himself spoke from on top of a large dissection slab with restraints still hanging from it.

'We have been apart for some time,' continued Sarpedon. 'Captains, make your reports. Karraidin?'

Captain Karraidin was one of the most grizzled, relentless warriors Sarpedon had ever met. A relic of the old Chapter, he wore one of the Soul Drinkers' few suits of Terminator armour and had a face that looked like it had been chewed up and spat out again. He stood with the whirr of both his massive armour's servos, and the bionic which had replaced his leg after he lost it in the battles on Stratix Luminae. 'Lord Sarpedon,' said Karraidin in his deep gravelly voice. 'Many of the novices have earned their full armour in the Suleithan Campaign. They intervened in the eldar insurgency and killed many of the xenos pirates. They have done us all proud.'

'What are your recommendations?'

'That Scout-Sergeant Eumenes be given a full command,' replied Karraidin.

Sarpedon spotted Eumenes himself among the Soul Drinkers – he knew Eumenes as a scout, one of the new recruits of the Chapter, but now he wore a full set of power armour and he seemed perfectly at home among its massive ceramite plates.

'Sniper Raek has distinguished himself in scouting and infiltration duties,' continued Karraidin. 'I recommend that he remain a scout and take command of other novice forces. Given our current situation I believe the Chapter would benefit from veteran scouts like Raek.' The slim-faced, quietly-spoken Raek was the best shot in the Chapter – as good, some said, as the late Captain Dreo.

'Then it shall be so,' said Sarpedon. 'And of the latest recruits?'

'The harvest has been bountiful again,' said Karraidin with relish. 'They are born soldiers, every one of them.' The Soul Drinkers recruited new members from among the oppressed and rebellious people of the Imperium and turned them into Space Marines as the old Chapter had done, but without such extensive hypno-doctrination – Sarpedon wanted to ensure their minds were as free as the Chapter itself. For the last several months Karraidin's novices had been earning their place in the Chapter, intervening to fight the Emperor's enemies around the scattered worlds of the largely desolate Segmentum Tempestus.

'Then we are winning our greatest victory,' said Sarpedon. 'The forces that deceived once wanted us broken and desperate, whittled down one by one, reliant on those forces to keep us from sliding into the abyss. We have clawed our way out and built ourselves a future. Some of our best have been lost to win this victory. And I have no doubt there are those who will still try to stop us. As long as we take new novices who believe in our cause, and those novices earn their armour fighting the Emperor's foes, our enemies will never win.

'But those enemies never tire. Ever since Gravenhold we have had to rebuild ourselves and now I believe we are ready to fight as a Chapter again. The Eye of Terror has opened and Abaddon has returned, it is said. More and more of the Imperium's military is diverted to countering the tyranid fleets. The underbelly is exposed and the Imperium is too corrupt to defend itself. We are sworn to do the Emperor's work, and that work is being neglected in the galaxy's hidden and isolated places.'

'Such as the Obsidian system,' said a voice from among the assembled Soul Drinkers. It was that of Iktinos, the Chaplain, distinguished by his black-painted armour and the pale grimacing skull that fronted his helmet. He was surrounded by his 'flock', the Soul Drinkers who had lost their sergeants and gone to Iktinos for leadership. They accompanied him in battle and often led the other battle-brothers in prayers and war-rites.

'Chaplain?' said Sarpedon. 'Explain.'

'The *Brokenback* picks up many signals from across the galaxy,' said Iktinos. 'We are far from the Imperial heart-land but nevertheless there is chatter, transmitted from ship to ship. I have been sifting through these to find some indication of the Emperor's work remaining undone.'

'And I take it you have found somewhere?'

'I have, Lord Sarpedon. The Obsidian system, in the Scaephan Sector, to the galactic south of the Veiled Region. The planet Vanqualis has been invaded by the greenskin scourge. The people there have begged for assistance from the Imperium but as you well know, the Imperial wheel is slow to turn and the orks will surely devastate their world.'

'So there is the Emperor's work to be done?' asked Sarpedon.

'They are people of an independent spirit,' said Iktinos. 'They have resisted the Imperial yoke and remaining true to their own traditions. They have survived for a long time alone, and we may find adherents to our cause there.

Certainly there are many billions of Emperor-fearing citizens who will perish without help.'

'We are not a charity,' said Librarian Tyrendian sharply. Tyrendian was a lean and handsome man, seemingly too unscarred and assured to have seen as many battles as he had. Like Sarpedon he was a powerful psyker – unlike Sarpedon his power manifested as devastating bolts of lightning, like psychic artillery, hurled at the enemy. When Tyrendian spoke his mind it was with a self-important confidence that won him true friends in the Chapter. 'There are countless worlds suffering.'

'This one,' said Iktinos, 'we can help.'

'We should be at the Eye,' continued Tyrendian. 'Chaos has played its hand.'

'The whole Inquisition is at the Eye,' retorted another voice, that of Captain Luko, the Chapter's most experienced assault captain. 'We might as well hand ourselves over to our enemies.'

'It is also the case,' said Iktinos, 'that our Chapter is not rich in resources. We are lacking in fuel and ordnance. The *Brokenback* cannot go on forever, and neither can we. The Obsidian system has a refinery world, Tyrancos, from which we can take what we please. Tyrendian is correct, we are not a charity, but we can both help secure our future and help an Emperor-fearing world survive without being ground down by the Imperial yoke.'

'And it's better,' said Luko, 'than sitting on our haunches here waiting for battle to come to us.'

Luko was known throughout the Chapter for the relish with which he approached battle, as if he had been born into it, and Sarpedon could see many of the Soul Drinkers agreed with him.

'Lygris?' said Sarpedon, looking at the Chapter's lead Techmarine.

'The Chaplain is correct,' said Techmarine Lygris. Lygris's armour was the traditional rust-red and his face, and a servo-arm mounted on his armour's backpack reached over his shoulder. 'Without significant resupply soon we will have to reconsider using the *Brokenback* as a base of operations. We would have to find ourselves another fleet.'

'Then I believe the Obsidian system may be our next destination,' said Sarpedon. 'Iktinos, assist me in finding out whatever we can about Vanqualis and its predicament. Lygris, prepare the warp route. We must be ready for—'

'Let them rot,' said yet another voice from among the Soul Drinkers.

It was Eumenes who had spoken, the scout-sergeant who had recently earned his full armour. He pushed his way to the front, close to the anatomy stage at the centre of the auditorium. He was a brilliant soldier and looked it, sharp intelligent eyes constantly darting, his face as resolute as it was youthful.

'Scout Eumenes,' said Sarpedon. 'I take it you disagree?'

Eumenes grimaced as if the idea being discussed left a bad taste in his mouth. 'The people of Vanqualis are no better than any of the rest of the Imperium. They will be as corrupt as the rest of them. You say you have turned your back on the Imperium, Sarpedon, but you keep dragging us back into its wars.'

'On the Imperium,' said Sarpedon darkly. 'Not the Emperor.'

'The people are the Imperium! These vermin, these murderers, these are the corruption we are fighting against! If we have to bring the whole damned thing down, if we have to set worlds like Vanqualis aflame, then that is what we do! The Imperium is the breeding ground for Chaos! The Emperor looks upon this galaxy and weeps because none of us have the guts to change it.'

'Then what,' said Iktinos darkly, 'would you have us do?'

Eumenes looked around the assembled Soul Drinkers. 'The underbelly is exposed. You said so yourselves. We strike while we can. Break it down. The Adepta, the bastions of tyranny. Ophelia VII or Gathalamor. Imagine if we struck at Holy Terra itself, blotted out the Astronomican! This tyranny would collapse around us! We could help rebuild the human race from the ashes! That would be the Emperor's work.'

'Eumenes, this madness!' shouted Sarpedon. 'If the Imperium fell the human race would follow. Destroying it is not the way to deliver its people.'

'If what I say is madness, Sarpedon, then a great many of us are infected with that same madness. Do not think I am alone. And we could do it, Sarpedon! Think about it. The Imperium has been on the brink for thousands of years. We are the best soldiers in the galaxy, and we know what the Imperial vermin fear. We could bring it all down, if we only made the choice!'

'Enough!' Sarpedon rose to his full height, which on his arachnoid legs put him a clear head above the tallest Space Marine. 'This is insubordination, and it will cease. I am your Chapter Master!'

'I have no master!' Eumenes's eyes were alight with anger. 'Not you. Not the Imperium. No one. You cling to the ways of the old Chapter so dearly you are no more than a tyrant yourself.'

No one spoke. Sarpedon had fought the Chapter before – he had led the Chapter War when he had overthrown Gorgoleon and taken control of the Soul Drinkers, he had battled adherents to the old Chapter's ways and even faced one of his own, Sergeant Tellos, who had become corrupted by the dark forces against which the Chapter fought. But a conflict like this had never come into the open so brazenly.

'I see,' said Sarpedon carefully, 'that the Chapter does not unite behind me and cast down the rebel.' He cast his eyes over the assembled Soul Drinkers, reading their expressions – anger and offence, yes, but also apprehension and perhaps some admiration for Eumenes's boldness.

'Then you cannot ignore me,' said Eumenes. 'As I said, I am not alone.' The young Soul Drinker smiled and stepped forward into the centre of the auditorium, face to face with Sarpedon himself. 'They used to say that the Emperor would give strength to the arm of His champion. That Rogal Dorn would counsel victory to the just. Do you believe He will lend you strength, Sarpedon, if we settle this in the old way?'

The old way. An honour-duel. One of the Soul Drinkers' oldest traditions, as old as the Imperial Fists Legion, the Legion of the legendary Primarch Rogal Dorn, from the ranks of which the Soul Drinkers had been founded almost ten thousand years before.

'First blood,' said Sarpedon, with a steely snarl on his face. 'I would not grant you anything so noble as death.'

IN THE HEART of the *Brokenback* lay the dark cathedrals, the baffling catacombs and ornate sacrificial altars that once adorned the *Herald of Desolation*. Nothing was known of the *Herald* except that it had at some time in the distant past been lost in the warp and become a part of the ancient space hulk, and that its captain or creator must have been insane. Hidden cells and torture chambers, steel tanks scarred with acid stains, tombs among the catacombs with restraints built into the stone coffins – the purpose of the *Herald of Desolation* was lost amid the hidden signs of madness and suffering, smothered by the dark, ornate magnificence that blossomed in the heart of the *Brokenback*.

The dome that soared over Sarpedon's head was crowded with statues, locked in a painful, writhing tableau of contortion and violence. Below the sky of stone agony was a thigh-deep pool of water broken by oversized figures who had been sculpted to look as if they had fallen down from above, and reached up towards the figures of the dome as if desperate to return.

The dome was vast, easily the size of the Chapel of Dorn in which the last honour duel among the Soul Drinkers had taken place.

The Soul Drinkers standing observing around the edge of the circular pool seemed distant and dwarfed by the strange majesty of the place. In the centre, Sarpedon and Eumenes stood, armoured but unarmed. This was their fight, and theirs alone – when it was done the results would affect the whole Chapter, but for now it was a matter between them.

'Why have you brought us here, Eumenes?' asked Sarpedon. 'You could have come to me earlier. There was no need to bring the whole Chapter into this.'

'It's not just me, Sarpedon.' When Eumenes spoke there was always a mocking note in his voice, as if he couldn't help but scorn those around him. 'There are dozens of us. And you can't hold out forever.'

'Are you just here to threaten me, Eumenes, or to decide this?'

Eumenes smiled. 'No witchcraft, Sarpedon.'

'No witchcraft.'

Eumenes darted forwards. Sarpedon ducked back and raised his front legs to fend off Eumenes but the younger Space Marine was quick, far quicker than Sarpedon anticipated. Eumenes drove a palm into Sarpedon's stomach and though the impact was absorbed by his armour Sarpedon tumbled backwards, talons skittering through the water to keep him upright. Eumenes jumped, span, and drove a foot down onto Sarpedon's bionic front leg. Sparks flew as the leg snapped and Sarpedon, off-balance again, dropped into the water and rolled away as Eumenes slammed a fist into the floor where his face had been. Stone splintered under his gauntlet.

Eumenes had learned to fight twice. Once, among the brutalised outcasts amongst whom he had grown up – and again with the Soul Drinkers, under the tutelage of Karraidin. He was dirty as well as quick, brutal as well as efficient. And he really wanted to kill Sarpedon. Sarpedon could see that in his every movement.

Eumenes followed up but Sarpedon was on his feet, backed against a huge broken stone arm that had fallen from above. Eumenes struck and parried but Sarpedon met him, giving ground as Eumenes tried to find a way through his defence. Sarpedon's front bionic leg dragged sparking in the water as he skirted around the fallen arm, watching Eumenes's every flinch and feint.

'What do you want, Eumenes?' he said. 'Why are we here? Really?'

Eumenes ducked under Sarpedon's remaining front leg and darted in close, spinning and aiming an elbow at Sarpedon's head. Sarpedon grabbed him and turned him around, using the strength of Eumenes's blow to fling the young Soul Drinker over his shoulder. Eumenes smacked into an oversized sculpture of a contorted figure, his armoured body smashing its stone head into hundreds of splinters. Eumenes slid down into the water on his knees but he leapt up immediately. His face had been cut up by the impact and blood ran down it as he snarled and charged again.

This time Sarpedon reared up, bringing his talons down on Eumenes and driving him down so he sprawled in the water. Eumenes struggled under Sarpedon's weight as Sarpedon reached down to grab him.

A stone shard, sharp as a knife, stabbed up from the water. Sarpedon barely ducked to the side in time as Eumenes tried to stab him in the throat. Eumenes swept his legs around and knocked Sarpedon's talon out from under him and now Sarpedon toppled into the water.

Suddenly he was face to face with Eumenes. Eumenes had the knife at his throat, Sarpedon gripping his wrist to keep the weapon from breaking his skin. He was looking right into the youth's eyes and what he saw there was not the emotion of a Space Marine. Eumenes might have been implanted with the organs that turned a man into a Space Marine, and he might be wearing the power armour so emblematic of the Astartes warriors – but Eumenes was not a Space Marine. Not in the way that the old Chapter understood it. Sarpedon had not understood what he was doing when he began the harvest anew and made Eumenes into the man fighting him now.

Eumenes tried to force the point home but Sarpedon was stronger and the stone blade was slowly pushed away. Sarpedon held up his free hand, which had a dark smear of blood on one finger: blood from the cuts down Eumenes's face.

'First blood,' said Sarpedon. He held up his hand so the watching Soul Drinkers could see. 'First blood!' he yelled, signifying the end of the fight.

For a few moments Sarpedon saw nothing in Eumenes's eyes but the desire to kill. The honour duel was forgotten and Sarpedon was not a fellow Soul Drinker to Eumenes – he was an enemy, something to be destroyed. Eumenes really believed in his own cause, Sarpedon realised. To him, Sarpedon was as foul an enemy as the daemons that preyed on mankind.

Eumenes's grip relaxed and the stone shard fell into the water. Gauntleted hands took Eumenes's shoulders and pulled him back away from Sarpedon. The hate in Eumenes's face was gone, replaced with something like triumph, as if he believed he had somehow proven himself right.

'Take him to the brig,' said Sarpedon, pushing himself up out of the water with his seven remaining legs. 'Post a guard.'

Apothecary Pallas hurried up and shook his head at the ragged state of Sarpedon's bionic. 'This will take some fixing,' he said.

'Be grateful it's the same one,' replied Sarpedon. Had Eumenes shattered one of his mutated legs and not the bionic, Eumenes would have won the duel to first blood. It had been that close. Sarpedon might be stronger, but Eumenes's ruthlessness had almost brought him out of the duel as the victor.

'Your orders, Lord Sarpedon?' asked Techmarine Lygris.

Sarpedon looked up at Lygris. Like Pallas, Luko and others, he was one of Sarpedon's oldest and most trusted of friends, veterans of the Chapter War who had been with him through everything the Chapter had suffered. He realised then that such old friends were becoming rarer, and the Chapter would have to rely on its new recruits.

'Take us to the Obsidian system,' said Sarpedon. 'Find out everything we have on it. And make the Chapter ready for war.

The story continues in
CHAPTER WAR
by Ben Counter

Available from the Black Library
in Spring 2007